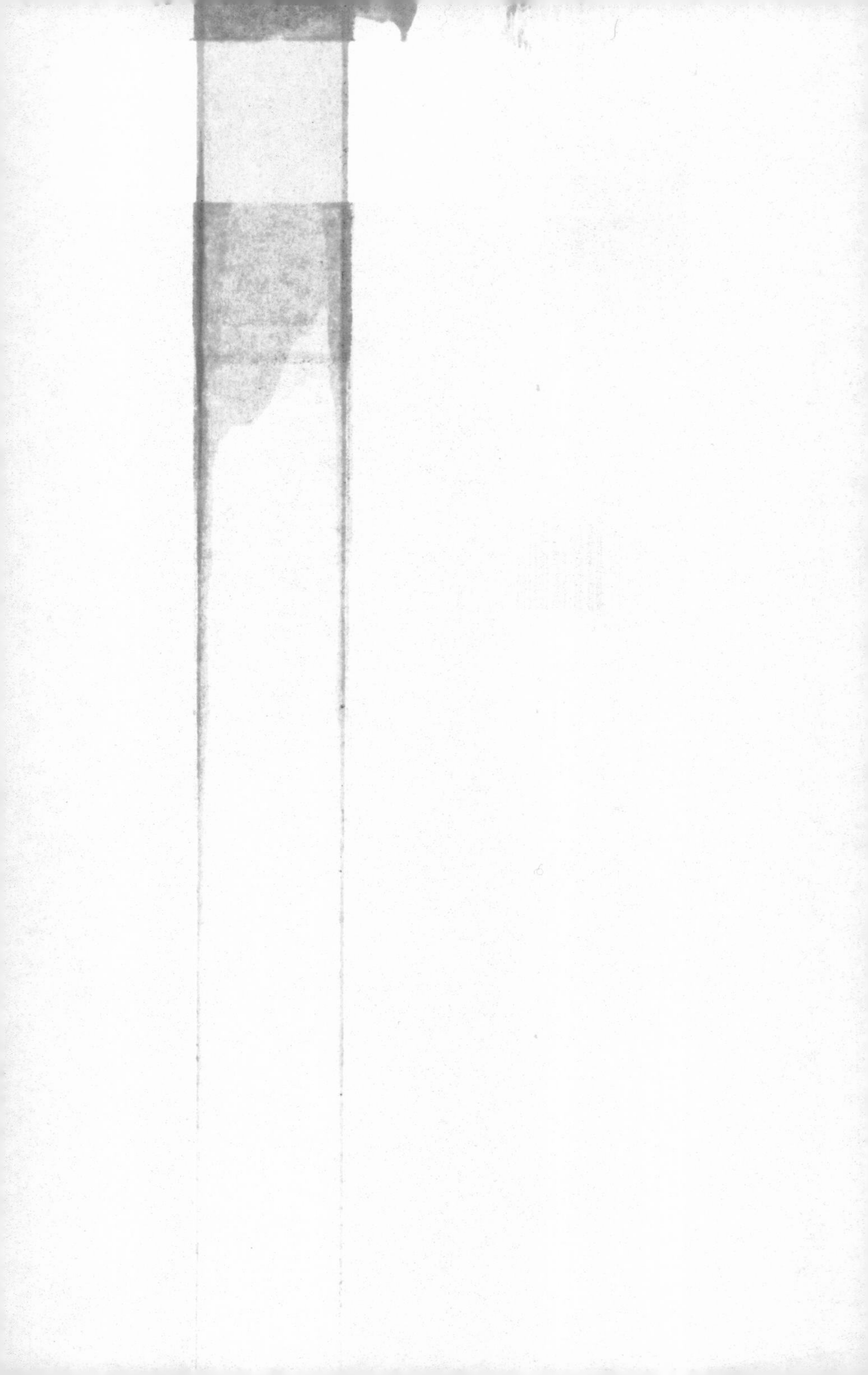

The Findlings

A novel based on a real event

by

Joanne Wilshin

Anacortes, Washington

VOYAGER

VOYAGER

A Voyager Book
519 Commercial, Ste. 1942
Anacortes, Washington, 98221
www.joannewilshin.com

Publisher's Note: This is a work of fiction. Names, characters, places, and incidents are a product of the author's imagination. Locales and public names are sometimes used for atmospheric purposes. Any resemblance to actual people, living or dead, or to businesses, companies, events, institutions, or locales is completely coincidental.

Book Layout © 2021: P. B. Sargent/ Anacortes, Washington
Book Typography: Palantino by Hermann Zapf and Avenir Next by Adrian Frutiger
Cover Design: P. B. Sargent/ Anacortes
Cover Typography: Eurofurence by Tobias B. Koehler and Alike by Cyrean
Cover Photograph: Shutterstock
Author Photograph: David Wilshin/ Anacortes, Washington

The findlings: a novel based on a real event/ Wilshin, Joanne Rodasta. -- 1st ed.

Library of Congress Control Number: 2021908099
ASIN : B0924ZPC1J
ISBN 978-0-578-86741-0

To Davy,

Lisa, Nicolas,

Cecilia, Jim,

and the poem voice

The straightaway causeway

lays at our bay. Take it

Contents

One

Her Children Were Leaves

November 4, 1948; The Ether

Before I begin, I need you to know that I am not alive, not in the carnal sense. Neither is my younger sister Delilah, though our time is nigh. For now, we content ourselves with hovering over our life to come, above the Earth and its goings-on.

I also confess I should have known what I had initially witnessed was not the whole truth. Retracing my steps, so to speak, I remember sensing something was amiss, but Delilah, bless her soul, insisted all was lovely, and I followed along. I knew better than to do that.

As my saga begins, we were in the ether above the Southern California coast. Far below me, I could see Grace, my future mother, gathering stones and storing them in her pockets, or something like that. For her mantel, I supposed, or for her door stoop.

Scanning the shoreline, I noticed, perhaps a mile beneath me, Delilah's lacy, cotton-candy pink aura motioning for me like a beckoning neon sign. "Anna!" she called to me. Her pinkness quivered with bliss.

Before streaming down toward her, I hesitated for a fleck of time. Delilah seemed her happy and untroubled self, while within me swirled a hint of worry. Perhaps my perception of Grace was off, or perhaps it was in fact correct. Grace, you see, was a soul with closets; she thought nothing of locking their doors to make life easier. Today could be one of those days where I found her doing something so poignantly reckless the devastation would be far-reaching and deep. I hoped not; I chose to believe not.

I dropped to Delilah's level, which at first disoriented me. You have no idea how glaring Earth can be with the ocean and sky reflecting back and forth their roaring azure shades. But Delilah's welcoming aura reached out and bathed me in its steadiness. "I am so glad you have come! Follow me."

"How is everything? Are they doing well?"

"Of course, everyone is fine. Look for yourself. If you would visit a little oftener, you would save yourself a lot of stress."

I ignored her last comment, because, well, she did have a point. Admittedly I am a roamer of this vast and fascinating world.

She nudged me. "Perk up, Anna. Let us see what the world offers us this day."

Yes, I thought, let us go for a visit together.

Below, I saw a familiar sandy beach. Waves curved around the air like Corinthian ferns, then dashed onto its shoreline and devoured stones and seaweed bits in their path, and left a contented, white tatted edging along the sand. Around me, swirling gulls cawed and peeped, and the aerated scents from shells and seaweed textured the air. How lush it all seemed, albeit temporary.

Delilah fizzed. "Do you see where we are?" She plunged even closer to the surface.

Keeping pace with her, I assured her, "Certainly I do."

As usual, a thrill rushed through me. We were near La Jolla, California, where our whole family, prior to our incarnating process, had selected as the best place to raise our family. It had really been Grace's idea. "I love how the ocean saturates the air and gives it a salty sparkle," she had told us before she incarnated. She believed the moist air would act as a prism rosying how we would see the world. She had thought it important that her children be idealists and that we be a forward-looking family. And that we strove to make life better and sweeter with everything we said and did. So strongly did we four children believe this that we swore upon our eternal lives that we would, as a quartet, embody this in our lives and in our vocations.

We just never suspected the current obstacles that would get in our way.

The hint of worry returned, along with the sound of grinding stones. I edged close to Delilah; her pinkness tickled with innocence. "Delilah, I have this feeling things are not what they appear. Do you know about what I am talking?"

She stared at me with a quizzical froth.

"Do you hear stones grinding against one another? It seems off."

"Oh, Anna, you are always thinking something is wrong or something needs to be fixed. No, nothing is wrong. In fact, today is particularly lovely."

She motioned for me to accompany her as she dove to just a couple of yards above the beach's surface.

Ashore, past the seaweed strands and driftwood chunks basking at the high-tide line, the first thing I noticed were two young couples clad mostly in white strolling together on a path that would eventually lead to the beach. At the end of the path, I spotted Grace and her two small children, my siblings already born, who were playing among the sand and stones near a cliff.

Relief wove through me. I recognized firsthand that my family was well and safe. But before I could savor this feeling, it vanished. The closer I drew to Grace, the more I could see how wrong my summation was.

Because a dull, gray light about an inch thick and resembling a smog layer emanated from her body and encased her, she appeared more like a storm cloud than my future mother. Then, perhaps because I was quite near to her, I could hear the stones again, griping and grumbling, trapped in circular arguments.

I dropped down eye level with Grace. Her details shocked me, and I despaired at how I could have missed her recent deterioration. Please understand that Grace had been a brilliant woman, glamorous in her own right, and quite the survivor. What I found in her place was a disheveled mess. Atop her head of unkempt, black, wavy hair, she had perched a brown cowboy hat, which she wore backward. Her boxy plaid jacket clashed with her flowery slacks. Her worn, brown brogues lacked laces. She seemed a bit thicker around the waist. From under her arm, carelessly dangled the children's yellow cardigans. Her alabaster brow seemed permanently furrowed with twisted thoughts; her cuticles and nails, what was left of them, were swollen red and jagged. You would never know by looking at her that she had once been a concert pianist.

Like marbles spilled on the floor, Grace and my brother and sister padded off in their own directions combing the sand and rocks at the foot of a cliff which rose to the road. Atop the cliff and accessible by a flight of stairs, lived Grace's best friend Sadie, where, I assumed, she and the children had spent the earlier part of the morning.

Freckled and chubby-cheeked Beatrice, with her bouncing copper curls glinting in the sunlight, removed a turban shell from the collection amassed in the pockets of her worn, red corduroy overalls. She held it to her eye and peered out at the ocean, then at the sky, and then all around her. With each new view, her pink lips opened or shut, smiled or grimaced, oohed and ahhed. By the time her body had fully revolved on its axis, she aimed the turban shell at her brother Evan several yards away, and broke into a smile. "Evvy! I tee you!" Then she kissed the air, as if it were him. Who could not love that!

Evan, older than Beatrice by a year, looked at her and smiled, before crouching down and gathering sand in his fists. His dark eyes stared into hers, and one eyebrow lifted authoritatively, signaling that she must watch him and learn. His cowboy hat, with its overcast-stitched brim, just like his mother's, fell low over his ears and neck. When he rose, he splayed open his upturned palms, as though he were releasing a butterfly or a fireworks extravaganza. His mouth opened in delight, and his focus darted this way and that as it tried to follow each sand particle's path sifting through his fingers and floating away. Particles landed everywhere. On the beach. In his sleeves. Between his scuffed, brown shoes' laces. Over and over he did this. He picked up sand. He held it tight in his hands, as if he had captured a treasure. Then he released it.

Beatrice, in response, imitated Evan exactly. She picked up a handful of sand, proudly freed it from her grasp, and squealed in delight. That complete, she returned to viewing her world through her turban shell.

Delilah cuddled beside me. "Are they not precious, Anna? I can hardly wait to join them."

Delight bloomed within me. "Me too." For this was exactly what I wanted. To be with Beatrice and Evan, and eventually Delilah, living life as a family, helping each other remember who we were, what we were capable of, and what we had come to do.

A golden orb, like the sun on a summer day, came to my awareness, reminding me of the moment we all agreed on our Destiny. Bringing idealism to humanity was our singular purpose. Evan would accomplish it through music and Beatrice through the arts. I would accomplish it through architecture and Delilah through medicine. What we would add to life!

A cotton-ball cloud scudding overhead cast a cinereous shadow over Grace as she hiked head down, through the worn-smooth stones and bleached driftwood piled at the base of the cliff.

The stones! Icy, metallic fear cut through me as I watched her.

Methodically, yet randomly, she picked up a white or brown stone about the size of a ring box, thumbed its surface, and dropped it into one of her pockets. Her jacket and slacks bulged and drooped under the weight of the stones she'd already collected.

"Delilah, do you see what is happening? Grace is collecting stones in her pockets."

Perplexed, Delilah studied Grace. "Maybe they are for her garden."

"Stones," I said. "Not pebbles."

"Like I said, maybe they are for her garden."

"She has no garden, and you know it. Look at her aura. Look how she is dressed. She is having a hard time. Listen to her thoughts."

We both paused to listen.

I knew what I heard, and I did not like it. "Do you hear her, Delilah? Dear, God. You hear it, right? To you, what is she thinking?"

"She's thinking it is a lovely day and the stones will add to her garden's pathway. And I am thinking we need to remember our place as spectators."

I know I should have maintained my composure, but I failed. More exactly, I flailed. I could not believe Delilah's naivete. "You mean you do not hear what she is saying to herself?"

"I refuse to listen. I consider it snooping."

Delilah was right, to an extent. But when someone's thoughts make it difficult not to be heard, one ought to be absolved for prying. "Well, Delilah, here is what she is saying: 'He won't help. No one will help. I have no other choice.'" I could have gone on, but Delilah had turned away from me.

Frustrated, I returned my attention to Grace, who had left the stone area and was trudging through the sand. Her back stooped sad and low, as if from a weight heavier than the stones in her pockets. Beatrice and Evan scrambled around her like puppies circling their mistress. Grace stopped and slipped the sweaters on the children, atop their overalls.

Delilah could not be contained. It was as though Grace did not exist for her. "Are they not dear! Look at Beatrice's dimples. And Evan's rosy cheeks. Pictures of joy and health, they are. Is not Evan a gentleman, buttoning Beatrice's top button? They are so darling."

"What do you mean, 'Are they not darling'?" Delilah's blindness irked me. "Have you not been watching Grace at all? There is nothing dear or darling about her right now. She is having a very difficult time. Clearly, things are not going well here."

Haunting memories from previous lifetimes streamed through my awareness. I had seen Grace like this before, in other incarnations. Her slim, aristocratic figure clad in bright, mismatched garments, with a martyred expression tarnishing her patrician face, as though none of what happened to her was a bit her fault. Come to think of it, every lifetime of late, it had been the same thing. She would insist on being the mother, she promised to do it right this time, and always we acceded. You would think we would learn, but instead we always held out hope.

Delilah ignored my concern. Her shimmer softened. "I mean the children. We will look just like them one day."

I shuddered at Delilah's blindness and continued watching. Grace picked up a stone the size of a sandwich half and stuffed it in her rear pants pocket. It barely fit. The sight caused me to feel strangely vulnerable and unsteady, something a receding wave could easily snatch away. I was unsure if I was feeling her or myself. "Grace!" I yelled. "Go back to Sadie's house! There always is a way, there is always hope."

Grace showed no sign of hearing me. The skin between her dark eyebrows furrowed deeper and longer. Her eyes, restless and anxious, searched the sand for direction. In ostinato fashion, her sturdy hands gripped the children's, then just as firmly she released her hold, for the children begged to play.

"Grace! Sadie will help you. This is not a time to make decisions. Go back! Hope is the greatest virtue! Hope creates. Remember?"

Grace continued walking toward the shoreline. I presumed she did not hear me.

Then, without warning, when she was halfway to the shore, she stopped and gazed at the horizon. Something had captured her fancy. The creases between her brows dissolved, and her lips moved imperatively. The children stopped in their tracks and faced her. When Evan grabbed Beatrice's hand, she sidled tight to him. Both their tiny mouths froze in little O shapes.

"Maybe we will live by the shore." Delilah swirled. "That would be terrific. Life cannot come too soon."

I let her words pass through me. Delilah was the baby of the family. Her inexperience had to be tolerated. Why, it has been how many lifetimes that she has never even made it to adulthood?

Besides, my attention was on Grace. Her gritty mind chatter grew more visible to me, along with a glum green light now leaking from her. She wanted someone to save her, or at least lend a hand, but thought no one would. It was that kind of a green. Muddy and hopeless.

Then the green vanished completely.

I waited for a new color to replace it, but nothing emerged.

Grace, I then realized, had not only taken the children's hands stiffly in her own, but she was marching them toward the water's edge.

With Grace's hand clutching his, Evan was forced to run to keep up. His hat dangled against his back, bucking like a bronco, while its chin strap cut into his neck. The sunlight lit his ears in such a way that they appeared as two, glowing red wings. His short dark curls jiggled against this scalp, like nervous music.

The pace proved too much for Beatrice. Not quite two years old, her little legs had to take three steps for her mother's every one. Thrice she tripped over seaweed limbs and landed flat on her face. Specks of sand and seaweed leaves stuck in her hair and eyebrows. Tearfully she would rise, arms stretched high, and beg, "Mama, pick up. Carry me." Each time, Grace merely stood and waited for Beatrice to catch up, all the while clenching Evan's left hand. His right hand reached toward Beatrice, urging her to hurry.

"Coming, Evvy, coming," she called to him, her voice low and determined.

When gathered together, with Beatrice on Grace's left and Evan on her right, Grace resumed her march.

Oh, the children's faces! The nearer Grace dragged them to the water, the rounder their widening eyes became. I could not stand it. Evan's cries, "No, Mama, no," went unheeded. Beatrice's mouth fell open in horror, as if she recognized she was no match for the sea.

I rushed in close, yelling scarlet tones to stop them, but Grace walked right through me, leaving her bourbon scent wafting in me. I should have known.

Beatrice's hand wriggled against her mother's pull, and she halted in my midst. Looking up in me, she whispered, "An Na. An Na."

I nearly melted into a puddle. Beatrice recognized me! Do you know how rare that is? To have a loved one confined by skin, sinew, and corpuscles, actually see your soul and know your name!

Grace tugged at Beatrice. "Come. Keep up."

Little Beatrice obeyed, but not without first looking back at me and whispering, "Carry me."

It broke my soul. I had to do something. But what? There is a fine line that separates helping, which is acceptable, and interfering, which is not. But I could hope. I could create.

The moment the trio reached the moist sand, pristine, white ocean foam swirled around their feet like famished hyenas, darkening the children's shoes and staining their red socks a burgundy hue.

Beatrice leapt to escape the water's chill. When she splashed back down, cold, dark droplets drenched her overalls. She screeched and howled. Wispy parts of her, rainbow threads, rose into the sky, congregated, and hovered above her.

Evan's teeth chattered, and his stunned eyes froze at the sight of the colossal, roaring surf about to devour him. His thwarted efforts to save his life alternated from struggling to unleash his fist from his mother's strong hands, futilely turning against her strength to run for the beach, and biting her hand and socking her in the belly. Oh, the shrieking terror in his eyes, like those of a wild, trapped animal.

Grace's grip on the children's hands tightened. Her knuckles whitened. Her back stiffened, soldier ready; her shoulders leveled like a yoke. Her teeth gnawed at the insides of her tightly sealed lips. Worry had left her brow. A decision had been made. Step by step, she drove herself and her children forward into deeper water.

This had to stop! I buttressed my vibration, making it as dense as possible, which I knew was not dense enough. Nevertheless, I placed myself before Grace.

Alas, to no avail. She walked through me as though I were a mere fog bank.

"Help here, will you!" I rattled at Delilah, who I knew had been watching.

"Anna, we should not interfere." Her shimmer scolded.

"I am helping, not interfering."

"No. Clearly you are interfering."

"For heaven's sake, how could you think that?"

"You know the rules. Only help when asked, and then help sparingly."

"Surely you of all souls should remember how quickly life can be stolen away."

"That has nothing to do with it. Things happen for a reason."

"Let's not forget things also happen for the wrong reason, the unintended reason. Do you want your siblings to die? That is what is about to happen here. How will we manage if they are gone? Or if Grace dies? Or she goes to jail. How will we be born?"

"But if we interfere . . ."

Obviously, I was talking to a wall, which Delilah can sometimes be. Except this was no time to discuss the intricacies of free will and limitless possibilities. "Dear, we are not interfering. The children are asking for help. It is in their faces. Look at them."

As I watched Delilah accept my point, a rogue shore wave broke on the trio. Somehow Beatrice managed to remain standing. Evan, did not. He stumbled and fell backward; sea foam and green water covered him completely. With her left hand still holding Beatrice, Grace hoisted Evan to his feet and patted him between the shoulder blades, as if burping him. He coughed and cried and staggered, but she took hold of his hand and continued on. His soaked locks glinted like quicksilver. The sea's froth bubbled about his waist. His hat bobbed toward the shore before the sucking tide carried it back out to sea. He did not seem to notice.

Back on shore I searched for, and spotted, the foursome I had seen earlier. The two young ladies seemed like friends in their matching movie-star hair-dos, each laughing and strolling with an enamored white-clad man. Sailors most likely. There were a lot of them in the vicinity.

I condensed hard with all my will and rapped each lady on her cheek that faced the ocean.

The taller woman, the one with Springer-spaniel brown hair, turned to see what tapped her. In the process, she noticed Grace and the children, who now, because of their size, were shoulder deep in the water. She pointed and hollered, "Isn't that the lady with the kids in yellow sweaters? What's happening? She's going to drown them!"

Both men dropped their ardor and looked out to sea. Without so much as a word, they raced down the beach. Sand kicked high behind them like rooster tails.

Pleased as I was, I had no time to spare. I rose past the long cliff-side staircase rising from the beach to Sadie's patio and her sleek, mahogany-sided home. I condensed and flung myself full force against her huge, mirror-like oriel. It even rattled!

Glancing down to where Grace stood waist deep in water, I noticed Beatrice completely submerged and looking up to me with pleading eyes through the water's blurring surface. "Help is on the way," I called to her. Her eyes followed my movement, and a half-smile appeared in her eyes.

I then hardened myself again, in case Sadie had not heard the window rattling, while simultaneously keeping track of the sailors who were now within feet of reaching the children.

Fortunately, Sadie hurried toward the window, perhaps expecting to save a bird. She felt to make sure the yellow towel she had wrapped around her head was secure, and she tightened the belt around her black lounging robe. Her bath scents left behind a florid wake.

Once outside and discovering no bird on her patio, Sadie admired the surf. Her perfectly plucked eyebrows leapt when she caught sight of Grace standing in the water, her children perhaps submerged, and two sailors diving under the water's surface. "Damn it, Grace," she whispered, then hollered, "Grace, come back! Now!!" though she must have known the crashing shoreline muted her words.

She raced back into her home, not bothering to close the double doors behind her. In her kitchen, she dialed a number on her black telephone. The nails of one hand clicked on the tile counter as she waited. And waited. Each second seemed a day. Furious and frustrated, she slammed the receiver down and rushed back to her patio.

The sailors, who had plucked the children from their mother's and the ocean's grasp, said something to Grace. She turned her back to them. Her shoulders had lost their level. The sailor holding Beatrice shouted something at Grace, and waved his hand for her to follow him. Getting no response from Grace, he scrambled to catch up with his friend rushing Evan to shore.

The sight of the two little ones in the men's arms set Sadie in motion. She ran down the flight of wooden steps; one hand held the metal rail, and the other minded her towel.

Evan's eyes lolled in their sockets and his arms and legs dangled lifelessly. Water droplets dripped from his fingertips and sock toes. The man carrying him was in tears, racing faster than he could breathe. He howled and panted, and prayed to every lord he could name. Beatrice was a tight, sopping wet ball in the other man's arms, a little sow bug curled into herself.

Once on the sand, mere feet beyond the tide line, both men yelled above the thunderous surf at their flames, "Get an ambulance. Call for help."

Sadie stopped her bustling descent and spun around. She galloped back up the steps to make the call. Seeing Sadie, the girlfriends kicked off their shoes and raced toward their men.

Both men worked on Evan, pressing his back to expel the ocean he breathed. Sad little Beatrice, who'd evidently kept her lips sealed while under water, wandered in manic circles around the men, whimpering, and stooping low to see. She did not seem to notice when the girlfriends arrived. Her plump, dimpled hands kneaded her knee caps. One of her brown leather shoes had managed to survive intact, while scratchy sand caked her other foot's sock.

Delilah and I floated above Evan. I was desperate. He had to live. I could not dismiss our family's destiny as easily as Delilah seemed to.

I conjured the thought that Evan lived, and I thought it. The more I thought it, the more it thickened. With all my will I wanted this thought to exist.

I wafted backward to watch the thought become.

Down on all fours, shivering from the wet, Beatrice crawled through the colonnade of arms and legs. She petted Evan's lips and ears with her tiny fingers. She leaned over him and kissed him on his cheek, leaving a shiny sparkle of spit. Though her tiny teeth chattered, she cooed into his ear, "Evvy, wake up." Her little voice was kind, as though she genuinely believed Evan was simply napping.

Then the man pressing against Evan's back hit the magic spot, and water shot out Evan's mouth. A circle darkened on the sand beneath his cheek.

"Do it again," the other man told him.

"Be gentle," the tall woman said.

The man pressed again, his hands trying hard to be firm yet thoughtful.

"Evvy, wake up," Beatrice chanted until Evan did open an eye, and then the other, and then coughed and sputtered, and threw up, and cried.

My energy collapsed in momentary relief, only to tighten itself once more when I realized that trouble still brewed.

I focused on Beatrice, who had turned toward the surf to watch her mother.

Grace stood waist-deep in the water, her back to the shore. Her hat dangled against her back, and her hands lay piled atop her head. Evan's hat bobbed to her right, maybe fifty feet away.

Beatrice ran to the water's edge and cried, "Mama!" When her mother ignored her, Beatrice howled, "Mama, Mama." Her trembling hands reached out toward her mother, spread wide like free-falling starfish.

Still her mother did not turn her way.

Beatrice stomped her socked foot on the sand. She stormed in little circles. She threw sand at her mother. When she dashed into the water to drag her mother to shore, she froze the instant the water touched her. Screaming and sobbing, she backed away from the water. "Mama, Mama, Mama," she whined.

But Grace never turned around to answer Beatrice, never made an attempt to see how her children were, never said a word to soothe them.

"Mama, Mama," Beatrice whispered, her voice trailing off, as if coming to grips with the fact that her mother was refusing to be her mother. More wisps of Beatrice rose, purples and yellows, to assemble with the others, high up and safe.

From behind, a sailor's arms scooped Beatrice up to take her to Sadie's house.

Knowing Sadie, I did not have a good feeling for what would happen next.

§

I rose to the cliff top, near Sadie's home, while Delilah stayed with Grace. I wanted to be alone. I had thinking to do and decisions to make. Saving the children had been dangerously close, and confounding. I decided I best simply watch what happened next, to let life unfurl. Perhaps Delilah had been right. Perhaps not. Chances were good that I had already overstepped my bounds, but with good reason, in my opinion.

But no one really knows.

The women helped their sailor men carry Beatrice and Evan up the steps to Sadie's.

With pristine white towels in her arms, Sadie was ready for the sopping men and the children they carried. Behind her, the double doors stood shut. "I can't thank you enough for your help," she told the men, as she took first Evan, then Beatrice, and swathed them in towels and sat them in two of her wrought iron patio chairs. Both children, thumbs in their mouths, kept their eyes locked on their mother standing like an islet in the sea.

"Glad to be of help," one sailor said, his teeth chattering from the cold. "Did you call an ambulance?" He perked his ears to listen for sirens.

Sadie handed both men towels. "Everything's being handled. I'll make the reports and see this is taken care of correctly. And keep the towels." By taking minuscule steps toward the staircase, she tried to make it clear that the four should leave.

"You're sure?" the other sailor asked. "Don't you think we should talk to the police? Tell them what we saw?"

Sadie smiled meticulously, the way powerful people do when faced with adult naivete. "I'm sure there'll be no need. I saw it all."

"But that lady was going to drown her children. That's against the law."

Sadie looked at him quizzically. "You don't know that to be true," she said with a straight face, while inching closer to the staircase.

The tall girlfriend grabbed the arm of the sailor with chattering teeth. She held his soaking hat in her other hand. "Come on, Hank, we better get back. You'll catch pneumonia out here." Then, leveling her focus at Sadie, said, "This lady obviously knows what she's doing."

Sadie's chin rose ever so slightly in triumph and inched another step closer to the cliff.

When the four finally disappeared down the staircase and were on their way back to wherever they came, Sadie stood between Beatrice and Evan. She placed her palms on the backs of their heads to send comfort, and watched their mother get herself to shore. Once there, Grace walked back into the water and sat a few yards from the tide line, where she faced the cliff that stared back at her. Here she wailed and bawled and lifted her arms like swan necks before letting them splash down in the incoming tide. Waves crashed at her back, giving her the flogging she deserved.

§

I assumed that what happened next was a result of phone calls Sadie made. Three fancy dark cars arrived in quick order and parked against the cypress bushes in her ample U-shaped driveway. A Cadillac, a Lincoln, and a snazzy Healey convertible. Men in worsted, wide-lapelled suits stepped out of these cars, two carrying fine-skin brief cases, and the other a black leather doctor's satchel.

I recognized the latter. He was Ernest, the children's father, and presumably mine in the future. I initially thought he arrived to bring his children to his home. But that would make no sense. He was married to another woman who happened not to be our mother, and who had no knowledge that Evan and Beatrice even existed.

I looked back at Grace, washing this way and that in the waves, and I recalled the pact she had made with Ernest before they were born. He had agreed to father us, and she to be our mother. Unfortunately, there were details they had failed to address.

Which sent me worrying about my future. A Thomas Eliot line repeatedly streamed through me, like a warning, "In my beginning is my end."

Though I knew what the line meant, I did not want to think about what it signified for my future. Worried, I went out to the driveway and awaited more cars.

I admit I half expected to see a police car arrive, or a fire truck, or an ambulance. Perhaps Sadie had forgotten to call them. But that was unlikely. Sadie was too clever to forget. When she had opened her front door to let the men enter, Sadie took the hand of the man carrying the cordovan alligator brief case, pulled him aside, and whispered to his cheek, "Lawrence, we have to find someone to take the children off Grace's hands." He nodded without looking at her, as though he had precisely the same thought.

This baffled me, for I considered Sadie to be a real friend to Grace.

What happened next added to my surprise, perhaps because I had not spent copious amounts of time watching my siblings play around on Earth all day, as Delilah had.

Ernest removed his suit jacket and tie and hung them in Sadie's entry closet. He then rolled up his white starched shirt sleeves and bathed Evan and Beatrice in Sadie's tub. When they were clean, he wrapped them in cozy, white blankets to dry. By the awed way the children studied him, I had the feeling that he was a stranger to them. Was this to be my fate too?

While Ernest bathed the children, Lawrence and Sadie Lacharite drove their Cadillac to Grace's tiny apartment and let themselves in using the key with which Grace had entrusted them. She removed two days' worth of children's clothes from the clean-laundry pile on the bed, folded them neatly, and packed them in a grocery box she found on Grace's kitchen counter. Lawrence added Beatrice's dirty stuffed bunny and Evan's giraffe to the box, along with dry shoes for each, before they headed back home.

The third man, who sported a thin white mustache, remained in Sadie's living room. He removed an envelope from inside his suit coat, counted the stack of one-hundred-dollar bills found inside, tidied the stack, and replaced it in the envelope. His eyes looked absently at the fineries appointing the room. A Ming moon flask. Two black leather Eames sofas facing each other. Vast, drapeless windows, which rendered the ocean view into seascape paintings. He moistened the envelope flap with his tongue and folded it shut. The heel of his hand secured the seal. Using the pen from his lapel pocket, he wrote "Grace Winslow" on the envelope's front. He then propped the envelope against the black vase filled with pink roses Sadie had positioned atop her hand-carved Steinway.

All the while, Grace lolled on the shore flogged by the sea. No one went to retrieve her. No one even called for her. Delilah took it upon herself to watch over her while she sobered up and could then get herself home.

"See, Anna!" Delilah called to me from the beach. "What did I tell you! Everything always turns out for the best."

I perched outside, near the roof. "You did not tell me that. You said, 'Everything happens for a reason.'"

"Same thing."

I dulled myself to show I disagreed. "Actually, what happened may not be for the best."

At that moment, Sadie, who had been home for perhaps fifteen minutes, brought the children and their stuffed animals out to the Lincoln and bustled them into the back seat. Both children screamed for their mother, while Sadie shut the door with an unintended slam.

Delilah, still pondering my words, rose up the cliff to also watch Sadie. She asked me, "You do not think everything happens for a reason?" Her aura seemed mottled and confused.

"It may happen for a reason, but not necessarily for a good reason." I had to remember how young she was, how few life times she aged enough to gain any kind of wisdom.

"But who are we to know what is best?"

"Best feels good."

Delilah crystallized for a second, then relaxed, as though smiling. "I like that. Best feels good."

"Do you feel good about what is happening right now? Would you want to be them in this moment?"

She weighed my question. "Not really."

"Nor would I." Grace's thickening waist came to mind, and what it could mean for me. "In fact, what is happening has me rethinking this coming lifetime."

Delilah froze. "What? Whatever do you mean?"

Her reaction startled me. But so did the abrupt decision I had just made, or was making. I had not given a thought to Delilah or Grace. Why, just as I experienced relief in the possibility of not living out this lifetime, it occurred to me how badly Grace might take my early death. And how she might respond as a result. I did have Delilah's future with Grace to consider. She would be an only child. There were no easy answers. "Please, Delilah, pay me no mind. I was just thinking. I was not deciding."

The man with the white mustache came out the front door, kissed Sadie on the cheek, and opened the driver's door of the Lincoln. The children's crying blared in the courtyard until the man shut his door.

Delilah came so close she touched me. "Why are the children in that car?"

"I think he is taking them away with him."

"But they are our children. They are our siblings. He cannot do that."

"Maybe you missed it, but he put money in an envelope for Grace. He probably thinks they are his children now."

Delilah sank for what seemed minutes, then suddenly rose and puffed out. "This is terrible. We have to fix this. What will you do when you are born? You will have no siblings. We have to think of something."

"That is why I was reconsidering this coming lifetime."

Her color startled, then shattered. "Are you planning to skip this life time?" She moved in closer. I could feel her shards penetrate me. "You cannot do that. You promised you would be with us. With me."

I tried to appear calm. "I know. But perhaps I will be more helpful not alive as a human." I focused on the driveway and hoped Delilah's attention would follow. I really did not want to discuss my thoughts until I was clear. "Look, he has started the car."

Delilah wobbled, and she withdrew from me, just as the Lincoln snaked its way out the Lacharite's driveway and into the neighborhood. I could see the sobbing children standing on the back seat, looking out the rear window, searching for their mother. The bunny and giraffe lay sprawled on the rear window ledge. Then, dreamlike, Beatrice spotted me. She pointed my way and stared at me, as if to memorize me, or to fathom what she was seeing.

I kept myself steady, so she would not miss a bit of me. Our futures together would depend upon this memory. How I wanted to lunge into that car and rescue my siblings from what was happening, but wisdom gained from lifetimes and soul-times stayed my reaction.

Eventually the Lincoln turned right onto Pacific Coast Highway and headed south toward San Diego.

"He will bring them back, I am sure." Delilah jittered with worry.

"Not if he thinks the money he left is a fair price." I could not help muse at the irony of our parents, Grace and Ernest, in the pre-life, adamantly pushing a unified Destiny, a family effort, but then undermining it in this lifetime to such an extent it is practically impossible to manifest.

But, when I really thought about it, I realized it was not impossible to create. Nothing is impossible.

"How much money did he leave? Did you see?"

"Ten one-hundred-dollar bills."

Delilah shrank to a small ball. "But our family's Destiny? What is to become of it?" Her vibration dimmed enough that I worried she would dissipate.

I, on the other hand, had resolved my conflict. My mind was made up. "That explains why I think we will all be better off if I opt out of life."

"But—."

"Hear me out. I care about our Destiny. I care about it more than ever before. I know this is our moment in time. Science and art are ready for us. Picasso and Einstein have paved the way. Thinking which once would have made our Destiny more difficult has changed. You, Beatrice, and Evan are incarnating into a whole new age on Earth. As for myself, I will hold back, for in one's beginning is one's end.

She appeared a splash of colors. Amused, quizzical, perturbed. "That sounds familiar. What are you telling me?"

I beamed. I loved that she recognized words from *Four_Quartets*. "Dear, if I am to meet my end, I will need a new beginning, different from the one originally planned."

She seemed to understand. "But what about me? How will I meet my goals?"

"I will help you. Because you will not have Beatrice or Evan there to remind you of your destiny, I will take it as my duty to remind you. One of us has to remember how pliable the world really is. One of us has to remind the others that possibility is in itself a seed. I will be the reminder."

Her aura swirled and tightened, like a movie of an explosion run backward. Then she brightened into an innocent yellow glow. "I will remember. Trust me. I know I will."

"No, you will not. None of us ever do. Not without help."

Delilah fidgeted. Then she suddenly formed a column. "Then, swear to me you will be with me in life."

I let my energy surround her. "That is what I am telling you. I promise I will be with you. I swear on my soul. My whole purpose in skipping this life is to be there for you, and Evan and Beatrice, as you try to remember."

Delilah glittered, popped, and sprayed.

I cozied even tighter around her. "Everything will be fine. You will see."

That was the best I could hope for, and thus create.

§

September 14; 1981

My three siblings, now incarnated, have no idea how close I stay to them. Even though I have skipped this lifetime, I live with them every day of theirs. I believe in the promise I made Delilah more than thirty years ago and have made it my primary purpose.

Which means a lot of work for me.

Consider managing your kin's destiny when practically no one is in the same family. Then factor in how blind and deaf they are to me. They have no concept that I even exist.

But, all things considered, I am satisfied with my progress. I show them pertinent things by focusing my light into a hotspot, which they notice approximately three percent of the time. I put things in their way, like books and magazines they should read, which again they detect less than five percent of the time. I move things out of the way. I conjure visions. Sometimes I'm a complete chatterbox around them, or I wax poetic, even though they tune me out. They would be famous if they ever wrote any of my lines down. (Others have, which thrills me more than you would suspect.) Regardless, I care not; I love to hear myself think. And I need to keep pace with their growing vocabularies. I've even come to adore contractions!

You might think my success rate intolerably low, but actually it's not bad. I mean, I'm not around in order to live their lives. That's considered illegal, in some circles. I can offer my services, which their own free will can either accept or reject. Pretty fair, in my opinion. Besides, it keeps me engaged, and I've saved their lives a surprising number of times. Literally.

At this moment, the Monday sun has already set in Lubbock, Texas. In the dimmed light of her bathroom, Delilah, who was born a year after my stillbirth, readies for an early bedtime. Her kitchen's cleared and cleaned of tonight's pizza dinner, and her tub's filling with water. She's exhausted from yesterday, which was her twenty-ninth birthday. First there had been a quiet little party around her kitchen table with her husband and two young sons. Lots of chocolate cake, ice cream, and sprinklies for them; a pack of cigarettes for her. Her boys had gotten her Foreigner's latest tape, and Big Joe'd bought her little diamond studs. Too bad they couldn't give her what she really longed for and has been going to extravagant lengths to achieve.

Afterward, just before the babysitter arrived, she moussed and teased her dark, wavy hair and coaxed it away from her face so it surrounded her like a lion's mane. She donned a lavender silk shirt, tight Calvin Klein jeans, and gold stiletto sandals. Big Joe removed his tie, but kept on his starched dress shirt and suit. Together, they drove off in his white Camaro, which doesn't show the Texas dust, and stopped in at Stubbs for a couple of ribs and a cup of slaw. Afterward, they proceeded to drink their way through every bar, honky-tonk, and dive still open in downtown Lubbock.

Morning came early.

Without wanting to taint your impression of Delilah, I must admit life has toughened her more than I expected. Her life, as we originally planned it, should have been much easier: plenty of rest, intellectual encouragement, and the financial support needed for her to become a doctor. Instead, she spent her formative years foiling Grace's attempts to pass her off to family, friends, and even complete strangers. It is by Delilah's sheer fortitude that she remains Grace's daughter, or that Grace remains her mother.

Two time zones west of Delilah, a couple hours of daylight still remain along the California coast, where Beatrice and Evan live in Huntington Beach and Santa Barbara, respectively. I must warn you; they have new names. That often happens to adopted children.

In Santa Barbara, with the low western sun spraying his hillside home with golden light, Victor, whom you've known as Evan, pounds and kneads a heap of sourdough on a thick, cornmeal-strewn chopping block, while singing along to Wagner's "Pilgrim's Chorus"_playing on the stereo. He hits most of the notes on key, but gets every word of the German libretto correct. Two cigarettes of different lengths burn in a Madonna Inn ashtray resting on the denim-blue tiled counter. A breeze steals into the house through the partly-open kitchen door. Victor considers closing it, but refrains. Openings to the outside world are exactly what he wants.

The phone rings.

Victor stares at it, while a thrill surges within him. Fortunately, he's home alone. His wife Phoebe and toddler daughter Katie haven't arrived yet. Giddily, he waits for the second ring before answering. Horribly, the thought of Phoebe walking through the door grows immense in his mind. He imagines hearing her car coming to a stop in the driveway. "Hello?"

"It's me," the voice on the other end of the line says.

A guillotine slams down in Victor's mind. "Don't ever call me again. Even if I beg you to."

The caller says nothing for a moment. His breathing can be heard. Then, with a quick one-two, he says, "I don't believe you," and hangs up.

Another gust blows in the kitchen door, widening it. Victor slams it shut and returns to his dough, kneading it, pounding it, strangling it, killing it with his bare hands. He's got a lot to sort out in his life.

A hundred miles south of Santa Barbara, Bibi, whom you remember as little Beatrice, stands on the sidewalk in front of the Beef Palace Meat Shop, a block from her home. Here she absent-mindedly tends to her two little kids as they ride the almost-life-size steer statues, which they always get to do if they've been good in the grocery store next door.

In reality, it's not her kids she sees. Paintings float before her mind, haunting and taunting her like the New World must have coaxed Columbus. These paintings are the ones she'd love to paint, but won't. Thick, heavily textured paintings, rich in color, vibrant with motion, made deep with layers and tiers like chapters of a book, each fabricated to reveal the wonders of the mundane world. Her physical body and psyche respond alike, soaked in the moment, whisked to another zone where she knows and understands things from another plane.

"Mommy, watch!"

Her daughter's voice snaps Bibi's out of her trance and shoves her back into her real life, where painting is an impossibility with small children around, or with her life around, for that matter.

"C'mon, sports fans, time to go home," she tells her kids as she hauls them off their colossal mounts and walks them to the car. The paintings linger burned in her mind as an afterimage. She imagines the day, hanging out in front of her like a beckoning carrot, when the needs of everyone in her life finally quiets enough for her to pick up her paint brushes again.

But that day is not today. She buckles the kids into the sty they've made of her back seat. When she gets into the car, she slams the door so hard that the car shakes and the air inside it convulses. The movement surprises her, but not the fact that she slammed the door. She stares into the rear-view mirror, trying to detect how much of her anger shows in her eyes. When she decides she looks normal enough, she puts the key in the ignition and starts her car. She'll be home in two minutes. If only she could elongate that to two hours.

§

I feel you must also know that Bibi and Victor have no connection, legal or otherwise, with their birth mother Grace's family, the Winslows, or their birthfather Earnest's family, the Borgs. Their new parents, Leif and Signe Andressen, adopted the children the day after the beach incident. Or rather, they took possession of the children that day. The official adoption would take another seven years. That was the Andressens' money in the envelope.

Immediately, they renamed the children Bibi and Victor. Well, actually, they named her Ingrid, but Victor refused to call his sister that.

From my perspective, Victor and Bibi lost a lot more than a mother that fateful November day in 1948. Victor lost his mirror, and Bibi lost the threads that sewed her together.

Since then, Victor has spent his days wondering who on Earth he is, because it was for Grace to show him. Like her, he was to be a pianist. An absolutely fantastic one. But the chance for that has passed. He is not with Grace, and the Andressens have little understanding of his talent. It's as though he were a Stradivarius bequeathed to a tribe of Papuan aborigines. Not that there's anything wrong with Papuan aborigines.

On the other hand, Bibi, out of self-preservation, tries to ignore who she is because with her threads no longer holding her together, she's not present enough to actually suffer. She's like a cashmere coat whose every seam, every placket and lapel, every button and pocket insert, is held together with safety pins, duct tape, and paper clips. As for her threads, they're up here, safe in the ether. They visit her from time to time, hoping they can be of use. But really, a thread repair here or there won't fix this coat.

You know, most animals have a way of shaking off a frightful experience so it doesn't pester them for the rest of their lives. A rabbit finally safe in its warren, having just escaped with its life from the jaws of a pursuing coyote, allows itself time to literally shiver and quiver the trauma from its bones so it can once again leave its warren tomorrow morning in search of food.

Bibi is no rabbit. That whole experience at the beach will stay with her for the rest of her life, doing its thing, incessantly recreating itself, until she finally stops and shakes it off.

We all know this before we are born, but how easily we forget: You have to do something with your traumas, even the little ones, or they will rule your life.

Two

Whispers in the Air

September. 14; Huntington Beach, Calif.

This moment, when Bibi parks her four-year-old Volvo she's christened Lars O'Leary in the family's garage and opens the passenger door so she can unbuckle her little monsters, is the moment when whatever peace she's experienced during the fifteen-mile drive home from her teaching job abruptly ends. If she downs a couple cups of coffee, categorizes her to-do list and focuses like a shot gun, she can get her stuff done by nine, or maybe ten. But then there's the question of what she'll find in her bedroom. That's a priority.

Noah tumbles out first; the left strap of his railroad-striped Oshkosh B'Goshes is twisted over his shoulder like a wrung rag. A tiny chip from a grape lollipop dangles from a teddy-bear brown curl near his crown. "Momby, Sesmee Treat. Okkar." He races past his father's mailbox-blue Plymouth Reliant, which looks suspiciously like a narc's car, to the steps leading from the garage into their home's entryway. His fat, untied tennis-shoe laces trail behind him, despite the double bows Bibi ties and the lace guards she keeps buying, which are, hopefully, somewhere in the car. With a splat, he stumbles on the garage's concrete floor, starts to cry, but stops and gets back up. "Sesmee Treat!" Using both hands, he climbs the steps leading into the house, pushes open the door that's been left ajar, and disappears.

"Good boy, Noah!" Bibi calls after him. "Be a little trouper. You're going to need it in this life." She hates that she's said this. If she had time, she'd hug him, or kiss his knees. But she's got so damned much stuff to do.

Bibi's tow-headed four-year-old daughter Ella sits unbuckled, but not yet out of the car, because she's adorably pushing the stuffing she removed from her turquoise plush elephant back in through its fanny.

Figuring Ella's project will occupy her for at least another ten minutes, Bibi follows Noah into the house, her arms burdened by the three brown paper grocery bags she removed from the trunk, a wheat-toned canvas book bag thick with self-inflicted essays to grade, and the kids' Smurf sitter tote, which now weighs a lot less since Noah got off the bottle and diapers. She checks behind her to make sure she hasn't lost anything.

"I am the Count. Ha, ha, ha, ha," the Transylvanian in the TV booms. In the back of her mind, Bibi registers that Noah has mastered pulling the TV's power button. Not a good thing.

Bibi plops everything she's carrying a foot away from the spot where her gray-and-white fluffy-cat Ceres naps on the ugly, brown Naugahyde settee in the family room, the one she'll replace when she hopefully works summer school next June. She gives the cat a quick love pat between her ears, lowers the TV's volume a quarter turn, takes the matchbox car out of Noah's mouth, and heads down the hall to her bedroom.

Ceres patters right behind.

Having heard his family come home, Michael has rallied. He sits by the side of the bed, his jaw slack, his shoulders heaving as he pants.

Bibi hesitates and slows her steps. She's still not used to Michael being sick all the time, but it's been going on so long, she can't imagine him well either. What fate has wrought.

As she nears, Michael puts on his horn-rim glasses. A day's worth of fingerprints mar their transparency; she glances to his bedside table to make sure he still has a supply of Kleenex. She walks around the bed in order to face him. "How're you doing?" Behind him, her side of the bed is just as she left it this morning. A dimple remains on her faded glen plaid pillow case where her head had rested. The amethyst crystal she holds when she sleeps peeks out from under the pillow. Jean Auel's *Clan of the Cave Bear* lies open and face down on her table. What she'd give to be back in bed reading a book. That one especially.

Michael looks up at her and grimaces from some internal pain.

She judges his coloring and touches the back of her hand to his cheek. She kisses his forehead and smoothes her hand across his crown, where just a couple months ago he sported a full growth of fine, brown hair. Now he looks like a Saturday Night Live cone head, which she hates because she thinks people will tease him or think he's a goon. His stomach feels rotten; she can feel it in her own. And she senses a headache near her sinuses where just minutes ago she felt fine. "You have a headache?" She watches him closely. He's the forty-sixth person in the whole world to be on that experimental drug Interferon; no telling what it'll do to him.

His eyes close, as if he's tired of complaining. Then he nods.

"Want some Tylenol? I'll get you some."

"Nah, I'm okay." Dried-crisp saliva accentuates the corners of Michael's lips.

Elvis Presley lips, she reminds herself. Full and devouring. At least that's what she used to think. She wipes them clean with her index finger and thumb and removes his glasses.

Ceres bounds atop the bed and immediately caresses her head against Michael's back and arm.

Michael gifts her with an under-the-chin scratch. Her whiskers quiver, her mouth grins, and her motor purrs.

"She's a fool for love," Bibi laughs, ignoring the envy she feels. She exhales on his lenses and wipes them with a Kleenex.

Michael reaches for Bibi's shoulders. "Yep, definitely knows how to get what she wants."

She braces herself; he weighs eighty pounds more than she. It amazes her how easy carrying the weight of others seems, as though she was built for it. She realizes the ache behind her sinuses has quickened. "You sure you don't want a Tylenol?"

His hands press deeply and trustingly into her shoulders, and he hefts himself up. "I'm okay."

She holds her breath; it makes her feel stronger. When he's standing on his own, she studies him more deeply. She can't decide whether to believe him or not. Sometimes his stoicism aims to gain him sympathy. She replaces his glasses on his nose.

"Talking about headaches, Bibi, your mom keeps calling."

The air around Bibi eddies. She searches Michael's dark, equine eyes for emotional clues, but sees only his sick tiredness and his gratitude that she's finally home. If he were feeling better, he'd be yelling about her mom calling a bajillion-William times. She's like an obsessed squirrel in the fall, he says. She never knows when enough is enough. It's just one of the thousand things about her mother that drives him livid.

But Michael's not feeling better. He just finished another round of chemo yesterday, and she knows he doesn't give a rat's ass about anything. His words, not hers.

"I'm sorry. I'll call her." Bibi straightens his black-and-indigo plaid terry robe around him and reties its belt. It was her father's robe, when he was alive. Her mind goes blank for less than a second. She hates men in bathrobes. They look stupid, or something. It seems wrong that Michael should even consider wearing it, much less own it. But he likes its feel.

He reaches in his pocket. "First." He hands her the folded note he'd written earlier. His square thumb covers her name, which he'd neatly printed on the outside. "The lady in C has a clogged toilet. Can you get it unclogged so we don't have to pay a plumber?"

Bibi tastes bile. She manages to smile enough for Michael to know she'll take care of it, but not enough for him to believe she's happy about it, which she is not. Who would be? Another goddamned responsibility that only she out of all the people in the whole stupid world can do. And if she doesn't do it, everything in her well-organized life will crash down upon her. God, she could use a cigarette. But, no, the hypnotist told her to count to fifteen and promised the feeling would go away.

She counts to fifteen, files the note in her blazer pocket while also feeling around for a stick of gum which she doesn't find, spins around before her anger reveals itself, and marches down the hall, past her paintings she did in college, past Ella's room on the left and the hallowed study on the right, past the entry and family room where Ella has joined her brother in front of the TV, and into the kitchen for crappola-snacks to feed the kids during the drive to Costa Mesa where their apartments are. Forget getting her chores done by nine. She'll be lucky to be in bed before midnight. It won't be the first time she's fallen asleep standing up.

Ceres, having heard the pantry open, weaves herself around Bibi's legs, purring and marching her little feed-me-now dance. Bibi stuffs a packet of cheese and peanut-butter crackers in one pocket and a box of animal crackers and a pack of gum from the cannister atop the armoire in her other, and then satisfies Ceres with a fresh catnip mouse she's had cached way back in the cupboard. God knows, everyone can do with an altered state now and then.

Michael's footsteps shuffle down the hall. "Punkin, I'm sorry. I'd do this if I could." His dark eyes bleed honesty.

Bibi thaws. This is not his fault. When he thought it would be a great idea to own some apartments, it was three months before his cancer was discovered and a third of his lymph system had to be removed. If the two of them knew then what they know now, she doubts she'd be worrying a whit about the lady in C. She goes to him and takes his hand. "I know," she tells him. "I'm sorry I'm cross. I'm so tired. I have so much to do. I just want some rest."

He holds her to him, his arms warm, but not what they used to be. "I know you're tired. This is unfair to you." How she longs for the Michael she married. His illness has turned him into a third child, something she vehemently refused to have. She muses at the irony; his doctor discovered Michael's cancer when he went in for a vasectomy. She wills herself to let him hold her for as long as he needs.

But the phone rings.

Bibi grips Michael harder, grateful for the pang of guilt he must feel in this moment. "It's my mother," she says into his chest. She pauses for this to sink in. "Will you answer it?"

He pulls away and stares at her like she's asked him to leap off a cliff.

"Please." She feels stupid begging him, but what little time she has keeps washing down the drain. Worse, she doesn't have the stamina. Michael's view of her mother being a squirrel is hypobolic. No, Bibi's mother is one of those torture mechanisms found in horror movies where the walls move in closer and closer, inch by brutal inch, until her prey is massacred, bloody, and trapped.

Michael releases her and goes to answer the call at the kitchen wall phone.

When he flips on the light switch next to the kitchen phone, their sunken great room, where they entertain guests and listen to music, lights up. Bibi's old ebony baby grand gleams in this light, as does the now half-crazed Ceres, who lolls luxuriously and completely out of control in the huge room's center.

After listening to the phone for a moment, Michael nods at Bibi. "No, Signe, she's not home yet."

At which point Ella gets up from the family room floor, and, holding forth her elbow, runs to Bibi, while the plush elephant she holds in her other hand spills kapok all over the floor. "Mommy, Mommy, look at the scratch I got today."

Damn it! She could kill the world. Bibi hurries past Ella to the kitchen and grabs the phone from Michael. "Mom, we just got home." She snaps her fingers at Ella and points to the spot on the family room floor where she wants Ella to sit down on and watch television with her brother. "Yes, just now. How are you?" She holds the phone away from her ear so Michael can hear and stretches the phone cord enough so she can reach Ella's head. She gives her innocent daughter an exaggerated love pat on the head and a love touch on the end of her nose. It's not her daughter's fault Bibi has the mother she has.

Bibi's mother clears her throat, waits a beat, and then announces, "I got a call from Victor." Bibi's back in Michael's orbit, so they both hear her mother's words. They lock eyes and give each other that here-we-go-again look. This means one of two things. Either Victor wants something her mother refuses to give. Or vice versa. Such a dance. "Mom, can I talk with you later? I gotta take care of one of the apartments."

"Can't Michael do that?"

"Mom, he's sick. Remember?"

"Of course, I remember. I don't know what you're talking about."

Michael and Bibi's eyes meet again, but this time express their struggle to keep from laughing.

"So why did Victor call?"

"He wants a family gathering."

The idea of a family gathering sounds like fun to Bibi. She loves being around Victor because she always feels lively and creative. Besides, she hardly ever gets to see Victor and his family now that they each have children, and, of course, Michael's illness. "And you want some dates?"

"Yes, and I want the gathering at your house."

Michael shakes his head, as if Bibi needs prodding to reject her mother's idea.

Bibi pats his shoulder to still his rising anger. "Why not Charlie's?" After all, her oldest brother Charlie's house, while a suburban tract house like hers, is newer, and larger, and better looking. Heck, it's a veritable mansion. Besides, neither he nor his wife works, the lucky bucks.

"He's too busy now that Christmas is coming."

Busy at what Bibi cannot guess. "And I'm not?"

"Well, you handle things so beautifully."

"Actually, I don't. But why don't you have it at your house."

"It's too far for Victor to drive."

Michael shakes his head adamantly and his hand cuts his throat. His eyes demand: Just tell her no.

"Please, Mom, don't make me do it. I have too much going on in my life. It's not fair to Michael."

Her mother holds her words for a moment, as though purposely creating an uncomfortable silence. Then, "Bibi, poor Victor needs your help. You know how he is. And you know how to handle him. Is this weekend free?"

Victor needs Bibi's help? The only things that come to her mind are the usual. He needs money, again; or he's getting a divorce, which seems unlikely; or he still wants his money from their father's estate, even though the trust says it goes to his mother. Whatever, Bibi doesn't want to talk about it with Michael standing right here. "Mom, I can't."

Like a warning salvo, her mother clears her throat. Bibi recognizes the tone and knows her relentless mother has fully loaded her rifle, which she now, in the privacy of her lovely home, aims directly at Bibi.

Michael pulls out one of the captain's chairs set around their antique oak, claw-foot kitchen table and slumps into it. He reads the mottled brown carpeting under his feet as if it's a cup of tea leaves explaining to him why Bibi's family is so screwed up. Then he looks up and puffs out his cheeks like a trumpeter.

Bibi drags her eyes away from him and looks at the ceiling. "Why don't we all drive up to Santa Barbara, and Victor can put on the dinner? We can all bring things."

"Bibi, you are making this very difficult." Her mother's words tighten around her like a vise. "I can't imagine why you think you just can't have it at your house. It would be easier for everyone."

Bibi holds the receiver to her chest and leans her forehead against the fake mahogany-paneled wall upon which the phone hangs. Scattering psychedelic shards spin in her mind. She feels perforated and exposed. There's no way she can please everyone. Telling her mother no now will not solve the problem, because her mother will just keep calling and doing everything she can think of to get her way. Everything. But doing the opposite from what Michael wants also has its repercussions. He'll accuse her of having no backbone or of not putting their family first, both of which she hates because they're not true. But they seem true to him, and so there's no talking him out of it. At least he's forgiving. This will blow over in two days.

Bibi tsks. "Okay, Mom, this Saturday. At five. But you make the phone calls."

With great protest in each movement, Michael gets up and walks to the sink; his head shakes in disgust.

But he says nothing to her, which is a good thing, because she needs to get to Costa Mesa with the kids in tow and fix Apartment C's stupid toilet and then drive back home in what should, by then, be full-on, stopped up, totally constipated Southern California evening freeway traffic, so she can make and clean up dinner, bathe the kids, correct a piss-pile of essays, do the laundry, oh, and, figure out what this Saturday's meal will be, before she can finally lie down and get some sleep before tomorrow's here-I-am-again rat race starts up. Whatever Victor wants, it better be good.

§

I am constantly rapt by how any singular experience can send one human being careening in one direction, and another human in a completely opposite one, as if the incident were not the same event at all.

Why am I rapt?

Because always the direction starts with a decision, right or wrong, which has the herculean power to hurl a person toward success, or failure, or somewhere in between.

Which is why I wish upon the stars that I can find a way to remember what I know as a soul the next time I incarnate. One of those warning bells, like they have out at sea, would be handy. Or a congenital tattoo. That would be perfect! It should read: Note to Anna: Be willful. Make decisions consciously knowing they are seeds which germinate into your future. Do not plant weeds in your life!

§

Saturday, September 19

Bibi surveys the spread she'd created for Victor's oh-so-necessary Saturday family dinner. Inwardly, she applauds herself for the milieu she's created, though no one else at the table seems to have noticed all the work and effort it took. Just minutes ago, Victor had tried to take credit for the meal. "Isn't this the recipe you got from me?" he'd loudly announced. "It almost tastes good." How unlike him to be so cruel and needy toward Bibi.

The table, tightly set for thirteen, mirrors the picture she'd seen in July's *Architectural Digest*, with a brown-on-brown print Michael's mom, bless her heart, hemmed up from fabric she'd bought for a song at Marimekko's end-of-summer sale. At each place, Bibi'd inserted ivory roses from her garden into a little black beaker she'd gotten on sale from Horchow's, and set it next to a brown-rimmed Dansk plate, upon which she'd served a fine scampi and capellini meal made from her Vincent Price cookbook. If the table looks good, the food's yummy, and you're surrounded by your family, even if they can at times be the world's biggest jerks, what else is needed? Maybe a cigarette. And a thank you.

She counts to fifteen as her attention focuses first on her oldest brother Charlie, and then to Victor, who is up in the kitchen searching for something in Bibi's refrigerator.

If Bibi's brothers were planets, Charlie would be Mercury, and Victor would be Pluto.

Charlie, her elder by seven years, sits next to her at the dinner table, regaling the family with his tale about how he took a train to Catalina Island. He's still wearing his Stetson, which he's paired with a blue and white Reyn Spooner yachting shirt (size XXL), deck shoes, and loose Bermuda shorts. Being a Gemini and a guy's guy, he pulls off such irony with aplomb, even pushing the limits further with his puffy, curlicue handlebar mustache.

Victor, on the other hand, reminds Bibi of a Ritalin-deprived bohemian. Think Edgar Allan Poe. Victor has now bolted from the table for the sixth time during dinner, leaving behind his half-eaten plateful of pasta. He has abandoned his refrigerator search, and is now opening and slamming cupboards and drawers in search of God-knows-what. He's wearing what he's probably worn for the last five days. Dark, rumpled jeans. Thin, barely-white t-shirt. Crumpled, plaid work shirt, sleeves rolled up and completely unbuttoned. And bare feet. His hair resembles Mark Twain's head of curls, unlike Charlie, who is balding. The ashtray next to his plate sits filled to the brim with ashes and butts.

Bibi's inner clock ticks away; she's moving closer to interrupting Charlie and telling Victor to sit down and stay put. Because he's the one who wanted this dinner, he should be sitting at the table holding court, and not Charlie. But she holds back. It'd be just like her family to insist Victor do what he wants while Charlie entertains the family with his exploits.

Gun shots blare from the family room, where Noah, Ella, their four cousins, and Ceres loll about the floor and furniture like noodles, their attention snagged by some Clint Eastwood movie. Evidently Clint's just shot a bad guy and now he's pulling the reins on an irritated, whinnying horse.

"How's it possible to take a train to Catalina?" Bibi asks, even though her mind has already conjured several ways. At the same time, she watches Victor's every move and senses his internal clatter, like he's a growing pile of dirty dishes waiting to be scraped off and rinsed. If only she could see the clock. It feels hours have passed since her family arrived. From where she sits, she realizes how dark outside has become. She touches Michael's wrist under the table so he'll show her his watch.

Instead, he checks the time without showing her. Then, from his seat to her right and at the head of the table, he nudges her with his foot. She picks up on his signal and stares wide-eyed at Victor's wife Phoebe across the table. Hint, hint, her eyes scream. Get Victor down here and make him talk.

Phoebe smiles patronizingly. The pony tail gathered high on her head flits. Such ballerina poise. Her eyes beg for patience.

Charlie rattles on in his slow, entitled way. "We went with the Zeppos. Rented an old railroad dining car, loaded it on a barge, and rode it across the Catalina channel into Isthmus Harbor. Had a wicked little meal on the crossing, right off the Santa Fe Super Chief menu. Kippered herring. Griddle cakes."

Charlie's description of his preposterous adventure distracts Bibi and kindles her jealousy. How fun it must be to live Charlie's gilded life.

From the other end of the table, where Michael had insisted she be seated, Bibi's perfectly-coiffed, white-haired mother chirps, "There isn't anything you two can't do."

It's clear to Bibi that her mother admires Charlie and Rose's life as much as Bibi does. But not enough to ask them how they achieved it, since neither of them work, nor have they done so for years.

Rose, with her Farrah Fawcett looks, puts an arm around Charlie's shoulder, making it impossible to miss her golden trove of rings and bracelets. Auntie Sparkle, the family calls her good naturedly, for she is fun to be around. She smiles her pleased grin and looks down at her plate, because there's really no way to answer her mother-in-law without making the rest of the family hate her.

"Next, we're going to Vegas." Charlie pauses and pretends to smell the air. "By boat."

Of course, thinks Bibi. "Let me guess, a boat on a truck?"

Michael's foot nudges harder against Bibi's.

Irritated that Michael's foot means he's monitoring her stupid jokes, Bibi turns and glares at him. But swiftly realizes Michael's attention is rightly on Victor, still in the kitchen.

Bibi twists left in her chair, raises her hand high and snaps her fingers. "Hey, Vic, get down here!" It's a gesture that always works on her students.

While Charlie fills in the details of their Vegas passage, Victor turns at the sound of Bibi's voice and snapping fingers, and, without closing the cupboard he's been in, hurries through the kitchen past the breakfast table, takes a quick peek around the corner at the cousins, and trots down the three steps. His huge, Elliot Gould piano-player hands smother the Eiffel Tower salt shaker he's carrying, the one Bibi recently shoved behind her platters because she didn't know where else to put it.

Charlie stops talking and stares at the horde of shakers amassing around Victor's plate. Like the rest of the family sitting at the table, Charlie has noticed that Victor's twitching forays to the kitchen, which everyone has pretended to ignore, have yielded four different salt shakers (embarrassingly drawing attention to Bibi's shaker fetish), two water glasses, a now-filled ashtray, and a Marks-a-Lot pen, with which he drew a fat, black arrow on the inside of his forearm.

Victor plops in his chair, pulls it up to the table, and then pushes it back out. He crosses one leg horizontally over the other and grips it in his hands. When Phoebe pats his arm, he shrugs her off. His eyes are lit like fuses.

"Are you okay?" Bibi asks Victor. She wants him to talk, but not when he's like this. He seems inflamed and ghostly all at once, as though he could concurrently explode and deflate.

His nostrils flare, and he pours a salt pile in his palm and heaves it into his mouth, all the while staring vilely at Charlie. "Yeah. I'm fine."

As usual, Charlie reacts to Victor's force with lightness. He stretches out his arms and rests them on the backs of Bibi and Rose's chairs. "So, brother Victor," he asks, with a lilt of humor, "what's going on?"

Before Victor can respond, Phoebe tries to divert the conversation. "Bibi, it was so kind of you to have us. Signe said you insisted on having it at your house."

What nerve her mother has! Bibi glares daggers at her mother. Michael makes a show of clearing his throat, adjusting his glasses, and staring aghast at his mother-in-law.

For a split second, her mother's terrifying eyes stare through Bibi. Round like cannon muzzles, yet made small and covert by shrouding double lids. Stiff, blond lashes rim her lids. Her beady pupils pierce through her ice blue irises, aiming, drilling, and gutting Bibi with one look.

Bibi inwardly shudders, and blinks.

Then her mother shifts her concern to Victor. She reaches to touch Victor's plate, but stops short. "What *is* going on?"

Victor grips his leg tighter, and his fingertips redden. His bitten fingernails seem ironically pale. He glances about the table, from person to person, disgust oozing from his eyes. Then his expression softens. He looks at Phoebe, then at his mother, before taking a deep breath and saying in a clear, deep voice, "I'm going to look for my birth mother." He turns to Bibi. "Our birth mother."

Victor's words suck the air out of the room, leaving nothing for Bibi to breathe. He must know, as they all do, the words he spoke are a sacrilege. He knows Bibi will never agree to look. Never, ever, has she expressed such a desire. He knows this.

Bibi glances at her mother and sees what she expected. Her mother, whose normal complexion carries a lovely ivory cast, burns crimson. Bibi brings her wine glass to her lips and takes a gulp.

"I've come to ask you for your help," Victor tells his mother.

His mother's eyes are on him like nerve gas. Her faint eyebrows have jerked together so that deep ruts have formed above her nose, resembling little horns. Bibi recognizes the look and fully expects her mother to get up, fetch a wooden clothes hanger from the closet, and give Victor a good whipping on his bare legs.

Without responding to his mother's explicit disapproval, Victor turns and looks solely at Bibi. "I can't do it alone." His tone has changed from cold and demanding to poignant and verging on tears, revealing what he thinks destiny owes him.

Burning from the limelight and the dripping sadness in Victor's words, Bibi looks down and studies the uneaten shrimp and pasta she's molded into a mountain on her plate. Victor's pitiful tone draws her in, and she fights her urge to rescue him. He has always been her soft spot. Yet her instincts scream at her to run like hell.

She looks up and stares blankly at him, daring him to continue his course. He should know she won't help him on this. Any other request? Fine. But her birth mother? No one should force that search on another person.

He turns back to his mother. "Well?"

Rose briefly pats Charlie's arm, stands, picks up her dirty dishes and heads up the steps to the kitchen.

Bibi's mother sits stone still. Not a twitch reveals what she might say until she speaks. Then, only her top lip moves. "No." Slowly and certainly she plants her edict, challenging Victor or anyone else to change her well-made mind.

Charlie lets out a sigh and smooths his mustache.

Michael's chair creaks as he sits back and looks out the sliding glass door to the patio.

Bibi glances at the piano, remembering that rare and sickening time she and Victor went toe-to-toe over something, then returns her attention to Victor. If their father were still alive, Victor wouldn't have the nerve to do this. But Dad's dead, so here they sit, Leif and Signe Andressen's three adopted children living out the moment they've seen coming, but have dreaded, for most of their lives.

Phoebe caresses Victor's arm while turning her attention to her mother-in-law. "Signe, Victor's therapist suggested he look." She glances around the table for support.

Victor winces, but says nothing, though his eyes, for a wink of time, suggest a desire to reveal what's locked inside.

Her mother's cheeks pulse in protest. Carefully, she asks, "You mean Victor wants to find her for Dr. Westoff?"

"No, Signe, it's part of Victor's healing."

"Healing? I thought his therapy was for your marriage. That's why I'm paying for it."

Embarrassment stains Phoebe's neck and cheeks. "According to Dr. Westoff, our marriage is being destroyed by Victor's distrust of women." Her voice cracks; her eyes mist. Phoebe, so poised, so resolute, so close to bursting out in tears. Bibi wants to jump up and rescue her from this family. Of all of them, Phoebe is the kindest, the classiest, and the one most willing to forgive.

"Distrust?" Bibi's mother presses her palm to her heart and speaks directly to Victor. "Didn't having a loving mother help you at all?"

Charlie leans forward. "Mom, don't do this."

She ignores Charlie. "We did everything we could think of for you. We gave you everything. And you weren't easy. You know that, don't you?"

Victor slams his hands against his ears. "Stop! Stop! You've been saying that to me all my life."

Bibi grips her hands to keep from also covering her ears to avoid her mother's familiar drone. God, how she hates the drip, drip, drip of indebtedness.

Victor lurches out of his chair, and walks toward the patio, and back again, his fists opening and shutting, holding on, letting go. He clutches his chair's back. "Don't you understand? I have these memories. The memories come to me in dreams in the middle of the night. Hell, in the middle of the day when I'm wide awake. They're so familiar I can taste them. I can't sleep. I don't know what to do about them. It's like I've left part of myself behind somewhere. I was three years old when I was adopted. Not babies like you both were." He stops and stares at Bibi and Charlie, then sits back in his chair. "I know things. I can't just shove everything inside like you can."

He's right, of course. Bibi does shove things under covers, beds, in closets, you name it. So what? Sometimes there's no other choice. Her favorite is to stack all the dirty dishes in a sink and cover them with hot water to soak under a duvet of Ivory liquid bubbles. When she comes back in half an hour, all the rinsing's done. The only thing left to do is run the disposal and load the dishwasher. What's the matter with that? It certainly beats hand scraping everything, dish-by-dish. What a waste of time and effort.

Her mother's words shake Bibi from her self-talk. "I will not agree to this," her mother says. "Tell Dr. Westoff, from me, that he must find another way to help you."

"Can you at least give us the papers?" Phoebe asks.

"No."

"Why not?" Victor hollers at his mother.

The television mutes. Six heads pop up to see what's happening, but pop right back down as a single unit, because Bibi, Michael, and Charlie in unison motion for them to go back to the television or they're dead meat.

"Because I am your mother. You don't look for another mother when you already have one."

Victor smirks. "Depends on how many you have in the first place. Ever thought of that?"

Bibi's mother does not answer, does not move, does not stray from how Bibi would expect her to behave. She's made her decision, and her gestures echo it.

Victor's face reddens, as do his ears. He turns his rage toward Bibi. "Will you? Will you help me?"

Stunned, Bibi stares back at him. She feels her mother's eyes on her and cannot speak or think. She takes Michael's hand under the table.

Michael leans close to Bibi. His breath warms her ear. "Say as little as you can," he whispers to her. "Stay out of this."

Victor's lips twitch and grimace. Obviously disgusted with Bibi, Victor turns back to his mother. "Answer me this, then. Why did you spend all those years telling me I was adopted and then not expect me to be curious? Did you think saying I was adopted erased my first three years? If you were adopted, wouldn't you be curious?"

His mother's frigid eyes weaken and tears tinge their rims. "We took you in when no one wanted you. You needed a mother. Where would you be without us?"

His eyes flash, and a faint smile surfaces on his lips, as if he's just gotten her to say the day's bonus word. "And where would you be without someone else's kids to adopt? You'd be childless!" His hands grip his chair seat.

Bibi groans, not realizing she'd been holding her breath. Such a low blow to her mother, but not unjustified.

Her mother's head bows, silent and stalwart, and hurt. She scoots her chair out and reaches for an embroidered handkerchief, something she always carries in her pocket.

Satisfied with himself, Victor turns back to Bibi. "Aren't you curious?"

Michael squeezes Bibi's hand and holds it tight. She can't read his signal. He could be telling her that he supports however she chooses to answer. But that's unlikely. He's never been interested in the fact she was adopted.

Without flinching, she answers, "No."

"You're not curious?"

She hesitates at first, but repeats, "No." Which she realizes may be a lie.

"Always playing it safe, huh?"

"Stop it."

"Explain to me how you cannot be curious?"

Bibi hears his question, but her eyes follow her mother as she stands up, touches her handkerchief to her eyes, and exits the dining room, through the family room past the kids, and down the hall toward the bathroom. Michael's, Charlie's, and Phoebe's eyes follow too, as do Rose's, from the kitchen.

Victor doesn't bother to look; he bears down on Bibi. "Ignore her. How can you not be curious?"

"Because I don't want to know her." Bibi's breathing shallows. She needs time to be alone, to think. She feels ungrounded, like floating detritus in a Chagall painting. She tries to let go of Michael's hand, but he's holding her tight. Phoebe pats Victor to shush him.

Charlie brings his arms off the chair backs and folds his hands on the table. He leans forward. "Sis, why not help him look? You don't have to meet her."

Bibi's jaw goes slack. Charlie's betrayal stuns her. How can he suggest such a thing? Then she remembers. Charlie's the only one in her immediate family who shares no allegiance with anyone. She and Victor are tied by blood. Her parents are tied by matrimony. Charlie has only himself to be loyal to. Thus, there's nothing like it when Charlie's on her side. But when he switches, like now, the betrayal feels staggering. Slowly, Bibi manages to speak. "No. I'm not interested."

"But, Sis, you don't have to meet her."

"Yeah, Bibi." Victor pulls his chair in tighter to the table. Hope fills his eyes.

"You never have to meet her if you don't want to."

Bibi swallows. "It's not that simple."

Michael lets go of Bibi's hand and sits forward in his chair. "Charlie, Victor, she said no."

"Come on, Sis. It's simple. Think about it." Charlie's voice mocks her resistance.

All the years of being the youngest child come back to her in Charlie's tone. She was always the stupid one, always the naive one. And Charlie, being the oldest, was inherently the smartest. Except now they're adults. Age no longer implies intelligence; he doesn't have all the answers anymore. "Let's just say it's different for me than you, Charlie."

"I don't see how?"

"How would you like it if I came to you one day and said I found your birth mother? I know her name, where she lives, what she looks like. How would you like that?"

Charlie fumfers before admitting, "I wouldn't like it at all."

Inwardly, she grins. "Why not?"

"I don't want to know her."

"Because?" Unconsciously, Bibi taps her index fingernail on the table.

Charlie studies the ceiling, perhaps observing the memory he's conjured to depict that exact moment when his birth mother chose to walk away and leave his fate in someone else's hands. His eyes mist ever so slightly, and his mouth slowly opens and shuts, like a guppy taking gulps. He shakes his head and raises his eyebrows, as though surprised by his thoughts. "I'm really pissed at her."

Bibi's eyebrows rise in conquest. "I know what you mean. I feel exactly the same way."

Victor looks from sibling to sibling. "I don't care what either of you do." His voice is higher and more frantic. "I'm looking for my birth mother. If you want to meet her on your own someday, Bibi, go find her yourself. I don't need your help. Sorry I asked."

Victor turns to Phoebe and points to the arrow on his forearm. "We're driving down to Mom's, and I'm going to look through her stuff. I'm going to find those papers."

Phoebe resists. "We can't do that. Let's wait and follow her home."

"No. She had her chance."

"But that's breaking —." She stops, for Victor's not even listening.

Bibi's rarely seen Victor move so fast. He gathers their backpacks and little Katie, dashes out the door without hugging good-bye, all the while assuming Phoebe's following in his wake. Then they're gone. Whoosh. Vacuumed out of sight.

The sudden quiet stares everyone in the face. Even the television is turned low. Or the movie's over. Bibi has no idea. A horrid angst swirls in her belly, like dirty drain water filled with debris, which she knows has something to do with Victor.

Maybe she was wrong to be so harsh to him. Maybe he really meant it that he needed to find their birth mother. If only there was some other way to help him.

Rose comes down the steps, drying her hands with a dish towel. "That was fast." She studies Signe's empty chair and looks to Bibi for her thoughts.

Bibi rolls her eyes. "Mom's probably still in the bathroom."

Charlie snickers. "She's probably locked herself in."

Bibi bets Charlie's right. When they were growing up, when it looked like her mother wasn't getting her way, her mother would lock herself in her room for hours or days, however long it took. No one in the family ever verbalized this, but her locking herself up was generally considered, as it is now, a hell of a relief, and terribly rude. "I'm amazed she'd do this here."

Michael mutters, "It's the only place she has an audience."

Isn't that the truth. Bibi rests her head in her hands, with her elbows on the table. "Screw Mom. I feel bad for Victor. I wish I could help him."

Michael touches her elbow. "Not if helping him hurts you."

Bibi raises her head. The air seems light and crisp, like morning. "That is the question. Is it better to do what hurts? Or what helps?"

§

The five of them, Bibi and Michael in their robes, the kids fleeced snugly in their Dr. Denton's, and Ceres peeking through their legs, stand in the half-dark hallway talking to Ella's bedroom door, which is shut and barricaded from the inside.

Ella slaps her door with her palms. "Bestamor. Open the door. I have to go to bed."

Bibi knocks with her knuckles, higher up and faster. "Mom. Why are you locked in there?" She knows of course, but wants her mother to tell her anyway. "You're not being a very good role model."

Noah kicks at the door's bottom. "Amor. Amor. Ope."

Michael wiggles the knob. "Signe, open the door. The kids have to go to bed. If you don't open up, I'm going outside and break the window."

They hear a chair move from inside the room, and wait for the door to open.

When nothing happens, Ella turns the knob and slowly opens her door to utter darkness. Both Michael and Bibi have hands on her shoulders, just in case.

Michael reaches in and flips on the light switch. Bibi eases the door open wider.

Ella gasps and screams.

Ceres's back arches in fright and scrambles toward the great room.

Ella races toward her bed, not because her grandmother's arms open for her, which they do not, but because her stuffed animals are strewn about the room, along with assorted other toys. Plastic palominos. My Little Ponies. She-Ra. Underwoman. Hello Kitties. Ella rescues her green-legged Jeremy Fisher and blue-bonneted Jemima Puddle Duck from the wicked floor, clutches them to her heart, and howls, her eyes scrunched shut, her mouth wide open, her lungs at full belt, big gloppy tears streaming down her cheeks.

Jesus. Bibi covers her ears. She can't stand it when Ella screams. It could go on all night.

Noah scampers in to help. He grabs two large, pastel teddy bears crushed between the wall and Ella's mattress, holds them upside down against his chest, and wails even louder than Ella.

Snot decants from his nostrils. His howls have a weird roaring rhythm, as though he were a semi engine.

Michael and Bibi stare at the three children left in their care. Two hysterical tots and Bibi's mother, a full-grown, platinum-haired adult with a driver's license, who has dripped herself off the bed and into a weeping puddle on Ella's olive-green shag carpet, curled in a fetal position, her feet shoeless, and her face so red Bibi thinks she might pop. Or maybe she has to pee. She's been locked in here for what, three hours?

"Mom, you gotta get up." Bibi straddles her mother and tries to lift her as one would a bag of fertilizer, but her mother's gone limp.

Michael comes to Bibi's rescue. "Signe, get up." He leans down to pick her up, but Bibi stops him.

"Mom, don't make Michael pick you up. If he tears something inside, I'll never forgive you. Stand up."

Michael and Bibi step back and wait a minute while the kids mourn and her mother decides what to do. When the kids calm down and find solace in Noah's room, Michael and Bibi go in the kitchen and kill time by decoding her various family members' behaviors and motives and debating whether or not Victor is gay, which they decide he couldn't possibly be.

When her mother finally appears in the kitchen, she looks the same as when she arrived six hours ago. Hair neatly arranged, sky-blue polyester pantsuit on with the seams in the right places, a touch of coral lipstick happying up her face, and pearl earrings hanging from the appropriate spot on her lobes.

Behind her, Ella and Noah can be seen staring at her in wonder and fear.

"Bibi and Michael, it's been a lovely party," her mother says without an ounce of insincerity. "You've been lovely hosts. I must be going. My, how time flies."

They follow her out the door and make sure she's in her car properly. "Don't forget to turn left when you get to Springdale," Michael reminds her in his most innocent tone.

Her mother rolls down the window before putting her car in reverse.

The beads in her mother's eyes jackhammer into Bibi, and she combats her urge to escape into her house.

"You could have stopped him." Bibi's mother puts the car in reverse, but holds it still with her brake foot. "And you should have." She rolls up her window before either of them can answer and releases the brake.

They watch her mother's blue Olds Cutlass disappear down the street. The brake lights blare and she stops at the sign. The left turn light blinks gaily.

"You know, Bibi," Michael says, "I'm amazed you're as sane as you seem."

She nestles closer to him. "I'm amazed I'm even —." She catches herself before she blurts the word "alive." That word, because of how precious it is in their lives right now, always requires vetting before being spoken.

§

I have worried about Michael.

As soon as he learned of his illness, I took it upon myself to help him. Mind you, if Delilah were up here, instead of down there, she would have shamed or harassed me into not interfering. But I was free to do whatever I wanted to help him help himself.

You see, Michael had decided long ago that, because he was named after his father, he would, like his father, die in his mid-thirties. What had really convinced Michael that he'd have a short life was the fact that his father had been named after an older sibling, also named Michael, who had died in early child-hood. Thus, while Michael had no intentions of giving his newborn son Noah the cursed family name, he also had no idea how to rid its effect on his own life.

I sent him dreams, which he did not understand. I laid books in his path, and poems like Wallace Stevens's "Sea Surface Full of Clouds," which he neither noticed nor read. I even hollered in his ear, "Michael, think about what you decide. Decisions be-come beliefs. They become your future. They become your illnesses. And your health." Nothing he did led me to believe he heard me at all.

When at last it dawned on me how adamantly football held his interest, I switched my tactics. I must have yelled, "Think be-fore you punt," into his ears maybe two-hundred-fifty times before I heard him repeat it.

It was the middle of last December. He lounged on the family room's long sofa, his feet propped up on Bibi's prized art nou-veau foot stool, watching the last minutes of the Holiday Bowl. Watching football was considered therapeutic for him. It helped him recuperate. The two-hundred staples that trussed him to-gether after the surgeons removed a third of his lymph system in early November were healing nicely.

A hefty bowl of popcorn rested to his right, from which he ate between plays. On his left side, Ceres snoozed belly-up; her snowy white tummy and toes heaved and twitched with her dreams. On the floor, between Michael and the television, Noah shoved his Tonka trucks along his imagined highway, and Ella saddled up her plastic horses and released them from their corrals to run in the pasture. Bibi was off doing laundry in the garage and correcting another set of essays in the study.

The game had been going on for hours, it seemed. Southern Methodist was way ahead of Brigham Young, 45-25. Michael didn't care about either team, but given it was a competition, he set his heart on SMU winning. And they were. SMU's cheerleaders urged their crowd on. "Go Red! Go Blue. Go Mustangs, S-M-U!"

Then, like cats unexpectedly springing from behind a door, BYU's Cougars earned a touchdown with just a few minutes left on the clock. And then another. The score was 45-39, with less than a minute remaining. The Cougar mascot, clad in his blue and white uniform, raced up and down the sidelines in a conceited pre-victory run.

The Mustangs' kicker jogged out on the field to punt.

Michael frowned and sat up. He didn't like the kicker's demeanor. Something was wrong. Michael had been a C.I.F. track finalist, had run with the best in the state, and had placed second. He knew a thing or two about the athletic psyche. The kicker's shoulders appeared more slumped; his steps had lost their bounce. This kicker, Michael could tell, was distracted, or had lost his confidence.

Michael could stand to watch no more. He stood up. Popcorn spilled on the floor like jack stones. His arms shot up. He grimaced with pain and shouted, "Think before you punt!"

I swooned. I swirled around him. I slapped him on the back in congratulations.

None of this he noticed because what happened in the game's last moments swept Michael away. Brigham Young blocked the punt, which resulted in Michael switching his allegiance to the underdog BYU.

Then, with seconds to go, BYU's squad took their positions. Brigham owned the ball. It was third down. Clay Brown, caught a forty-one yard, what do you call it, a hail Mary pass thrown by the quarterback, and was quickly buried under a stampede of Mustangs.

It looked like a loss. But Brown was on the winning side of the goal line when he hit the turf. After the conversion point, Brigham Young had won by one. The stadium went wild, as did Michael. "Jeez, what a game," he kept repeating, until the kids chanted it too.

Michael got up and found Bibi in the garage folding laundry. "I swear to God. I kept telling him, 'Think before you punt,' but he wouldn't listen."

"Who?" Bibi stuck the toe of one of Ella's Popeye socks into the opening of the other and dropped it into the half-full, white laundry basket.

With his thumb, Michael pointed behind him. "Eric Kaifes. The punter."

"Is that who you were in there yelling at? I can't believe he didn't hear you."

Michael grinned. "Smart ass." He turned to go back in the house, but stopped on the top step and poked himself several times in the chest with his index finger. "But you know what? I knew he was going to screw up. I knew Kaifes wasn't going to kick it high enough. He wasn't focused. He wasn't thinking. Your old man saw that coming. Remember that. 'Think before you punt,' I told him. But he wouldn't do it. Dumb fuck."

Bibi dropped the black-and-brown face towel she was folding into the basket. All she could imagine was how helpful Michael's new talent could be in Las Vegas. Or the stock market. Or Hollywood Park. God knows they could use the money. They paid too much for their apartments, and had a fourteen-percent variable loan to maintain.

I left Bibi to her dreaming and followed Michael back into the family room. He'd switched channels to a golf tournament and sat on the sofa panting. Besides eating the popcorn they found on the floor, Noah loaded tiny handfuls of it into the beds of his trucks, and Ella lined her horse barn with it so her horses would be comfortable when they lay down. Ceres hadn't moved an inch.

Suddenly Ella and Noah stopped what they were doing and gathered up popcorn in their bowled hands, which they brought over to their father. "Here, Dod," Noah sang. "Popporn!" Ella let her handful fall over her father like rain.

Michael smiled one of those million-dollar grins that can't be forced or contrived. His eyes grew dewy. He leaned forward and spread his arms to capture his children. With effort, he snuggled them close. The bubblegum scent of their hair filled his nostrils. "I love you guys," he told them. "I'm going to be around to see you grow up. I promise."

Again, I swooned and fell in love with hope and possibility. He'd made a decision. And a good one at that. I swished around the room's ceiling and praised myself. Two giant steps in one afternoon.

§

Because they had decided at the start of Michael's illness to keep the phone on his side of the bed for the days he was bed bound, the phone's ring in the middle of the night forces Bibi to blindly fumble over Michael's sleeping body and grope through his nightstand's medicine bottles, dusty candles sticks and family pictures for the phone. She catches a glimpse of Michael's empty barf bucket on the floor, lit by moonlight, and makes an extra effort to rouse him as little as possible. At the bed's foot, Ceres stretches her legs and splays her toes apart, before settling back to sleep between Michael's feet.

The phone cord slaps Michael's forehead. He groans. She pats the spot lightly, her touch begging forgiveness. When she brings the receiver to her ear, she pauses momentarily. If it's a prank call, she'd rather not have her voice heard. "Hello," she finally says.

"Bibi, you never called to see if I was alright."

She silently gasps at the sound of her mother's voice. A vague terror burns in the fog of Bibi's mind. She reads the clock's glow-in-the-night hands. Quarter to midnight. Michael perches himself up, but flops back down when some pain deep inside rears its fangs. She holds the phone away from her ear so he can hear. "But I did," she tells her mother. "You didn't answer." Her hands make the yakking motion for Michael.

He rolls his eyes and blows up his cheeks.

Her mother's voice lowers and deadens its aim. "You didn't call."

"I went to bed. I was exhausted. I did the dishes and collapsed. Michael was pooped too. You know how it is." Her eyes apologize to Michael for blaming him.

He touches her cheek softly and closes his eyes.

Her mother's voice lowers more. "Frankly, he didn't look good today." She pauses for this to sink in. "Is he getting any better?"

Bibi pushes the receiver into the covers to muffle the sound. Michael and Bibi look at each other. Her friggin' mother. It's been a little over a year since her dad died from bone cancer.

You'd think her mother would have an ounce of sympathy. God, for a cigarette. She counts to thirty.

"Bibi, Bibi, are you there?"

"Mom." She presses the receiver close to her ear.

"Have you talked with Victor?"

"Since he left? No." Suddenly Bibi remembers that Victor said he was going to their mother's house that evening, and wonders if he actually did.

"Are you going to?" her mother asks.

Bibi knows where this is going. "No. Mom, I have a lot of work to do. Laundry, essays to grade, and a house to clean. And I'll be exhausted. Morning comes early around here, you know. I have two little kids. My house doesn't stay perfectly neat and tidy like yours does." She glances at Michael, and smiles when his face shows he recognizes why she's rattling on and on.

"But are you going to help him look?"

Bibi's disappointed her mother didn't take the bait, but not surprised. "No, Mom, I'm not. I don't have time. Nor do I want to. I don't want to know anything about that woman." Or man, for that matter, though she rarely thinks about her birth father. Which seems odd to her now. Fathers are important. Her mind shuts, then opens, as she searches for a good memory of her dad. Always what shows up is when he insisted on buying her a dishwasher when she earned her master's degree.

"Then I can rely on you?"

Bibi closes her eyes. She can taste her stomach's acid. She hates situations that trap her into unintentionally obeying her mother. It makes Bibi look weak and satisfies her mother's need for power. She half whispers, "Yeah."

"What?"

Bibi holds the receiver out in front of her face, as though it were camera taking her picture. She could just repeat the word yes, but the defeat she feels deserves to be painted red. She yells into the phone, "Yes, you can rely on me."

After a pause, her mother responds, "Good girl."

Again, Bibi mashes the receiver into the covers. "Good girl," clangs in her ears and reverberates in her mind. She detests herself for allowing her mother to have power over her. Good girl. Worse, she hates herself for not knowing how to thwart her mother. Good girl. Those words her mother said, knife sharp and able to pare her down to size. Good girl. What her mother really meant to say was, "Thank you for being obedient. It's the least you can do for me after all I've done for you. That's the price of your debt."

Eventually, Bibi picks up the receiver and hears silence. "Night, Mom," she whispers, wondering what her mother's last words were before she realized Bibi wasn't listening to her. Carefully she stretches over Michael's still body and returns the phone to its cradle. Just as carefully, she eases herself back to her side of the bed, placing one hand on the bed and using the other to support herself with the headboard. She congratulates herself for not once pushing against her fragile Michael.

Michael stares blankly at the ceiling, obviously irritated.

"What?" she asks him. "What are you all Jesus-Christ-in-Heaven about?"

"She called you a good girl?"

As if Bibi didn't hear her! She scoots further under the covers and turns her back to him. "So what?" she harrumphs. Her eyes focus on the book, face up on her night stand, and barely visible in the moonlight. The main character Ayla stands on a cliff, confident and ready for the next obstacle her Neanderthal clan throws in her path. What Bibi would give to feel that same way. She searches under her pillow for her amethyst stone and finds it.

"Your mother's manipulating you. She doesn't care what's best for you. Or for us. She only cares what's good for her."

Helpless tears boil in Bibi's throat. Michael doesn't understand. He didn't hear the whole conversation. The amethyst feels warm in her grip. She's not as weak as he thinks she is. She swallows and turns to face him.

With obvious pain, Michael turns on his side and faces her. He studies her eyes in the moonlight streaming through the window. His eyes brim with distrust.

Bibi releases the amethyst and puts a hand on Michael's shoulder. Her touch begs him to stay on her side. "Mom asked me if I was going to help Victor."

"I heard that part."

"I told her no."

"I heard that too."

"She never mentioned that Victor'd been to her house."

"Hmm. That's interesting. I wonder what happened."

"I don't know. Then she asked me if she could rely on me. I know you heard me answer."

"I did." He rolls on his back and her hand drops to the bed. He doesn't look at her. "And then that's when she called you a good girl?"

"Uh huh. What else could I say?"

He inhales this information deeply. His eyes focus on his own thoughts. Then he exhales the air in a gust, like wind that blows after a front has moved through. "What are you going to do when Victor really presses you for help?"

She wasn't ready for Michael to change the subject. She'd almost forgotten about Victor. Almost. "Nothing," she tells him.

"It won't be that easy. He'll plead and beg, you know." Michael glances at her. "I bet he calls you tomorrow."

"I'll tell him no."

"Are you ready for him to fail? You know he'll never find her on his own."

Michael's words shock Bibi, and then nauseate her. She hates the truth his words reveal. Worse, she cannot stand the idea of Victor failing at yet another thing. But she tamps these fears down. "I'm not helping Victor. I told him I'm not getting involved."

"What if your mother asks you to help him?"

"But she won't."

"Your mom is capable of just about anything to get what she wants, and you know it. Two words: wedding dress."

Michael's right, of course. She presses her cheek into her pillow. It can't be denied what her mother did with Bibi's hand-knit wedding dress, saying she was following the pattern Bibi picked, but in fact using a pattern she preferred. When Bibi discovered this, it was too late. Bibi'd never consider doing anything like that to Ella. Or to anyone. She rolls on her back. "I just can't imagine her wanting our birth mother found."

"I guess what I'm asking is, are you doing this just to keep the squirrel off your back?"

She laughs because she loves when he calls her mother that. It's the perfect description. She rolls back toward him and nestles in close. "No. I have no desire to find my birth mother. None. Zippo. Nada. Nyet. And even if he finds her, I don't want to meet her. It's bad enough having one mother." She pulls the covers tight around her neck, wondering if she really believes herself.

§

Bibi's eyes won't shut. She needs the sleep, but it's not coming. Her mind spins. Besides her mother's words, "Good girl," taunting and haunting her, the day's events repeat in her mind like an old lover who won't go away. She doesn't want to think about them. There's nothing new to think. The lovely table, Charlie's adventures, her mother's obstinacy, Michael's health, and Victor's craziness. Or is it his sanity? Bibi understands his desire to find their birth mother; just leave Bibi out of it.

But that's the rub. Her shoulders tense tighter. Her fretting morphs into whispers of sadness. Her heart hurts as though pining for something important, yet unknown to her. Maybe it's because she hates being left out or abandoned. But that can't be it because she's deciding to count herself out. Maybe it's because she ought to help Victor. His pain has always been her pain. But she can't help him. Not this time. She hears her mind revving up again and needs to stop it.

Bibi slips out of bed and tiptoes a zigzag path down the hall, past Noah's room on the right and Ella's further down on the left, and into her dead-of-night place of refuge, the study.

To Bibi, the study is the quietest room in the house, even though it faces the street and it opens to the family room and front door. The previous owners had installed floor-to-ceiling oak bookshelves along the wall by the door, which helped put the house on the top of their list when they decided to move from Long Beach to Huntington Beach. The bookshelves don't give the room its hush, however. Their hundreds and hundreds of books on myriad topics do. Opposite the bookshelves, Michael had placed an old banker's desk and chair he'd bought at a fire sale. It is everybody's desk.

Bibi switches on the little Brew 102 lamp nestled on one of the shelves. Surrounding it, other beer paraphernalia glow in its light. Dos XX and Tecate trays picked up on Michael's many drunken forays to Rosarita Beach and Ensenada. A glass Pabst Blue Ribbon ashtray. An old Falstaff bottle still unopened. Michael used to always display these in the living room, but when the kids came along, Bibi vanquished them to the study. They add a deplorable Early-Swap-Meet feel to the study. But she's trained herself to ignore them.

When she hears Ceres's curious high-pitched mews coming down the hall toward her, Bibi holds the door open to let her kitty enter before sealing it tight behind her.

Above the shelf of antique beer stuff, tucked under some books, safely sits Bibi's red lacquered Chinese candy box. She removes it from the stack without disturbing the books much. The box feels warm and comforting to her, like a familiar teddy bear. Its gleaming black glyphs carry great meaning for her mind, but not for her brain; she has no idea what it says, but trusts it anyway.

Before opening the hexagonal lid, she hesitates in order to contemplate her intentions. Solace, she decides she's after, and information, which she hopes will give her the solace. That way she'll know what to think about this day and she'll be able to get back to sleep. She's glad she remembered this step, which she often forgets.

She sits cross-legged and sets the box in front of her on the carpet, whose brown, mottled ugliness jumps at her and revolts her. She tunes the carpet out so it literally disappears. The painful revulsion evaporates and is replaced by a discreet, tolerable, and dull sadness.

The box lid comes off easily. Bibi places it top down on the floor. Ceres sits across from her staring at something on the ceiling; her tail's end twitches quietly.

Bibi glances up, but notices nothing. Silly kitty.

The box's six pie-shaped chambers reveal their contents: raw crystal stones, feathers, a small brass Tibetan bell, a slim pen and pad of paper, and her dowsing chain. Michael knows this box exists, but they rarely talk about it. The subject arises once in a while when they're around her brothers, who half-kiddingly regale how they fully expected to come over and find a palm-reader's tent erected on the front lawn. It didn't take much for her to realize how taboo this skill of hers was, especially how she sometimes depends on the nothingness for answers to real questions. But to her, the nothingness seems organized and logical, even steady.

She lifts the dowsing chain from its compartment by its amethyst pendant. The cool silver neatly coils as she lowers it into her left palm. Its rough, lavender gem backshines in the dim light. She lifts the chain by the clasp and lets the slim, inch-long amethyst dangle. Holding the chain gives her the same confidence having a fairy godmother might.

She takes the gold pen and paper from the box, and clicks the pen. It fits neatly in her palm.

On the paper she prints: "There's no point in finding my birth mother." Something about her wording peeves her, but she discounts the feeling. She stations the chain's clasp between her index finger and thumb and holds it over the paper as steadily as she can, and waits. The chain moves left and right a bit, then builds up momentum as it unfortunately circles counterclockwise over the paper, revolution after revolution, until Ceres nabs it in her paw.

A chill envelopes Bibi. Counterclockwise circles mean no. In other words, yes, there is a point in finding her birth mother. But Bibi can't be sure that's correct, or she doesn't want to believe it is. Anyway, she should have written it in the positive. Stupid her.

On a new paper she prints: "I should find my birth mother." She positions the dowser clasp between her finger and thumb and readies it over the paper. She shields the chain from Ceres with her other hand.

The amethyst starts its turn to the right.

Bibi's left hand grabs the stone before it can complete its first orbit.

She doesn't want to get a yes, and she certainly doesn't need a yes. Doesn't even want the opportunity to get a yes. Her life is crazy-complicated enough.

But temptation and curiosity beckon her, for her dowsing chain rarely lies to her, even though it's considered totally stupid and scientifically unreliable. If she ignores its wisdom tonight, it may make itself unavailable in the future. She can't take the chance, not on her life. Besides she wants information. That was her intention. Information to give her solace. She's a big girl; she can handle it. Screw it, here she goes.

Ceres eyes Bibi, curious about what's next.

Bibi again positions the chain over the paper, asks the question, and watches.

The amethyst makes a movement to the right and arcs toward her, a wider arc than before, and swifter.

Her chest constricts. She drops the chain in a heap. A positive answer again. An adamant one. Quiet as a cloud, the room holds her as her mind clicks from one thought to the next, as she rejects each as impossible for this reason or that: looking for her birth mother, then finding her, and ultimately living life with her birth mother in it. It's all too much. It can't happen. If it's forced upon her, well maybe, but it would take a lot to force it upon her. The frightening possibilities her future holds slap her and propel her to break its spell. Enough of this.

Ceres meows her signature clipped soprano mew.

Grateful for the distraction, Bibi studies her cat for a moment. Its life seems so simple. Play, eat, sleep, with an occasional feral hunt thrown in. What a life. Bibi picks up the chain by its clasp and dangles it before Ceres.

The kitty cannot resist. She holds her paw out and steadies its aim, as though she were a batter on a mound. Then she swats the chain at precisely the right moment and captures it in her claws. When she brings it to her mouth for a taste, she spits it out in disgust.

This time Bibi drags the dowser along the floor for Ceres's delight.

The little gray kitty rises on her hind legs, exposing the precious white fur heart on her chest, and then lunges for the pendant. Once she has it in her clutches, the joy has apparently left the game. She dismisses the pendant as a mere nothing.

Bibi chuckles to herself, and then realizes how the room seems less quiet and her mind less fogged. She strokes Ceres's brow and coos, "I hope you live a good long life." Then she rips her papers into little bits, throws them in the trash, and returns her dowser to its candy box. As she fits the lid back on, it occurs to her that her fingertips quite possibly managed the dowser's output.

On second thought, she doubts this. Too many times the stone on the end of the chain has given her the correct answers she's needed. It told her to buy this house. And it told her not to buy the apartments, even though they did anyway. It knows her fate, and will reveal it to her if she asks.

She picks up Ceres and circles back toward her bathroom. Maybe if she pees, she'll be able to sleep. Maybe that's all she needed in the first place.

But the pendant's orbit has etched its line in her mind.

§

September 20

I had watched Bibi and Michael earlier this evening listlessly sit through the first program of the Sunday night line-up, while Ella and Noah looked through picture books in the great room. Shortly before eight o'clock, Bibi left *Sixty Minutes* to Michael before Andy Rooney had his turn at the mic. Something about the folksy commentator's ability to see through b.s. totally bugged her tonight. She tucked the kids in for the night, sang them a couple of verses of "You Are My Sunshine," before falling in bed herself, exhausted from her day. Michael joined her twenty minutes later. Now they're all totally conked out.

I love how Bibi's home sounds at night. A symphony of breaths.

Tonight, it's more Shostakovich than Debussy. As I float from bedroom to bedroom in the darkness, the family's fitful slumbering punctuates the quiet. Even Ceres, curled in a ball between Michael and Bibi, snorts and squeaks in her sleep.

I drift into Noah's room, where the littered floor teems with unparked trucks and trains, tennis shoes, plush gorillas, and picture books. The room exudes a specific dirty sock odor, oddly like a Dorito chip. In this moment, Noah, in his Superman Underoos, lies on his side facing his window. He is still, save for his fists, which open and close, as if kneading Silly Putty. He snores, sometimes quickly, sometimes not. The Tommy Tugboat comforter Bibi tucked around his shoulders at bedtime has woven impossibly around and through his legs. If he were to bound out of bed in a flash, he'd instantly trip into a voluminous pile. I hope his dreams improve. I throw some pink his way. How Bestamor acted yesterday still troubles him, you know.

Down the hall, Ella, in her sleep, reminds me of those old scenes of Snow White lying in a tomb, fast asleep, and surrounded by her protective dwarfs. Except Ella's surrounded by her stuffed animals, each of whom suffered during Bestamor's visit. Frown lines form ridges between Ella's brows. Her fingers, which lie flat on her tummy, drum rhythmically, then stop, then drum again. As pink and pretty as Ella looks, last night's events have not washed away. I dash creamy white light her way and watch it fall upon her like snow.

In Michael and Bibi's room, I see them as stars from different galaxies, asleep together, and yet not.

Michael's pillow lies slumped on the floor, where he must have thrown it. He sleeps on his back, with his head on the mattress, as if giving credit to the belief that the world is a hard place in which to live. The white tank t-shirt he wears adds to this look. He groans intermittently. The dribble of a dried tear lies caked down the side of his face. I try not to worry about him. It's not helpful.

Bibi, like Ceres, sleeps in a ball. Back in some womb she is. Her teeth gnaw on the fat skin of her index finger. Her brows purse like quotation marks. The covers barely stir as she breathes.

I move in closer to sense Bibi's being. Without warning, jealousy spasms my substance.

I recognize this feeling. I have felt it often since my stillbirth. Bibi has what I want: Life. I want the feeling of being so dog tired

I cannot take another step, and then crawling into the fresh linens of a cozy, soft bed and pulling up the covers snug to my chin, then closing my eyes and drifting off into sleep's comforting arms. I'd love to experience the feeling of being utterly famished after a day's work, and then sitting down to a bowl of chicken noodle soup, or a grilled cheese sandwich, or a chunk of ice berg lettuce dripping with dressing. Or taking a long, hot shower on a cold night, just before bed. Or walking into a bakery and tasting the cinnamon, and vanilla, and fresh baked bread through my nose. Or being vexed by those I love, and who love me. And then being unvexed. It astonishes me how profuse the human experience is. I miss it profoundly. I miss death loitering near my back. And I miss perceiving through contrasting highs and lows, darks and lights, louds and softs.

But I do not miss how I can now always perceive possibilities and potentials. Problems do not seem insurmountable to me. A way always exists. It's really quite lovely. And it's why many of us keep returning to Earth. We want with all our souls to experience life as a body and a soul simultaneously. The best of both worlds. If only, once born, we could remember what we knew as souls.

I hear Noah's whimpers stream through the air, like the arms of a drowning person reaching for help.

I flow out into the hall where the scent of the remains of reheated chicken Florentine lingers, and into Noah's room. I poise myself mere wisps away from his face and focus on his being. Sadness hangs gravely in the air touching him. My focus quickens. I see images of his father appearing in his awareness, one after the other, like a Kodak slide show. Selective images of Michael throwing up, of Michael ashen and frightened, and of Michael unable to awaken. Again, Noah whimpers, and I recognize what is once again happening. Noah feels his father's sadness and worry in his own body. This pain serves as his only proof of what he knows: something is terribly wrong with his father.

I whisper into Noah's ear, "Everything will be fine."

He covers his ear with his chubby hand.

I draw even closer and whisper, "Noah, he'll be fine."

Noah squirms, as if resisting the meaning of my words.

I inch away from him. The many lifetimes he and his father have lived together appear to me. This sympathy he feels for his father is not new. It's been repeating itself over and over for centuries. I recall how Eliot began his first Quartet by telling how the past and the present are both present in the future. Yes, for Noah and Michael, today may be today, but it is still yesterday. Without intervention or evolving, yesterday will be their tomorrows.

I conjure images where Noah dreams of sitting upon his healthy father's knees, of seeing his father's head full of hair and his father's body free of the two-foot scar that courses down the middle of his torso like a maroon river. I imagine Noah feeling confident in his father when he watches these dreams.

For those other images Noah had watched in his dreams caused him to fret and bleed with sympathy for his father. Pity is the last thing Michael needs if he is to heal. In subtle ways, what is believed today becomes tomorrow's experience.

I focus on these new, helpful images to intensify until they seem to bubble over.

Then I move away from Noah. He will see these pictures, I'm sure. How he responds, I do not know. I have done what I can. I cannot make him think these things. I can only make them available. I feel complete.

Except that I feel drawn to Ella's room. Upon entering, I grasp that this evening I am on a mission for the whole family's sake.

I waste no time. I suspend myself just above her forehead. I listen for and hear her angry chatter and her confusion regarding her grandmother, Bestamor. Internally, Ella's been grousing about it all day. Her other grandmother, Grammy, would never come into Ella's room and tear it apart. Grammy loves Ella with all her heart, this Ella knows. They'd spent the day with Grammy today, and she got five hugs and ten kisses and a new coloring book filled with circus and farm animals, because they're her favorites. Why would Bestamor be so cruel? Because she hates Ella? Maybe. Or she loves Noah more. Bestamor never touched his room. That has to be it. But Ella had been such a good girl all day long. If only Ella were an even better girl.

I steady myself so as not to become involved in the painful poison Ella's angry chatter invokes. I want to pick her up and tell her face, "Your jealousy means you want something. It does not mean you can't have it. Think about what you want, because you *can* have it. You can experience Bestamor's love; just dream about having it." Jealousy can be maddeningly misunderstood.

But this is what life is like. Things happen and illogical judgments get made. The judgments result in decisions. The decisions become beliefs. The beliefs replicate in like experiences. Bestamor, who is tidy to an extreme, became angry with her younger son and turned Ella's room into a wreck. Because of that, Ella thinks, and therefore decides, that Bestamor loves Noah more because Ella's not a better girl, which is so untrue it makes me want to scream. Unfortunately, if this belief is not replaced, the future will give Ella more experiences to prove this because this is what she has decided, and therefore believes, and therefore creates. Yesterday becomes tomorrow.

I'm sure you see how things can go wrong.

I pet Ella's pink cheeks. I kiss the end of her nose and tell her how loved she is. She does not fight or resist me. I nestle on her pillow and sing little songs about her, hoping they'll get through to her subconscious in the quiet of the night. "You are my sunshine," I sing. She smiles in her sleep. Then I sing four made up verses of, "You are the Bestest Girl in the World." For she is.

I then slip back through the hall toward Michael and Bibi. Oddly, neither has moved since my earlier expedition into their room. Ceres, who now has her head resting against Michael's leg, opens an eye. I can tell she sees me, because she follows my motions. She meows ever so quietly, as though I were a fly on the wall. I whisper for her to hush, which I guess satisfies her, for she closes her eye and drifts back to sleep.

From the moment I enter the room, Michael's aura disturbs me. I suspend myself in a column on the floor next to him. His worries become clear to me. He doesn't trust Bibi to do the right thing for their family. Her manipulative family always twists her to do what they want her to do. He's glad they spent the day with his mother because Bibi wouldn't have to field phone calls from her family. This birth mother thing can only lead to trouble. What kind of trouble, he cannot see. But he can smell it coming, and it burns him to the core. He and I are at cross-purposes on this. I'll need him to change his mind, but not tonight.

I slip back to better see his energy field.

And then I see what I initially missed. He translates his fear that Bibi won't stand up to her family to mean Bibi won't make him a priority. Which means he's not important. Which he instantly generalizes to mean no one loves him. Forget how illogical this seems. It's what he and all humans do when they're not paying attention.

In truth, what he really wants is to feel loved. Even by himself. Everyone wants this, even those who protest against it. Especially them.

In his ear I tell him, "You are a wonderful man. You are a loved man. You deserve a pillow." He pulls the covers up to his ears. He is the father of the son, is he not? I repeat, "You deserve a pillow." This time, his arm reaches out from beneath the covers and down to the floor where his pillow rests. He pulls it up and situates it under his head without waking. Success of this sort is infinitely satisfying.

I then lie next to him and caress his aura. I want for him to feel loved by everyone. I imagine this. Just thinking it soothes my substance. I feel like I'm in heaven, blissful and sweetened.

Until I remember Bibi on the other side of me.

I revolve to face her.

Her skin glows cold, as though she were dead. I must focus hard to gain clarity. Her horrible habit of cramming her feelings down deep makes her difficult to comprehend at times. She's like Grace; she has closets, only hers are more like tombs. But I get what's going on.

At first, I thought it had to do with her father. But, no, it's Victor.

He's disturbed all those memories of her birth mother which lie dormant, along with her other unthinkable memories, in a chained and padlocked crypt hidden deep in her psyche. Victor's needs have provided just enough heat to rattle those memories to bubble and stew, like molten lava. One timely schism in her surface, one weakened link in her chain, and all hell will break loose.

Fortunately, this morning, as soon as Michael awoke, he'd insisted they spend the day with his mother. "Well, my stars,"

Judith had said in surprise when she opened her small condominium's front door and saw them standing on her porch. In they had marched, and sat in their accustomed places. At noon, Judith surprised them with a grand lunch of dilled carrots, chicken Florentine, candied beets, slaw, and twice-baked potatoes, the leftovers of which they brought home for dinner. Michael had sat glued to the television. The Falcons had beaten the Forty-Niners, despite Joe Montana; Michael's team, the Rams, had beaten the Packers. The kids had built a lopsided Lego castle and cut pictures from Judith's magazines. And of course, Ella had colored. Bibi had corrected essays and read fifty pages of *Clan of the Cave Bear*, which she had to stop reading because she felt rude and the kids showed signs of cabin fever.

Going to Michael's mother's had given Bibi the relief she needed, but it didn't eliminate what was to come.

I worry about Bibi. The urge to tell her to just go find Grace rises in me. But I taste my own judgment pressing on me, keeping me from crossing some preordained boundary. And yet...

I take time to comfort Bibi's aura, to soothe it with love and hope. That's all she needs, really.

That's all any of you need. For love is the absence of fear and the presence of all that is possible. Hope is the catalyst allowing good to happen.

Then I imagine her making the right decision, whatever it might be.

The house is soaked in peace. Satisfied, I slide into the skies and wait.

Three

Darkness Being Precarious

August 1981; Santa Barbara, Calif.

My brother Victor is going through such a patch. Watching his predicaments unfold, as I have over the last month, has been difficult. It's bad enough he found nothing at his mother's after Bibi's dinner yesterday, but Bibi not helping him, that drives him crazy. He'd counted on her. She's trained him that way.

In this moment, the sun has just dropped beneath the horizon and casts a pumpkin glow throughout Victor's home. This orange splendor even bathes the rooms at the back of the house.

Victor wishes he too were dropping behind the horizon. He has just picked up the kitchen phone, and realizes who is on the other end of the line. Please, he silently prays, don't let Phoebe walk in right now. Behind him, the dishwasher churns. The stereo in the living room blasts Prokofiev's *Romeo and Juliet*.

"Vic?" the caller asks.

Victor closes his eyes and forces himself to say, "Don't call me again. This has to stop."

There is a pause, like a deep indentation before a new paragraph. "You know you don't want that," the caller says and hangs up.

Victor drops the receiver into its cradle, just as the dark "Dance of the Knights" cut booms through the speakers. His arm swings like an inverted pendulum to the music's profound rhythm; he snaps his fingers to each slow beat. The music portrays his mood perfectly: caged and torn. The harder he tries to live a life of truth, the more his life seems a lie.

A small, framed black-and-white photo of Bibi and him, posed and shot on someone's patio a decade ago, catches his eye. There's something about her hands, her face too, that make Victor ache, make him want to dial the number back. But he can't. He mustn't.

A month ago, Victor had gone to Jurgensen's Market to pick up cookies and berries for his beloved daughter Katie, along with the fixings for that night's dinner.

Victor had stashed his shopping list in his shirt pocket, certain he hadn't forgotten a thing. He studied the items in his cart, visualizing that night's dinner. Lamb shanks with garlic, *à la* Alice B. His wife Phoebe's favorite. Mélange of local root vegetables. A nice 1972 claret. His salivary glands had bubbled beneath his tongue.

He felt his wrist for his watch, for a sudden feeling of lateness overcame him, as though he hadn't given himself ample time to complete his family's dinner on time and still get to theater practice by seven. So many people depended on him for direction, literally, that he personally could not tolerate his own tardiness.

He glanced along the grocery store's upper wall for a clock, but no clock could be found. He scooted his cart into the shortest line; he'd ask the checker for the time.

His attention naturally observed the food selections already placed on the conveyor belt by those in front of him. Often, he'd guess the dishes that would be made from the ingredients. On more than one occasion, he'd asked a patron how a specific ingredient they'd bought would be used. Not today. He internally snarled at what he saw. How people could feed their children processed cereals, he did not understand. Or spending the premium required to buy ordinary, prepared salad dressings. In most instances he'd rather make his foods from scratch than speculate at the ingredients.

Impatient, Victor's attention moved to the checker, or more correctly, to the checker's back. The young man was Victor's height and approximate build, but he had dirty-blond hair, and such a nice, tight ass. Victor admired it while he could, then quickly pulled his list from his pocket and pretended to read it.

Feeling how flushed he must look, Victor breathed in deeply, and exhaled slowly, as though in the early minutes of a yoga session. The young mother in front of him moved forward, giving Victor room to place his items on the conveyor belt. He felt the checker's eyes upon him as he emptied his wagon, but he did not look up to make sure. His cheeks and ears burned. Christ, he hated when he felt this way.

Victor lit a cigarette. The lady in back of him coughed, but he ignored her. He felt more in control. That's all that mattered. He pushed his cart forward and took plenty of time to fumble in his pocket for his wallet. When he inadvertently looked up, his eyes met the checker's.

Victor's mouth dropped open. He couldn't move a muscle. He felt himself free falling into the young man's eyes, the young man's life, the young man's past and future, his heart, and his soul.

"Check or cash?" the young man slowly asked, as though he too were going through the exact same experience as Victor.

Victor steadied himself by leaning against the counter. He couldn't help smiling. The checker's face was vernal and handsome. Long eye lashes. Pouty cheeks. Full lips. Hands like Bibi's, which was odd. Chiseled jaw. But he became aware of the patrons around him and the possibility that someone he knew may be watching him.

He forced himself to appear serious and detached. "Check," he replied, while scribbling out the name of the store and the amount tallied on the register. He tore out the check, but hesitated, realizing that his name, address, and phone number were printed on it. If only he had chosen a different check-out line.

The young man took the check from Victor's hand and studied every line of it, giving Victor a chance to note the checker's name: Quentin. Somehow Quentin's California surfer-boy face and prison-inspired name didn't quite jive, in Victor's opinion.

Quentin removed the pen perched over his ear and focused on Victor. "ID please."

With distracted eyes, Victor removed his driver's license from his wallet and handed it to him. He studied the ceiling, he pushed up his sleeves, and stuffed his wallet in his back pocket, forgetting he still had his driver's license to replace. He could stand it no longer. He looked at Quentin.

"Thanks," said Quentin, meeting Victor's eyes, while returning the driver's license. He pursed his lips slightly, drawing Victor's attention to them.

Victor heard himself inhale, as if suddenly overcome. He wanted to stay; he had to leave. No part of him could afford ever seeing Quentin again. Victor was a married man, wed to an amazing woman, and they had a child, a beautiful, brilliant daughter, who deserved the best life possible, which meant he must remain married to her mother, and that was that. Besides

Phoebe was his greatest asset when it came to finding his birth mother. Phoebe could talk his mom into just about anything. For a very cruel reason, he believed.

Hence, no more questions.

He snatched his license from Quentin's fingers, slipped it into his shirt pocket, grabbed his bags as quickly as possible, and practically ran out the store.

§

August 1981; Santa Barbara, California

That August day when I had watched Victor run from Jurgensen's Market in Montecito, I followed him as he headed his truck west toward home through the coastal mountains on Sycamore Canyon Road. His encounter with Quentin had heated his psyche and physiology; I worried he'd get lost or drive off a cliff.

In his unsettled condition, he twisted his car radio's knob this way and that in search of something to support his state. Not the news; he wanted to think. Nor an opera on KFC; *The Magic Flute.* Hardly. Nor rapid-fire jazz. The dial settled on a sort-of-oldies channel airing "Love the One You're With."

A mix of anger, loneliness, and guilt flooded him. His hand reached to turn the knob.

But I brushed against his right forehead, causing him to turn his head enough to see his eyes in the rear-view mirror, at the exact moment Stills sang, "Love the one you're with."

Profound sadness lurched through him. His eyes welled. If only he could love the one he was with: himself.

That's progress, in my opinion.

He parked his truck under a pepper tree in a turn-out on the wrong side of the road. From this height, he could see the Pacific Ocean spreading fifty, maybe a hundred miles out. The Channel

Islands, which at beach level always appeared as mountains on the horizon, reminded him of small turtles swimming north against the current. The Earth's bigness made him feel small and meaningless. That night's practice never crossed his mind.

For the moment, he relished this feeling. Insignificance granted him the possibility of doing whatever he wanted without there being any effect. The look in Quentin's eyes and shapes his lips made played over in Victor's mind, like mordent trills.

He allowed himself the extravagance of wondering how Quentin's touch might feel. And what one night, or maybe just an afternoon, with the young man might mean to his total experience.

This extravagance was short lived. His mind slammed shut. Images of Katie and Phoebe slid into view. He scanned the horizon one last time and turned on the truck's ignition. No way would he do anything to disturb his happy, orderly life.

Except, when he'd gotten home and was preparing dinner, the kitchen phone rang, freezing Victor mid-step.

He stood gripping the handles of the copper roasting pan filled with beets, carrots, parsnips, and garlic that he was about to pop in the oven. Options flared up his mind. It could be Quentin. Probably not. But maybe. Or it could be Katie's sitter. Or Phoebe. If it's Quentin and he doesn't answer now, Quentin might call later. Regardless, if it's Katie's sitter, and something's the matter, he'd never forgive himself for not answering the phone.

On the third ring, Victor set the pan on the counter and picked up the phone and listened.

"Victor Andressen?"

Victor's heart leapt at the sound of Quentin's voice. He loved the feeling of being sought, being found. But then his throat tightened in terror. His hand dropped the phone as though it were a potato right out of the oven. Quickly, he retrieved the clattering phone from the floor and made the adamant decision to let this fancy go no further. Without an ounce of hesitation, he set the phone back in its cradle.

The cruelty and finality of his action seeped into his awareness. Victor knew that if Quentin didn't call him back, which was a huge possibility, he'd stay up all night thinking about him, and then he'd be back in Jurgensen's tomorrow looking for Quentin, and would have to apologize to him for being such a schlub.

Victor dialed star-five-four, hoping that was the instant-redial number. He thought of Phoebe and Katie, but other images quickly replaced them. He thought of his year in New York City when he was an experimental nineteen-year-old trying out drugs and lifestyles; he thought of the actor in L.A. who'd taken him in and taught him to cook, among other things; and he thought of the debonair lawyer in San Francisco who'd taken him to Algiers that same summer as his pet.

He'd always passed these off as mere adventures, even though they weren't. These were times when he'd felt most himself, when living seemed most honest and alive. These were corrupt times, but orderly. Now his life was considered moral, but he felt corrupt.

The call was picked up. "Victor?" Quentin asked.

"Yes."

"Do you have a pen?"

"I do."

"778 Garden."

"Got it."

Pause. "Will I be seeing you today?"

Victor looked at the clock, and knew he was driving off a cliff.

"Yes."

He turned off the oven, put the pan of vegetables in the refrigerator, and left the house. One must meet one's destiny rather than let fate toss one's life about.

§

With slow, slinky naughty-dog movements, Victor eased himself away from Quentin's naked, sleeping body. The darkened bedroom's curtains and blinds were drawn making it difficult for Victor to estimate the time. Spots of sunlight peeked in from outside; he knew night had not yet fallen.

He spotted the corner of his watch lying on the carpet under his clothes which he'd torn off in the heat of passion. He picked up everything and moved into the bathroom to clean up and dress.

His watch, an old Omega that had once belonged to his father, explained his predicament. It read quarter-to-five. The weight of what he'd just done sickened him. Hopefully he'd arrive home before Phoebe. Using Quentin's shabby blue washrag, Victor wiped his parts, his face and his hands. Inside his head, he rationalized his actions as following his honest instincts. He could not, however, rationalize how his actions were honest with regard to his wife.

Hurriedly, he completed dressing. With each button he buttoned and snap he snapped, he alternated between dreaming about what it would be like living with Quentin and thinking up a reasonable explanation for why he left the house with dinner still in the refrigerator and the stereo on. He decided that he'd tell Phoebe he needed to think. Which bore some truth. Phoebe, being an artistic type, would understand and forgive him.

Victor found his way to the front door of Quentin's tiny, nondescript apartment. When he creaked open the front door enough for a sliver of light to shine through, he heard Quentin's voice from the bedroom. "What's next?"

Victor closed the door enough to seal out the light. He wanted to lie, but hated the chaos that would create. Shoot to kill, he tells himself; it's more humane. "There will be no next."

Quentin laughs. "Yet."

§

I followed Victor that day in August, just before he grabbed his watch and left his kitchen to go to 778 Garden Street, I followed him into the living room and watched him replay the "Dance of the Knights " cut on the stereo.

As before, his arm swung back and forth to the masculine beat, like a throbbing metronome. Back and forth, to and fro. The music held some truth that reminded him of himself, or that made him ache for himself.

He knew this truth was linked to his desire for Quentin, but it was greater than desire. It had to do with all of him, with his physical origins, with his future, and with his soul. It had to do with all that he'd been separated from when he was adopted by the Andressens. The music offered him a path back into himself, and he would follow it.

The truth was all he wanted.

He straightened the cowboy hat he kept on the piano's top, a seeming ornament.

He was sick of living a lie.

He was ready to be found.

§

September 21; Lubbock

My sister Delilah's fingers clamp around her Celica's pearl-white steering wheel; her thumbs tick against the crossbar. She squints, as the late-afternoon sun blares in her vision. Just outside her window, her mailbox stands idle and benign. She likes the new sign Big Joe put on its top. The Storms, it reads. The Storms of Arapahoe Rd. Visually framed in the windshield, she recognizes her pear-shaped neighbor lady from maybe seven houses down waddling across the street in Delilah's direction, but not much else about the woman.

Delilah rolls down her window, allowing the sizzling Lubbock air to overwhelm her car's coolness. The heat waves over her like detonating grenades. She reaches out and unlatches her mailbox door with a sharp flick before the metal burns her fingers. If her eyes were closed, she might guess her arm was in an oven. The mail door flops open, exposing a neat stack of mail leaning at a tight angle against the side.

A thrill darts through her. This could be her lucky day. She waits a second for her fingers to cool and then reaches inside the box for her mail. If what she's been hoping for is in the mailbox today, she'll want to deal with it privately, without the comfort of prying, neighborly eyes. Delilah guesses at her neighbor's range and figures it'll take at least a minute for her to reach the Celica.

She extracts the stack, which includes next month's *Redbook*, all of which she sets on her white-cotton lap. Her breathing stops. Her fingertips rifle through the letters, while she divides her attention between her approaching neighbor lady, who's pressing a small bundle to her chest, and the return addresses of her mail. An alumni reminder for Big Joe. The new tax assessment from the county. A shower invitation and a letter from her mother in California. Some credit card bills and advertisements. Her possibilities dim. The last letter, the one she'd been pinning all her hopes upon, is from the electric company. She looks up and exhales old, bleak sadness.

So that you know, Delilah does this every day. I mean the mailbox ritual. She opens her mail-box door. Gets her letters. Holds her breath. Searches through the letters for something from Sadie Lacharite. Or from La Jolla, California. Exhales disappointment. Doesn't hear me when I say, "Find Sadie's daughter." Never hears a word. Triggers her garage door opener. Throws her gear shift from neutral to drive. Over-accelerates. Squeals into her garage. Brakes in the nick of time. Marches into her house, while her blond, gum-chewing, denim-clad babysitter marches out with her black Sony Walkman plugged into her ears. Drops her purse and the stupid mail on the antique sideboard by the front door. Maybe greets her two boys, who are either outside or in front of the television. Twists on her tub's hot water faucet. Plops down at the end of her bed. Wrenches off her white oxfords without unlacing them. Slides down her white nurse's pantyhose. Unbuttons her shirt-dress uniform from the hem up. Stops with two buttons to go. Dissolves into tears. Suddenly grabs a shoe. Throws it at her closet mirror. (At first, I thought she was aiming for the closet; now I realize it's her reflection she has in mind.) Finishes disrobing. Lights a cigarette. Sinks into the hot, bubbly water. Breathes the vanilla scent. Feels like a queen again. Cheerily answers, when her five- and seven-year-olds knock on her door, "I'll be right there, sweeties."

But not today. Yes, Delilah does hold her breath while going through her mail. And she does exhale disappointment. But instead of then punching her gas pedal, she yanks her brake and clicks her gear into park. "What have you there, Marsha Lee?" she asks her Mary-Kayed neighbor, though it's obvious to her that Marsha Lee holds in the palm of her bejeweled right hand the dearest and most frightened bawling runt of an orange-striped tabby kitten.

"Want it?" Marsha Lee drawls and shoves the kitten at Delilah. Tangerine hair clings to the turquoise t-shirt covering Marsha Lee's hefty breasts. "Why, there I was in Donner's parking and heard this miserable mewing. I couldn't just leave it. But I can't keep it. Billy's allergies. Could y'all?" She squints at Delilah and smiles her perfectly outlined fuchsia lips.

Delilah cradles the kitten in her two hands and rocks it just so, whisper-kissing the air, filling the space with love.

The kitten's bawling stops. It looks at Delilah, eyes wide open, and playfully reaches a pink-toed paw at Delilah's nose. Then its purring starts, loud and audacious, as though it were an important part in a movie soundtrack.

Tears choke Delilah's throat. She bites her upper lip to keep her sorrow and happiness inside, for she does not want to explain how this moment with this motherless, furry ball of precious represents both the worst and the best in her life. For Delilah, the best would be for her to find her own lost and motherless brother and bring him into her family where he belongs.

When Delilah thinks she can talk, she rolls up her window a quarter way. "I'll take him, Marsha Lee. Thanks for thinking of me." She rolls the window up the rest of the way, places the kitten atop the letters, and carefully drives into her garage.

Before getting out, she cranes high the kitten's tail and inspects its pink behind. An upside-down exclamation mark is what she sees. "Ah, you're a girl. You look like a Baby Bee. Lucky me."

I do what I can.

§

About the only thing Delilah adores about her garage is how cool it feels on these blistering days, and thus how safe from the real world she feels. But why her boys can't keep the garage as neat as they do their rooms erases this little pleasure. She yanks the Celica's hand break and twists the ignition key to stop the engine. Her mind sees a way all those toys can be made to look beautiful, lined up, sequenced by size or color spectrum. Something less upsetting than the current debris she sees: prone bikes, baseball gear, shin guards, potato shooters—the stuff of boys. A little harassing just before dinner ought to get them to accomplish that mission.

She scoops Baby Bee from her lap and makes sure all the mail's in her purse before getting the kitty litter and cat food from her trunk. A bitter taste loiters on her tongue. Mail, mail, everywhere, but not the letter she wants.

Inside her home, she smiles. Compared to the dives she lived in growing up, this is a mansion. And it's hers. Well, hers and Big Joe's. It's new, it's modern, and it's clean, as are its furnishings. She chose beige for everything because it calms her, which makes her seem less brittle to others, she thinks.

"Okay, Mr. Hart. Is that Hart like a buck or Heart like a Valentine?"

To Delilah, it sounds like her sitter Tammy's on phone. Then it dawns on Delilah that Tammy's talking to Mr. Hart. She tries to drop everything and race to the phone, but her purse and shopping bags tangle and she almost strangles Bee. "Wait, Tammy! Let me talk to him! Don't hang up."

Delilah's too late. By the time she gets to the kitchen phone, Tammy has hung up the phone and is straightening its cord, which never lies flat on the little desk, or Command Central, as Delilah refers to it.

Delilah, eyebrows peaked, stares at Tammy in disbelief. "Why'd you hang up? Couldn't you hear me?"

Tammy turns to Delilah and sees Bee. The pony tail on top of her head bounces, and her arms stretch toward the kitty. "Aww. Can I hold it? How cute. Aww."

Delilah blinks loudly and hands Bee to Tammy before grabbing the notepad Tammy had written on. Shouldering the handset near her ear, Delilah dials the number Tammy had written in her low, fat writing. 714. Clearly, Mr. Hart's calling from California. Orange County to be exact. Why there, Delilah does not know. He should be in San Diego. Delilah wonders how many rings until he picks up; it's already been four. She reads the rest of Tammy's note while she waits, her mind filling in what Tammy did not. "Not good nws. Call him tomor afterno."

Delilah slams down the phone. Not good news, whatever that means. Maybe her brother has died. Dear, God, let that not be. It's one thing to have your brother stolen from your family, but then to have him stolen from life itself. This can't be happening. Or maybe it's Mrs. Lacharite. She's dead. Or really sick. Or a senile old bat like Delilah's mother. She can't wait another day to find out.

While her mind calculates what to do, Delilah's eyes study her command center. Next to the phone rests her five-by-eight notebook containing all the phone numbers and addresses and information her family will ever need. At least almost all. Above the desk, the framed cork board reminds her of all the appointments and dates everyone in the family must keep. Not just a calendar, but Post-Its noting what to wear and what time to actually leave in order to get there. The world's a lot easier when one is organized and holds the reins.

Suddenly inspired with a solution, Delilah snaps both her fingers and smiles at Tammy, who's sitting at the kitchen table with Bee in her lap. Delilah's toes do a little dance inside her shoes. "Cute, huh?" she asks Tammy. "Her name's Baby Bee."

Tammy's head lilts back and she smiles relief.

"Check on the boys, will you?"

"Sure, Mrs. Stone. They're outside."

"I know. Tell them to stay out there. In fact, I'll pay you extra if you can keep them out there for another half hour."

"Sure. That's great."

When Tammy passes by Delilah to go out the back door, Delilah grabs Bee from her; she trusts her boys, but they're boys.

As soon as the back sliding door clasps shut, Delilah scrambles to her bedroom, sets Bee on the floor, and gets out the step stool she uses for retrieving top of the top-shelf items. In this case, she's looking for her gris-gris box, an ancient, dirty-white train case with rusty, pitted hinges that she bought at the Pasadena swap meet her senior year of high school.

Except she doesn't see it.

She gets off the stool, first making sure Bee isn't underfoot, and kneels down to search her closet's floor. Nothing there but all her shoes in their perfect line. Maybe she moved the box in a panic; she can't remember. Maybe she moved it on purpose. That's more likely. But where? She's an extremely tidy person, if it's okay to admit such things, even for a Virgo. Where the hell is it?

She climbs back up the stool and scans the top shelf inch by inch. Her head feels clogged. Her fingers snap to a slow beat thumping in her mind. It occurs to her that someone could have taken her box. Stolen is more the word. That's the story of her life, which explains why she's never met her brother. Her eyes narrow and boil. Tammy comes to mind. As does Big Joe. For the first time since entering her bedroom she hears her boys' voices and Tammy's outside. She only has so much time.

Off the stool she descends. Down the hall to the boys' room she runs. Plan B snakes its way through her mind.

The smell of their room hits her before she even crosses the threshold. Dirty socks. Crayons. Grass stains. Dusty basketballs. Their bubbling, algae-ridden aquarium.

But upon entering, their room tells another story. Tucked in. Clean. Everything managed. Such good boys.

Delilah sets Baby Bee on the floor and scans the room. She knows what she's after. Right above Matt's and Little Joe's desks, she spots them. There's over a dozen of them, so she can take her pick. She only needs two. The green Troll with the woolly, yellow hair will work for Mr. Hart. The red Troll with the blue hair is perfect for her mother. Bee disappears under Little Joe's bed before reappearing near the door.

She takes the two Trolls to her bathroom, while listening for her boys' voices to make sure they're still outside. It occurs to her that she's stealing from them, but decides she's really borrowing. From one drawer, she removes her glass bowl of safety pins; from another she removes a small, yellow notepad and pen.

She tears one paper from the pad into rough fourths.

On the first fourth she writes, "Hart." On the second she writes, "Find him." She then opens a large safety pin and straightens it to remove its vertex. The point she stabs into the two papers and then aims at the green Troll's rubber flesh. So as not to actually hex or hurt Mr. Hart, she stabs the pin horizontally into the top of his head. She winces at what should be the Troll's pain. It matters not. She has a point to make.

It proves harder than she expects, and the pin bends in the process; its point exits the Troll's forehead. A subtle shudder careens through her. The pin seems directed at her. She backs the pin out a bit and sees the point disappear into the doll, but not the hole it made.

She reads again what she'd written. "Find him." Doing this has worked before. Not always, but enough. It's worked often on her father. All the times she'd wanted protection, it was from him she'd gotten it, because she'd pinned the idea to his head.

Now for her mom. On the third fourth, she writes, "Mom." On the fourth careen, she writes, "Tell D everything." She straightens a safety pin and stabs the papers. As she aims the pin at the red Troll, she recognizes her urge to stab her mother directly in the center of her heart, a spot she can exactly identify on the Troll. How satisfying and deserved that would be. Something brushes against her check, but it's nothing. Instead, she inserts the point in the Troll's right hind cheek. Something to get her mother off her ass. Delilah congratulates herself on her restraint, as do I.

She then gathers the two Trolls and places them on her side of the bed, between the box springs and mattress. No one but she will know they're there.

On her way out the bedroom to look for Bee, she refolds the step stool and replaces it in her closet. Her eyes scan the shelf one more time. It drives her crazy that someone stole her box. Except now, with her very own eyes she sees it where it had been all along. Right where she thought she'd left it. Her dirty-white Samsonite overnight case with its crummy bronze hinges resting on top of the Stetson hat box.

She feels like mush, a person of no substance, someone she cannot trust not to be outwitted. There must be some explanation. She feels another brush against her cheek and slaps at it.

§

September 21; Huntington Beach

Cripes, Bibi could use a cigarette and the solace it would provide.

She removes the wad of while-you-were-out memos from her skirt pocket, squashes them flat with her palm onto the kitchen table, next to the laundry basket full of clean clothes she'd put there this morning so she couldn't avoid folding them. The papers' sharp corners visually jab at her psyche; something new and uncontrollable cutting into her life.

She mindlessly raps her knuckles on the table top, as if it were a door she'd like opened. It calms her to do this. She breathes. One, two, three, four…

Dinner! She remembers not because she's hungry, but because her family's needs constantly knock on her mind's door. She should have stopped at the grocers on the way home, but, because of the memos, she'd panicked and sped home from work, after picking up the kids at the sitter's. Luckily, she didn't get a ticket. She can be a cop magnet when she doesn't pay attention.

In her mind, she recalls the freezer's contents. She half smiles, and removes a frozen Tupperware container marked Stew, while wondering how long it's been in there. Maybe a year, and she's not kidding. Her family's lucky they get fed every night. She fills the sink with hot water and submerges the container in it. Liberated bubbles percolate to the water's surface where they float. She wonders if this is a good sign; she'll check later.

An image of the memos flashes center stage in her mind. The stack of maybe ten yellow, pink, and white papers she'd found in her school mail box after last period seemed innocent at first. Probably from a parent, she guesses. Nothing unusual about that except there were so many. But when she read "Call your brother," "It's an emergency," she'd stuffed them in her skirt pocket, where they crunched and crumpled. Nothing about the messages led her think he was in a life-or-death situation. Still, calling Victor from work seemed stupid. No telling what he wanted to talk about. Worst case? Maybe he'd found their birth mother. The thought had terrified Bibi. It's one thing to not want to look for her birth mother, it's another to have the woman found.

Bibi faces the kitchen's wall phone. Anything can result from the call she's about to make.

Ceres circles Bibi's ankles, her fluffy tail tickling Bibi's calves. Except Bibi can hardly feel it. She picks up her kitty, massages its cheeks and the insides of its ears, and walks over to the pantry for tuna treats. Bibi sets down Ceres and puts a handful of fishy pellets on the floor, rather than in a clean dish, which is not readily available. That way Ceres can play with what she doesn't eat. A little entertainment never hurt anyone.

Bibi again faces the phone. She should plan how to respond to her brother, rather than just call and blurt things out. But thinking's hard. Her mind's fixed on the possibility that Victor's already found their birth mother. No telling how Bibi'll respond if that turns out to be, or how she should respond. She pushes her mind to come up with another possibility. Maybe Victor's trip to their mother's was a failure, and now he's angry, which means he'll be cruel. Like his mother, he can be impossible to argue with. He'll shame her, and ridicule her, and wear her down with his rants and judgments. Relief only arrives when she acquiesces.

Or he'll whimper. That's almost worse, because he never fake whimpers. All her life Victor has been her most constant worry. His suffering was her suffering. When he was punished, it seemed to hurt her worse. Easing his suffering eased her own. Making sure he stayed, meant she stayed too.

She has no idea how to unbind herself from this loop. She's just wired this way. He's the reason she drove eighty in a sixty-five mile-an-hour lane. He's the reason she's panicked out of her mind. He's the reason she needs to find a way to say no to everything he wants and begs for. Because, right now, what he wants is the exact opposite of what she needs. Maybe it's always been that way.

On the other side of the wall, Scooby and Shaggy blare from the Panasonic baby-sitter; the kids are happy. Down the hall, Michael sleeps in the bedroom, having worked half the day. She could tell he serviced his cigarette route today because a bunch of empty Kool, Raleigh, and Belair cartons protruded like skyscrapers from the garage trash can. Across from her, the dishwasher stands ajar, waiting for her to push the button to make short work of this morning's and last night's dishes.

Bibi's drained. Her head swims, and she realizes she's stopped breathing. She reaches for a chair back to grab, and grips it 'til her knuckles pale. Mentally, she reminds herself why this phone call should be easy. She's a grown woman, she's on the teacher's negotiating team, and she has a master's degree, more than either of her brothers have earned. She's a junior high school teacher, which by itself proves her bravery. She can do this.

She fans the memos out on the table's oak surface and notices their different layers of intensity like the Frank Stella she saw at LACMA. One message leaps out. "Bro. says, 'I need to tell you something.'" Of all the messages, it's the scariest. Bibi wants to know what this something is before Michael wakes up.

She picks up the phone, and dials. Her eyes scan the sink counter, which relaxes her because it's clean and clear. Ceres has stopped eating and is making noises at some phantom she spots on the ceiling.

"Bibi, is that you?" Victor answers after the second ring. He sounds frantic and hollow, a specter of himself. Another voice, a male's, can be heard in the background.

"Victor, what's going on? I got your messages. How did it go at Mom's?"

"Are you kidding? I found nothing."

Bibi plops in the chair next to her and exhales in relief. Her kitchen seems brighter, neater. The children's television less loud. Her body makes room for her soul. Thank God, she mouths to the ceiling. This conversation is already better than she expected. She can afford to be light. "That's too bad. Did you look under the bed?"

Victor sniffs. "She probably stuck everything in her bank safe."

"Hmmm, probably." Bibi would do that if she were her mother.

Bibi hears the other voice again. Definitely a male saying, "Just tell her."

"Tell me what?" Bibi asks. "Who's with you?" It's obvious the other man knows Victor's talking with his sister and cares very much that she be told something. Which is weird.

Bibi hears muffled noises and a door slamming before Victor says, "Nothing. No one. Tell me what happened on Saturday night? After I left. She must have stayed at your house a pretty long time. Is she going to disinherit me?"

Please don't let the conversation go in this direction, Bibi prays. "Of course not. C'mon."

"Really? Then what did she offer you to not help me?"

Bibi ignores his insult. "Actually, Mom didn't talk because she did her usual thing and locked herself in Ella's room for forever."

"Which one of you sat in with her?"

"No one. We ignored her for a really long time. Until the kids had to go to bed."

Victor cackles. "That must have pissed her off."

"Yeah, I guess it did." It feels good to be on the same side with Victor, making fun of their mother's manipulative ways. It's how they spent most of their childhood; just the two of them, taking care of each other, defending whoever was the weaker from the more powerful family members, even though it was usually Bibi defending Victor. But she could be wrong. In many ways they were identical, even soul mates. Because Victor was the older, Bibi naturally followed his example, and she liked it that way. It felt comfortable being like him.

"Listen, Bibi. I know you don’t want to help me look. I get that. I don’t understand it, but I get it. I’m just curious about what my sister the fortune teller thinks my chances of finding our birth mother are."

Bibi’s Sunday night session with her amethyst pendant pops fresh into her mind, but she won’t tell Victor about it. That would reveal a possible interest on her part, of which she has none. “I don’t really get anything. Maybe it’s because I have a ton of stuff to do.”

"Can you check it out?"

"Now?"

"No, when you have time." This she can do, even though the whole idea that she, a rational person, can predict things based on an irrational, moving pendant baffles Bibi. "Okay. I'll let you know. I just hope you can trust what comes up. I don't want to give you false hope."

"I've trusted it before. I'll take my chances. And, Bibi, one more thing. Can you at least find out if the folder's in her bank box?"

This seems easy enough. She could do this, but resists telling him so.

"At least if you find out, Bibi, I'll know. Because if she's locked the folder up, I'll never get it."

"But if it's locked up, how's that going to help you?

"It won't help me. I'll just know it's hopeless. I'll have nowhere to turn." Victor's voice betrays his sadness. "Then what'll I do?"

"Wait. I feel like I'm not understanding you. You're not telling me everything." In her mind she sees the sad face Victor carried everyday as a little boy. It broke her heart then, and it breaks it now.

"I have to find her," his voice catches. "I don't have a choice. I keep crying, and I don't know why. And if I'm not crying, I'm angry, and I don't know the reason for that either. I have to figure this out. I'm more fucked up than you think."

Bibi looks around the kitchen for an answer. Victor's despondency lodges in her throat thick as porridge. She needs him happy, because when he's not, her life suffers. Her amethyst dowsing chain, making its wide, rapid, clockwise arc, flickers through her awareness, which she tries to ignore, but can't.

"Vic, does your therapist help you with this? I mean, I'm just an English teacher."

"I need more than a shrink. I need—." Invisible tears roll through the telephone wires and out the phone's mouthpiece.

"What? Tell me what you need." Bibi's practically in tears herself, except she never cries. Or hardly ever. She tries to think of some way to help him without participating, but cannot. His words and tone act like a crying kitten on her resolve. She is a child again in a family that never understood his needs or would never help him. He didn't fit in either, nor would he try. She had to step in. She'd lie for him, or take blame for him, or take sides with him. It was the two of them against the world. If they gave him away, they'd give her away too. And she was done with that business.

Victor's teary voice reaches for her again, "I need you to help me find her."

Just as the heartbroken balloon in her throat threatens to burst, Bibi hears Michael's voice saying something to the kids from down the hall. The clock on the stove reads quarter to five. If only she could trust time to be on her side. It slows when she needs it to race by, and it evaporates when she needs it most of all. She glances around for a cigarette, then remembers. She counts, tapping her foot to get her all the way to fifteen, and eyes the armoire's monkey cannister where she's taken to stashing Juicy Fruit and Double Bubble.

"Bibi, tell me you'll help. You're all I have."

Bibi holds the phone to her belly. She can't listen. Michael is now by her side, looking first at the phone and then at her eyes. When he mouths, "Victor?" she nods, aware that from this moment on, her conversation with Victor is no longer private, and that she's not at all happy about that. She puts the phone back to her ear.

"Bibi, are you there? Answer me. You're the only one who gets me. You always help me. Remember when we were little. You always could figure things out. Don't let me down. I cannot do this by myself."

Michael's not listening anymore. He stands a foot from Bibi. He holds his left hand level with his face, palm toward Bibi, fingers spread. With his right hand, he holds first his thumb, then his index finger, then his middle finger, while he whisper-yells at Bibi, listing with all the heat and vitriol he can muster the reasons why she should never and will never help Victor find his damned birth mother.

When Michael holds his ring finger, the one on which he's never had to put a wedding band, Bibi turns her back to him.

She feels numb, like dried out clay.

"Listen, Bibi, could you just ask Mom where the papers are? Do it for me."

She weighs the possibility of actually pressing her mother for the information Victor wants, but knows, one way or another, she'll come out on the losing end. Besides, Michael stands right behind her adamantly protesting her family in general and her brother's request in particular.

"Victor," she says slowly. "Please stop asking me. You know I'm going to say no."

"Give me one good reason you won't help."

She leans her forehead against the wall's paneling. If Bibi helps Victor, she can count on three things. Her mother will make Bibi's life miserable. Her husband will be furious that she let him down, which doesn't sound all that awful, but it is. And third, Bibi might be humiliated into meeting her birth mother, which is the last thing she wants. "I don't want to pay the price."

"Price?" he yells. "There is no price to you."

"Oh, but there is. Anyway, why don't you ask Charlie? Mom's a sucker for him. Does she ever get mad at him? No."

Victor says nothing, which Bibi takes as confirmation that she speaks the truth.

"Anyway, be brave. You're the one who can talk her into most everything. Even better than Charlie. Cripes, she pays your shrink bill, doesn't she?"

"She's threatening to cut that off."

"Well, which do you need more? Finding your birth mother or keeping your shrink?" She hates that she asked this question, because she knows the answer.

He pauses. "It's because of my shrink I need to find my birth mother. My shrink said, 'How can you know yourself if you don't know your gene pool?'"

Bibi wonders if therapists actually say stuff like that. "Yikes. What would your shrink say to an orphan?" As Bibi says these words, her curiosity ventures into unpermitted territory. She has viewed herself as anything except the antithesis of her birth mother. Or an orphan. She blinks.

"Don't you feel that way? Bibi, don't you want to know who you are?"

Her mind swirls with thoughts which she refuses to see, but knows are there.

"No."

§

I slide outside the window that's by the microwave. The sun sinks lower in the western sky, casting a cool shadow the entire length of the narrow side yard outside Bibi's kitchen, giving it the feel of an *al fresco* tunnel. Chlorine from the next-door neighbor's pool has escaped; it floats unrestrained in the side-yard air.

Above, gangs of crows soar overhead, heading northwest to their staging ground before leaving as a flock for their roosting spot, where thousands of birds perch together for the night. Rare are the animals that prefer to sleep alone at night.

A pair of ruby-throated hummingbirds whir and buzz, darting in and out of the morning glory blooms to suckle what last sugary sweetness they can before the flowers curl in for the night. Such a dance of colors upon the grape stake fence.

The male's iridescent red against the flowers' regal purple, all set against a dense, lawn-green background of leaves.

I move in closer to watch the last of today's minute energy rays beaming to Earth from the sun. Photons you call them. They're more akin to energy gusts, bursts of wind. My attention is now on the bubbly surface of a morning glory's leaf. From this close, the leaf resembles rows upon rows of green corn clinging to the cob.

I cannot see each individual energy gust, for each is too small and swift for even me to follow. Rather, I sense them as a unit, as you would sense the wind. Unlike the wind, the photons do not deflect off the leaf's surface. Instead, they enter it like cars hurling forward onto freeway on-ramps. And like these cars, photons move into the leaves, a lane at a time, and become included in the leaf's energy traffic. In doing so the photons become part of the solar-system-like structure of the leaf's atoms. Therefore, they become part of the leaf's molecules, which means they become part of matter.

Think of it! One teeny-tiny energy gust from the sun first becomes part of a leaf. Then, when the leaf falls off the plant and decomposes, that photon is now part of the soil. If a tomato plant is planted nearby, that photon may become part of the tomato. When you then eat, that photon becomes part of you. Amazing! Elegant!

And, of course, it's the reason life would cease without the sun.

§

The amethyst pendent arcs a path inches above a small, white slip of paper upon which Bibi has written, "Victor's having a hard time." From north to east, south to west, round and round it goes, with the energy of a bronco, its adamant path etching an invisible circle in the air —a circle that confirms what seems blatantly obvious to her. Victor needs help.

Annoyed, she stops the silver chain with her free hand and lets it puddle in her palm. When Phoebe married Victor, his big problems became hers, not Bibi's. At least that's the way Bibi sees it. She doesn't disrupt Victor's life with her problems, of which she's got plenty. Her fingers curl around the chain to shush its message, before dropping it on the floor where she's sitting.

Except it has spoken; there's no shushing it.

Victor's need for help whines and barks within her like a dog tethered to a tree. The thought makes her cringe, but not because she doesn't want to help him. Of course, she'd help him with the usual. But something about how Victor's been lately, and the way the pendant swung, as if trying to free itself from the chain so it could really express itself, is not usual.

The part of her conversation with Victor that keeps retracing its steps in her mind was when he said he was angry and didn't know why. Multiple possibilities scramble for Bibi's attention. His marriage. His health. Money. And obviously his birth mother.

Out of the corner of Bibi's vision, she spots Ceres paw pulling the study's door open wide enough so she can enter. Bibi does nothing to encourage her kitty, who suddenly seems fascinated with some apparition in the corner behind Bibi.

On a new little slip of paper, Bibi writes, "His marriage has problems."

After placing it on the floor, she picks up the chain, steadies it between her index finger and thumb to remove all bias, and lets it pend over the paper.

The purple stone springs alive with fraught, clockwise momentum orbiting over the paper. In an instant, Ceres lunges at it and tugs it from Bibi's grasp.

Bibi pets Ceres carelessly. Her attention focuses squarely on Victor, whose marriage appears to be in trouble. She thinks back to the family dinner and wonders how Phoebe can even stand being around him when he's like he is. With all Phoebe's poise, it must be alarming to be around someone with such crackling, invasive energy. Maybe that's it.

She writes, "Phoebe doesn't love him anymore."

Feeling every bit the voyeur, Bibi gets the chain from Ceres's grip and dangles it over the paper.

This time the chain arcs a counterclockwise circle over the paper, negating the words she'd written.

Which, thinks Bibi, is good. Phoebe still loves Victor. That's a relief.

She then writes, "Victor loves Phoebe."

The chain calmly circles clockwise above the paper, over and over, like a second hand on a wall clock.

Until Ceres can no longer hold herself back. Up she rises on her hind legs. Down she pounces with her forepaws.

Bibi doesn't care. She lets the chain go. The cat can have it. She could use a cigarette. She counts. She counts again. After getting up and getting some gum in the kitchen, she circles back to the study and sits on the floor.

She doesn't want to do what she does next, but she does it anyway. She writes, "Victor finds his birth mother." She grabs the pendant from Ceres and positions it over the paper without first trying to still it.

At first the chain makes no movement other than its residual, sloppy dangling. Then it stops, like the last period of a poem.

Bibi waits. Maybe she should have worded the thought another way.

But then the chain awakens and makes tiny clockwise movements, which grow larger and faster, outlining and fencing in the words, "Victor finds his birth mother."

This message framed in the amethyst's orbit forces Bibi to imagine the unimaginable. Except she can't comprehend what she sees, as though she doesn't have the ability to see a fourth primary color. Her mind blanks.

The chain then slows and transitions to side-to-side swings, which Bibi knows is not a good sign, or it's a mixed-up sign; she can't remember. Whatever it is, she's relieved the chain stopped its clockwise circles. She dares not think what the back-and-forth movements could mean, except they augur Victor's failure. God, please let him fail.

Bibi's heart pounds. She rises. Her palms open and close. The spines of the books in her full-wall library face her. She knows their titles at a glance: the fiction, the non-fiction. Knowledge is power. She knows in which ones she's cached little pieces of papers between pages. Papers with questions, like the ones she's just written. She doubts Michael will ever find them. He won't know what they mean anyway. Yes, here is her safe spot, here is where she finds her answers.

She sits back down on the floor and writes, "I am okay."

The chain swings back and forth.

Bibi nods. She believes the chain's message. On some level, she knows it's more than believable; it's true. She probably isn't okay, and, considering her life in this moment, anything could go wrong in a heartbeat. Except it's a horrible omen about her future, one that she doesn't want to think about. Michael. His health. Ella and Noah. Their finances. Her sanity. She wonders what awaits her.

On a new slip of paper, she writes, "I find my birth mother." Without a doubt it will curve to the left.

It doesn't. The chain, like a ballerina sweeping around the stage, curves an elegant halo above the paper. Before it can start its second loop, Bibi drops the chain so it splatters on the carpet. There's no way this is right. There's no way she'll let this happen. No way.

§

I watch how the light over Bibi's kitchen-sink counter shines on her and the work she's doing. Using a tablespoon, she guides the partially-thawed chicken stew out of the Tupperware container and into a white baking dish. The stew's scent rises into the air and draws Ceres into the kitchen from the family room.

The kitty seems ready for her dinner now. She stands on her hind legs, her forepaws stretching to reach whatever that divine scent is that's luring her from the counter. She's a good kitty who has learned not to jump on working surfaces. And, despite her scent-induced hunger, she's got me on her radar. I make a sudden move from kitchen light to the fireplace in the great room and then circle back to the kitchen. She forgets her hunger and follows me. It's our little game.

Back in the kitchen, I notice Bibi's aura and the self-talk emitting from her body. Her aura seems predominantly lawn green, like the leaves outside. However livid red light sparks out from her heart, head, and throat. The more she scrapes stew into the baking dish, the redder and sharper the sparks grow.

I move close enough to her that I can read the curly Lanz tag inside the Alice-blue pique robe she's changed into. I sense the White Shoulders cologne, weakened now since she dabbed it on this morning.

I pick up the sound of Victor's words playing in her mind's echo chamber. "Don't you want to know who you are? Do it for me. How can you know yourself if you don't know your gene pool?" They repeat over and over, sometimes overlapping one another in a mental fugue.

Then I notice her self-talk emanating from her skull like mortar shells. At first, I hadn't noticed them, but now I can't not see them. Little explosions, shooting out of her head: I'm always the one who has to give up things . . . I'm always the one who has to make others look good . . . It's always on my shoulders . . . And if I say no? They'll abandon me, or they'll ignore me. Same thing; they'll set out to make me miserable.

I watch these thoughts leave her skull in fiery, energy gusts, like photon particles leaving the sun. If I had a head to shake, I would do so. All these negative thoughts radiating from Bibi's mind will not just die and cause her no harm. Like photons from the sun, her thought energy will become part of matter, and thus will inform it, and even develop gravity and magnetism, and will be part of the great collective unconscious.

All of us out here notice this happening to you on Earth. Your thoughts get thought. They leave the confines of your skull and venture out into the world and become themselves. Some of you were victims, so you think you are victims, and because you think you are, you will be. Others of you were fortunate early on and always think you're lucky, and so you are. Still others of you always think traffic will be a pain in your neck, and so it is. Some of you, like Delilah, expect to be stolen from, and so you are. Some of you, like Victor, expect to be ignored when you cry out for help, and so you are. And some of you, like Bibi, think too much is expected of her, and so there is.

I'm just reminding you of what you already know.

And, yes, I know when I'm born next, I, like you, will forget this.

Still, I hope. Hope creates.

Four

And Then Desire Moved

September 22; Orange County, California

Some days unravel before they start.

Bibi has tuned the radio to an AM talk station during her early morning drive north on the 91 Freeway. It helps cancel out her mind rerunning last night's conversation with Victor and the last question she asked her amethyst. Two men on the radio discuss what the negative implications are for the country now that Sandra Day O'Connor's on the Supreme Court. Really? She can't imagine how these men think the country will get worse with a woman in a lofty place. The guy with the higher pitched voice complains that O'Connor was only nominated because she was a woman, which he considers discriminatory. Really? The guy evidently never considered how discriminatory it was to hire men just because they were men.

Bibi switches the radio to the FM classical station to soothe her jangly nerves. Her insides churn, maelstrom-like, and her inner chatter crabs and maligns. She could shoot a kitten if it got in her way. Not really, but almost. She's surprised how on edge she is this morning. She thought she slept like a log last night, until she remembers the dreams that woke her and the two-in-the-morning non-stop rerun of Victor's choicest question, "Don't you want to know who you are?"

She turns up the volume.

Bedroom towns zip past her peripheral vision as she speeds toward work. She should slow down, but her foot, heavy with fret, won't let up on the pedal.

The piano piece streaming into the car through the speakers barely touches her attention.

Her mind keeps agitating over what she just heard on the news. She can just see it all now. All those white men, who've lucked out all these years, are going to start moaning and groaning because they have to share the wealth. Women are taking their jobs, they complain. So are ethnic people. No, guys, nobody's taking your jobs. They're our jobs which you wouldn't share for the last bajillion years. Jerks.

But gradually the music becomes less transparent. A couple of notes here, a glissade there. For a moment she forgets about O'Connor and the chauvinist men, and listens to the pianist's next slow, single notes exuding from her speakers, soft and caressing like baby powder.

Then her mind returns to its churning. She thinks about that creepy school board member for whom she works. An old codger with gray-brown skin that matches his lips. He had the nerve to tell the teachers they didn't need a raise because their husbands made plenty. She remembers how well that went over when she quoted him to the male teachers.

Her ears pick up a couple more musical phrases. A trill. Maybe this is Liszt. Or Chopin. She can't really tell.

Anyway, it's probably going to take a few generations before men figure out how to deal with women being treated as equals. Especially since it's not in their interest to get used to it. Cripes, she can't even get Michael to help with household chores, even when he was well.

This is Chopin, she decides. Familiar chords. Perhaps an etude. Obviously Chopin. She knows she's right. The crescendos. The double timing. Harmonies so unlike Beethoven or Handel. Bibi turns up the volume a notch.

She shifts Lars into overdrive and moves into the left lane. Here she can zone out and relax for the next twelve miles in her own peaceful little heaven. This is the good thing about leaving for work just after six-thirty: light traffic. Bibi's foot calmly presses the gas pedal, and she drives a mile or two or ten above the speed limit.

In her rear-view mirror, she checks the back-seat status. The kids have both fallen back asleep. Noah's blowing one of his famous nose bubbles, and Ella's head lags back far enough that Bibi can see the roof of her mouth. The light from behind makes her pale curls shimmer like the cellophane wrapper on a lollipop.

It still amazes Bibi how much Noah looks like his dad and Ella resembles Michael's mom. She sees nothing of herself in their looks. Neither child has Bibi's red curls, her deep-set eyes, or her sun-kissed freckles. Noah has Michael's lips, while Ella has her grandmother's. Her two kids are clearly part of the Amato clan.

Bibi tastes her sadness, as though tears she's never wept before have come forward for her to cry. Her mind wanders to imagine her genetic family, living somewhere in the world, wondering where on Earth she and Victor, their lost relatives, are. How strange that must be for these family members, because they probably once knew Victor and her, probably saw their baby pictures which is something she's never seen, probably even sent presents when they received the birth announcements. These people must look like her and Victor, in the same way all her current cousins all seem to look alike. Blond Norwegian manes. Shortish thumbs. Thickish calves. Flawless complexions. How weird it must be to look like you fit in a whole family. Or how wonderful, how very wonderful.

She turns down the base a bit to better balance the music. The pianist's fingertips seem to caress the sound from the keys, even though the fingers move lickety-split. Bibi's heard this piece before, somewhere.

It feels horribly poignant, though it really doesn't sound sad. She looks around the front seat. If she found a cigarette in her glove compartment, she'd be so tempted. She hates how her sadness burns her throat. Part of her wants to change the channel back to the news or something, maybe KROQ, but her hand won't leave the steering wheel, stuck there as if by some higher order.

And no, if she really thinks about it logically, this can't be an etude. Not elaborate enough. But then the tempo slows into the loveliest strains. Majestic. Heavenly. Full of big love. It's as though she'd never heard it before, but suddenly remembers having heard it a million times. It is so beautiful, and impossibly sad.

Tears push at their floodgates. She puts on her blinker. For God's sake, she's about to cry.

She barely makes it to the freeway's emergency parking lane, when she can no longer contain herself. At first, she only whimpers; her mouth turns down like an overturned bowl. God, she needs a cigarette or a piece of gum. She bursts into huge tears while managing to put the Volvo in park. She sobs and sobs and cannot stop.

Noah awakens and joins the crying.

Bibi ignores him, for she can do nothing but let this bottomless sadness weep out of her. She has never cried like this before. Damn. Her mascara's going to be all over her face, and she'll be late for work. She can't be like this.

But she cannot stop. Everything is wet with tears. Her face contorts in a pain worthy of Dante. She must look like Munch's screamer. She doesn't even know why she's crying, and remembers Victor telling her the same thing, "I keep crying, and I don't know why."

She holds her head in her hands and gasps for breath, so pressing are her sobs.

Both kids are now screaming loudly, as though Godzilla were just outside.

Bibi hears a sound to her left rapping on her window.

"Open the window," a man's voice says, followed by more rapping on her car window.

Bibi forces her eyes open and through their blur sees red lights flashing in her rear-view mirror. Outside her driver's side window, from which the rapping came, she sees an oval, pewter belt buckle forged with a six- or seven- sided star containing a blue circle reading California Highway Patrol.

Jesus. She covers her mouth, forcing herself to shush. But the tears will not stop.

The kids cry even louder.

Ella screams, "Mommy, Mommy." She rolls down her window a little way, because her little hands can barely manage the knob.

"Ma'am, step outside the car."

Bibi opens the door and it swings away from her. She's done nothing wrong, that she knows. It's not illegal to sob your eyes out. God, her head throbs. At least Ella and Noah have eased up on their crying. She struggles with her seat belt, but can't remember how to undo it.

"Ma'am, can you show me your license?"

She wants to give him what he requests, but she cannot stop crying. His very question seems to make her tears worse, and her head sinks into her hands, and she just bawls her living heart out.

"Ma'am, are you all right?"

She shakes her head no.

Noah resumes his screaming, and, thank you, dear Jesus, Ella is not. She'd get them all arrested if she got started again.

"Ma'am, if you don't stop crying, I'll need to take your keys away." He opens the back door. "These your kids?"

If only she could stop the tears. She nods, holding her breath to see if that will calm her. She looks up at him through her fingers, because God knows she must look a wreck. His aviator glasses reflect her upside-down image, and his helmet strap bites into his neck. His boots squeak authoritatively, forcing her to realize this guy is in charge of her future. He could arrest her. She coughs, which only makes her crying worse. Nothing will make her stop.

"Gum." Ella says.

"What?" The officer drops his hand to his gun. "No. Don't look at the gun."

"Give my mommy gum."

"Gum?"

"Give my mommy gum."

It shocks Bibi that Ella knows about her gum habit. And delights her too, because, yes, officer, it would be the grandest thing if you would please give Bibi some gum so she can stop this freako crying jag. Or a cigarette. That would be even better.

The officer practically runs back to his motorcycle. His steps sound more like a dance, than those of a peace officer. He's back in a flash. With Juicy Fruit!

She takes the whole yellow pack from his hand, and yanks the red opening strip. She pulls out one, unwraps it from its silver paper and pops it in her mouth. The first chomp provides her the sweetness she's been looking for. She chews again, slowly, using her tongue to fold the gum between her teeth. Moisture springs alive in her mouth. Each jaw movement calms her and restores her balance. She chomps again, while opening another stick. She lets the silver paper and yellow wrapper fall between the seats. As she chews her tears subside, and her face slackens. "Can I have one more?" she snivels politely.

"Yeah, sure."

She reaches into her now spotlessly clean ashtray and extracts a dime. "Here, sorry for taking your gum."

He takes the dime and steps back from the car and bends down to observe the backseat. "I'm not sure you're fit to drive." He walks to the back of her car, but returns.

Noah starts screaming again.

"Look, I've just had a really bad morning. My husband's dying, my father just died. My mother has leukemia. I'm okay now. Really I am."

Ella starts screaming, right along with Noah. The cacophony is unbearable, and Bibi realizes she has said the worst thing possible about Michael in front of her kids.

"I mean, my husband is really sick, my kids' dad is really, really sick. "She tries to whisper this to him in hopes the kids can't hear.

"Ma'am, can you undo your seat belt and get out of the car?'

"Officer, really I'm okay." She wipes her eyes and face. She must look like shit. She stretches her upper lip over her teeth and then smiles for him. "Really." Bibi again struggles with her seat belt, but it won't release its grip on her.

Ella stops crying long enough to tell the policeman, "Her p'incipal will get mad at her."

"Huh?" he asks Ella.

After Ella repeats herself, the officer peers into Bibi's eyes. "You're a teacher?"

Bibi swallows. "Un huh. "This could turn really ugly if the officer hates teachers. Silently, she begs, please, officer, don't take me in. Don't arrest me. Don't institutionalize me. I'm really a very responsible person, and you just had the luck of seeing me like this today. You don't understand. I never cry. And I'll never cry again. Because if crying gets me arrested and I lose my job because of that, because that's what they do with teachers who get arrested, they fire them. And they'll take my childr—.

"I'm going to let you go. Get yourself some more gum. Take it easy on the road. Maybe take the surface streets."

She shudders in relief. "Oh, thank you. I'm so sorry to have taken your time. I'm much better. Thank you for the gum."

She leans out and grabs her car door and closes it. Her hand is about to turn on the ignition, when her eyes notice Noah and Ella in her rear-view mirror.

They're craning in their car seats to watch the officer's every move.

It's as though she's watching Victor and her as little children. Something about the sight seems familiar. And then a wave of horror grips her chest. Her heart races. She knows she came an inch away from losing everything important to her. The officer could have thought she was crazy. He could have hauled her in and arrested her. They'd have taken away her children. She'd have lost her job, and her health insurance.

No, she thinks, she's got to be better than this. She's got to be more careful. She turns on the ignition, and straightens her posture. Shoulders straight, back erect, tummy in, radio off. She's never going to be one of those women who lose their kids. She'll make sure of that.

§

September 22; Buena Park, California

Bibi sits in the teacher's lounge, alone, because a substitute was called for her class when the school hadn't seen or heard from her. The end-of-class bell will ring in moments and break will start. She sips the coffee she poured for herself, and wipes the fresh lipstick off the rim. She smells a hint of banana in the air and scrunches her nose. Browsing the headlines of the *LA Times* sloppily stacked in the middle of the table, she reads: "China Launches Three Satellites into Orbit," "Proctor & Gamble Initiates Campaign Regarding Toxic Shock Syndrome and Tampons," "Stewardess Crushed to Death in In-Flight Elevator." Thank God Bibi's world is tame compared to what the rest of humanity has to deal with. Nothing about Sandra Day O'Conner, though. It'll be in tomorrow's paper.

The bell hasn't even rung, and Mr. Hickman, the history teacher, walks in. He brushes back his Vitalis-ed hair with his palm, pours himself a cup of coffee from the urn, leans against the sink and crosses his ankles. He inspects Bibi. "Well, look what the cat dragged in."

Shut up, creep, she thinks. She reaches in mid-stack for the Calendar section, finds the radio playlists and folds back the movie-listing pages and television program line ups. Near the back page she spots what she wants. KUSC. Six forty-five a.m.

A happy chill runs through Bibi. It *was* Chopin she heard this morning. She congratulates herself, and writes "Ballade No. 1" in her little brown Ghurka pocket calendar. She should pick up a manuscript at Heffen's Music on the way home. It's not like she has time to learn some new music at this point in her life. For some reason she wants to.

"So where, might I inquire, have you been all morning?"

Blessed be, the bell rings. She ignores Delford Hickman and puts her calendar back in her purse.

"The whole school thought you'd succumbed or something."

Succumbed. The whole school thought she'd died? What a jerk. "It's none of your business, Delford."

He cranks his neck and adjusts his green tie. The chalk on his right plaid sleeve matches the lounge's yellow walls. "I object to your rudeness. It is my business since your absence disrupted my class."

"Car problems, Delford. It's pretty hard to make a phone call when you're stalled on the freeway."

The lounge door opens. Three teachers walk in and nudge Delford away from the coffee pot. He brings his cup to her table and sits diagonally across from her. His chubby nose always makes her thinks snot is about to drip out. She considers moving to the end of the table.

"I must ask what exactly was the matter with your car, since, if I'm correct, it is now parked out in the lot directly adjacent to my classroom?"

Bibi's fellow English teacher and Mary Poppins look-alike Gloria plops a book in front of Bibi. "What are you guys talking about?" She nods at the book and then looks at Bibi.

Bibi reads the book's dark blue title, *Astrology for Karmic Understanding* and silently counts the stars making a C formation on the cover's illustration. She looks up at Gloria and smiles her genuine gratitude.

Gloria points at the book while setting her cup next to Delford's. To Bibi, she says, "There's some really good stuff in it." When she sits next to Delford, he sighs, as if quite put upon.

"Her car," Delford explains to Gloria. "Evidently it broke on the freeway and now it's fine."

Gloria looks at Delford and then stares at Bibi and frowns quizzically. "Are you okay?"

Bibi's brows rise and she nods. "Oh, sure. I'm great." She flips through the book, from back to front. Her fingers tingle. She spots a logarithm chart in the middle and inwardly smiles. When she quickly scans the table of contents, the word "node" stares back at her, whatever the hell that means in this context.

Pamela, the math teacher who's worn the same pixie hairdo since Bibi met her a decade ago, sits next to Gloria and stirs her tea; she stares at Bibi with concern. "We know you're great, but you look like you've been crying."

Bibi looks pleadingly at the two women to change the subject.

Delford clears his throat. "So, woman, what did happen to your car?"

The air around Bibi suddenly becomes shallow and hard to breathe. She does everything in her power to keep from throwing her coffee in Delford's face.

Gloria and Pamela both turn to him. "Bug off, Delford." "Yeah, twerp."

Pamela turns to Bibi, serious as all get out. "How's Michael?"

Usually, she's not that grateful for this particular question. Her whole torso nods, or bounces, like she's trying to soothe herself. "He's doing okay. He had chemo like ten days ago. But you already know that."

Gloria nips at her lower lip.

"And the kids?" Pamela sips her tea, but her eyes don't leave Bibi.

"They're alright."

"You're sure? You tell us if you need anything. Promise?"

"Promise." Bibi hates she's said this. She can't tell them what's really going on. Not these two. They'd be her biggest fans. They'd dive in helping and urging. They'd make sure she found that birth mother of hers, because to them that would be a really good thing. She folds her hands atop the book. She could, of course, share with them the horrible mistake she made this morning. Nope, she thinks, not a good idea.

Pamela hasn't blinked. "Part of being brave is asking for help." She nods her head a tad and lifts her eyebrows, checking for comprehension.

Bibi feels herself choking up and her face redden. She swallows. Oh, for a cigarette.

Gloria leans in. "Okay, cough it up. What's going on? You promised."

Bibi inhales for stamina. “Okay." She swallows again. "Help me with this one. I was on the freeway this morning, and I, well, I had to pull over. Car trouble or something. And this highway patrolman stops. And Noah and Ella are screaming their brains out because this cop scares the hell out of them, and they won't stop screaming, and he's looking at me like I'm beating up my kids or something, and I start telling him that my father just died and my mother has leukemia." She waits for their reaction.

Pamela and Gloria sit spellbound, while Delford turns sideways in his chair and studies the ceiling, probably in an effort to show her how little about her life he really cares.

Pamela makes circles with her hand. "And?"

"And then I said, and I don't know why, I never should have, I said, 'my husband's dying,' which really set the kids screaming. Jesus. They cried all the way to the sitter's. I kept telling them their father wasn't dying, because he's not, damnit. But now they're going to go home and tell their father what I said."

Pamela moves her cup to the side, and reaches over for Bibi's hands, which she takes in hers. Gloria puts her hands atop Pamela's. A pact is being made without Bibi's permission. "Listen, kiddo, you made a mistake. When you pick up the critters today, tell them the truth. Daddy is sick, but Daddy is getting good medicines. He has a great doctor. He's getting better and better every day. Tell them what Mommy said before was untrue. She was wrong. And that it would upset Daddy very much if they repeated this wrong thing Mommy said. Do that. Everything will be alright."

Gloria, whose head has been bobbing during Pamela's whole spiel, says, echoing the faculty's current buzz word, "This too shall pass."

It makes Bibi laugh, though she really wants to cry some more. Yeah, this too shall pass. But she doesn't know with what consequences it will pass. Maybe she'll have to face the fact that she's crazier than she thinks. Or that Michael will hate her for the rest of her life because of what she said. Oh, sure it'll pass, but that doesn't mean it will have no effect. She glances down at the book in front of her. Karmic understanding. She could use a little of that.

§

September 22; Huntington Beach

Ella's low-profile bed is a mess.

And Bibi sits propped up right in the midst of it, her back resting against three white egg-shaped pillows, and her feet cozy beneath Ella's chicken comforter. Despite hating to sew, Bibi had hand-appliqued a huge, Revlon-red, nesting hen on a white duvet so Ella could have bedding unique to her. She's glad she did and loves how it looks.

At the end of the bed, Ceres lies spun into a ball and sound asleep, oblivious to anything not found in her kitty dreams.

Above Bibi, on the wall shelves, Ella's animals have recovered from Bestamor's visit. In other words, they're stacked on top of each other in disarming positions, pretty much matching the freakish poses taken on by the animals she has stuffed in her large, glass-based lamp. For a sweet little girl, Ella definitely has some quirks.

From down the hall in the family room, a cowboy's voice sings about a hard-workin' dog." The kids' laughter splashes about the house.

Bibi cringes at the thought they might wake their father. If he slept for the next three months, it would be fine with her. She dreads the inevitable moment when the kids ask their father if he's dying, even though she spent practically the whole trip home today telling them not to. The thought of the confrontation nauseates her.

Spread around Bibi, like the result of someone having just played fifty-two-card-pick-up, are note pads, pens, astrology books, and her horoscope notebook, in which she's carefully drawn out her family and friends' horoscopes after having diligently checked the ephemeris and logarithm charts and calculated to a second the placement of constellations and planets. The charts look like ancient clocks covered with hieroglyphs and doodles.

On the floor, but still reachable if she stretches, lies the buff-colored Shirmer's piano book containing Chopin's four ballades she purchased this afternoon at Heffen's. While in the store, it shocked her to realize she hadn't been in a music store since the kids were born. Or an art supply store come to think of it. Or a gallery. or a classical concert. Cripes, she hasn't been to a classical concert since before she married Michael. And every time she plays her own piano the family starts hollering at her to stop. It's as though she deserted part of herself when she entered the marriage door.

Such is the price for getting to stay.

She picks up the piano music book and opens it. The excitement of seeing music on a page for the first time arouses old memories of being a teenager, picking out music to spend six months learning, committing to it, memorizing it, and letting it inhabit her to the extent she could play it blindfolded. The table of contents includes the first several measures of each ballade. She hums the First Ballade and smiles. It's what she heard this morning on the radio, and can't wait to set about learning it. When she opens the book to the actual music, she realizes this one might not be as difficult as some of Chopin's other works; there's more white on the page than black. Giddy with potential, she decides to start work on it the next time Michael's in the hospital. That way she avoids having anyone hear her practicing, what with all her screeching notes, constant repetitions, and incomplete riffs.

She sets the book down on the floor, patient that she'll soon know this piece, play it when no one's listening, and, most of all, figure out why she's irresistibly drawn to it.

Her attention returns to her charts and pages of calculations. She clicks her pen a couple of times, then, by casting out nines, she rechecks her math to make sure she's got the accurate positions for the Moon's nodes she read about in the book Gloria gave her at school this morning. Success!

She opens her notebook containing her horoscope and draws an upside-down horseshoe in her first house, by the nine-o'clock position. It represents the South Node. Next, she draws a right-side up horseshoe in Gemini, which happens to be in her seventh house.

She turns to Victor's horoscope, ready to do the same for him. His South Node goes in Aries, and his North Node in Libra. But, before she inks in the node symbols, she pauses at what she considers a wild chance in hell.

Victor's South Node, like hers, is in his first house, by the nine-o'clock position. Though her mind cannot logically explain why this is important, the shiver coursing through her tells her she's discovered a prime clue in a treasure hunt.

She opens Gloria's book to its index so she can look up South Node, to see what it all means.

When she does, a small, oblong, yellow paper falls out and cascades to the floor. In black ink, ten digits written in old script span the paper. A phone number, Bibi assumes, before dismissing its existence.

Her attention returns to the astrology book Gloria loaned her, for she's been inexplicably curious about this node stuff since she stumbled across it in the book's index earlier this morning. On page four-hundred-sixteen, she spots what she's looking for.

Three words pop out at her, grab her psyche's shoulders and shake them. Death. Drowning. Young. Danger of death while young, possibly by drowning.

The words chant in her mind. They ricochet; they bounce and ping. She knows the words have something to do with her, and yet she doesn't. The morning's bizarre sadness again saturates her being. Her throat burns, and her heart chokes. The words and the coincidence of Victor's and her horoscopes make no sense, and yet they do. She puts her head in her hands and allows herself to momentarily weep.

Moments later, Bibi lets the book close and fall from her lap onto its face. Numbly, she walks through the family room to the kitchen. On her way, she lowers the volume on Sesame Street and picks up half a graham cracker one of her kids left on the floor uneaten. She hesitates a moment and stares at her kids, whose faces reflect Bert and Ernie's orangeness.

But they ignore her, which is good. She's not quite sure how she appears to others in this given moment.

In the kitchen she has a change of heart. It's sheer lunacy to call her mother about this. There's nothing her mother can add. And there's nothing she can add to her mother's life by bringing it up.

She heads back to the family room and stops. Noah and Ella sit cross-legged on the floor in front of the television. Their shoulders touch because they're leaning into each other. Neither of them notices she's looking at them. They seem like replicas of Victor and her hiking the forest paths near June Lake, lost in the world that only the two of them shared.

She returns to the kitchen and dials her mother from the wall phone. She walks diagonally across the kitchen, the long, coiled cord stretching to accommodate her. God, for a cigarette. She turns around and opens the monkey canister. At the third ring, she picks out a Double Bubble, which she unwraps and pops in her mouth by the seventh ring. Chomp. Chew. Chomp. Oh, the relief. The cartoon she leaves on the kitchen table.

At the eighth ring she hangs up and heads to Ella's room, on the way again lowering the TV volume and grabbing her dowsing chain from the study. The Cookie Monster is downing another chocolate chip cookie. What a role model.

Not without noticing the yellow paper on the floor, Bibi sits back under Ella's covers, picks up a pad and pen, and wriggles her toes under Ceres.

The kitty attacks the toe-creature dashing about under her.

On the pad, Bibi writes: "The nodes tell the truth."

With the dowsing chain clamped between her finger and thumb, she dangles it over the paper and wills herself to not give a hoot what direction the chain follows.

The chain immediately begins swinging widely, like a Chair-O-Plane, in positive, clockwise circles.

She stops the chain's movement with her hand, for she realizes she does in fact care very much what direction the chain follows. For if the chain moves in a clockwise pattern, it means the statement she wrote is most likely true, which in turn means the nodes' messages are true.

She feels hollow inside, as if something has been sucked out of her. Her fingers have lost sensation. Surely the chain can't be correct. In this moment her thoughts are greater than she can think. Bibi must move around and do something; she can't just sit here and stare.

She crawls out from under the covers and sits on the bed's side. She bows to her urge to shake the tensions from her fingertips; she shakes and whips them, while her world spins within her mind's eye. Then she catches a glimpse of the paper on the floor, which seems an even brighter yellow.

She picks it up and takes it to the kitchen, where she studies it. The numbers, written in a nineteenth-century script, draw her in the arcanest of ways, like a magnet, or beautiful music, or a long-forgotten and much-loved aroma.

None of this makes sense to her. But the numbers, if they express a telephone number, have a California area code. What the heck!

She dials the number; her fingers can barely stay still, so strangely excited is she. The air about her moves in gloppy heaves, like Jell-O.

A woman answers, "Kettenburg Marine."

"Oh!" Bibi says with genuine surprise, and slams down the phone. She hadn't prepared for what to say in the event someone actually answered. She feels stupid for having dialed, like a teenager calling random people and asking if their refrigerators are running.

"Who're you calling, Mommy, who're you calling?" Always curious, her Ella, who in this moment sits on the floor before the television, adding the finishing touches to her terrorized Barbie which she has tied to the red wings of one of Noah's plastic airplanes.

"No one." Bibi crumples the paper before Ella comes out to see what she's doing. When the paper looks the size of a pea, she throws it basketball-style into the trash, watches it earnestly arc into the container, and returns to Ella's room, momentarily sizing up how long it will take her to clean up her mess and get dinner started before Michael wakes up.

Ceres opens one eye slightly and seems to be looking at something moving about the ceiling, and then shuts it. Bibi glances up, but seeing nothing, tries to refocus on what she'd been working on in Ella's room.

But Bibi can't think straight. Her thoughts start and stop and sputter up again. She wants something practical to focus on, but she can't. If she were a kid, she'd be sucking her thumb; instead, she chomps on her gum.

Then, without prompting, myriad fascinating words saturate her mind, as though she has found herself in a great, acoustically-perfect lecture hall. She's heard voices before, but nothing like this. She sits on Ella's bedside, grabs her pen, turns one of her calculation sheets over, and writes, hoping it makes sense in the end. Ceres moves from her spot to where Bibi is, and leans against Bibi's back until the writing stops. "Intersections, overprotection," Bibi writes, "hovering, hollowing space." The words repeat in her mind, as though expecting to be transcribed.

To the words' rhythm, her shoulders move, and then her torso. She hears more words and writes them down. Her curiosity has come alive with the desire to have it all make sense.

This day, which started out horridly, which had the potential for ruining her life, and still does, seems suddenly like a new kind of day to her. For something deep down in her knows this all makes sense, even though she cannot in this moment understand why.

At some point she realizes the words are done, and that whatever it is that she was writing is complete.

She goes into the study and retrieves her brown and red paisley, cloth-covered journal, into which she transcribes the words as a poem, which seems appropriate to her. Then, instead of signing it with her initials like she usually does when she writes poems, she merely puts the date. September 22, 1981.

Intersections,
overprotection,
hovering, hollowing space.

Making illusions of
artificial premises,
disguising enlightenments by
deeming the shallow deep,
while raping the depth from the ether.

It is only a matter of time,
that our trials,
heaped high,
burdens piled in an inverse triangular trilogy of strife,
will finally be self-sufficient,
occurring without thought,
without plan,
without prior commitment,
will occur solely from past failures,
from past futures not realized.
So shrill the plot seems,
doting upon our every shadowy bruise,
poking at it (not in jest)
but for the lust of our screams.
But, for the tunnel we search

Oh, freeway to freedom
that gateway to glory,
where piety is proven
and choice chiseled at.
Until finally a straight path
is seen
is ventured upon,
taken.
The straightaway causeway lays at our bay.
Take it.

§

I hover close to Bibi, watching her inscribe my last words. She dots the i high above it, like the sunshine in a child's picture. The tee she crosses with a long, happy dash. And the period? She almost forgets it in her hurry to write the date.

I tingle and froth with excitement, then uncontrollably twirl and spin from the thrill of it all. My substance sprays around me like glittering stardust. Such a hay day this has been for me. Even I am not so blasé to be unaffected by the events of the last hour. You may think it was easy to conjure that yellow paper with the numbers just right. I assure you it was not.

And, and I say this with a capital a, Bibi heard me. No, more than that, she understood me, for an extended period of time. She wrote my whole poem, word for word. For ages, I have been trying to get through to her like this. Eons, I tell you. If only I could have such success with Delilah, or Victor. You should read what Williams and Eliot got from me and from others. Poets are such sponges, and I mean that in a good way.

Bibi, whom I now watch from outside her home, pets the journal page's surface. Slowly her hand draws over my words, her eager fingertips listening for their complete meaning. Her violet, radiating thoughts appear clearly to me. She feels herself in a profoundly new world, as if she's dropped out of a Star Trek's Transporter into a strange, mythical land. Certain of my words she finds provocative and realizes they remind her of something she knows, but does not comprehend.

A faint smile embellishes her face as she rereads my words. Outside her door, unbeknownst to her, Ella and Noah have turned off the television and are creeping on hands and knees toward their father's room, where he soundly sleeps.

I slip further from Bibi's home, where I balance myself maybe forty feet above the street. The light of the late-day sun blanches her front-porch bricks. Noah's red steam roller lists on the entry mat; unfortunate, flattened bugs bedeck the rollers like decals.

From this distance, I'm aware of the neighborhood's teeming life. Shade trees and ornamentals, flowering shrubs and annuals, carpeting lawns, thriving molds, wispy algae clinging to aquarium walls, slumbering cats, family dogs, worms and moles tunneling beneath the surface, foraging birds, web-spinning spiders, scampering children, nibbling termites, and a nation of mites caught in the throes of a territorial feud. All, from where I perch, seem bulging with effort to have what they need to live their best life.

It makes me wistful. Life is such a gift.

I'm aware of others, like myself, suspended over houses. Most of these souls I recognize, for our humans live here. We watch, we care, we do what we can without living their lives. They're our family, not our puppets. Usually, we're ignored.

And I'm aware of all the concrete and plaster walls, the picket and grape stake fences, the privet and oleander hedges, the locked side-yard gates, and the inviting front doors, and the battered back entries, and the many, many doors found within each home.

For all that is good about life, I consider these partitions a tremendous downside. Don't get me wrong; I understand why they're necessary. It's just that they reinforce something tragic. Have you ever heard someone remark about someone else, "What a wasted life for one with such talent"? That's what I'm talking about. Walls and doors and fences and gates all help you forget your most incredible talent. Open those doors, unlock those gates, and tear down the fences. See what else is available.

§

Bibi's in the act of squeezing her paisley journal into a row of books in the study, when the phone rings. It sounds like her mother, but she can't be sure. Quickly, she picks up the phone in the study, and closes the door behind her to keep her kids from hearing her. She prays hard that Michael will go back to sleep if the phone woke him up.

"Bibi, do you have a minute?" her mother asks, though it sounds more like a demand.

"Not really. But I do have a question for you."

"The only reason I called is because I want to know if you've heard from Victor."

"Mom, can I ask you a question first?"

"I'm sure Victor has called you by now."

"Mom, stop. I did Victor's and my horoscopes, and the same thing showed up. There was a danger of us drowning as children. Isn't that weird?" She hopes her mother simply answers the question instead of going into a winded explanation of why Bibi should stop with the occult stuff and attend the local Lutheran church on a regular basis, which is what their whole family has done for lifetimes.

Her mother is indeed silent, for too long in Bibi's opinion.

"No," her mother finally says. "That's not strange. It's what happened. She tried to drown you."

A faint, "Oh," is all Bibi can manage. The air feels suddenly sopping, as if in this moment Bibi were once again drowning. "You're sure? I have no memory of that."

She opens the study door several inches and looks at her kids, whom she expects to see sitting there, entranced by Oscar the Grouch or The Count or whomever, their innocent faces glowing and changing colors in the television's reflected light. Her mind is thick like felt. She cannot imagine for the life of her how someone, especially her own birth mother, could attempt to drown her. She could never do such a thing to her own children.

"Bibi. Bibi, can you hear me?"

Bibi now realizes she has dropped the phone. She picks it up. "Sorry."

"Bibi, you were saved. People saved you. They brought you to the shore. Then her friends found us because we were looking for a daughter, and a son. You were saved. We saved you."

"Wait. Does Vic remember this? He should. He'd have been almost three. Older than Noah."

A sucking whirlpool spins in Bibi's mind; memories she dares not see regurgitate from her past, appearing in random, nanosecond-long visions that flash in her consciousness. The water's surface, dappled white, as seen from below. Men in white. Victor asleep. The images carry no meaning, except that she feels her body tighten in dread.

"No, Bibi. Victor has no memories of this. He's never said a word about it. It's best this way."

"But how could we both forget it happened. Or maybe we haven't tried to remember." The thought of something happening to her and Michael so the kids end up with new parents becomes a solid worry. Ella and Noah can't just forget her and Michael. That can't happen.

Bibi's mother's voice seems miles away. "I hope you understand why I want to protect you from that woman."

Numbness walls Bibi into herself. "Yeah, Mom, I get it. I don't want to find her. Trust me."

§

Bibi painstakingly hangs up the phone, as though it were made of porcelain. The sound of the phone settling into its cradle, like teeth chattering, seems to be the only noise in the house.

She's aware she can't hear the television, which is such a nice respite. The faux-leather desk chair invites her, and she sits in it, comforted by its arms.

The family pictures arranged evenly on the desk, call to her as random memories. The first steps her darling Noah took last Halloween; his plastic Superman cape stuck out perpendicular from his body so it looked like he was running. Michael's and her wedding picture. Ella in her car seat eating a Happy Meal hamburger, with bun crumbs sticking to her rosy, slick cheeks. Charlie and Rose on their boat. Victor and Phoebe in their hen house. Ceres sitting on a tree branch just before she fell off it, as she is wont to do. The kitty's always falling off tables, walls, trees, beds, you name it. To Ceres's right, sits a black-and-white of three-year-old Bibi, irresistibly cute, sitting on a boat seat with her brothers, on Gull Lake in Mammoth. All three of them were out-sized by their fat cotton life vests. She rues. How her birth mother could have taken Bibi, so irresistibly cute and cuddly, into the ocean to die dumbfounds her.

A deadly logic settles in Bibi. Her birth mother must be a creep to have done what she did. If it were indeed true, Bibi herself must also be a creep capable of God knows what. Bibi takes this thought as a warning and inwardly promises to be part of an entirely new generation.

As she thinks this, she notices the odd, golden quiet of her home.

She positions the picture of her brothers and her in the boat to her extreme left, and Noah's picture to the desk's right edge. She selects her wedding picture next, with the intent of arranging it on the left to be in chronological order, like organizing a memoir.

But a child's loud wail coming from her bedroom causes her to hastily set the picture face down in the middle of the desk. She hears another wail. And then another. The bedroom door knob bangs against the closet door. The children's full-on screaming and howling moves out the bedroom and down the hall. Michael's moans lie low in the soundtrack. The cacophony is ruthless.

Bibi lurches from the chair and opens the study door, ready to call an ambulance, or the fire department, or the police.

Then she recognizes what this is about.

Standing in the hallway, strangled by anger, Michael staggers toward Bibi. Weeping Noah clings to Michael's left leg, and screaming Ella to his right. Michael's eyes bleed from betrayal. "How could you, Bibi?" he roars.

Bibi moves toward him. She can explain. It's all a mistake.

His jabbing index finger thwarts her. "You can't do this to me!" Spit sprays with his words. The kids wail louder.

She recoils to avoid his fire, but again moves toward him, holding out her left arm to herd him into the family room. "I can explain. I promise, this is not what it seems."

Michael flinches. "Don't you touch me!" The kids grip their father's legs all the harder, as though he were a toy they refuse to give up. "Don't you lay a hand on me."

His hatred shatters her like a grenade. She knew he'd be upset, but carelessly miscalculated how much. This was preventable. She should have closely monitored the kids. Stupid kids. Stupid naive kids. Stupid her!

"Please, Michael, let me explain." She takes the kids' arms softly in her hands. "C'mon, you guys. Let Daddy walk."

The kids whimper and step back. Their necks crane impossibly to see his face; their eyes stare questioningly.

Michael relents. He shuffles into the family room, the rest of his family in tow.

The kids walk no further than the room's middle, where they stand, side-by-side, skin-to-skin, silent and curious. Their moist red faces glisten like the insides of a persimmon.

Bibi resists her horrid, nagging urge to slap both of them for being such stupid little tattle tales. But it's not their fault. They're just repeating what she stupidly told them.

Michael situates himself on the long sofa that faces the television. He tightens the knot of his robe's belt, and leans his arms on the sofa's back in a crucified sort of way. Above him, lined perfectly as an homage to their college years, hang three framed Haight-Ashbury posters Michael had carefully removed from telephone poles in San Francisco in '67, which are now, because of their condition, worth a mint. His eyes reek of hostility and skepticism; he's primed to find her wrong.

Bibi stands before him accused of betrayal, and rightly so. "Michael, I apologize."

He looks toward the front door. His jaw shifts back and forth impatiently.

Bibi realizes he's about to erupt again. She searches for words with which to appease him.

Noah, his little attention span spent, spots an acid-green GTO Match-Box car by the fireplace to Bibi's right. He kneels next to the car and drives it along the hearth. "Dine, dine, dine," he chants. "Daddy's dine, dine, dine."

Michael whips his head around. His nostrils flare; his eyes bug.

Horrified, Bibi warns, "Noah, shut!" She realizes her son has no idea what dying means.

Noah giggles. "Dine, dine, dine." He gets up to please his father with his cuteness. He races the car on the sofa cushions. "Dine, dine, dine."

Ella races toward her brother to stop his antics, but is too late.

In a booming voice Bibi rarely hears coming from her husband, Michael hollers, "Shut the fuck up!" His trembling hands ram against his ears. Pulsing veins rise like mountain ridges on his temples. His eyes squeeze closed. "Shut the holy fuck up!"

The kids freeze, as though ice water had been thrown in their faces and then tear around the settee and down the hallway to Ella's room. The door slams behind them.

"Oh, God." Bibi sinks to her knees in front of Michael. Her hands fold prayer-like under her bowed chin. Shame and horror deluge her. What hath she wrought? She rests her hands on top of his knees. "Michael, Michael," she pats his thighs. "Honestly, it's not what it seems."

He glares into her eyes. His spine presses flat against the sofa's back.

"I got stopped by a policeman this morning. I was on the side of the freeway because I'd started crying and couldn't stop."

Doubt shows in Michael's eyes.

"I know. Me crying. But I couldn't talk. I couldn't get out of the car. All I could do was weep, which made the kids cry. It was horrible."

Michael's eyes narrow and his lips purse like a tight sphincter.

Bibi knows this look and what he's thinking. His deduction shoves her into a chasm impossible to escape. She's a terrible mother whom he cannot trust with his children. She's genetically identical to her wicked birth mother. "I know how crazy this sounds, but it's true."

"So, did he let you off?"

"No. I mean yes. Well, he was going to take me in. For crying. He said he wouldn't let me drive."

Michael's brows furrow. He bites the corner of his lower lip.

"I had to tell him something so he'd have sympathy and let me go. I didn't want to get arrested. I'd lose my job and our insurance. The only thing I could think of to tell him was that my mother had leukemia, which was a big fat lie. And that my father just died, which was kind of true. And that you were dying, which is a lie, and I never should have said it. Never, never. But I did it so he wouldn't arrest me. And I worried all day that the kids heard me. Especially Ella. She still wonders where my father is. But I figured they didn't know what it meant."

The anger in Michael's eyes subsides. His hands come down from the sofa ledge and rest near Bibi's.

"Just in case, on the way home I told them about how good your medicines were working and that you were getting well."

Michael sits enormously still.

The silence of his body makes Bibi feel like a criminal awaiting the jury's verdict. She waits, and hopes, knowing she'll continue appealing for his forgiveness until she at last has it. For she is innocent, even though she is not.

A movement out of the corner of her left eye distracts her. She glances toward the action and sees terrified Ella standing in the hall, her thumb in her mouth, listening intently to their conversation. Ella, the innocent culprit. And Ella the one who can verify Bibi's alibi. She smiles genuinely at her daughter, silently begging her to confirm the truth in Bibi's words.

"Daddy?" Ella asks softly, while inching her way into the family room.

Michael turns to her. "Yes, Ellie Belly."

"A policeman talked to Mommy this morning. He gave her gum so she wouldn't cry."

Michael's conciliatory hands cover Bibi's, still resting atop his knees.

His touch dissolves her. She sinks forward; her head rests in his lap, her nose between his thighs. "Please forgive me. I'll do everything I can think of to change what they think."

The fingers of his right hand gently thread through her curls.

His gesture should make her feel loved and forgiven. Instead, it haunts her and kindles a drive in her to race out the front door and hurl herself down the street for safety. She lifts her head several inches and stares at his lap, unsure how she really feels, for the weird and unexpected panic she has just experienced is subsiding. Still, his lap seems foreign and of another era. The remnants of her panic warn her that she needs to be a certain way and do certain things in order to stay, to be kept, to not be abandoned.

A new feeling then takes over. Nostalgic sadness snivels in her throat. It's been such a long time since she's felt any interest in his lap. She can't even remember what it was like. All she cares about now is protecting him and keeping him alive. He's lost his mantel of being her knight in shining armor. Now he's another dependent, another one of her children. She shudders at this thought, and the fact that she even thinks it.

Bibi hears Ella's voice behind her. "Mommy said the doctor's making you well."

Michael reaches both hands out to Ella, who is joined by a relieved Noah. Bibi straightens her back upright and watches their children flock to his lap. "Careful," she warns them.

They stand on the sofa and hug him around his neck, as though he were their big teddy bear. "Daddy," they purr.

Bibi watches his face redden and his eyes mist. Little furrows fold between his brows. His lips tighten and quiver. When he at last chokes up, he clasps his children tight, and hides his face in theirs. When he can talk, he says, "All I want is to see my children grow up. That's all I want."

Tears well in Bibi's eyes and throat and heart, for she, with all her soul wants the exact same thing. She wants them to have him for all their growing-up years and beyond. And then her eyes are helpless to not notice what surrounds Michael and is visible on the wall behind him.

Steadily emanating almost a foot out from Michael, and also her children, are dazzling silver and violet lights. Without knowing how she knows, she accepts the light's meaning. She wills it to become a fact that Michael Amato, father of Ella and Noah, lives to see his children grow up.

"Yep, that's all I want. And for you, Bibi, to stay focused on our family. Stay focused on what's important."

§

Michael's request that she stay focused on what's important has plowed right into Bibi's two versions of herself.

She scoots the polished ebony bench she sits on a few more inches away from her piano and readjusts the brass lamp to glow more directly on the open pages displayed on the music rack. Except for where the lamp's trained beam glows, umber shadows drench her great room giving it the feeling of a cathedral. With the lamp's round glow upon her and the piano keys, she could be on stage at the Met or part of the chiaroscuro section in a centuries-old Caravaggio painting. Her fingertips tingle, as does her spine, and the crown of her head. There is something she wants so much in the moment, something she remembers about herself. What it is, she cannot grasp. She feels connected, alive, and devious. The fact that Michael had admonished her earlier in the evening to focus on what's important didn't help. What an invitation he had given her.

The ball of her bare left foot rests ready on the piano's brass *unda corda* pedal.

The metal's smooth coolness momentarily surprises Bibi. Her left heel stays put on the carpeting. She parks her right foot under her knee and back a little, away from the damper pedal, which she's prone to over use. The carpet's uneven pile provides her right toes a woolly cushion.

Ceres, whom she thought was still outside, rubs her chin against Bibi's right ankle. Her whiskers tickle Bibi and cause her arms to shiver. She pets Ceres with her toes before bringing her foot back to its station under the bench.

Before she poises her fingers above the keys, she reads the dark, hollow space of her great room's cathedral ceiling. Her shoulders slacken, and she breathes in heavily. This room, this great room, which the previous owners added, is the only spot in her generic tract house where she experiences the elaborate space she secretly craves. This room could be her salon. Artists, musicians, and poets could meet here. And avant-garde thinkers. The conversations would explore ideas about social injustice, and the latest movements in the arts, sciences, and humanities. Her own paintings would command respect, at last. These images taste familiar to Bibi, as though this is how her life is meant to be. And yet this is not how her life is, not even close. Fate keeps handing her something different.

From up the three steps and to the right of the great room's other end, more than thirty feet away, Vin Scully or some other baseball announcer speaks through the television. "A low inside. Ball three." The stadium organ works on the crowd with a *Charge!* rift. "Charge!" Michael, Noah and Ella all sing in response.

Bibi positions her hands so they look ready to claw into sand, and steadies them above the age-stained, striated ivory base keys. She can't help but notice the cracks and glue marks on the six lowest keys. Noah had discovered that if he pushed up on the keys' ivory ledges, the ivory would snap off half way. Fortunately, she caught him before he'd done in her whole piano.

Her fingertips tremble, forcing her to see how truly nervous she feels. A weird taste generates in the back of her mouth, and her rib cage tightens. All hell will break loose in the family room the moment her fingers come down on the first chord.

She resists the urge to pull her hands back. There's no reason why she, like the rest of her family, shouldn't be able to focus on what she wants at the end of a long day. Besides teaching 'til three and running errands, she's warded off a policeman, assuaged a justifiably angry husband, discovered her birth mother tried to drown her, single-handedly made dinner, did the dishes, bathed and jammied the kids, corrected two class sets of papers, folded and put away a pile of laundry, paid three bills, got the trash out to the sidewalk, and found Barbie's red shoe in Noah's Lincoln Logs barrel. And what have they done since the moment she got home? Played. Slept. Made requests of her that they expected to be fulfilled.

Besides, she needs a real break before she reads another essay arguing which dog in Jack London's *Call of the Wild* would make the best pet. Especially after that last one she read. Jason from her third period non-honors class, whom she suspects hasn't read a page of the book, wrote his whole essay off topic. "Buck's the Best" he called it. He should have titled it, "The Repugnant Injustice of Lashing Fun-Loving Dogs to Dog-Sled Traces". Repugnant indeed, just like her life. It was as though he'd written the essay specifically for her.

She focuses on the sixteen identical chords that make up the first two measures of Beethoven's *Waldstein Sonata,* which must be played jack-hammer fast, yet softly, at least in the beginning. Her left foot presses down the *unda corda,* insuring her first notes can't be too loud. She winces and presses the pedal. It squeaks loudly. She glances toward the family room, to make sure the sound went unnoticed, then, bom, bom, bom, bom, bom . . .

How she loves these repetitive chords. It's as though she's riding a cantering horse. It takes guts and talent to write a sonata where the first sixteen notes are all the same. But it is, she'd decided years ago, a Beethoven quirk. Consider, for example, the repeating cello ostinato at the beginning of his *Seventh's* second movement.

Bom, bom, bom . . .

She imagines Victor standing next to her, and then in her place on the bench with her watching him. Of the two of them, he is hands-down the better musician. He should possess this piano, instead of her. Except he lived in a tree house when her mother decided the piano cramped her living room and gave it to Bibi. It's been a sore point between Victor and Bibi ever since.

Bom, bom, bom . . .

As if on cue, Michael has turned the television's volume up full blare, both jammie-clad and newly-bathed children race down the steps wailing their demands, and Ceres, faster than a flash, escapes to the kitchen. The great room, which moments ago reminded Bibi of a Renaissance basilica or a lush Paris salon, has mutated into a rumpled bowling alley.

"Mommy, read me a book," Ella pleads, as she crowds up against Bibi's left leg. Apple shampoo and strawberry soap tint the air; her beautiful child smells like dessert.

"I hate dat," Noah yells, his hands clasped against his ears. He marches around the sofa, his protesting footsteps smashing into the carpet.

From the family room, and over the roar of the television, Michael hollers, "God damnit, Bibi!"

"Momby, don't play dat," Noah yowls.

"Mommy," Ella screeches. Her fists pound on the piano's very lowest keys. "You promised me you'd finish *Babar*. I want to hear *Babar*."

Bibi blocks out their voices and demands the best she can. But it's hard. Ella's arrhythmic, discordant pounding drives Bibi to distraction. Bibi's well-practiced treble fingers manage to tap out the cascading bird-like notes in the next two measures. Inside Bibi, she's aboil. Her mind chatters and curses and prods her to anarchy so she can focus on what's important.

"Bibi!" Michael, she can see, stands next to the television. He turns the volume low and faces her. "Can't you do that when I'm not watching television?"

She glances at him quickly, letting her look speak volumes. Her voice, however, does not utter what she's thinking: Sure, I'll play while you're sleeping; I'm sure you'll love that more. Her fingers now attack the base keys for sixteen more repeating chords.

"Bibi, stop. Read to Ella. Do something else."

The kids are crying.

She wills herself to keep playing, just this one piece. Even though she's actually thinking about the last page of *Babar* she read to Ella, and what possible gene Noah could be missing to hate classical music so, and the thirty-five more essays she still needs to correct, and the fact that her birth mother tried to drown her, and that her husband never lifts a hand to help her, and the Chopin ballade she may never have the time or space to learn because there is never time or space for her to do anything she wants.

By the time she's three-quarters of the way down the page, she realizes she can't remember playing or enjoying any of it except the first two measures. At least she had that.

She slams down the piano's fall board. It snaps at the wood in front of the keys like jaws.

Life shouldn't be like this. She ought to be able to play the piano when she wants, even if her family detests hearing it. And she should be able to paint without the kids running around, smearing their hands in her palette. But her house, like her life, is set up to accommodate her family, not her. All she ever does, it seems, is serve others. Their needs always come first, because they scream at her and distract her. Their needs are spilled milk in the middle of the floor. Their needs have to be met before she can tolerate even acknowledging her own.

The end result: she winds up making everyone else's life easier, while they don't do the same for her. And for that, in this moment, she hates herself, and them. And wonders if Victor has found their birth mother yet.

Five

The Demanding Path

September 23; Huntington Beach

Garbage disposals. Such an invention. Bibi guides the clump of carrot peels down the growling drain. If only all the garbage in her life could disappear as efficiently. Yesterday morning's crying jag on the freeway and everything that followed, for example. But then she thinks of her birth mother getting rid of her in the ocean, and the idea doesn't seem terrific after all.

Bibi hears clanking from inside the drain. Cripes. Nothing like the sound of forks and spoons getting mangled in the garbage disposal. She guesses it drives her as nuts as the Beethoven she played last night annoys Noah. She reaches for the disposal switch on the wall.

At the same time the phone rings.

She clicks off the disposal, tunes into the phone for a second and guesses it's probably her mother calling to tell her she'll be late or that she's not coming. That would be good. Bibi hates it when her mother comes over on a school night and expects Bibi to feed her a proper dinner.

Without first drying her hands, she gets to the phone just after the second ring, and picks up the receiver. The phone's long cord allows her to return to the sink to fish out the spoon or fork that must have slipped down the drain with the carrot peels and bread crusts. Except her slimed hands retrieve a potato peeler instead. "Hello," she answers. Bibi rinses the peeler, and, pretending it's a spear, launches it into the dishwasher's utensil basket. She sets the pot of carrots and dill on the stove.

"It's me," Victor announces with a hesitation that makes his words seem more like a question. A chorus singing *Lohengrin*'s "Bridal Chorus" plays in the background. "What did Mom say?"

Bibi tsks and wishes she hadn't answered the phone. She eyes the two-week-old copy of *Time* featuring the new star Meryl Streep awaiting her on the kitchen table. That's how far behind she is on the news. She figured she could read some of it before her mother arrives later.

"She's coming for dinner. I'll call you tomorrow," she tells him. This phone call needs to end before Victor has a chance to start in on her, and before she blurts out something she can't take back.

"What about, you know, your gypsy stuff? Get anything? You said you'd call."

"Let me call you tomorrow. I haven't had a chance to do anything," Bibi tells him. Yesterday rekindles in her mind. She considers telling him about the meaning of their horoscopes, but senses this is not the time. Something about his voice is fraught. "I gotta go, Vic."

"Wait."

She glances at the clock; her mother should be here in the next half hour, or really an hour the way her mother drives.

"C'mon, you caught me at a bad time." She twists the dishwasher dial to START, listens as the machine ticks twice before water gushes into the interior. That set, she opens the oven door and adjusts the rack for the chicken-and-rice casserole she'd prepared. Life would be easier if she were an octopus.

His voice softens. "Do you trust who you are?"

Bibi thinks Victor's question sounds too simple or it's a facade. "Yeah, I trust who I am." Maybe not, she wonders. She pops the baking dish on the middle rack, shuts the oven door and awaits Victor's explanation of why she can't trust who she is.

"How can you be sure?"

Exasperated, Bibi stares at the phone's mouth piece, half expecting her brother to jump out through the little holes and demand she take his question seriously. Around the corner in the family room, Michael's watching his hero Louis Ruckeyser on *Wall Street Week*. Her children are back in their bedrooms and can't be heard. Their silence is golden. She switches the phone to her other ear, walks back to the counter, and reaches into the sink for the sponge. The phone's bouncing coiled cord follows behind her like an ecstatic snake.

"Well?" asked Victor.

It registers in Bibi's mind that *Lohengrin* still strains in the background. Elsa's singing, which probably means it's not long before the swan arrives. She's not that much of an opera buff, but she gets the connection. When the swan shows up, that's when the audience discovers the swan is really Elsa's brother.

Bibi knows she's no masquerading swan, even though Victor might be. "Honestly, with my life, I don't know any other way to be," she finally tells him.

"But what if there is another way?"

"I gotta go." She tosses the sponge in the sink. All these questions. She doesn't have time for this.

"No. Answer me first. What if there's another way?"

She guesses where his questions are heading. He seems the same as always, just more intense. Except he's all screwed up about this birth mother thing. And he was truly weird at the family dinner last week. Heck, it makes her feel screwy, and she's not even involved in the search, nor does she want to be.

"Look, Vic, if there's another way, I don't know how to find out."

"I know how," he beams. "That's why I'm searching. That's why you should be involved."

So, she's right. His questions are his rococo way of getting her to do the looking. "I don't want to look," she tells him. "Stop asking me." An image of her two mothers, standing side-by-side, chases flickered in her consciousness. Her mother, the white-haired monster shoulder-to-shoulder with her other mother, the faceless, female shape. Each waits, arms folded, tapping her foot, and ready to extract her needs from Bibi.

"What if you're more than you think you are? What if you're really different from how you see yourself?"

This question startles her. Last night, in her great room, while playing the piano, she was thinking this exact thing: Bibi Amato is living in the wrong life.

Bibi glances at the kitchen table because she can no longer bear her thoughts. The *Time* magazine, with Meryl Streep's endearing photograph on the cover, waits courteously atop it. "Magic Meryl," the editors have labeled her. Her straight and probably easy to manage hair's pulled back in a pony tail. Gold studs decorate her ear lobes. Her right hand hooks around the back of her neck so her elbow points at the photographer, and her left hand clutches the neckline of her white knit top, as though she just recently decided to cover herself up. How nice it would be to have Meryl's life right now, to be calm and relaxed. To have other people cleaning up after you. To have only one mother. To have lots of lives to try on.

She's tempted to gently lay the phone in its cradle and back away, as though this conversation were an automobile accident she just witnessed, but didn't want to get involved with. The selfishness this requires shames her.

"I'm going to call you tomorrow," she tells him. "I don't have time to concentrate on your questions."

Just as Bibi says this, Michael comes in from the family room. He frowns quizzically.

Bibi mouths, "Victor," and holds the phone so Michael can hear.

"Look with me, Bibi. You won't regret it."

She breathes in deeply, aware of how oddly close she is, in this moment, to appeasing Victor in order to calm down his life, and therefore hers. But she says words for Michael to hear instead. "Please stop asking me. You can't make me. I have too much going on in my life. I work, unlike everyone else in this damned family. I have kids. I have a sick—." Her eyes meet Michael's. "We have a lot to deal with." She instantly regrets saying the word sick, and it pains her that Michael heard her. She covers her mouth with her hand and looks sorrowfully at him.

Michael ignores her eyes. His attention waits for Victor's answer.

"Victor, I can't," she adds.

"Ah, but you can."

It's hard for Bibi to think with Michael monitoring her every word. She turns her back to him. His head remains close; his breath gusts along the surface of her neck. Her mind tries to digest what looking and finding would entail. Time, for one, which she already doesn't have enough of. Her mother's anger and subsequent revenge. Michael. Their kids. Strangers suddenly becoming family, and maybe family suddenly seeming like strangers. Having to change herself because of what she finds. "Maybe you're right, Vic. I can look, but I don't want to."

Bibi reaches back to touch Michael. In her head Stephen Stills croons, "Love the one you're with."

§

September 23; Lubbock

You may wonder where I focus my attention to bring about the gathering of my born siblings. Quite simply, I imagine each of them satisfied with the efforts they made to create the reunion. That's important, I think.

Which is why I now focus my attention on Delilah, who, as usual, unwinds from a hard day's work in her creamy white bathtub. Jasmine and rose scent the air, frothy bubbles fizz and pop. Baby Bee reclines on the peach bathmat, licking the crevasses between her toes. Little nuzzling noises rise from her mouth.

Perched among Delilah's many potions and lotions amassed on the tub's shelf is her little personal phone book and her bedroom's pinkish princess phone. She'd had Big Joe wire it with an extravagantly long wall cord, because he'd refused to allow their bathroom to have its own phone. "You'd live in there if we did that," he'd protested.

Balanced on Delilah's shoulder, nudged close to her ear is the phone's receiver. Its speaker smells of Lysol. Her index finger flicks at the white coiled wire connecting the receiver to the phone, making it bounce above the bath's bubbles. Next to her, on the ledge, rests a yellow pencil and a pad of paper. In Delilah's school-girl perfect script, she's written 351 Avalon Place,

Seal Beach, and 596 465 4889. Seal Beach, she thinks. Right next to Huntington Beach, if her memory serves her.

Suddenly she sits up. Water sloshes against the tub's sides. Rivers of water stream down her arms and breasts and drip into the suds below. "Is that all you found?" Her right eyebrow arches. "Tell me you're joking, Mr. Hart. "She slides the paper and pencil along the tub shelf so they're where she can use them.

"No ma'am. I'm not kidding," the man's voice coming through the receiver says in a Texas drawl. "These cases are difficult. The records are destroyed. No one wants to tell what they know. Mrs. Lacharite doesn't answer her phone. I don't think she even lives at the La Jolla address you gave me. The Seal Beach address? That's her daughter. Only reason I know's because one of the La Jolla neighbors told me. Wouldn't say another word. Tight-lipped bunch, those richies."

"Her daughter? What's her daughter's name?"

"Laura Sorenson. Better write that down. Laura Sorenson, with an o. Think her mom's living with her, but not sure."

Delilah could kick herself for not writing Mrs. Lacharite's neighbors before hiring this guy. There could have been a way. What a dumb ass. "But I've paid you three thousand dollars." She hates getting screwed like this, especially when she could have prevented it. "That's nearly a year's house payment."

"I'm sorry, ma'am."

"You have to give me more than this. I had to steal from my boys' college fund to pay you. I demand you give me more than one address and phone number. I demand it! Or I'll turn you in."

"I did what you paid me to do."

Delilah thinks back to their agreement. She knows he's right. She should have been smarter. People are always trying to cheat her. "Look, you came highly recommended, you know."

"Well, there is one little piece of information that I have that I'm, say, seventy percent sure is correct."

"And that is?"

"I believe you also have a sister."

Delilah almost drops the phone in the water. She switches the receiver to the other ear. Her fingers jitter with excitement. She rests an arm on the tub shelf to steady herself. The only sister she knows of died at birth before Delilah was born. Anne Marie was her name. "What leads you to believe that?"

"When I talked with Laura Sorenson, the daughter in Seal Beach, she said the only children she knew about who might be connected with her mother and yours were a boy and his little sister. But she didn't want to talk about it. She hung up on me three times."

"A sister? How old would she be? Is that the five-nine-six number?"

"It is. Don't know the sister's age. But she couldn't be much younger than your brother."

Delilah imagines a replica of herself somewhere out in the world. I have a sister, she repeats in her head. "And the Avalon address?"

"Not her most recent one."

"She moved?"

"I believe so."

"What do you mean?"

"Early September, I staked her house for two days and watched her come and go. Then I hiked down to San Diego looking for more records. When I returned, no one was home. Curtains drawn. Morning paper stopped. Looked like they went on a long vacation. I have my suspicions, though. That was a few days ago. I'm not doing any more looking until you pay me more. That's our deal. By the hour."

"I can't spend any more. My husband will kill me. Where did you have to look to find Sadie's daughter?"

"Sorry, that's a trade secret."

"I believe I paid for those secrets."

"Nope, you paid for solid information, and you got what I got, and then some. Next time, little lady, save yourself some cash and hire a detective in California. You used up a lot of money sending me to the West Coast, putting me up in hotels, renting cars, and feeding me."

"You could've told me that when I initially called you."

"Could've. But you seemed like a smart lady. Knew what you wanted."

Brittle with disgust, Delilah hangs up on the guy. She'll never talk with him again. He deserved her rudeness. She should have slammed the phone in his ear. She shoves the paper and pencil off the tub shelf. They fly in tandem over Baby Bee and ricochet off the oak vanity. The paper glides to a landing; the pencil hops on the tiles a couple of times before Baby Bee captures it in her paws.

She dials the phone number Mr. Hart had given her. It rang once and clicked to an official recording. "This number is no longer in service."

Damn it all!

She dials information. "Sorenson. With an O. Laura. On Avalon in Seal Beach."

"Sorry, no listing," the information lady tells her."

"Any Sorenson in Seal Beach?"

Delilah waits. Finally, "I'd say about ninety, with an O. A lot more with an E."

She slams down the receiver, knowing full well whoever's ear it was in California that suffered her anger, Delilah remained anonymous. She forgives herself.

Delilah dials her mother. The phone rings six times, then seven. Her mother could be out in the hall with all the other convalescing old farts, or she's purposely ignoring her. Delilah considers hanging up, but she hears the phone pick up before the eighth ring.

It takes her mother a few seconds to say, "Hello." Her voice trembles and fades.

"Mom, are you a wake?"

"What?"

"Mom, I have a question."

"Dear, I'm tho tired."

Her mother's lisp annoys Delilah. She considers asking her mother where she's put her false teeth, but decides the timing's wrong. "Mom, I need you to tell me the truth."

"Yet. Of courthe."

Delilah wishes she had a shot of whiskey handy. "Do I have a sister?"

"Anne Marie? You know she died at birth. Pleathe. Leth not talk of her."

"No, Mom, do I have another sister?"

Delilah listens intently for her mother's response. She expects her mother to mumble words. Or to breathe laboriously into the phone. Or to choke. Or to set the phone in its cradle. But she hears nothing. Images from Delilah's past emerge in her awareness. The day when her mother left her on a public bus with a complete stranger before getting off the bus to go home. The summer when Delilah was six, and her mother dropped her off at her uncle's Narragansett, Rhode Island, home and drove off without checking to see if anyone was home. The time when Delilah was still in kindergarten, and the grocery store manager drove her home when it was clear her mother had no intention of coming back to the store for her. Each time Delilah was able to scream and fuss enough to get some adult to get her back home where she belonged, even if her mother wasn't on board with this fact. Delilah's missing sister evidently wasn't so fortunate.

"Mom, answer me."

Still no sound.

It's an ugly, ripe interlude that leaves Delilah empty and alone, and unmothered. "Mom!"

Delilah finally hears her mother's slow breathing. Some of the aloneness disappears. There is hope. At least her mother's not lying to her.

"If you don't answer me, I'm never going to call you again. Do I have a sister?"

Her mother's frail voice slowly speaks up. "Anne Marie? My heart breakth to think of her."

"No, I mean a different sister."

Her mother sighs. Then she hums just a little bit, before answering, "Yeth."

"Yes?"

"Yeth."

"Is she younger or older than my brother?"

"Younger."

"What was her name?"

"Beatrith."

Delilah shudders when she realizes she named her adopted kitten after her lost sister. "Did they disappear together?" Delilah and her mother have agreed, after two decades of arguing, to label her mother's giving away her brother a "disappearance."

"Yeth."

The inside of Delilah's body plummets, as if the floor holding her life level suddenly gave way. Her chest heaves to capture air. Goosebumps appear on her flesh. At last she knows; this is the truth! Delilah half-wishes her mother had lied. "God damn it, how could you do this to me?"

Slowly and without shame, her mother said, "I didn't do it to you."

"Oh yes you did. You had no right to give them away. They didn't just belong to you. They belonged to me too. They belonged to our whole family."

There is quiet on the other end of the phone. And then soft, monotone humming.

"I can't believe this is happening! You've known this all along and never said a word?"

Her mother's humming continues.

"Did you think I'd never find out?"

Her mother's humming fades to silence.

"How would you like it if I gave you away? Because I'm tempted."

And finally, as Delilah fully expects to hear, her mother artlessly clatters the receiver into its cradle. The familiar, dull sound droning through the line rekindles the constant loneliness she fights not to feel.

Lonely for what?

She has friends galore and a lovely family. Two strapping sons and a husband to die for.

Lonely for what?

Her siblings, of course. Her family. It's only natural. But how does she explain this to the logical masses? She's never met her siblings. Didn't even know she has a living sister until now.

Lonely for what?

§

I'll tell you why she aches.

She has met her siblings before, though not in this lifetime. She knows them already, and deep down in her subconscious remembers their promise to be there for each other.

I watch Delilah's aura steadily collapse until it resembles the same despondent gray Grace had emanated that day at the beach in La Jolla.

Delilah returns her receiver to its cradle. Her hand smears against the phone, pushing it off the tub shelf to clatter on the floor. She lies back in the bathwater. Her big toe turns the hot water faucet on. She sinks deeper into the tub, so she's completely submerged. Her long, dark curls fan out in the water, like spilled ink.

Then, as though washed of her despair, she sits erect in the tub. Her aura perks up with lush reds and vivid purples. Hope and a scent of larceny shine in her eyes. Her hand reaches over the tub shelf for the telephone on the floor.

§

September 23; Huntington Beach

Bibi's front door creaks its lumbering groan, the way it always does when just opened. The sounds of traffic, airplanes, herons, and children playing flood the entryway.

Bibi checks the oven clock, and realizes her mother, who has just opened her front door, is really quite late. She scoots her chair away from the already-set kitchen table and dog ears the

Time magazine page on which she'd been reading the Saki review. Bibi savors the last second of quietness that descended on the house a mere hour ago, when, as if each had been forced to swallow a potion, Michael and the children went to their respective rooms and fell fast asleep, or so she thinks. If only this could happen every night. Her chicken casserole, done to perfection an hour ago, infusing the air with its herbal saltiness. When she places the *Time* on the baker's rack top shelf, she's none too pleased to notice a little, yellow-Crayola drawing Noah left on the wall near the bottom.

"Knock, knock." Her mother's cheery voice precedes her from the front door.

Suddenly, both the kids' bedroom doors fly open and slam against their respective walls. "Bestamor! Bestie!" the children sing. Their feet run down the hall toward their grandmother, galloping like puppies.

Bibi doesn't bother to greet her mother, for her mother will find her soon enough. Besides it's fun to let the kids make over their grandmother; it just does something for her mother's mood.

After wading between the kids and their usual grabbing of her legs and peeking in her purse for candy, which they find, and unwrap in front of the television, Bibi's mother peers around the kitchen armoire and finds Bibi scrubbing at Noah's crayon markings.

Without even glancing at her mother, Bibi moves a pottery canister in front of the mark to camouflage it and pitches the rag into the sink. She can smell bananas. Her nose scrunches in protest.

"It's so busy in here," her mother exclaims.

"Yeah, well . . ." That banana scent still wafts in the air. Bibi stares at her mother's purse. "Did you bring a banana into this house?"

"I could use a scotch." Her mom sits down at the kitchen table and looks around, presumably for Michael.

"He's sleeping. Open your purse."

"My purse? Oh. I must have forgotten. I was going to snack on it." She opens her purse and removes the banana, which she hands to Bibi.

Nausea overwhelms Bibi. She takes the banana out to the garage and tosses it onto Michael's workbench. Bleck. Damn her mother. She knows how ill bananas can make Bibi. It's not that hard to remember. Just don't bring bananas into the house.

Back in the kitchen, Bibi looks way in the back of the cupboard for the Cutty Sark whiskey, and gets ice from the Tupperware container in the freezer. She pours her mother a stiff, amber highball, because that's what she always wants and needs. As teenagers, Victor and Bibi survived their mother's menopause because they learned early how to put her in a good mood when she asked them to mix her and their father evening high balls. Each would fill a jigger with scotch and dump them into her glass, something they never did to their father. He was a one-shot-a-night kind of guy.

Her mother takes a sip, then another. Bibi watches the strain around her mother's eyes ease and her temples soften, so the mountain ridges her blue veins create seem more like foothills.

Bibi notices how old her mother seems, but reminds herself that her mother is old, seventy-six years old to be exact. And that she was adopted after her parents' silver wedding anniversary.

"There's nothing like a high ball." Her mother's pudgy fingers grip the glass carefully, as though it were a package. "I've had such a day. The Bullock's sale was worth it."

Bibi looks at her mother's purse to see if it's accompanied by a little gift from Bibi's favorite department store. But no such luck. She'll have to wait until Christmas, which isn't that far away, come to think of it. Cripes, more to do.

"Anyway, I wanted to finish telling you about," Her mother pauses for another sip. "About the —." She stops suddenly, her focus turns to the doorway leading into the kitchen.

Bibi turns around. "Oh, hey, hi. Did you get a good rest?"

"Yeah," Michael says sleepily. His mis-buttoned and partly-tucked-in shirt makes him look like a rummage-sale find. He sits down next to her mother.

"Hello, Michael," Mrs. Andressen says to her daughter's husband, as though she has just been introduced to him.

"Yeah, Signe."

Her eyebrows lift imperceptibly. "Anyway, I wanted to tell you about the drowning incident." She looks at Michael for the go-ahead. "People saw you, and brought you both to the shore. The Lacharites called our lawyer, and we came down and got you the next day."

"The Lacharites?"

"It doesn't matter. All that matters is that you were saved and we were able to bring you home to a new, safe life in Palos Verdes."

"Wait. Did you adopt them then?" Michael asks. "Just like that? Isn't it illegal to drown kids? Wouldn't the kids have become wards of the court? Weren't the police called?"

Michael's questions alarm Bibi. She'd never considered the reality of what had happened after Victor and she were saved from drowning. "Did she get arrested?" she asks her mother.

It all seems like a new story, not like the one she's previously imagined to be true, the one where a lovely, married couple decided they couldn't keep their kids and found the Cooks to take over their duties, similar to selling a car or something. At least she and Victor weren't foundlings, unlike Charlie. He has the family honor of being its singular, certified bastard.

"No, her friends took her in. She was a drunk. I don't know what happened to her."

"The Lacharites?"

"I said it doesn't matter. What matters is that you had a lovely, safe life. Think what you've gotten that you would never have had."

Bibi's tempted to think about it, but doesn't. She hates the subject and the implication that there exists an ever-lengthening list of obligations she owes the Andressens for their very kindness. Sometimes she wonders if they adopted her because, instead of a daughter, they wanted an indentured child.

"We're very grateful you adopted Victor and Bibi." Michael looks at Bibi and smiles. Probably one too many times he's had to listen to Bibi bitch and complain about her mother's tally sheet and seen her act on this belief that she owes the Andressens for her very life and sustenance.

Bibi nods and thanks Michael with her eyes. She wonders how fresh Victor's previous conversations are in his mind. Michael might think Bibi's capable of drowning Ella and Noah.

Michael turns back to Signe. "This woman who tried to drown Bibi was pretty bad then."

Her mother's eyebrows pop up again. "Bad? I should say so."

Her birth mother was bad? Bibi detests hearing these words. Michael and her mother have no right saying things like that about her birth mother. That's something only Victor and she can say.

"We want you to know Bibi has no intention of looking for or meeting her."

Bibi nods. But his mere words make it sound like his decision. And she wants this to be her choice, and hers only, even though he's right. It should be up to her whether or not she wants to meet someone who tried to kill her.

Her mother looks at her watch and downs the rest of her scotch. She sets her glass on the sink. She picks up her bag and walks slowly across the kitchen. "Charlie and I spoke," she says, as though it has no real importance.

Bibi's attention is immediately drawn to her mother, and to the image of her talking with Charlie. No one can change her mother's mind like her older brother. He never forces his point or challenges the views of another. He simply makes statements with the assurance and entitlement of a first-born son. His tone alone renders him sage. But he's also naughty as hell. High school beer parties. Automobile accidents. Firing a shot gun into the family furnace. Chasing Bibi around the house with his b-b gun. He is, she thinks, the most innocent and guilty person in the family.

Her mother keeps walking toward the front door.

Michael and Bibi glance at each other, trying to decide whether to follow her or not.

"Mom," Bibi asks, "aren't you staying for dinner?"

"Dinner? Why how lovely of you. I'll have to say no. It's getting late."

Damn! Bibi went to all that trouble making that stupid casserole for nothing. But she has free time she wasn't expecting. "It's okay. Don't you want to say good-bye to the kids?"

Apparently not hearing Bibi, or purposely ignoring her, her mother opens the door leading down into the garage. "Bibi, Charlie and I both think that you are extremely responsible."

Bibi looks at Michael. They both know that coming from Bibi's mother, this compliment has other purposes than the obvious.

Her mother holds the work-bench shelf with her right hand and adjusts her trifocals before descending the three garage steps. "You always do the right thing and make the right decisions."

Michael switches on the light, then he and Bibi follow her mother. They're both on high alert, trying to understand what Bibi's mother is up to. This is notoriously unlike her mother to be complimentary without there also being a price to be paid. Everything with her mother is a transaction of some sort.

"Unlike your brother." Her mother's pace slows. "Of course, Victor thinks so little of you," she says, as if this should surprise no one.

Bibi and Michael look crossly at each other. Her mother can pack a hell of a lot of meanness in a short amount of space.

"I just don't know why we keep him in the will."

This gets Michael's attention. He perks his ears, alert to what Bibi's mother might say next.

But she keeps walking through the garage, past the banana left on the work bench, and down the driveway. "And so..." She pauses her thoughts while she gets out her car keys and walks around Noah's Tonka trucks that he's parked in a bundled-tight circle on the lawn, like they're sharing a joint in chilly weather.

Bibi and Michael follow close behind, waiting to hear what she's really got on her mind. The clear night sky feels like velvet, as they each bend over and pick up two Tonkas. Bibi sees Ceres perched all comfy on the study window ledge watching their every move.

Her mother unlocks her blue Oldsmobile's back end, revealing Bullocks bags galore, neatly lined up in three rows. Crisp, crackling white tissue paper adds to the total sumptuousness.

Her mother retrieves a Joyce Shoes box, which she offers Bibi. "Charlie and I have decided to let you keep this information. You must know Victor will drive all the way from Santa Barbara every chance he thinks I'll be away so he can scrounge through my things for this. I don't want to change my locks. I'll tell him they're in the safe deposit box at the bank."

Bibi's hands do not extend to take the box. "Why don't you just put them in your safe deposit?" She's not sure at all that she wants to be the possessor of this information, especially since she'd hoped to tell Victor the letters were in their mom's safety deposit box. If he finds out she has the letters, he'll want them. It dawns on Bibi that she doesn't want to give them over, at least not yet.

Her mother looks at Bibi as though she were nuts. "The bank box is too small and I don't want to rent another one." She nudges the shoe box closer to Bibi.

Bibi puts down the two Tonkas on the lawn and takes the unblemished ecru shoe box in her hands. Electricity shoots up her arms. A stranger's disembodied voice urges, "Open it," in her ears. Her grip on the box tightens and she presses it to her chest. She wants to know everything that's in the box. Yet, she doesn't. But really she does, as though it's the last page in the novel.

Michael sets down the trucks he's holding too and tries to take possession of the box, but Bibi's grip won't let it go. Ideas for better containers fill her head: a kitchen canister, a small tool box, a lined sewing basket.

Her mother opens her car door and stands in its angle. "I know I'm doing the right thing giving it to you. You understand how important it is to keep our family together. You know to do the right thing. I'll tell him they're in the safe deposit box at the bank."

Bibi doesn't believe a word her mother says. There's some reason her mother gave her the box, and it's not because she always does the right thing, because she doesn't, as her mother recognizes all too well, and reminds her all too often.

§

Such a moment for me!

I know Bibi heard my urgings.

I watch her mind's energy-hues shift and change in response to each of my words. Her kaleidoscope thoughts blossom brighter, then fold into dimness, then again burst brightly, alternating from yellows, to red, to purples, to greens, and colors you've never seen. If I had hands, I would clap them in delight.

More importantly, I know what this all means. I shiver sparkles at the thought. This means my words have been planted. Their radicals have taken hold. My words, my thoughts, stand ready at the threshold of germination.

I scoot in close to Bibi and focus with all my will on the inch of air abutting her skull and copper curls. For here is where I can, if I'm clever and perceptive, see her thought particles, which can be particularly difficult to observe. They dart and spin, and they're impossibly small to see.

I don't see many, which either means there are only a few them, or that my perception is lacking. I assume the latter is true and intensify my focus and consolidate my substance so that I appear to others as a singular speck of light. I know Ceres notices me from her window ledge perch; her ears turn toward me.

I move near to Bib's temple, where her skin's tiny pores are deep canyons punctuating a vast, flat, pinkish plain. Coming from within Bibi and out through this surface, I think I find the evidence for which I am looking. I adjust my sight for my task at hand. At first, I see only the wakes of her thought particles, like contrails and comet tails. Each stream away from Bibi's skull, sometimes in a straight line, sometimes in ornate loopdeloops, before disappearing into a nearby atom's outer valence.

When my sight normalizes more, I see trillions of these thought-particle wakes shooting about her head, like a sky full of silvery sardines.

I steady my gaze for I have yet to actually see what I'm looking for.

The effect is akin to a theater curtain being abruptly pulled back to reveal a conspicuously-lit stage; an entirely new world now appears before me. I watch at close range as Bibi's actual thought particles streak past me. Flying concepts. They appear not as wakes, but as wind gusts. Pure energy on the go, their dutiful journey just beginning. Out into the world they head, to become part of this atom, then that, then the next, and so on.

I sharpen my focus even more and listen. The noise! I concentrate to discriminate one thought from another. The din is overwhelming as Bibi's thoughts flash past me. Some I recognize, some I do not. "I'm ugly." "I want everything perfect." "I love being surrounded by beauty." "I have so much to do." "I have to be good." "I refuse to meet her."

Then I clearly hear it: "I want to know her." I hear it again. And again. I glance around and see them breaking through her skull at full speed, running into atoms and hopping on first one, then another, for a ride, like hobos chasing trains.

I soften my focus and feel my substance expand. With the ease of one who has achieved her conquest, I slip higher into the sky. Bibi becomes fully visible to me, standing there in the middle of the street, next to Michael, watching her mother drive away into the night.

Her aura glows, and I sense a certain magnetic pull generating from her that I've not noticed before. I tune in, and quiver, for I realize that in my beloved sister a new gravity was forming.

Six

The Intrinsic Design

September 23; Huntington Beach

A silent anxiety eddies between Bibi and Michael. They stand in the middle of their street as they watch her mother's car disappear down the street, the devil's hearse masquerading as a guileless chariot. The street lamps light up and cast a yellow tinge upon the darkening neighborhood. Her mother's car reaches the stop sign at the street's end. Its brake lights stud the evening sky an alarming red. A moment later, the left signal light blinks an orangish red. Finally, as if she'd remembered what time it is, her mother turns on her car's headlights.

It makes Bibi laugh, imagining her mother having so much to do just to drive her car. Everyday things can seem complicated when her mother's involved.

Michael makes another feeble attempt to pry the box from Bibi's resolute grip. When it's clear to him that she's not giving it up, he asks, "Promise me you won't look for her."

She doesn't look at him. "Okay." His need to manage what she does about this irritates her, and she's not sure why.

His doubting eyes study her. It's clear he doesn't trust her. He probably thinks, given the smallest opportunity, she'll open the box, and start looking. She's that kind of girl. A real Pandora.

Too curious for her own good, sometimes. "You don't want to cross your mother on this," he tells her. "You saw the look in her eyes when she talked about Victor. Pure evil."

Her mother's cold blue eyes rekindle themselves in Bibi's mind. She inwardly shivers. "I know. I've never seen her like that about him. She always has a soft spot for him."

"Well, fuckin' A, look how he's been treating her."

"It's like he needs to humiliate her."

"And you know she'll make him pay for that. You know your mother. What the hell is he thinking?"

Bibi nods, remembering the steep price her mother exacted from her when she dared to beg for her own birthday cake as a child, instead of always getting her father's leftover marzipan cake from his party the day before. Even that was too much for her mother, being called out like that. Bibi got what she wanted alright, except her mother made sure it was a banana cake. Her thumbs hold the box's lid shut tight.

Michael crosses his arms across his chest, underscoring his confidence in his position. "Mark my words, here's what she'll do, if she hasn't already. She'll call him and say, 'Victor my boy, if you want to find your birth mother, go ahead. Just don't look for any inheritance when the time comes.' Yep, that's what she'll do."

"In other words, if I help him, I'm helping him disinherit himself."

"And you might get yourself disinherited, while you're at it. Why do you think Charlie was all gung-ho about you helping Victor look? More for him."

This Bibi had not considered. Gad, she hates intrigue. She can play a mean piano and paint a portrait that captures a person just so, and stand up for teachers' rights. But real, conniving political gamesmanship? No way.

Michael's breathing palpably slows down. His hands slide into his pockets. His lips purse. He steps away from her, but faces her head on, so she's riveted by his attention. "Face it, Bibi. I'm sick. I don't know how long I'll last."

Bibi gasps. She can't bear the tears in his eyes. With the box still in her hand, she moves into him and squeezes him hard to her, both to keep him for herself and to stop her own tears.

He strokes the hair on the back of her head, as if to tame it. His voice quivers. "I can't have Signe make life worse for my family." He chokes up. "I just can't." He buries his head in her hair.

God, she silently begs, please let him live. Just let him live.

"Promise me you won't look." His voice is soft and solicitous.

Bibi nods. "I promise." She has no choice. He deserves having his wishes fulfilled, what with all he's gone through. She can ignore the box. Pretend it doesn't exist. It can't be that hard to do.

He puts his arm around her and takes the box from her.

She watches it leave her possession as if she were giving away her life.

He leans down and picks up Noah's cheddar-yellow Tonka with his free hand and heads to the garage. His posture has straightened, and he walks with a bit of a strut, as though he finally settled some nettlesome score.

With a dirge in her steps, she follows him into the garage, the other three Tonkas held awkwardly in her arms. She sets the trucks in front of the old marigold refrigerator. By the time she's got the trucks in a line, Michael's climbing the old wooden ladder to the rafters with the box in his right hand. The box emanates a sheer, yet inviting light. She notices six little dots of light, tinier than pin points, spark around it.

He sets the box on the ladder top and removes the lid. He studies the contents without touching them, then replaces the lid, and places the box in the blue Coleman cooler, which he snaps shut.

Bibi swears an aura now emanates from the cooler, and the same six dots of light flash on and off around it. She catches him staring at her, as he descends the ladder.

"You promised."

Bibi wraps her arms around herself, as if tying herself to a post. "I know. I promise."

§

September 23; Huntington Beach

It is one thing to wake up screaming or hollering from sights seen in a bad dream. It is a far other thing to be awoken by your psyche weeping its heart out.

For Bibi, at this very time in her life, waking to her own spontaneous and uncalled-for tears is tantamount to wetting the bed. It is an invasion of the marriage bed. Here is Michael, going to sleep every night wondering if in fact he will wake again the next morning, or if his death will be in a month, or six months, or as far away as a year. Her weeping can only make him feel worse because he'll blame himself for her sadness.

She slips out of bed heads for the hall. To seal in her sobs, she presses her hands against her eyes. Michael mumbles something, but she figures he'll go back to sleep. She finds her purse on the cane chair in the entryway and unwraps two pieces of gum and crams them into her mouth. With each bite she chews into the gum's powdery hardness, she senses her mouth's warmth and moisture breaking down the gum, making it pliable, elastic, and comforting.

Her tears at last abate. She catches her breath, pats her heart, and tries hard to recall the dream that caused her such sorrow. But her memory retrieves nothing except the image of a long, skinny light shining brilliantly through the darkness, like a white-hot wire. Which makes no sense. Come to think of it, her freeway crying jag made no sense either. Surely it's too late to have the postnatal blues. Noah's almost two.

She wipes her wrist across her nose, thinking that would do. But she's a sopping mess. When she steps into the garage for a new Kleenex box from their supplies, she turns on the light because it's so darned dark. Ceres races ahead of her, down the garage steps.

With the light on in the garage, she doesn't trust herself. She dares not look at the Coleman cooler, but she can't help thinking about it.

Once she removes a new Kleenex box from the stash by the refrigerator, rips open the slit, and removes a couple of sheets. She blows her nose, assured that the noise won't wake Michael. Then she climbs the steps from the garage to her entry, flips off the lights, enters the house, calls Ceres, and closes the door behind her, safe from the shoe box's beckoning call.

Just this morning her garage resembled a warehouse stocked with stuff she needed but refused to have inside the house. In and out she'd go on a regular basis, glad for the luxury a storeroom provides: a way to hide her family's junk. The laundry, her pantry, Michael's cigarette stash, their sports gear, and the kids' big toys.

Tonight, however, it's been transformed into another woman's purse: a place she best avoid.

The shoe box image returns to her mind's eye. If only she could just have a look. That's all. Nothing more. She spins around and peeks back into the garage, but proudly does not enter. To her amazement, the aura remains, though it is not as bright or pulsing as when Michael was holding it, and the little dots still dance and blink.

No, she cannot do this. She quickly shuts the door, sealing herself off from the horrifying greatness of her temptation. She must not do this. Mustn't even consider it. Michael is right. Their family needs all the help it can get. Every single dime of it.

She slides back into bed, but cannot sleep, for random words again fill her head like jigsaw puzzle pieces thrown back into its box. Singular words articulate louder and louder in her mind, followed by random phrases. Underestimate. Expand. Fluids flow.

The poem voice is back.

Rising softly, she leaves her bed. She touches her right hand on Noah's bedroom door and senses his well-being. Then she presses her left palm against Ella's door to know that her daughter too is safe.

When she reaches the study, she turns on the desk's gooseneck lamp. She focuses the blown-glass shade so the lamp's light creates a bright circle where she will work. The family pictures sit arranged how she left them yesterday, before Michael and the children came down the hall at her. Quietly, she sits down at the desk and opens the drawer. Ceres jumps up on the desk to help; she sniffs the pictures, rubs her cheeks against the lamp shade, bats at a paper clip left on the desk top, and then looks up at a moth or something flying near the ceiling

From the drawer, Bibi pulls out the lined steno pad. The poem voice speaks up:

Underestimate yourself and you'll never find or know
Just how far your cells will expand, your fluids flow.

Bibi transcribes the words onto the steno paper, while Ceres stands on her hind feet, batting and mewing at the imagined moth. Random, distracting images slide through Bibi's' mind's eye. A Polynesian warlord with bones in his ears. Red chevrons. Jagged teeth. She involuntarily drops her pen, but picks it back up and continues writing. Her ears hear more words, or is it her mind, or her imagination? The words come as monotonous tones, like the beginning of the *Waldstein*. A memory of her father's hand nears her awareness, but it disappears before she registers its presence.

She studies the first two lines. The words make sense to Bibi, and yet they don't. If her cells expanded, she'd be fat, which is not something she wants in her horizon. And if her fluids flowed, there'd either be a mess or a death. Yet something about the words do seem true, as if they were talking about her spirit's cells and fluids, if that were at all possible.

Recognize the impossible, don't stop your walk too early.
Or inventions will cease, straight hair ne'er be curly.

She thinks the last line could use some work. It's a bit too crude for her tastes. She rereads it, considering how it could be changed. "Recognize the impossible." A pang of resentment rips at her. Her father's hand again appears to her, but she blinks hard. Poems like this drive her crazy. They always tell you what, but never how. She would love in every way to know the impossible, even live it, but that's not possible.

Her writing hand moves again toward the paper, and, as if having its own free will, writes: Look.

"Look?" she asks aloud.

"Look." The poem voice speaks in her ear, clear and assuring.

"Now?" She asks and writes. At the same time, she wonders why she should trust this voice or the way her hands move. It could be an evil demon, like the one she thinks abides in the Ouija board she almost sold at a garage sale last year.

"Yes," the voice answers her question.

She writes this too, on the next line. "But . . ."

"Now," the poem voice tells her emphatically.

Emphatically enough, that Bibi feels compelled to obey.

As if in a trance, she slips out into the garage, shuts the door behind her and Ceres, who has tagged along. After turning on the light switch and positioning the ladder, she stops for a moment to look and listen.

She hears the usual garage noises. A rafter tweak. The refrigerator motor turning back on. The low whisper of the gas water heater. A moth snapping against the window on the door leading out to the side yard. None of these sounds persuade her that what she's doing is the least bit normal, or honest, or worth the effort if she gets caught. She hopes she can climb the ladder without it grinding across the concrete floor or its steps creaking under her weight.

And then she sees what serves to strengthen her. Besides the usual garage sights of cars, toys, cigarette boxes, lawn mower, and paint cans, there is an unusual garage sight. The six light dots dancing around the blue cooler are visible despite the competing light. Ceres jumps on the Volvo's hood to be nearer to them.

Bibi scales the ladder quickly, but carefully. When she looks down, she notices how much larger her car and the garage itself seem. With the cooler's bottom at eye level, she realizes she must climb higher if she's to retrieve the shoe box.

She steps one rung higher. The ladder bounces in reaction. She takes one more step, knowing that death could come to her at any moment.

Though she cannot see into the cooler, her hand reaches inside and easily finds the shoe box, removes it with a bit of effort, and rests it on a ladder rung.

Her fingers tremble as they lift the lid. She half expects to find a soft little bunny living in the box, or a cobra. Anything could be inside.

With the lid finally off, the box's contents lay open to her. In a way, the contents look like her classroom trash can. Photographs, news clippings, and letters, some still with their envelopes, lie in assorted angles. For her mother to have collected the contents seems logical, but for her to leave them in such a messy disarray seems totally out of character. She spots an envelope addressed to her parents and removes the letter. It reads:

> February 11, 1949
> Dear Mrs. Andressen,
> I do hope you are well. For your sense of wellbeing, I want you to be aware that Grace still resides in the San Diego area.

Grace! Her mother's name is Grace. The name bathes Bibi in comforting warmth. And Grace lives in San Diego.

She reads on.

> Grace is most upset about the children and keeps asking for them. We are running out of excuses and will be forced to tell her the truth soon enough.
>
> We are quite concerned about her behavior of late. We loathe seeing her in such drunken states, but we can understand her need to forget her

troubles. At the same time, she has been running up quite a florist tab in our name, sending generous bouquets to friends and hopefuls.

Yours,

Sadie

With her mind whirling from the denseness of Sadie's words, Bibi studies the handwriting with its thin, uniformly-slanted letters, so precise and from another era. Even the syntax seems ancient and removed, as if none of this has a thing to do with her.

Yet this is her birth mother about whom Sadie writes. Bibi's own flesh and blood, who, thirty years ago, had been caught trying to drown her children, and then went on a binge.

"Bibi? Are you out here?"

Ceres jumps off the car and races inside.

The blood rushes from Bibi's face. Caught! Guilty! She turns to face Michael entering the garage from the house, for she knows he's thinking the worst. She cannot tell him a voice told her to look, but she'll have to think of something.

Frown lines emerge on his brow as his eyes travel from the bottom of the ladder to its top, then to the Coleman cooler with its lid cocked open, and to the box in Bibi's left hand. Horror and anger spread across his face as his eyes settle on the box lid and letter Bibi holds in her right hand. His eyes shoot bullets.

"Put it back. Get down from the ladder and go inside."

Bibi swallows, and secretly weighs whether what she has just done justifies the problems she has just created for herself. Instead of putting the box back in the cooler, she clings tightly to the ladder's edge and climbs down. It seems to bend slightly with each step. She marches past him and into the house, never for a second looking him in the eye. She has broken his trust, and he will be watching her like a stalking cat.

He slams the door behind her, making it known she's not welcome.

This is the wall she deserves. In fact, she deserves worse. Listening to voices that tell her to do what is wrong. What was she thinking! She rushes back to bed. More words from the poem voice stream into her head: fishing tackle, fishing tackle. She pulls the covers up hard over her ears. Stupid fishing tackle. Stop talking to her, poem voice!

Michael comes back to bed, lies flat on his back, and glares at the ceiling.

Bibi waits for his pronouncement, because he won't remain silent for long.

He folds his hands over his chest. "Remember your promise?"

She digs her head into her pillow in an effort to hide. "Yes," she whispers.

"Then there must be a good reason why you went back on it."

She can't tell him about the voice. "I made a mistake. I was just curious."

"Don't be. There's nothing in that box you need to see. In fact, I think I'll burn it tomorrow."

She lifts her head from her pillow and glowers at him. "You can't do that. It's not yours."

"It is now. What's mine is yours, and yours is mine."

Bibi can't argue with this. It's been one of their mottoes all through their marriage. Even though they have never taken possession of things the other acquired before they married. Nor have they purposely destroyed what belonged to the other. "But, Michael, it is mine, just as the pictures of your father are yours.

I treat them as yours; I don't disregard them just because I've never met him."

His jaw juts.

She knows better than to bring his father into the discussion. "Besides, we can give the contents to Victor after he finds our birth mother. They should go to him." Which she doesn't believe for one minute.

"His birth mother."

This takes Bibi aback. Michael can't pretend that Victor and she are not siblings. How dare he! But she resists her urge to battle him on this. "Michael, the box belongs to Victor as much as to me. If you burn it, you may regret it someday. Think about it."

He rolls over and turns his back to her.

She waits in silence for his answer. And waits. She rests her hand atop his hip. He doesn't move. He barely breathes. He's a turtle who has retreated into depths of himself, and all that remains is his thick, impenetrable shell.

She lets her hand drop from his hip to the bed. A quiet chill swirls around the room. Bibi feels like an imperceptible island in the midst of a vast ocean. Alone and unknown.

§

I hover close to Bibi's temple. I know she senses my presence because she wipes her cheek thinking she's brushing away an ant or a fly. Her mind clatters and chatters; the din sets me aback.

I gather myself tighter and examine her thoughts, which sound thorny and brittle, like pretzels. Michael's right, she thinks. The box must stay off limits.

Except Michael's wrong too. Who is he to keep her from her past?

"Don't let Michael stop you," I tell her. "He will get used to it." But her mind jangles on, deciding this and deciding that, making me impossible to hear.

Her thoughts then swing away from the box itself, and focus on the downsides of meeting her birth mother. Grace might want to spend time in Bibi's home, which would be like having a fourth child.

Or she might want to assume the role of Bibi's real mother. Bibi can't imagine that coming to fruition.

Anyway, the last thing Bibi wants is two mothers. The current one is a noose around her life as it is.

Maybe Grace will like Victor, but not Bibi, which seems plausible, and painful.

Or maybe her birth mother's dead. Or senile. Or maybe she has five other kids, and they'll all want to be part of Bibi's life. They'll expect things of her, and they'll take up her time, which she doesn't have. Or they'll hate her. Or they'll love her too much, and she'll feel guilty for not loving them back like she should, or like they want.

For some reason Bibi suddenly thinks her father is watching her from heaven. She pulls the covers tight around her neck. A fleeting memory of him passes through her awareness. His hand. The darkness.

The memory leaves before she can attach words or feelings to it. She prefers thinking about him eating sardines out of the can; him coming home from work, emptying his pockets into the leather box atop his dresser, and giving her the three peppermint Certs left in the roll; and him giving her a carved Chinese camphor hope chest for her twenty-first birthday, because he thought she'd love it, which she did and does. She's not used to him being totally gone. His passing has left a void in her. He was the parent who loved her truly. He was the parent she trusted to be soft.

Like a train nearing the station, Bibi's mind slows, and tires. It slides back to Grace and San Diego. Bibi wonders if her birth mother ever thinks of her, which reminds her that Victor thinks Grace looked for them. He told her that once. It had seemed irrelevant at the time, but not so in this moment. Bibi would like to know the answer to that too. And if her birth mother would she be proud of Bibi? That's something Bibi would really like.

I loosen my energy and allow myself to recede into the sky, above the roofs and trees, above the town and freeway and Pacific coastline. There is nothing for me to say or do in this moment, except resort to what I know best. I imagine and feel the joy and love on Bibi's face when she sees Grace's eyes for the first time in decades, and when she meets her sister.

§

September 24; Santa Barbara

My brother Victor has his own struggles this morning in Phoebe's dance studio. Hunching over the old mahogany Steinway upright, his hands splaying across its keyboard like octopi, he types out the hectic, unpredictable notes from the score set before him: Stravinsky's "Piano Rag Music." Internally he grumbles. The music's bitonality requires attention from him that he should be giving to Phoebe's performance twenty feet to his left. Quentin on his mind doesn't help either. Nor the unrelenting memory of that woman whom he swears was his birth mother, the woman he saw from the living room window when he was a child, the woman who sat behind the steering wheel of an old '51 Ford staring back at him. That memory is back to haunt him this morning.

In the studio's center, Phoebe whirs and leaps to the staccatos and syncopations. Her ankles warmed in frosty pink wool, her form accentuated by jet black Danskins, her toes protected in matching Capezios, she does what she does best: bringing life and meaning to what others thought they had completed.

Except something is off.

Victor raises his hands above his shoulders and signals her to stop. "Let me see the last eight again, without the piano."

Phoebe's body stills, and her posture relaxes, though he isn't sure her attention has turned its focus to him. Her frown worries him. He needs to play nice.

"It's not you, Love. It's hard to play Igor and watch you at the same time."

Her frown vanishes, and her Jackie O smile appears. God, he adores her.

She glances down, then back up. "Maybe we should record it." Hope is in her eyes.

He nods, but wonders if he should have agreed. He can't miss a note when the recorder is on. Then again, it is Stravinsky. No one will know, except him. He goes to the shelf behind him, plugs in the recorder, and turns it on. It is just a practice recording, he reminds himself. Only eight measures. It can be erased. The word *erased* feels loud in his head. It always does.

"You'll record the whole thing, right?" Phoebe's head tilts slightly and her pony tail swings.

Crap, he hadn't thought of that. The whole thing. Beginning to end. He feels hot. But he is no coward. "Might as well. Good idea."

He sits down at the piano, flicks his wrists to loosen his hands, leans forward, focuses his eyes on the first measure, and plunges in. Reading three staffs simultaneously is a trick. But he's practiced a lot and done some conducting. Better yet, he's doing what he's designed for. The notes, at one time jarring and atonal to him, have their own beautiful symphonics, their own order, which he loves deeply. His job is to play them. His eyes read what has been written. His fingers go where instructed. Everything else in his life and world disappears. He is the music, and he is pleased. Perfect notes, perfectly placed, until all of this Stravinsky creation is on the tape to be relived, re-enjoyed, and replayed. He relaxes, smiles, and folds his hands in his lap. He wishes Quentin could have heard him. He wishes that woman in the Ford could too.

Phoebe, who has listened from beside the shelf, springs to life, clapping, ballerina-running to him, hugging him, kissing his forehead, tussling his hair. "Thank you, thank you. I know you hate recording."

He basks in this, and wonders how it would feel if Quentin did the same. But he clicks off that thought and remembers there is a reason he went through this recording hell in the first place. Pushing back the piano bench, he stands sharply. He points to the studio's center. "C'mon. I want to see what you've got without being distracted."

Phoebe ballerina-runs back to the center, assumes the third position, but then raises her hands above her head in a switch to the fifth. When the music begins, it seems to Victor that Phoebe's mercurial face has turns slightly and takes on a cubist sense of time and space. She is both frontal and profile, in the moment and all the moments. It can't be, and yet it is. All the elegance and swagger of ballet and rag imbue her arms and legs, steps and pauses, bends and struts.

Except, there is that place again. Those eight measures. Something is missing, or misplaced, or misused.

He stops the recorder. "I'm going back sixteen or so."

Phoebe's mouth twists to one side. He knows this perturbed look of hers. She'd said in the car on the way to the studio that she had it perfected. For a perfectionist, for an ostinata as she deems herself, admitting to perfection *is* something. But when she wants something, that's what she wants. Just like his mother. He presses PLAY.

She picks right up where the music demands, and he can see absolutely where the dance is off. He presses PLAY again to stop the machine.

Phoebe's face tells Victor that she too has noticed the error. Angry red colors her cheeks, forehead, and neck. Or maybe it's shame, or both. He needs to be kind. He nods toward the mirrored wall. "Did you see it too?"

Tears brim her eyes as she stares at the mirror. Determination furrows her brows. She watches herself as she makes some quick foot movements and torso twists, before briskly heading toward the bathroom.

Victor knows better than to stop her; she's his kind of a girl. He plucks a cigarette from his shirt pocket, lights it, and stands in the open doorway facing the street and their parked Toyota pickup. It's red, but he'd gotten it cheap. Give and take. He inhales on his cigarette. It crackles because of the dry weather. As he exhales, his eyes follow the tree line, because frankly not much is tall in Santa Barbara. Mostly palm trees, tall ones, like amazon naked ladies. The flower, not the person. The palms always seem accidental to him, like they were transplanted to fill some rich person's gnawing need. And now they're the backdrop for millions of Southern Californians' holiday pictures.

He hears a familiar motorcycle rev and he stirs from his daze. Inwardly he smiles; he loves being found. But reality clicks back in, and Victor panics. Something's happening across the street. The motorcycle's engine had gone silent. Shit! He slams the studio's door shut before he puts out his cigarette. Again, shit! There, in the corner next to the door, he tosses his cigarette on the floor and stomps it out so hard he worries Phoebe could've heard it. Victor picks up the flattened butt and stuffs it in his back pocket and waits for all hell to break out. He knows Quentin saw him. He knows Quentin was coming his way. His heart pounds in his chest. He presses the side of his head against the door and listens. He hears birds chirping, a car driving by, and then the motorcycle engine starting up again, gunning a few times, and then thundering down the street and into the distance.

Relieved, he exhales and looks about the studio. The last few years have been happy for him, he thinks. He'd probably still be living in a tree house if he'd not met Phoebe. Nor would he have Katie. Nor would he have the opportunities being married to Phoebe provides. The big extended family of people who actually belong together, and are intelligent, and understanding. He nods to himself. Understanding. That's a big one. He'd always had it growing up with Bibi. It seemed like she was the only one in the world who got him. He'd found the same understanding with Phoebe. He remembered the relief he experienced that day they'd met, that day she found him. It wasn't her words or her actions. It was her eyes, her open, open eyes.

The bathroom door creaks; Victor looks toward it. Out marches Phoebe. Her posture mirrors someone who's won an Oscar. Her Jackie O smile is full glint. Her nose wrinkles at the scent of cigarette. She stops in the center of the studio, assumes the fifth position, and dramatically nods at the recorder.

When the music begins, Victor is torn between listening to his own matchless performance and watching that of his own Miss Ostinata. That tug-of-war lasts until the eighth measure when the timing switches from 6/8 to 5/4. How Phoebe does it, he does not know. All that had been amazing is still amazing; all that had been wrong has disappeared. Part of it is in her foot work. Part of it is the angle of her torso. Because of how fast it happens, he considers asking her to do it again. But he knows she'll explain it all to him over dinner. God, he loves her. That he has to preserve.

Seven

Moving into the Dark

September 24; Lubbock

It has been a parched, lifeless day in Lubbock. With weather systems stymieing each other, it is also a windless Lubbock day. I have never enjoyed this type of weather in any of my lifetimes. I pity all those folks working outside, shining like oiled baked potatoes.

The usual mist that fogs the mirrors in Delilah's bathroom when she lazes in her tub is missing. Today she lies still as a lamppost in a bath of cool, foaming water. While her eyes absentmindedly search for imperfection in everything they see, Delilah's brooding mind replays the last time she spoke with the detective. Under the vanity, on a fluffy rug, Baby Bee sleeps curled up, a ball of orange angora yarn. To my delight, her left eye opens and follows my movements.

Delilah sinks lower into the tub so the water bobs against her chin. Her mind reruns the tarot-card spread she'd dealt when deciding on the detective. The second card had shown upside down, which she'd reversed so the illustration of the workman chiseling the pillar appeared standing, rather than falling. What's a little cheating? Except if she'd paid attention to the meaning of the card, she never would have hired the jerk. She hates incompetence.

Especially her own. If she's going to cheat, she should at least benefit from it.

Suddenly, Delilah sits up and snaps her fingers, castanet style. The idea that germinated in yesterday's bath has had a day to gestate. The chill air against her skin strikes her as both glorious and cruel.

She draws her bath tray toward her and hurriedly takes a note card from the box resting atop it. There's a right way to do everything, she reminds herself with a grin. Such a good brain she has. She lights a cigarette, drags the smoke into her lungs, and luxuriously exhales. The smoke meanders around her head, as though she were Saturn.

She takes another drag, and bites on a tobacco strand caught in her teeth.

"Dear Mrs. Lacharite," she writes, not sure what to say next. If Mrs. Lacharite lives with her daughter, like the detective said, then obviously her mail will get to her.

Words flow into Delilah's mind and through her pen. She smiles and imagines Mrs. Lacharite reading her words.

From the hallway, she hears her sons whispering. Her toes turn on the tap to add warm water to the tub. She drags on her cigarette and longs for the quiet she had before their births.

"Mom!" Delilah's seven-year-old Little Joe knocks on the bathroom door. "We have to be at practice."

"Can you drive us?" his older brother Matt pleads.

Damn it. Don't they ever get tired? "Call your father."

"Mom, he's at work".

"Yeah? Well, I've been at work, too. You can't call me either."

"Mom! Coach said not to be late."

God damned soccer. Why don't they teach it in PhysEd and let the kids get some rest after school? She douses her cigarette in the tub water and drops the butt on one corner of her bath tray. "Aren't there any other moms who can drive you?"

"I think Teddy's mom is getting tired of always driving."

"Can I have ten minutes? That's all I ask."

The boys whisper behind the door; Delilah figures they've accepted her demand. She lights another cigarette, inhales, and reads what she's written, which isn't more than a paragraph.

Her writing is beautiful, and sweet. But it's too soft, too easy for Mrs. Lacharite to dismiss. She needs something to snag the lady's attention, make her drop everything she's doing, and feel obligated to correct the wrong she committed all those years ago.

Delilah eyes Baby Bee still asleep under the vanity. How safe the kitty seems, unlike how Delilah felt with her mother, her mother who somehow lost Delilah's brother, and, as it turns out, her sister, about whom she'd purposely forgot to tell Delilah all these years.

She draws deeply from her cigarette and realizes what her letter has to say. It will be a lie, of course. None of it will be true. But she has no other choice.

Words fly onto a new note card. Perfect phrases. She'll tidy them up tomorrow. At least she's got the tone right.

The whole idea of avenging the detective's failure fills her with glee. Even Big Joe warned her she'd never get her money's worth. Imagine, three-thousand dollars with no guarantees. Three thou and what does she have to show for it? Sadie Lacharite's daughter's old address and a useless phone number, plus the knowledge she has a sister. But that's it. Period. No brother. No trails to follow. No leads.

She can't blame Big Joe for refusing to spend another dime looking for her brother: His usual reasoning: "If your mother won't tell you what she knows for free, why should I spend a bunch of money trying to get someone else to tell me?"

Delilah rereads what she's written and grins. It's good. Damned professional. She should hire herself out. Too bad she wasn't this smart when she filled out that application to the Tri-Adoption Agency a year ago. Maybe then someone would have responded. Every time she calls them and asks if anyone has been looking for her, they always tell her no. She cannot imagine that her brother or sister don't know she exists. It confounds her that her siblings wouldn't be looking for her.

Without warning, the door bursts open. Baby Bee leaps up and flares around to face the intruder. Her hackles stand high, her tail hairs burst straight out, her arched stance dares her attacker to come closer.

Delilah scoots low in the suds before her boys can see her. "C'mon, Mom. We gotta go."

Behind them, Big Joe enters. She loves his lank, sophisticated ways. All decked out in his suit and tie, knocking the world dead with his charm and expertise. She'd married a college boy! And her boys are spittin' images of their daddy.

Big Joe's eyes smile at Delilah, then stop at her note card filled with words. "What are you writing?"

"Oh, nothing. Just a grocery list."

"C'mon, Mom," her boys chide.

"Ask your daddy. He's already dressed. You won't have to worry about being late if he drives you." She looks at Big Joe and gives him a wink. "And hurry back home, you hear!"

§

September 25; Lubbock

The next morning, which feels even hotter than yesterday, Delilah waits in her car for Matt to join Little Joe in the backseat of her Celica.

"Mom, why're we leaving so early? It's not even eight."

Delilah watches Little Joe in her rear-view mirror. There's no way she's telling him why she turned off *Toon Times* right in the middle of the good part and forced him and his brother to get their things and jump in the car. She watches him take another bite of his cherry Pop Tart while he waits for her to answer him. He looks like the cat dressed him. She reaches into her purse for a comb and passes it back to him. "Comb your hair."

Before Little Joe can complain, Matt opens the door and scoots in beside his brother. He's singing that stupid Pop Tart song. "Pop, pop, pop, pop. "Delilah could shoot the jingle writer.

When Matt's door shuts, Delilah's ready. She puts the Celica in reverse, scoots out the garage, activates the garage door to close, and backs down the driveway, almost running over a girl walking down the street.

The girl stands on the sidewalk a foot from Delilah's driveway and screams at the Celica. But her school books are still in her arms, so she can't be that bad off.

Delilah puts the car in neutral. She should at least give the girl a ride to the high school. It's not that far from work.

"That's Lily Rose," says Matt. "Look how scared she looks."

As soon as Delilah rolls down her window, the girl turns and runs. "That's her name? Lily Rose? She should've been looking." Why Lily Rose's mother couldn't just pick a single flower and stick with it baffles Delilah. It's like Tuesday Weld having Wednesday as her middle name. Or Mae June West.

"Hey, Mom." Matt watches his mother's gaze in the rear-view mirror. "Wasn't she pregnant?"

Delilah rolls up her window, puts her car in gear and heads for the boys' school. "Um, yeah. She was. You're right. I forgot." It disturbs her that he would remember this.

"Why doesn't she have a kid?

"You sure she doesn't?"

"Yeah. Jimmy said she came home with nothing."

"Nothing? That's a cruel way to describe it. Maybe her baby died."

"Un huh, maybe it died."

But Delilah knows better. Lily Rose, no doubt, had to give her baby away and pretend it didn't make any difference to her. Like those kids who raise cows and pigs and sheep for 4-H projects and then sell their animals for slaughter.

A pile of sorrow, that's what Lily Rose has got ahead of her. All those people who want their girls to give birth to their illegitimate babies, do they give a second thought to the wake that decision leaves behind?

§

Without moving a muscle, Delilah stands just inside the back door of Dr. Grout's medical suites. The door's pneumatic hinge stops whining and the latch snaps shut.

She exhales. Home safe. She slips the office keys in her pocket, grateful that Dr. Grout thinks enough of her to entrust the keys to her.

She scurries down the linoleum-tiled hall, past anatomical diagrams, vision charts, and serene mountain scenes. Her rubber-soled nurse shoes squeak and squeal in an urban, high-speed chase sort of way. When she gets to the head nurse's desk, she opens the drawer and spots the key to Dr. Grout's office. Using her index finger, she precisely measures the exact location of the key in the desk before removing it.

At Dr. Grout's locked office door, she inserts the head nurse's key into the slot. She counts to three for luck and turns the key with ease. Once inside Dr. Grout's office, she bends down low and takes five sheets of the good doctor's stationery and five envelopes from the box he keeps on his lowest book shelf. She only needs one of each, but mistakes happen.

With the luck of an aged mouse, she slips out of Dr. Grout's office, shuts his door, and enters the head nurse's office, where she opens the top desk drawer completely. She measures with her index finger and replaces the key with the precision of a NASA scientist. The world missed its chance by not allowing her the wherewithal to attend med school, much less college. Such a reconstructive surgeon she could have been.

From there she goes into the ladies' room and locks the door, in case someone should arrive early. She carefully folds the stationery, which she fits into her purse, along with the envelopes. Then she flushes the toilet, just in case.

Nonchalantly, she walks down the corridor, looks at her reflection in a framed picture's glass, and straightens her dark curls. Her heart leaps. She's going to get away with this.

She slips out the door and lets it bang shut on its own. The blaring Lubbock sunlight forces her to squint.

Deep in her beige Celica's trunk, she hides the stationery under the blanket she always carries in case she gets stuck in an ice storm. She can never be too prepared.

She quickly scans the parking lot and street, something she should have done first. How she forgot that little detail irritates the hell out of her. Someone could have seen her.

She checks her watch and realizes she has time for a Dunkin' Donut and a fresh cup of coffee before going back to work.

§

Have you ever seen a bird fly into a window and noticed how hard it smacks? The bird truly thinks the way to get twelve inches beyond the window is to fly through it.

Such a woeful misperception.

Humans are no better. I don't have the statistics in my sphere, but there are literally millions of humans who, like birds, mistakenly attempt to walk through sliding glass doors. Maybe you've done it yourself. Acted on a misperception, only to regret it.

§

When Delilah gets home and finds no letters postmarked La Jolla, California, in her mailbox, she does not burn rubber on her way into the garage, nor does she drop her purse and things on the sideboard, nor sit on her bed and cry before taking a long soak in a tub of bubbly, hot water.

Instead, she greets her baby sitter, as usual, turns off the television and tells her boys to go outside and play. When they balk, she asks them, "Would you rather do your homework?"

They go outside.

In the wonderful quiet, she enters Big Joe's den, plugs in his IBM Selectric, and sets Dr. Grout's folded stationery and envelopes next to it, along with the draft she'd written in the tub last night.

Carefully, she spools a fresh sheet of the stationery into the typewriter. Before typing, she does three things which should always be done before typing an important letter. She gets up and washes her hands. She arms herself with the blue, *Webster's Collegiate Dictionary* with its million words printed on onion-skin-thin pages. And she gets a fresh bottle of Wite-Out. About a yard from Delilah's chair, Baby Bee bats at imagined flies.

Delilah swings the carriage return, and Dr. Grout's stationery inches up a quarter inch. She then begins typing; the letter ball spins at break-neck speed with each key stroke. Plink a-choo, plink a-choo, plink a-choo.

> Dear Mrs. Lacharite:
>
> It is with great regret that our office has discovered a rare genetic disorder in one of our employees, Mrs. Delilah Stone.
>
> Mrs. Stone has been diagnosed with Polycystic Kidney Disease, which can, if untreated lead to extreme damage to the kidneys, as well as to the liver, pancreas, heart, and brain. People die from this.
>
> When we informed Mrs. Stone, her first response was to cry, "Oh, no, my brother and sister."
>
> Since the disease is passed on genetically, I naturally wanted to know about her siblings, especially since I thought she had none.
>
> But she informed me that you know where her siblings are and that you won't tell her.
>
> Therefore, I am taking it upon myself to ask you to contact her at the address below. Please provide her with the information she needs to help her siblings live long, healthy lives.
>
> It would, in my opinion, seem terribly unfair for you not to do this, especially since Mrs. Stone informed me that your own husband is a doctor. I would think you would be especially sensitive to the ramifications of not warning patients of potential health crises.
>
> Please do not contact me. Instead contact Mrs. Stone at the address below. I'm sure she very much

looks forward to hearing from you so she can save the lives of her siblings.

Yours sincerely,

Lloyd Grout, M.D.

§

September 29; Buena Park

Bibi has never been totally alone in her principal's office, left with her own ethics to keep her eyes where they should, left with her own guilt-prone psyche to remember she is not in trouble, and left with her giddy pride that she has been trusted enough to be allowed in this vault, where the school's secrets lurk. It's like she's been given permission to enter someone's house while they're away on vacation, and wonders on what grounds they base their trust.

She sits in one of the chairs where a parent would be asked to sit, or a naughty student, or the superintendent, or the President of the United States, and apprehensively picks up the phone's receiver.

Just minutes prior to this, Mr. Dillard had stepped inside her classroom and announced to her class, without first telling her why, that their teacher had an emergency to take care of, and would they please take out something to read or draw or do until she returned, which probably wouldn't be that long.

Fortunately, she was not in the midst of dictating them their weekly spelling paragraph. And fortunately, Mr. Dillard follows her out the door, because she is totally terrified by what her emergency might be. Michael's death flashes in her mind, then her children's and her mother's. Bibi's terror paralyzes her breathing.

"Your brother's on the phone," he explains to her. "No one can understand him because he's yelling. It could be an extreme emergency. We can't tell."

He holds his open palms up to face her, like he doesn't want to be accused of mishandling an emergency phone call that turns disastrous, and whispers kindly, "Please, go into my office and take care of this."

With Victor on the line, Bibi can hardly understand him either, because he's hollering and talking in disconnections even James Joyce could not understand. Mostly, she just holds the phone in front of her face and stares into the earphone, amazed at the energy that can be transported through a copper wire from, she assumes, Santa Barbara, all the way to Buena Park.

Finally, she's had enough. "Stop. I can't understand anything you're saying."

Bibi hears a gaudy silence coming from the other end of the line. "Tell me slowly," she asks Victor. She wipes lint off the mouthpiece. God knows how many people have used this phone. She puts the receiver to her ear and waits.

Victor does get himself together. "How can you do this to me?"

"Do what?" She races to think of what she's done wrong, other than not coercing their mother to help him. Surely that's not what this is about.

"I talked with Charlie."

She holds her breath. Since the family dinner when Charlie betrayed her, and since her mother's visit last week, when her mother said Charlie had talked her into giving Bibi the box of paper, Bibi no longer entirely trusts her older brother. Now that she thinks about it, she suspects Michael's right. Charlie is maneuvering his mother, and now maybe his brother, to place himself in a position to gain a greater share of their inheritance. Maybe he's trying to get it all. Her mind sees why this is logical, yet hates to think this is Charlie's plan. "And?"

"And he said Mom gave you the information."

Her jaw drops. "What!" She checks herself. Her mind boomerangs from one family member to the other, reconstituting the final moments of her mother's visit. "Bibi, you are extremely responsible. . . You always do the right thing. . . Make the right decisions. . . Charlie and I have decided . . . You keep this information . . . I'll tell him they're in the safe deposit box at the bank."

Surely when Charlie and her mother gave her the box, it wasn't with the intent that Charlie would then tell Victor. Or maybe it was. What a couple of jerks. She removes a pink eraser from the top of Mr. Dillard's desk and squeezes it in her palm.

"You heard me. Charlie says you've got the stuff at your house."

She slams the eraser onto the desk. Of course, she thinks, suddenly realizing what should have been clear from the get go. "Wait a minute. Mom told me she was putting it in her bank's safety deposit box." Technically this is true, Bibi reminds herself.

"That's not what Charlie said."

"Then call Mom and ask her. I'm at work. I've got classes to teach. I can't have you calling me in the middle of the day like this."

"I believe Charlie. You have it."

"Call Mom and ask her personally." If Bibi's mom doesn't keep her story straight, Bibi'll be on the losing end. She imagines her mother assuring Victor the papers are safely locked away. Then she imagines her mother's face when she hears what Charlie has done. Bibi so wants to rat Charlie out, if indeed he's acting on his own. "Then you'll know the truth."

"Why should I believe her, or you, for that matter?"

"Because—." Her instincts tell her not to answer his question.

"You're lying. I know it."

If only she were a better liar. The office walls tighten around Bibi. The plaques on the left wall loom larger and closer, awards from the Buena Park Rotary, Silverado Days, Knotts Berry Farm, and the Los Coyotes Golf Club. To her right, through the window, the sparkling cars parked in the lot seem mere yards away, caging her in. She cuts him off. "You think our birth mother is any better?"

This stops him dead.

Despite a voice saying, "No," somewhere in her mind, she decides to give Victor a spoonful of the truth he's in search of. "I don't know how to explain this, but, like on Monday, a friend gives me a horoscope book." She hears him exhale out of boredom or irritation. "I take it home and read it, and guess what?"

"I don't know. Tell me."

His tone says: I don't want or care to know. Bibi's used to his masked curiosity. He often wants to know what she picks up from the woo-woo-sphere. "There are these similarities in your and my birth charts. You know what they are?"

"Just tell me!"

A louder "No" yells in her head. She ignores it. "Okay, okay. Both of our charts say there was a danger we'd drown when we're really young."

She waits for his response, but gets none. At least his obsessing has stopped.

"When I call Mom and tell her this, I think she's going to laugh at me, except she doesn't. You know what she says?"

A prickly silence travels through the phone.

Suddenly she regrets saying anything about the drowning to Victor. Maybe he actually remembers it. He was almost three when it happened. "Are you still on the line?"

The silence continues.

The quiet mirrors to her what she has done. She picks up the eraser and squeezes it. Telling him about the drowning could have shoved him off a cliff. She doesn't want him to go crazy. She loves her brother. He's the only person in the world who actually understands her, because of how alike they are.

"Victor, are you there?" She stares at the silence in the ear phone.

Then there is a click and a dial tone. A boulder-thick wall hovers in her mind, separating Bibi from her beloved brother.

She cannot stand what she has just done.

§

September 29; Santa Barbara

My dear brother, Victor.

After his conversation with Bibi, Victor's anger spumes and storms into his kitchen's air. His mind incessantly chatters, "Fuck you, fuck you." His hands long to strangle something to death.

He swings open the refrigerator door, and considers popping the top on a Guinness. But the refrigerator's contents stare at him, as does his life. "Do something with me!" silently yell the days-old leftovers sealed in pasty Tupperware bowls and the half-eaten container of smoked oysters.

He removes three folded brown grocery bags from the pantry next to the stove, shakes them wide open, and, starting with the top shelf, rashly removes anything from his refrigerator that looks the least bit old. Milk. Pickled mushrooms. Lavender honey. Grape leaves. Watermelon pickles. Paddlefish caviar. Elk jerky. Duck *fois gras* in aspic. Echire butter. His relentless chatter amplifies. "Fuck me, fuck me." His blackened aura swirls erratically and counterclockwise around his head.

How conflicted I feel. I wish Bibi had waited to bring up the drowning with Victor. On the other hand, he yearns to hear the truth.

Yet, when he hears it, he goes mad with rage.

I feel compelled to do something, which is why I begin singing to him. Not words really, for they might be misperceived. He's even less tuned-in than Delilah. I sing him syllables that might calm him. Oms and las. I sing him a favorite his birth mother used to play on the piano, or hum on their walks. Something from Schumann's *Scenes from Childhood*, or *Kinderszenen* as he prefers to pronounce it.

His aura's swirling now and seems more circular, though still counterclockwise. He turns the spigot, and hot water fills the kitchen sink, which already contains today's unrinsed breakfast and lunch dishes. Using both hands, he squeezes the plastic Joy bottle so hard a sharp spurt shoots out. He draws a V in the water and then a B. Within moments, the dishes lie submerged beneath bubbling clouds of detergent.

His mind flashes on the early bath times he and Bibi had shared in their new home, right after they were taken from Grace. Mrs. Andressen had kept calling him Victor, and Beatrice she called Ingrid. "My little Ingrid," she would say. "Come to Mommy."

"Beatrice!" he'd holler back. "Her name is Beatrice. You're not my mommy. I'm Evan. Evan!"

Mrs. Andressen's eyes had alarmed him. Their blue had been so pale they seemed white; her pupils were two bottomless black holes into which he could fall to his death. When she'd smiled at him, she looked frightened rather than happy. "Yes, I am your mommy. Forever and ever."

His words, it had seemed to him, counted as nothing. He was the one who understood and knew his sister, not this strange, gray-haired woman with beady eyes. Perhaps she'd misunderstood. "Beatrice," he'd told her. Then he'd over-pronounced his sister's name. "Bee-a-trice. I'm Evan."

Mrs. Andressen had gripped his arm and shaken it. The blacks of her eyes had dilated, as if ready to eat him. "Ingrid. Ingrid. You're Victor. Vic-tor."

"God damn it!" Victor yells into the sink water. "Just God, fucking, damn it." He remembers fetching the floating, foot-long wooden battleship they'd given him as a tub toy and hitting Mrs. Andressen, clunk, over the head. The satisfaction this had given him was enormous at first, until he'd realized it made no difference. The Andressens had changed his sister's name and his own, and then covered over this fact by calling his sister Bibi or Sister. Bibi, so pliant and callow, betrayed him by quickly adapting to his new name Victor.

It had been galling, and it still is. He cannot stand his name.

I continue singing.

And then, as if he can hear me, he dries his hands on his jeans and walks into his living room. Through the oriel, he notices the eucalyptus trees rustling in the breeze gusting up the canyon on which his home sits.

He positions his piano bench away from the brown upright he bought at a garage sale, and sits down to play. A bound Bach collection sits on the piano's music shelf.

Bach is not what he wants.

He eyes the bookcase to his right where he stores his music, certain that he doesn't have what he needs because Bibi probably took it when she last visited, which he knows isn't true, but still entertains the thought. He thumbs through the books, all the while his mind chatters about Bibi always laying claim to what is rightfully his. Her piano, for example. She'll deny this, of course. Truth is not Bibi's forte. She'll never admit the piano is rightfully his. He's the one with the real talent; he's the one who should have had a real piano teacher, one that would have trained him for Julliard, for that's where he should have gone. He should be famous by now, one of those performers who brings audiences to tears, and then to their feet. He should be giving music its day in court like no day it's ever had. For music shows the grandeur of which humanity is capable. And composing music creates something magnificent out of completely nothing.

His fingers stop rifling through the books. He spots the thin, frayed, faded-turquoise book of Robert Schumann's *Kinderszenen,* Opus 15. *Scenes from Childhood.* His fingers shiver; his heart pounds.

He sets the book on the piano's shelf and opens to *Von Fremden Ländern Und Menschen,* "From Foreign Lands and People."

The notes, simply played, he recognizes in a heartbeat. They transport him to another time and place, and kindle in him a yearning. The setting is hazy, but he smells cinnamon and oranges and hears the ocean lapping the shore. A woman's voice saturates the air with the melody he now plays. Her fingers guide his as they press each note of the song. The more notes he plays, the deeper his melancholy bores into him. He knows this place and longs to be there with her. With her he was always safe, and known.

Suddenly he cannot play another note. Decades of sorrow and longing gush from their hiding places. His hands leave the keyboards and cover his face, giving him a bowl to catch his tears. He sits on the piano bench, head bowed and sobbing, a broken man, beaten down by a past he can barely remember.

I continue singing. I could change the melody, but I do not. He aches to hear the truth, just as truth aches to be heard. Truth adds a certain loveliness to the world, just as lies tarnish it. All Mrs. Andressen had to say to Victor was, "Yes, her name is Beatrice, but we're changing it."

But she didn't. Her dissonant words had jarred his psyche like wrongly played notes. By insisting his name was Victor, she had erased the truth of his first three years and had made him seem a liar. He knew the facts, but had no way to prove them, like a kidnapped king.

He's been here before in other life times. Victor, always the kidnapped king.

§

September 29; Buena Park

Bibi draws the wet sponge across her classroom chalkboard, washing it clean of yellow chalk and today's knowledge and making it ready for tomorrow's thrilling lessons on concrete and abstract nouns and on Friederick Nietzsche's superman theories that influenced *Call of the Wild*. She glances at the full-moon poster she put on the bulletin board for the book. Her students keep telling her it makes the room feel like a science lab. Two more weeks of *Call of the Wild* and they'll have a whole new appreciation for the moon. Heck, after her conversation with Victor in Mr. Dillard's office this afternoon, she feels like crawling up on some rock and howling her guts at it.

She hears voices outside her room, then two bodies appear in her doorway. "Hey, lady. What's the scoop?" asks Gloria.

Bibi smiles, because she's glad to see Pamela and Gloria, and she glances at the clock, because she's actually not that glad since, as usual, she has a ton of work to get done before bed tonight.

Pamela and Gloria set their purses and bags on the floor near the filing cabinet and make themselves comfy in the first two desks, because, apparently, they're planning to stay. Gloria repeats, "What's going on? Like, everyone's talking about Mr. Dillard having to take your class while you had some strange conversation in his office."

Bibi should have known the school secretary would let everyone know about that phone call. Victor's incoherent yelling must have been the talk of the lounge. She leaves the sponge on the tray and sits at her desk in front of the chalkboard. It's always best to get one's own side of a story out when it comes to staff gossip.

"It was just my brother. He was upset."

Pamela's look tells Bibi she not a believer. "What's your brother upset about? Is it Charlie or Vic?"

"Victor."

"You may think we don't notice, but you've been acting a little weird lately. You've stopped mentioning Michael. You talk about your damned cat all the time. You seem distracted. What's going on?"

Bibi stares at Pamela. Older than Bibi by almost a decade, she's also wiser. Bibi knows she has nowhere to hide, and, frankly, no desire to either. Pamela's been one of her truest teacher friends. Her mentor, really. "Victor's going through a lot of shit right now. My mother's not being very helpful." Bibi regrets saying the latter, because she's not sure it's true.

"A lot of shit? What does that mean?" Pamela asks.

Gloria leans forward. "What's the problem. Is it your mom?"

"My brother wants to find our birth mother."

Both women sit back in their seats as if to escape the conversation, which is when Bibi remembers Pamela adopted both her children. She's not going to love the tale Bibi's about to spin. Bibi peeks at the clock.

Gloria is the first to ease up. "Is he having any luck? Is that why he called? Did he find her?" Elements of worry etch Gloria's pretty face, and Bibi doesn't know why.

"No. He wants me to find her."

Gloria's eyes search for what this means, and then she shrugs. "Knowing you, that would be smart of him."

Pamela winces at Gloria's words. Pamela shakes her head while she says, "You don't want to look. I know you don't."

Gloria looks to Pamela for some clue. They're not clones of each other, but they make a formidable pair. "Are you going to help Vic? How does anyone just go and find a birth mother anyway?" Gloria asks.

All good questions, Bibi thinks. She starts stacking her piles of essays and grammar exercises that need correcting into a neat column. She does not want to have this conversation. Even Michael has no idea what she's thinking, although he's probably got a good guess. She stops gathering and looks squarely at them both. "What I'm going to tell you, you have to keep a secret. If you can't, I won't tell you."

They both nod.

Bibi looks at Pamela. "Maybe you don't really want to hear about this."

Pamela nods microscopically while she thinks. She smacks the desk with her palm. "Nope. I want to hear. You're part of my life. I'm part of yours. Here we go."

"My mother gave me a shoe box filled with letters and pictures that have to do with our adoption. She wants me to keep them so Victor won't get hold of them."

Pamela dead pans, "That sounds like a terrific idea."

Bibi chuckles. It is definitely weird her mother did that. "She wants Victor to believe she still has the box of information. Except Charlie told Victor that Mom gave it to me."

Pamela again dead pans, "Swell."

"But the worst part is that I told Victor that our birth mother tried to drown us."

"Whoa." Gloria is shaking her head and waving her hands. "Whoa, just a minute. How do you know that?'

"Remember the astrology book you gave me a week ago?"

Gloria frowns. 'Yeah."

"Well, Victor's and my South Nodes are both in the first house, which means there was a danger we'd die very early."

Gloria says, "Wow."

Pamela rolls her eyes.

"When I told my mom this, and she told me the reason we were taken from our mother was because she tried to drown us."

Pamela's jaw goes slack. "It's true? Really?"

Tears well in Gloria's eyes.

Bibi looks from one good friend to the other, surprised by their array of reactions. "Yeah. It's true. And when I look at my own kids now, well, I'm used to looking at them at wondering how anyone could have given me away, but now I wonder how anyone could have wanted to kill me."

Gloria bursts into tears. Bibi and Pamela turn to her in surprise, then rush to her, pat and hold her, and whisper to her until she stops.

Composing herself and wiping her eyes and nose with a Kleenex she's gotten from Bibi's desk, Gloria says, "I'm sorry, you guys. I didn't mean to do that."

Pamela frowns lovingly. "That? What was that about?"

Gloria sits back in her seat. She bites her lower lip to quiet its quivering. Her eyes count the tiles in the ceiling. "You may not agree with me about this, but I hope you look for your birth mother. I hope you find out what really happened. Because I bet it's not as simple as your mom makes it sound."

The three friends sit for a moment looking from one to the other. Tears and a little terror fill Pamela's eyes; sorrow and hope fill Gloria's. Bibi has no idea what her eyes reveal, but she hopes they spell gratitude, love, determination, and terror, because that is what Gloria's words have inspired in her.

Eight

Still Motion

October 1; Huntington Beach

The ends of Bibi's fingers tingle, as though magic were at hand. She picks up the phone in her darkened kitchen; its cord skids across the paneling.

A blustering gust of wind rattles the windows and causes the roof to heave and creak. Hopefully by morning, the hot, dry Santa Ana's blowing out from the desert will have eased. This weather causes her nose to hurt and her lips to crack. Bibi daubed Vaseline all over the kids' faces before kissing them night-night.

The rest of the house too is dark, except for the globe lamp hanging over the breakfast room. On the table lie the overly-detailed lesson plans she prepared for tomorrow's substitute.

Another gust blasts through. The kitchen light flickers. Tree branches claw at the great-room windows, begging to enter.

She fights her impulse to call her mother and ask what Victor's been told about the whereabouts of the adoption information. Seven, one, four, she dials, then the rest of the digits for the school district's absence line. It's weird that Victor hasn't called Bibi since Tuesday's tantrum in her principal's office.

And it's even weirder that Bibi hasn't called him, or her mother, or Charlie. But she can't do it. Whenever she builds up the guts to call them, the phone seems like a grenade waiting to explode. Given a choice, she'd rather suffer with not knowing. Though their silence, the longer it goes on, leads her to believe her mother told Victor she'd locked up the information.

When she worried about this to Michael, he told her this would pass. "Lie low," he'd said.

Nevertheless, she's been living in a swamp since Tuesday, mired in her need to protect herself and her desire to undo having told Victor about the drowning.

Her call to the school district rings twice before the service answers. "Buena Park School District absence line," a woman's voice says.

A thud crashes against the kitchen window, possibly a bird became a helpless missile in the wind. Bibi resists her urge to go outside and rescue whatever the noise was.

She inhales and focuses on keeping her words simple, honest, and worried. Everyone at the district office knows she has a sick husband. "This is Bibi Amato. Eighth grade English. I can't be at school tomorrow. I'm sick. I'll be there Monday."

"Okay, Mrs. Amato. Do you have a substitute you prefer?"

"Carla, if she's available."

"She is, Mrs. Amato. I hope everything's okay."

"Thanks." Bibi's index finger presses the switch hook. Click. But she doesn't hang up the phone. It would be easy to dial her mother, who's most likely had enough whiskey by now to be fairly talkative.

She decides against it, though, and hangs up. Michael's right; Victor was probably just testing her. Why show her hand when the cards haven't yet been dealt?

After checking outside the window for a bird and finding nothing, Bibi heads to bed.

Tomorrow is a big day.

§

October 2; Huntington Beach

It is Friday morning. The wind has died quite a bit; the sky is a brilliant robin's-egg blue. The weatherman predicts temperatures may rise as high as one-hundred two. What a perfect day Bibi picked; she hates teaching on blistering days when it's too hot for her students to even think, let alone learn.

Dressed for a school day, she stands in her entryway facing the door leading down into the garage. An excited chill gushes within her. In her hand she holds a ratty old, royal blue Xanadu cosmetic bag she got free from Nordstrom's, into which she's emptied nearly ten dollars in change from the secret slush-fund jar she keeps hidden in her closet's back corner.

Earlier, she'd gone to school and left off her lesson plans before taking the kids to their sitter in Buena Park at the regular time, and then driven the fifteen miles back home.

A pang of guilt slices through her about telling the district's night operator she was sick and would need a day to recover. Of course, she isn't sick, but she'd be docked a much-needed day's wage if she called in and said, "I have to find my birth mother, and no, this cannot wait." She's already taken too many days with Michael's illness. Too bad today's a Friday, because they'll suspect she's taking a three-day weekend, as if she even has the energy to enjoy one.

She opens the door to the garage. It swings wide and bangs against the water heater. Garage scents rise to greet her: paint thinner, burnt automotive oil, drying grass in the trash, and Downy from the dryer.

She tastes her guilt in the back of her mouth. Her promise to Michael that she wouldn't look for her birth mother was sincerely made, but that was before Tuesday when Gloria urged her to look.

With the garage unlit, she scans the Coleman cooler in the rafters. Light entering from the side door's window makes her search difficult. She closes the door to the house to darken the space. Her shoulders sink. The light she had hoped to see emanating from the cooler isn't there, nor the six light specks. Maybe Michael removed the box and hid it that night he caught her on the ladder.

If only she'd searched for the shoe box last night. Now she has to waste time looking. Her mind envisions a clock's minute hands spinning around lickety-split, devouring the time she needs.

She momentarily forgives herself. The reason she had chosen not to search for the shoe box last night was because she thought it more important to garner Michael's trust, which meant no funny business on her part. Besides, she'd only made her decision to look for her birth mother at the last minute, during her drive home from school yesterday. Persuasive images had flooded her awareness during the drive. The shoe box was in her hand. People helped her. Phone calls got answered. Her mind was showing her what to do.

Yes, that's exactly what happened on her drive home. Her mind was helping her. Okay, mind, she thinks, find the shoe box. Is that how it works?

Bibi snaps on the light and steps down onto the garage's cold, concrete floor. Everything appears as she expected. Michael's car is gone; the smeared brown oil pan holds its place. He'll be gone most of the morning, hopefully. He's driven himself to his doctor's appointment and maybe will get in some work after that. Later this afternoon, when she's home from supposedly teaching school all day, she'll take him to the hospital for another round of chemo that starts tomorrow. She tastes her worry and crosses her fingers when she imagines him calling her at school today.

She tosses the Xanadu money bag in through Lars's open driver's window. It jingles when it lands on the front passenger seat. Next, she presses the button on the door leading to the side yard, which is really just a concrete path. They always keep this door locked. Always.

Except she needs it unlocked for that just-in-case event where she must surreptitiously return the shoe box to the garage.

Then she drags the ladder in front of Lars and lengthens it to reach the rafters. She adjusts the feet so they're stable, and climbs the rungs until she faces the blue Coleman cooler and the sea of crap stored in boxes, bags, and mailing tubes. In one pan, she notices paintings still on stretchers, an old canvas tent, a cello, some witch hats they'd long ago stolen from a newly painted street, two Persian rugs Bibi got from her aunt, crates of oil paints, buckets, old garden hoses, the crib and bassinet, Christmas ornaments, and boxes of baby clothes.

Bibi lifts the cooler's lid. Her hand reaches in and feels for the shoe box. She climbs higher on the ladder and sinks her hand deeper into the cooler. She feels toward every corner. Her fingertips touch nothing but cool, smooth, plastic.

After adjusting her stance so she trusts she won't fall, Bibi pulls the cooler toward her and manages to turn it diagonally, so what's behind it is visible to her. All she sees are moving boxes sitting on the press board flooring Michael added to the rafters. She pulls the cooler out further and leans as far to the right as she feels safe. Still no sign of the shoe box.

Bibi shoves the cooler back in place. Damn. That was stupid of her not to have paid attention to Michael that night he caught her with the shoe box. She should have listened for him moving the ladder to another spot or for falling boxes, or timed how long it took him to hide the box. Now she's got the whole garage to search.

She inspects the rafters one more time, tuning in to unusual signs of light. Slowly her focus travels, from left to right, and then back again. A fat, black, October spider drops down from the ceiling beams and lands inches from where she stands. Horror races up her spine. She gasps and scrambles down the rungs, looking back up to make sure the spider didn't follow her.

Cripes, there's no way she can find anything in here. She rushes into the house to check the clock and realizes she doesn't have much time. Her body tenses. This cannot be a wasted day.

She reenters the garage and turns off the light. Ceres's padding steps follow close behind. From the dryer, Bibi removes a damp towel, which she drapes over the side door's window. She waits for her eyes to adjust to the darkness.

The angst in her chest tightens. The zits she awoke to this morning throb. It can't be time for the curse already.

She closes her eyes. A kaleidoscope of colored patterns scrolls down her vision. Reds, blues, and purples, intense against a black backdrop. Mind, she tells herself, find the box. She breathes in, and then slowly out. Tension leaves her like an ebbing tide. She repeats this, in then out, in then out. With each respiration, another bundle of anxiety washes away. Ceres's fluffy tail skims across her calves.

Bibi opens her eyes.

The garage seems brighter, though it is still dark. Lars's beige seats seem champagne pale. The kids' Hot Wheels glow tangerine orange. She rescales the ladder and observes what she sees. Nothing catches her eyes. No aura. No sparkling dots. She descends and methodically walks the garage's perimeter. She walks past the washer and opens the dryer's door. She looks above the rusting, refrigerator to the folded moving blankets stacked on its top. She continues past Noah and Ella's Tonka trucks, Michael's cluttered workbench, and dusty shelves holding house paint, motor oil, and car wax. Then down the side where the bikes, trikes and wagons are parked at perfect diagonals like military service stripes. And across the edge where the garage door rests on the concrete. Light from outside squeaks through the gaps between the door and garage floor. Spiders and crickets scramble to hide under the door. Then she treads up the other side of the garage, next to her car, where Michael keeps his large boxes of professional cigarette inventory, where she spots Ceres's tail, and where fishing rods lean against a stud.

She stops. Her skin feels cool and her mouth drops open. A faint glow emanates from the floor. And the dots, they dance above the aura, while Ceres hilariously bats at them.

Delighted, Bibi leans down and spots the shoe box, nestled, appropriately she might add, among the fishing rods, nets, creels, and tackle boxes.

She remembers the night when Michael was out here relocating the shoe box. She'd gone back in the house and climbed into bed. She kept hearing the words "fish rods" spoken into her ear. It made no sense then.

Bibi glances up. Something was trying to help her that night! Or someone. She thinks of the poems, and the poem voice.

The aura around the shoe box pulses a brighter silver light, and the dots quicken their flashing, and dance in circles and loops. Ceres is half out of her mind trying to bat them. Bibi crosses her arms across her chest and holds her arms tight. Tears well in her eyes. Beyond a doubt, she knows these dots are as aware of her as she is of them, and gratitude sweeps over her. For all the times she may have felt alone and disconnected in this world, this one moment atones for it. "Thank you," she whispers, "whoever you are."

When she picks up the box, something else catches her eye. Lying squarely in the middle of the spot where the box had been resting, is the little yellow paper with the phone number she knew she'd wadded into a ball and thrown away last week. She specifically remembers tossing it in the plastic trashcan under the kitchen sink. She even remembers the arc it traveled before disappearing into the trash.

Somehow it has come back to life and has been lying flat and new and hidden under the shoe box.

She blinks and looks around wide-eyed. This is all too strange. The paper wants to exist; why, she does not know, but she certainly has a hunch. She picks it up and puts it in the box before realigning the fishing tackle, making it harder to notice whether the box is there or not. Obviously, she's not as alone as she thinks she is.

Giddily, and much to Ceres's disappointment, she puts the shoe box in her trunk, next to the spare tire and the jumper cables, and counts on her fingers to make sure she has the seven things she needs. Money. Shoe box. Garage side door that's unlocked. Purse. Keys. Lights off. House looking like nothing has changed.

Doubting that she left the bathroom exactly as it should be, she rushes back in and closes the under-sink cupboard. Phew! She eyes herself in the mirror. Three swollen Vesuviuses have erupted over night. The one on the end of her nose is reminiscent of Rudolf. The other two give her the appearance of someone shot in the face. Not really, but almost. God, how embarrassing.

After having made sure Ceres was inside the house, she hoists up her garage door from the inside, then backs out the car, before closing the door again. She makes her way to the end of the street, then out of the tract and finally onto the main thoroughfare, where she relaxes. At last, she experiences the sumptuous feeling of anonymity and the relief of getting away with larceny.

She applies more pressure to the gas pedal, for she's got maybe four hours to find her birth mother, or at least get a whiff of her trail. Who knows what she'll discover.

She glances at the Xanadu bag next to her, chock full of coins, and imagines the shoe box in the trunk, all lit and happy to be found.

She tells the dots, whoever and wherever they are, thank you.

Then stops, and asks, "Who are you anyway?"

§

I answer, "Anna," in my very best elocution.

Bibi does not hear. Alas.

Truly, I'm grateful for the moments Bibi does hear. They're becoming more and more frequent.

And I know she knows I exist. She sees the dots and she found the phone number, for which she thanked me. I adore her for that recognition.

If only I could help Delilah more. Unlike Bibi, she picks up none of my clues. Perhaps it is her youth that makes it hard.

More likely, it is her anger, for she has been looking for her siblings for years, to no avail. I keep trying to help her find them. She even lived in Santa Barbara for a while, a breath away from her brother.

But isn't that just what happens when walls and doors exist. You cannot see what is literally inches away from your nose.

§

Bibi considers the beaming, lidded shoe box resting before her on the reading table of the La Palma Public Library, and swallows. To open it without ceremony would seem such a sacrilege, for in it lies her future, her past, and, most importantly, her present.

She opens the wheat-toned school composition book she'd purchased at a local drugstore on her way to the library, the kind that has the multiplication tables and measurements on the back. She needed something to hold all her thoughts and information, and keep them private. The last thing Michael would peek into would be a school composition book.

In it she writes the date: 10/2/81.

Resisting her urge to simply dump the box's content on the table, she places her palms on its lid and, without closing her eyes, speaks to whatever spirit it is that surrounds her and guides her through her fate. "Speak to me. Help me understand. I, with everything in me, will try my hardest to pay attention. Thank you."

Her fingertips fizz and simultaneously feel weightless and extraordinarily large. Awe and humility thread through her.

She hesitates before opening the box and acknowledges that her next actions will change the path of her life. Of course, she can forfeit this change, close the box, and go home. But, no, she can't. Not if she is to live with herself.

Right or wrong, she knows her best course is to systematically sort the box's contents into piles. Her spine shivers and chills despite the library's warmth.

The huge, institutional wall clock over the librarian's desk adds to her jitters. Its red second hand sweeps around the clock's face, vacuuming away the minutes, making the need for her every action to be all the more efficient. The minute and hour hands all align. Five 'til eleven. She's got to be out of here by two to pick up the kids and get home without Michael suspecting anything.

Get to work, she tells herself.

But the librarian behind the counter halfway across the room distracts her, even makes her jumpy. She's youngish to be a librarian, in Bibi's opinion, and pretty, like Pat Benatar, even with the aviator glasses. The librarian keeps glaring at the shoe box like she suspects Bibi has stolen money from a bank or it's filled with a bomb, or something equally dangerous or illegal.

Bibi tries to ignore her and stick with her plan. When in doubt, keep the order. She takes out the little yellow paper she found in her garage and copies the number into the book. She remembers calling the number before. Katzensomething. She can't remember.

She then pulls all the photographs from the box. The pile seems smaller than she'd expected: photographs of the ocean; a Spanish-style house with rounded roof tiles; and a little girl with dark, curly hair, who is definitely not Bibi.

Her lips twitch. She examines everything again, just in case she missed a picture. Her hopes were high that she'd find a picture of herself as a baby. She's never seen what she looked like as an infant, or when she took her first steps, or her first birthday. Even her birth certificate is a lie. Michael's birth certificate has his length and size, and a black imprint of his sole. Hers has her new and much detested name Ingrid and her new parents' names, but neglects to tell her birth size, which Bibi thought was incredibly important when her own kids were born. The earliest pictures Bibi has ever seen of herself were the ones taken right after the adoption, when she was almost two, and Victor was almost three.

She glances up. The clock hands have ticked away fifteen minutes of her time, reminding her to be more efficient. To her relief, the librarian has stopped scowling and staring, and actually seems approachable. Which is good, because it occurs to Bibi to ask her a question.

She walks over to the librarian's desk. To Bibi it looks more like one of those court room bars that stop people from approaching the judge. "Do you have any books about adoption?"

As soon as the word adoption leaves Bibi's lips, its meaning spills into her psyche, soaking her in its sadness and humiliation, saturating her with the knowledge that when she lost her mother, and her father, she became an orphan. No-man's child. Unclaimed and alone in the world. And that's the way it's always felt, even though she ended up in a family. That feeling of being dropped to earth from the sky with no genetic family to collect her, and nurture her, and show her how to be her. An ugly duckling.

The librarian studies Bibi's face, a worried expression on her own. "That would be in the one-eighty-eights."

Bibi turns around and looks at the book stacks, though she's really hiding her tears, for she's a sixty-fourth of an inch from bursting into a full-blown weeping session.

"Upstairs, in psychology."

Bibi can only nod in acknowledgment, her back still turned to the librarian, her hand reaching into her pocket for some gum.

"Are you looking?" the librarian asks.

Bibi again nods, and conjures the bravery to turn back around. If she tries to talk, she knows she'll start blubbering. She pops in the gum.

The librarian removes her glasses. Her dark-lashed eyes show genuine caring. She pivots and walks to the other side of her little desk, her right index finger raised. "Just a moment. I'm going to get you some information that might help you." Her footsteps sound feathery against the linoleum flooring.

Bibi chews and chews. She's calming down. Someone's here to help her, though she doesn't know how that help might look. Maybe there's a book about someone else's search, or a book that tells her what to do. She loves how-to books.

The librarian returns with pamphlets in her hands, which she spreads on the counter before Bibi.

Bibi reads their titles. In purple letters, "Finding Your Birth Parents." In white letters and black, *Where Did You Come From?* In brown script, "The Triadoption Agency." This one especially grabs her attention. It's a non-profit near here, in Westminster, that helps adoptees reconnect with their birth families. Evidently, she's not the only one looking, which calms her.

The librarian eyes the shoe box back on the reading table. "It looks like you have a pretty good start. You're lucky."

Bibi looks at her treasure chest filled with letters, envelopes, names, and pictures. Clues galore. She does have a good start. "Thanks so much. You're so kind."

The librarian then scribbles something on a white three-by-five card and hands it to Bibi. "Get these books. They'll help. Buy them if you can. When you get them, you'll understand why you need to own them."

Bibi arranges the card atop the pamphlets and reads the titles. *Lost and Found. The Adoption Triangle.* Every space in her tingles. "I will." She smiles at the librarian, grateful for her help. "What's your name?"

"Lilian."

"Thank you, Lilian. Thank you very much." Bibi's a child just given a horse by Santa. She's Cinderella whose foot has just been discovered to fit the glass slipper. She floats back to her table and resumes wading through her treasures.

She separates the letters with envelopes from those without, then carefully, checking her spelling, once, twice, thrice, copies every name and address she finds.

She then opens each letter, looking only for names, addresses and phone numbers, and likewise copies them into her book. Names like Lacharite, Kettenburg, Borg, Winslow, and addresses in San Diego, La Jolla, and Borrego Springs, out in the desert.

Kettenburg. Something about the name.

She shuts everything back in the box, including the pamphlets and card with the book titles. She goes back to Lilian. "Is there a phone?"

Lilian smiles knowingly and points to a series of little rooms along the side wall. In each is a pay phone.

"Thanks!"

"Good luck!"

All Bibi can manage is grin. She carefully gathers her stuff, enters the middle room, and seals herself and her treasure chest into its quiet, monochrome privacy.

She opens her book to a clean page, opens her bag of coins, and calls the first number, the one that keeps following her around.

"Good afternoon. Kettenburg Marine."

"What!" Bibi suddenly realizes she's seen that name on a return address or two.

"Kettenburg Marine."

"Where are you?" She tries to sound polite, rather than crazed with curiosity.

"Shelter Island, on Shelter Island Drive."

"I mean what city?"

"San Diego. Can I help you?"

"No, no, I think I have the wrong number." She hangs up and writes what she knows down. None of it makes sense, other than this is the phone number on the yellow paper, and the name Kettenburg is on some envelopes, which is beyond odd.

She should stop now and read all the letters, but then she'd have to make her phone calls from home, which Michael would ultimately discover. She looks at the clock. It's past noon. It seems whenever she needs time, time shrinks, or seeps away.

She calls information and gives the name Borg. "Any in San Diego? Yes? A dentist. Charlie Borg." The irony of Charlie's name popping up in her search startles and amuses Bibi. She takes down the number any way.

When she calls one of the last numbers on her list, a woman answers. Not knowing what to say, Bibi blurts, "Do you know Grace Winslow?"

The phone hangs up.

She calls back. The lady doesn't answer. She calls again, but hangs up before the fifth ring. Maybe it was a wrong number. Or the right one.

Bibi returns to Lilian, whom she guesses has been keeping an eye on her. "Would you happen to have a San Diego phone book?"

Lilian pulls three phone books out from under the counter and scoots them toward Bibi. “Three. It's a metropolis down there."

Back at the library table, Bibi sifts through the pages and writes down anything that might help, but gives up. It seems impossible, like finding a pin in a forest. When she looks up, it's quarter to two.

Pressed, Bibi arbitrarily singles out a letter to read.

Upon opening the letter, Bibi realizes it is written by her birth mother. She can't help but notice how Grace's handwriting lilts and dances across the page.

> Dear Sadie,
>
> Would you be so kind as to forward this to whomever is taking care of my precious Beatrice and Evan? They are such sweet children, so trusting and loving, I cannot bear to think of someone mistreating them in any way.
>
> Both children will usually sleep through the night if they've been bathed and read a story or two before bedtime. And, of course, they both love lullabies. Beatrice likes to sleep in her Dr. Denton's, because they help her stay warm when she kicks off her covers. Evan is in big boy pajamas now and knows how to get up in the night if he needs to go to the potty.
>
> Beatrice loves peas, peaches, and peanut butter, but she hates bananas. They make her gag. Evan likes to have raisins with every meal, and he'll eat

his vegetables if you melt a little butter on top. Do not feed either children liver. They will not eat it.

The little dears love animals so, and they'll want to pet every dog and cat they come across. And Evan can never have enough trains, ships, and golden books. Beatrice needs a good teddy bear or two to carry around.

The children have never been yelled at or spanked. They'll usually do as told the first time they are asked.

Please tell my babies I love them and miss them so much it breaks my heart into pieces. If I knew where they were, I would drop everything and get them to bring them home to me, where they belong, with their mother. Every child belongs with his or her mother. Every child.

Yours sincerely,

Grace

The incredible poignancy of Grace's letter both weighs and tears at Bibi's heart. She notices that her birth mother loved the same things about her that Bibi loves about her children—what they wear and like to eat. Bibi's heart cannot stop bursting. Her birth mother loved her with all her heart, more than any love she's felt from Mrs. Andressen.

She searches the letters for something her birth father may have written, wondering how he is, or who he is, and if he has been attempting to get her back into the family. But there are none. Her heart feels hollow and drips with sadness. She doesn't want to think about her birth father. The dad she has is fine. Even though he's passed on, he was always nice to her. Except—. Her needs were important to him, and he tried to give her things that would make her life easier. Like appliances and the new VW. Well, he didn't exactly give it to her, but he sure made it easy for her to buy. Her mother never would have been that generous.

Bibi glimpses the clock and immediately shoves all the papers back into the shoe box. It's two o'clock on the dot. If she doesn't leave this instant, Michael will know she's up to no good. She'll read some more of these tonight, after she's taken Michael to the hospital for his chemo.

For now, she must focus on picking up her kids, bringing them home, loving them, and letting them feel their father's love, for as long as it is possible. Hopefully a good long time.

§

I watch the papers Bibi shoves into the box nestle against each other. They wiggle and jostle ever so slightly in their search for the most comfortable position in which to rest before she replaces the lid atop them.

There they lie, waiting to be reread, hoping to be understood, and yearning to be linked with their kindred experiences. Not hoping and yearning in the way people do. Rather in the way letters and memories do; the causes and the effects meet each other and recognize their connection. Nothing ever just happens.

Grace's letter to her children's new parents, in particular, longs to know about the children. Both Victor and Bibi had loved bath time. Regardless of the day's happenings, their world became a soft pillow once they were set in a sudsy tub. Each loved the warm water against their skin and the Ivory soap smell and the way soap foamed so it would completely cover up their noses, or their eyebrows, or their chins. "I was born this way," they would tell each other, when they masqueraded in their bubbly new skin.

While you already know how bath time became a war zone for Victor, you do not know how entwined Victor and Bibi became.

When Bibi was probably three, I remember, and Victor was therefore four, they ventured across the street. There was rarely traffic in their neighborhood, so this was not a daring feat on their part.

Once across the street, they crawled, hand-in-hand, several feet down a simple path into the canyon that began mere feet from the side of the road. Indigenous pepper trees and volunteer palms framed the canyon's sides. Rocks littered the pathway, and dried grasses and weeds covered every inch of soil.

It felt good to be away from Mrs. Andressen's violent temper, livid forehead, and powerful right arm. Earlier, they'd both had their pants removed and were paddled with a clothes hanger for doing something Mrs. Andressen didn't want them to do anymore. When it had been Victor's turn for his switching, Bibi screamed and wept, begging Mrs. Andressen to let her brother live. She could not stand to see Victor's face howling in pain, or to watch his fingers being whipped as they tried to protect his fanny from lashings. She sucked her own fingers in her attempt to soothe his. She was never sure he would prove strong enough to endure Mrs. Andressen's resentments.

When it was Bibi's turn to be spanked, she sunk her face deep into the bowl of her hands, screamed out her horror, and decided that if and when she got yet another mother, her life could be many times worse. She hated mothers with all her heart. She hated them with the same fear she hated the queen in Snow White. She hated them with the same horror she felt for the lady who tried to bake Hansel and Gretel. Out of the corner of her ear, she heard Victor hitting Mrs. Andressen, and telling her to stop, and begging her to leave. Bibi loved him for doing this, but feared what Mrs. Andressen would do to him as a result. For Victor's safety, Bibi stopped crying. When Mrs. Andressen resumed hitting her harder, Bibi refused to cry. Rather, she refused to feel in order to keep herself from crying. She did this in the face of her new mother, whom she thought was the most frightening person in the world.

And that is what was on their little minds as they crept further down the canyon path. They really didn't go far into the canyon, even though, because of their size, they felt like they were miles from home. Because they couldn't see over the canyon's rim, in their minds, their house had disappeared from their lives.

They each found little spots on which to sit. Victor sat on a broad, limestone rock. Bibi nested in a clump of weeds.

It was here they had a very serious conversation, one which they would remember for the rest of their lives, for, in hindsight and in their hearts, they knew it was a conversation they really shouldn't have had to have. In this conversation they made plans for what to do when the Andressens gave them away, as they surely would because Victor and Bibi were bad, and because the Andressens kept telling them they would give Victor and Bibi back to the Indians. They shuddered at the thought.

Thus, it was in this canyon, soft and round like a womb, that they decided how they would survive on their own.

Of all the trees in the canyon, the old palm tree to their left seemed like it would shade them and protect them from the dark, though neither of them wanted to go near the tree. It made noises, even on windless days. And spider webs were everywhere. But in a pinch, it would do until they figured out something better. Next, they figured they would get the neighbor dog Biffy to help them find food, or maybe he'd share his food with them. They'd tasted dog biscuits at their cousins' house and thought they were pretty good.

Their options were limited, and they knew it.

But it was an important conversation, one they needed to have.

§

October 2; Santa Barbara

What a nightmare.

With all his might, my brother Victor struggles to comport himself so he can argue his case to Phoebe. Planted in the middle of their living room sofa, he cradles his head in his hands, and presses the heels of his palms against his eyes to stave the shame and remorse weeping from them. His mind refuses to clear. Haunting images replay before him. Phoebe opening their bedroom door and screaming at the site of Quentin and him together. Her roaring up like a lioness betrayed, shouting at Quentin to get out. Her cringing at the men's nakedness. Katie screeching and spinning in circles. Phoebe racing out to the driveway and pushing Quentin's motorcycle over so it lay there like a dead horse. Over and over, Victor asks himself, my God, why he would he do this to his family, to his life. He doesn't even love the guy.

Across from him, swollen and red faced, Phoebe sits cradled in their ancient, black Eames chair. Her poised hands rest folded in her lap as she awaits his explanation. So like his mother. Selvage that cannot fray.

Down the hall, little Katie sleeps. Hopefully.

Victor feels Phoebe's eyes studying him. He inhales, drawing his snot back into his head, and wipes the moisture from his face with the back of his hand. Now, he tells himself, is your moment. He looks at her face, so hurt and beautiful. Then at her eyes, into which he reads her pleading for him to fix this, to make it disappear and never, ever return again.

He closes his eyes and slowly shakes his head. "I am so sorry." He opens his eyes. "I can't blame you for feeling as you do."

She slides her left foot under her right knee. "And what am I feeling, pray tell?"

How dumb of him to have said that. He knows what she wants and deserves. "I can't explain why that happened. It'll never happen again. I promise. I swear."

"Are you attracted to him?"

He hears the horror in her voice. "No." His voice begs her to accept this.

"But then how did it happen? Do you know this, this jerk?" Her eyes flame.

He looks out the picture window and searches the patio furniture for an explanation that will save them for this calamity he's created. He looks back at her. "He found my address. He works at the market. I did not invite him here. I did not."

Her eyes bead. She's not buying it. "Okay, stop. We're not going to continue this if you're going to lie to me. You know him. You've been with him before. Or maybe not. But you know him. Right? Tell me the truth."

Victor glances left, looking for an honest way out. Finding none, he tells her, "I've had coffee with him. He writes. He acts. He wanted to know if I'd direct a play he'd written." Victor stops. He knows what can happen with these lies.

Phoebe nods and studies him. "And what exactly attracts you to him?"

The answer leaps from Victor's mouth. "He sought me out. He's spontaneous. Off the wall."

"Super creative? Rash?" She raises her eyebrows as she waits for him to confirm her suspicions.

He looks from her to the paintings on the wall, a couple of them Bibi's. They've had this conversation before. He loves that Phoebe's such a rock, but he always yearns for how life was when he and his sister were teenagers, when his sister would drop everything to do something crazy, like spending the entire day in a movie theater watching *Help* over and over until they practically had it memorized.

Before he can answer, Phoebe states, "I can't be your sister."

"I know. I don't want you to be her."

Victor knows Phoebe is marking her territory, so it doesn't surprise him when she gets up and goes to the kitchen and comes back with a broom, which she lays on the floor between them, turning their living room into an arena.

When she sits down again, she asks, "Did it ever occur to you that Bibi's like your birth mother? That they may be alike. You know, how you think my mom and I are alike."

Victor mulls this thought and the broom separating them. This little metaphor of Phoebe's could get ugly, and soon. "Never occurred to me until you said it," which is pretty true.

She smiles and looks at the broom. Then she points at it in a way that lets Victor know he is on the outskirts, a fringe element in her life, which both she and he know he has no wish to be. "Which side do want to be on, Victor? Be careful. I'll not ask again. You know how I hate surprises. And you know that as a forgiving person, I have my limits. But I love you with all my heart, but you recklessly tried to break it today. Don't ever do that to me again."

She's right, he thinks, as nausea engulfs him. He needs to get up and step over the line she's drawn, the threshold she's presented him to prove his love and devotion to her and their family and way of life. It is what he wants. It's what made him the happiest. He's a strong person. No need to be rash like Bibi.

Tears stream from his eyes. He gets up and goes to Phoebe. He takes her hands and pulls her up. With his arms surrounding her, he rocks her, and tells her how much he loves everything about her and how grateful he is to be with her. Tears continue to flow, as he rues the parts of himself he left on the other side of the broom.

§

These are the hardest times.

I watch Victor stare out the living room window, the one that usually takes in the Pacific Ocean as it stretches all the way to China. Phoebe, exhausted and terrified, has escaped to Katie's bedroom to recuperate and hide.

All the lies Victor has just told Phoebe roil in his belly. He cannot live like this, cannot deceive and cheat his way to authenticity. His imagination searches for unlocked doors that, when opened, show him the way. Failing that, he's trapped. His thought kill or be killed warps into die or be dead.

I cannot let him out of my awareness. I surround his head and his shoulders. It's the best I can do in the moment. I look around for help.

The view, he notices, is hazy, the horizon indistinct. Not from smoke, nor fog, but from the off-shore Santa Anas. His skin feels dry, a reminder fire season has arrived. Die or be dead. He swallows hard.

I put out a call knowing full well it might go unanswered. But I see tiny lights packed with help coming my way. The relief of that.

Outside, standing in the driveway, Victor studies his pickup in the garage. His chariot. His place to think. Phoebe's clean, white Corolla remains in the driveway where she screeched to a halt so as not to hit Quentin's motorcycle.

Quentin, the siren. He should never have come to Victor's house. Victor had told him to never under any circumstances contact him again. But Quentin just had to, he being so rash. I tried to stop him, but I failed. Now I fear I'll need to stop Victor. Failure is unthinkable.

Victor returns to the kitchen for his key ring. He stops for a moment and listens to the house sounds, all the silent screaming. His shoulders brace before quickly making his way to the garage and getting into his truck. He isolates the truck's key from the rest and imagines it will open one of his mind's fantasy doors. "Behind this," his mind entreats, "behind this door you'll finally have what you're looking for." He fastens his seatbelt.

I bunch my energy to form a tight cannon ball and smack him on his left temple. Not in anger, mind you, but in hope, which is always my motive. I hope that his attention will drive off the circular racetrack it's on and find a new path. Tiny lights swarm around the cab.

He glances to his left and touches where I'd hit him. Strange, he thinks to himself, he could have sworn something hit him. His brows furrow, but then relax. He toys with putting the key into the ignition, but pulls back. From the rear-view mirror, he catches sight of himself. This is how Phoebe will find him. He combs his fingers through his curls, takes one more check in the mirror, sets the keys on the passenger seat, unlatches the seatbelt, and gets out of his truck.

I send half the tiny lights to Phoebe. Get her!

Victor stands outside his truck and with seemingly new eyes takes in all that is his garage; he's a tourist in a new land.

I hover over Victor like fascia. I will for him to go back inside his home and lie down and sleep. I will him dreams that give him the answers he needs. I will him life and the desire to live it, and a clear memory of who he is so his search for Grace is a product of love and not fear or vengeance.

His attention focuses on the garage door's pull rope. My army of tiny lights still in the garage noticed this before I do. Clustered in the rafters, they lie wait. I join them.

Victor pulls at the rope, which does not budge. He tugs again, harder, to no avail. He shakes his head. This is not going his way. He steps backward onto driveway for a better view. His curiosity cannot withstand this boggling enigma. He goes back into the garage for the ladder, which he sets up in the driveway.

We cannot believe our good fortune; but then again, we can. Still, we remain focused. I, and perhaps they, wonder what success the other half of the army has achieved. I sense them coming our way.

Victor scales the ladder to inspect what's blocking the garage door.

A voice behind him asks, "What are you doing?"

He turns to Phoebe, hoping he's not ashen or shock-faced. Words don't come. He can't tell her the truth, nor can he lie. "The garage door's stuck."

"You're shutting the garage door when my car's still out?"

He stands on the second rung and smiles at her, Cheshire like.

She's waves for him to dismount. "C'mon. You need some rest." She holds out her hand to her child, her husband.

I calm myself and wave gratitudes at my army. But this is not over.

Nine

Rivers in the Sea

October 2; Lubbock

Delilah enters Dr. Grout's medical suite through the back door, as usual, except that she's a good ten minutes late.

The office seems unusually quiet, as though empty. Except everyone's cars are parked out back.

The quiet accentuates the screech in her footsteps on the linoleum. She tiptoes down the hall to the third door on the left, the room where she stows her purse and lunch for the day.

Resting perfectly centered on top of the room's small desk, Delilah discovers a large brown envelope. Her name, Delilah Stone, scrawled in black marking pen ink, blazes across the envelope's face.

Inside it, she finds two letter-sized envelopes.

The first, Delilah recognizes immediately. Her heart drops. She'd addressed this envelope herself, using one of Dr. Grout's official envelopes, and mailed it to Sadie Lacharite. The familiar red post-office symbol depicting a hand with a pointing finger and the words, "Return to Sender" has been stamped to the addressee's left. The envelope's seal has been ripped open.

Delilah heaves air into her lungs; she's been caught.

The second, a plain, white envelope, remains sealed. She recognized the office typewriter's familiar pica typeface spelling out "Delilah Storm" across the envelope's front.

Using her thumb nail as a wedge, she tears away the envelope's flap.

The letter, once opened, sends a mordant chill through Delilah. Crisp, but plain, white paper. No letterhead. No personal signature. Just simple and to the point.

> Mrs. Stone,
> You are fired.
> Lloyd Grout, M.D.

§

Timelessness has its advantages.

I have been traipsing the neighborhoods of Lubbock all morning, watching over Delilah as she makes one pit stop after another to fill what she's lost. The donuts and coffee she picked up at the drive-thru across from the record store temporarily stilled her jangled nerves. Beer and pool came next. That worked better. I'm obviously not in a judging mood. Two games she played by herself, even though a couple of patrons suggested they'd like to join her, given how they'd never shot pool with a nurse. Two beers later she was at the drug store testing lipsticks and blush. Using her credit card, she bought purple mascara, iridescent magenta nail polish, and a flacon of Lauren. The latter's cool, lily-of-the-valley scent never fails to calm her and to transport her to a magazine page where she is the prize. She'll worry about the money this all cost, forgetting there can be plenty. Money's like air, if only people would realize it.

Home now, she teeters on her foot stool as she takes her gris-gris box down from her closet shelf. It's the old travel case she couldn't find a couple of weeks ago, but was always in front of her eyes the whole time she searched. The human condition. She's already removed the two trolls from between her mattress and box springs and set them on her nightstand. She knows why the spells she cast a couple of weeks ago failed; she won't be sloppy this time.

Except she's a bit drunk.

Making every effort to not jostle the case, she places it on the bed, unsnaps its latches, and opens it wide. It doesn't exude a breeze, but it feels like it to Delilah. She draws closer and breathes in the altar's essence and meaning—her own private island.

In reality, it's an altar in a box, an idea she got from me. Its phantasmagoric aura emanates and blossoms to fill her room. Lined in red paisley, adorned with fabric figures and gold-framed images of saints and goddesses, it's replete with candles, incense, stones, and herbs. It's a working shrine.

She lights a cigarette and lets it dangle from her lips as she yanks free the safety pins from the Trolls. Honestly, what was she thinking? Safety pins. She wonders what adverse effect that had on her spells. Before she puts the pins and the papers attached to them in the ash tray on her night stand, she reads the notes.

"Hart." "Find them."

That disgusting conversation she'd had with Mr. Hart spews into her memory. "Sorry, that's a trade secret." "You seemed like a smart lady." His gall. She stubs out her cigarette and lights a fresh one.

"Mom." "Tell D everything."

Delilah's cheeks burn hotter. Her mother, her so-called mother, who can't remember a damned thing. "I'm tho thorry," she kept saying to Delilah. Well, Delilah muses, if her mother thinks she's sorry now, just wait. "Just you wait, Mom," she says out loud before torching the two notes with her cigarette.

I know where Delilah's headed, and it's the opposite direction from where she wants to go. I flit around her right cheek to distract her from the notes. I place myself behind an amethyst to make it glow. I yell, "What do you want?"

She picks out the beige burlap doll from under her pile of voodoo paraphernalia and smells it. Her nose wrinkles at the faint odor of dirt, pulverized dog shit, and pepper. This will do, she thinks. The last time she used it, she experienced some success. She writes "Mom" on a little piece of paper, folds it, and prepares to insert it into an open section of the doll's seam.

I cannot have this and have no other choice. Tightening myself into a bundle and steadying myself just inside the entrance to her ear, I shout, "NO!"

Do you know what she does when I yelled, "NO"? First, she blanches, which pleases me. She rubs at her ear, which, no, does not affect me, as I have already backed out. Then she sucks smoke from her cigarette into her lungs and lets it swirl and damage, which does not please me. I close in again, and whisper, "Ask. Ask for what you want. Be the magician of your life. It works far better than you'd believe."

My words have no effect. She tunes me out and inserting her finger into the space made by doll's unsewn seam. Without hesitating more, she tucks the paper upon which she has written "Mom" deep inside the doll so it is located in what would be her mother's rib cage. For this doll is her mother. White frizzy hair made from unraveled yarn. Fluid eyes made from opaline buttons. A mouth darned shut with gray twine.

Alas. Delilah creates that which she most detests, and then wishes to punish the results. No doubt I will do the same when I am once again human, at least until I remember the power of thought. One more time I whisper, "Ask. Ask for what you want."

§

October 2; Huntington Beach

It is late Friday night. Checking Michael into the hospital for his chemo went smoothly, but he had wanted her company, so she'd remained with him until nine. The sitter was good enough to stay. The kids are sound asleep in their beds. Now the house is Bibi's. She could go through the box in her trunk, but she has a better idea. After all, she'll have plenty of time tomorrow.

She adjusts the piano bench so her hands are the perfect distance from the keys. Not too close, not too far. She brushes her finger tips over the ivory keys of her seventy-year-old Weber piano, starting at the high notes, and skimming down to the last key on her left. Some of these low keys annoy her because when she glued them back on, she couldn't get them even with the rest of the ivories. But they also make her smile.

Her new Schirmer's edition, *Chopin Ballades for the Piano*, perches on her piano's lyre. She opens to the first Ballade. She's already studied it visually, humming how she thought it might sound, which is its own little tragedy since she's rather tone deaf when it comes to singing. At least she has some memory of hearing it on the radio, that day on the freeway.

When she actually plays the first measure, quite slowly at first, and softly for the kids' sake, she experiences surprise.

Something about each note, each chord combination, wakens her imagination, causing her to think she is not really in her own home, but somewhere else.

Irritated by how she stumbles with these first measures, she falls back on her normal ritual when learning a new piece. She plays just the right hand's portion until her fingers get used to their job. Likewise, with her left hand. When she at last puts them together, she smiles, for the melody, chording, phrasing, and tempo are simply divine.

So divine, it transports Bibi miles away from her home, into another space, another era. A beautiful home, with ecru, powder-smooth walls and towering ceilings, and filled with elegant, witty people. Men debonair in their tuxedos, and women glamoured to the nines in sleek, shimmering, jewel-toned satin dresses. Laughter and ideas sparkle the air. "Darling" and "Dear" the guests call each other.

It all feels close and familiar to Bibi, and yet distant.

She goes on to the next measures, first learning the right hand, then the left, and then in unison. It suddenly occurs to her how lovely this moment is, if, for no other reason, than her family is not present to silence her. Michael isn't shushing her because he needs to hear Chick Hearn or Vin Scully explain how well the Lakers or Dodgers are playing. Nor do her children scream and hold their ears at the sound of her classical music.

More measures she learns, before coming to a lengthy cascade, a cadenza of notes that will require her fingers to run up and down the keys in circular spurts, until at last they reach the low, irritating notes.

Phrase by phrase she practices the cascade. Slowly at first, then faster and faster. Her eyes follow the notes in the book. She is practiced; no need to watch her fingers.

With each new playing of the cascade, new images emerge in her awareness. She is no longer in the home with the men in tuxedos and women in satin gowns. Now she is in France, she thinks, in a wonderful country home bearing the same high ceilings, but of rougher plaster. Oil portraits of every size hang on, no, climb up the walls like vines. It could be George Sand's home, and Chopin could be in the next room, composing music under the light of an amber crystal chandelier, perhaps imported from Italy.

To live in such a house. It seems her natural lot.

Yet here she is, with her real fate, living in a copycat tract house, in Huntington Beach, in Orange County, in a home with faux paneling and blotchy brown carpeting, spending her days teaching about gerunds and prepositions and spending her nights correcting essays written by fourteen-year-olds.

Where the hell did her life go wrong? How did she ever end up in this place, which to her senses, in this moment, has the look and smell of a sty?

She shuts the *Ballades* and centers the book on the piano's music shelf. Then, without an ounce of animosity in her heart, she puts the third Brandenburg Concerto record on the player, turns up the volume enough to pretty up the house some, and heads to the hall closet for a dust rag. There's no one else she can blame for the state of her house but herself.

§

October 3; Huntington Beach

The Santa Ana winds have returned this Saturday morning, and have blown the L.A. basin's heap of smog back out to sea, where it hangs offshore waiting to creep back in. The world outside Bibi's home sparkles like a spring day, except it's so damned hot and parched.

For Bibi, this Saturday morning could not be over soon enough. From the moment she awoke, to this very instant right now, which finds her pushing and pulling, pushing and pulling, the vacuum over her despicable brown and beige mottled carpet, thirteen times, fourteen times, fifteen times, Bibi has wanted the day's responsibilities behind her so she can focus what spare time she has on searching for Grace.

Nineteen. Twenty. Despite the fact that the carpet does a fabulous job of covering her kids' tracks, it's beyond hideous. No matter how hard she vacuums, it never looks pretty, or clean. Especially here in the kitchen's breakfast room. If they didn't own those apartments, and pay fourteen percent interest, she'd have enough money to buy a new carpet in forest green. That would really look lush with her oak furniture. But Michael thinks now's the time to amass real estate, like he pictures himself to be some land baron or something.

Sweat drips from the end of her nose. She blows at it so it might fly away. She hates these suddenly-hot, arid days. Hopefully things will cool down by midweek.

Twenty-seven. Twenty-eight. She's aware she's counting to her vacuum strokes, somehow finding comfort in its rhythm. Hey, she counts when she gets blood drawn, and when Michael's in a yelling mood. Counting keeps her from feeling trapped. She counts when she wants a cigarette, and when she's waiting in line, and when her father—.

Thirty-nine. Forty.

The carpet under the kitchen table, which the vacuum draws away from, is superimposed by the memory of her father coming into her room in the middle of the night and sitting by the side of her bed. Her room, on these nights, had seemed so dark, but when he entered and closed the door, the darkness seemed incapable of hiding her. She felt obvious, frozen in space, and trapped. She'd close her eyes to increase the darkness and counted; still, he could find her. She'd held her arms rigid against her body and on top of the covers to make it impossible for his hand to reach inside for her, and she'd count. And yet he succeeded.

The idle vacuum roars beside Bibi. "Aaaaagggg!" she hollers. Her eyes press closed against the visions, her face contorts in outrage, and her fists sock at the air around her. She wants to think of something else, but realizes she's always thought about this even if she were blind to it.

Like a dike broken, pent up waters flood her mind. Dark, taboo film clips unreel before her eyes, blinding her to her real surroundings. Each vivid, livid memory screams its details. His quiet, strong hand pulling down her covers and moving over her stomach until it reached the elastic of her pajama bottoms. Here it did not stop. Always he would tell her what he was doing was for her good and for her pleasure. She sees herself enduring this as a little girl, and then a bigger girl, and then a sixth grader, and ninth, and—.

How could she have forgotten?

She's ice cold and burning all at the same time. The air around her shudders and steps back.

Leaving the vacuum roaring in the spot where her memory emerged, she shuffles zombie-like to the top step leading down into the great room.

Resembling a bomb that's exploded, dust and debris from her past whirl and twirl in her mind. She covers her mouth with her hands to stifle her rage; at the same time, she remembers this is exactly what she did the many, many nights when her father entered her room.

She stares in disbelief, for her flaring memories continue to show her as a teenager, and as a toddler, and a frightened prepubescent nine-year-old.

She sees the time when she was maybe fifteen and had asked her mother to make her father stop. They were doing the dishes in the kitchen, and her mother's sole reaction was to hold one corner of the sopping dishrag in her fist and to fling it at Bibi in such a way that it slapped Bibi across the face. Bibi sees in her mind the exact, slow-motion mid-air curve the rag made as it left the gray dishwater and flew toward her like a hurled snake. She remembers watching the rag coming toward her, and holding herself steady so as not to be knocked off balance the moment it slapped across her mouth and its end curved to smack her left cheek. Bibi never said another word about it while they finished the dishes, or any time after that. It was as though none of it happened. She never talked about it. Never thought about it, because there was nothing for her to think. At least, that's what she thought when she was fifteen. And that's the way she lived her life.

Yet it seems impossible to her that she could have forgotten all this, though deep down she knows she's always remembered it. And always, like a good girl, she remembered to forget, or refused to remember. And now, like her treasure chest in her car's trunk, it is making itself known and forcing her to see what her psyche knows.

She turns off the vacuum.

She wants to talk.

She needs someone, besides herself, to know what is happening.

A historian.

Or a reporter.

Someone to help her make sense of this craziness, or, if need be, to tell her definitively that she is indeed nuts.

But the house is silent. Ceres is outside somewhere fighting the forces of evil. The kids are down the street at the Brownleys; they always take the kids on chemo days, for which Bibi is extraordinarily grateful. Michael's at the hospital, and she'll see him when she's done with her chores. Perhaps she can talk to Victor, or her mom, or Charlie. On second thought, no she can't. She could call some of her friends, but it's Saturday morning, and if she says something, they'll all want to come and comfort her. She has no time for that.

Oddly, it came to her to call the Tri-Adoption Agency she heard about from the librarian.

Instead of getting the brochure from her car's trunk, she gets their number from information.

"Good morning. Tri-Adoption," a sweet, but business-like woman's voice answers.

Without first preparing her thoughts into coherent sentences, Bibi blurts, "I'm looking for my birth mother. I just remembered I was sexually abused. A lot."

"Oh," the voice sounds unastonished. "That happens. You wouldn't believe how many adopted children are sexually abused."

Bibi's almost relieved. "It's normal?"

"It happens."

"Is there anyone I can talk to?"

"We have meetings. Groups. You can talk about it there. Do you have our brochure?"

"Out in the car."

"Look in the brochure. It lists our regular meeting dates."

"Okay." Bibi wonders how anyone could have time to attend Tri-Adoption meetings. "Thanks." She hangs up without saying another word to the woman. There's no way she's telling what's happened to her in front of a bunch of people. All those faces; all those imaginations. Every time they'd see her, they'd imagine her father on top of her. She even imagines herself a fly on the ceiling watching her father touching her and seeing all the ways she tried to cope with it. It makes her cringe.

Nope. This is her little secret.

Except she'll tell Michael. Won't he find that ironic since he thought he was marrying a virgin. Even her parents wanted her to be a virgin when she married. Which is sick, in retrospect. And she went right along with it. She persuaded herself and then her husband that she was a virgin. How in hell's name do you go through that many years, what was it? She thinks back as far as she can. Three years old? Four? Until she was a senior in high school. That many years of sexual abuse and still be able to say with a straight face that you are a virgin. But she guesses that's what happens to a lot of adopted girls. Maybe boys too. Like them, she's no man's child. No taboos against what people can do to you.

The phone rings. She turns to face it as if it were a front door peek hole and someone on the other side had been watching her the whole morning.

It rings again. She should answer it, but realizes how much she really doesn't want to talk with anyone who might expect her to have a normal conversation.

But it could be the neighbors. Or Michael. She answers.

"Mrs. Amato?" a man's voice asks.

She swallows. "Yes?"

"This is one of Michael's nurses. You need to come to the hospital. He's experiencing injection-site cellulitis. His chemo spilled outside his vein. He's in grave danger. You need to come now. He could die."

"D-d-die? From his chemo?" That's like dying from penicillin, but then she remembers that people do die from that.

And then it hits her. A picture of Michael dead and lifeless clogs her mind. She loses all physical sensation and feels like she's floating outside herself. "I'll be right there."

She abandons everything on the floor. Vacuum. Chairs pulled out. None of it matters.

Realizing her latent nightmares are on the verge of hurling themselves into her life, she rushes to the sink and wraps her fingers around its front rim, as though she's about to vomit. Then she screams her bloody head off in spasms of grief and protest. She wails and hollers for one, five, fifteen minutes, who knows?

And then she stops, turns around, grabs her keys, jumps in the car and drives to Hoag Hospital in Newport Beach. She knows she's a mess, but screw it. If he's going to die, she wants to be there, princess pretty or not.

§

September 3; Newport Beach, California

Before taking the elevator to Michael's room, Bibi stops at the entry to the chapel on the first floor, which, thank the Lord, is empty. She knows the hospital's done its best, but it still resembles a funeral home.

Everything in the chapel sits in neat rows. The six bleached-wood pews. The brochures for every denomination. The crosses and lit wax candles on the altar. The vases of freshly cut lilies. Even the Bible seems open to the book's exact middle. It all leaves Bibi with the feeling that everything is in order and that life happens in rows.

Which better not be true.

She nears the altar and feels suddenly within God's hearing distance. She's had a sordid relationship with Him all these years. This morning's epic flashback doesn't help. Come to think of it, in most of her youth, she had regularly prayed to God to make her father stop, but saw nothing for her efforts. After that, she pretty much sidelined God from her life. Who wouldn't?

This time, she decides to take the chance that God will hear her. She looks directly at the tasteful, gilded cross hanging above the altar and carefully grants it the power to transform her life. To it she begs, "Please let Michael live. His children and I need him. He wants to live and deserves to. Don't let the thing that's supposed to heal him kill him. That's unfair. You have to have mercy. You have to let him live." She looks up. "Please do everything you can think of and do to help him live. I don't know what that is. Just help him. Thank you."

It's all she can think of to say.

Otherwise, she's totally out of control.

§

Bibi stands over Michael, taking in his hospital room's medicinal and antiseptic scents and its dripping and beeping sounds. He lies on his side, tubes sticking out from all over. Ice packets blanket his inflamed hand and arm. His paleness makes it obvious he's used the ralph pan lodged between his chin and pillow. She chokes. Everything that had happened this morning vanishes from her attention, for there's nothing she can do to help Michael. Her helplessness gathers around her like goading spectators, but she defies them. She rests her left hand on his side and wills energy, or whatever it is, to flow through it and into Michael to aid in his healing, to add to his life. Three starry dots, mere specks, spark in the air, which Bibi notices, making her smile.

After minutes, she weaves herself between all the tubes and kisses Michael on his nose. "How are you?"

His weak groan carries at least some hope for Bibi. She studies him. He looks like hell. His scalp is red and blotchy, and his lips are caked white. His fresh blue hospital gown offers a happier facade. Still, he's alive.

The male nurse who had phoned Bibi at home enters the room, his brisk walk taking her aback. "Will" she reads on his name badge. Will, with the jaunty demeanor and the cool slicked back black hair, motions for Bibi to move aside. Which she does. With obvious confidence he inspects every piece of apparatus connected to Michael. "He's a pretty sick puppy, but his signs seem to be leveling."

Bibi allows the comfort of this fact to seep into her. She nods with concern.

Will then removes a note from his scrub's shirt pocket and hands it to Bibi. "Your neighbor called and said they've got your cat. It's been hurt."

"Hurt?" Her head swims. Her neck feels cold. "What do they mean hurt?" This must be a mistake. She feels her loyalties being divided.

Will eyes Bibi over his glasses, as if deciding how much she can handle. "They said you should come home. And there's a car parked on your lawn."

"On my lawn?" Bibi's muscles tighten. "When did they call?"

Will's nonchalance makes it seem messages like this are commonplace. "About ten minutes ago."

Bibi can't assemble all this information in one picture. She looks at the note Will gave her. It's got the Brownley's number. It says there's a car on her lawn and her cat's been hurt. These two facts could be related, but she doubts it. She doubts a lot of things in this moment, to be honest. Cripes, an hour ago she just remembered she'd been sexually abused most of her childhood and didn't know how she was going to tell Michael.

She forces herself to prioritize. She presses her thumb against her index finger. The kids are safe, she guesses. Pressing against her middle finger, Bibi also guesses Ceres'll be okay, but she feels horrible pains throbbing in her head, which makes her doubt her guessing. Her ring finger and thumb touch. The car on her lawn could be anything, but compared to the rest of the day, it's near the bottom of her list. Her thumb folds over her pinky finger. The only thing, the one singular priority for her, and why this should even be a question escapes her, is Michael. "I'm staying here until I know what's going on with Michael." She rubs her forehead in an effort to relieve the pains she feels.

Will straightens, inhales while studying the ceiling, then steadies his gaze on Bibi. "You can leave and come back. I think Michael's going to be okay. I'm keeping a very close eye on him. I have your phone numbers. Besides, the doctor won't get here until after lunch." A slight nod and an intentional rise of his eyebrows underscores how he hopes Bibi will read the truth behind his words.

Bibi thinks she understands what the nurse is telling her, even though he won't say it. He knows Michael shouldn't be her main priority in this moment. Bibi's mind counts. Her hands clutch the hospital bed's metal frame. She reaches into her purse for a stick of gum and unwraps it in a practiced set of movements. "Jesus." What to do? What to do? One. Two. Three. Bibi stares at Michael. Both his eyes are now partially open. His pupils seem steady, but what does she know. He licks his lips, then moves them. He's saying something to her.

She stoops close to hear him.

"Go home," he tells her slowly. He sounds like he's on his death bed, but she realizes it's because he talked on his inhale. He smells of soap and rubbing alcohol, and whiskey, which she guesses is the Interferon. He smiles weakly, or maybe he's just pursing his lips. She can't tell.

Bibi stands upright. All around him tubes hanging from above drip and ping. Michael can't know how bad off he is. He's just being brave. She won't leave him. She'd never forgive herself if she went back home and he died.

But then the poem voice speaks in her ear, clear as a starlit night. "He'll be alright. He'll be fine. Go. You're needed. And then come back."

The voice sounds irresistibly true and logical, as though it knows the order in which everything should take place. Go home, fix things, come back.

She hikes her purse on her shoulder, and gives him one more good-bye kiss on the lips. She looks at him to memorize the moment, in case it's her last, but she knows it's not. "I'll be back. Hopefully in an hour or two." She smiles her worry at Will and turns to leave the room.

On her way down the hall to the elevator, she asks in her head, "Who are you?"

"Anna."

"Anna?"

"Yes, Anna."

Ten

There was Never Nothing

October 3; Huntington Beach

When Bibi's car is three houses down the street from her home, she spots the car Will spoke of, a red pick-up truck parked diagonally in the middle of her lawn. Her mind scrambles for people she knows who own red pick-ups and for why they'd have the audacity to park on her lawn when there's plenty of curb space

When she is two houses away from her home, she reads the tattered "Carter-Mondale" and "Stop Oil" bumpers on the truck's rear bumper and realizes it belongs to Victor. How dare he do this to her!

When she is in front of her next-door neighbor's house and about to turn right into her driveway, she sees what she thinks are Ceres's gray fur fluffs strewn hither and thither on her driveway like the remnants of a bird fight. She gasps. Bloody anger and worry thrash in her veins. She brakes her car just as it enters her driveway.

Once out of her car, it takes her less than a second to recognize Ceres's wispy, gray fluff with some white mixed in. The absence of shafts tells her she's not looking at feathers. But she also sees no blood.

She spins around, looking for witnesses. Seeing none, she squats to look under the truck to make sure Ceres isn't there, but remembers the Brownleys have her kitty, or at least that's what she thinks she remembers.

Wasting not another moment. she rushes up her front steps, because she assumes Victor's gotten into her house through her front door. Except she finds it locked, and has to go back to her car for her keys and purse.

With caution, she lets herself in. No telling what will confront her.

The first thing she notices is how dark and cool her home seems compared to outside. Then she focuses. Her home's interior is a wreck, and not just because she left it that way. The family room sofa that usually abuts the wall facing the television, is in the middle of the room. The matching settee is near the kitchen, and she'll have to climb over it to get to the sink, which for some reason is running. All the Haight-Ashbury concert prints hang askew on the wall, and her favorite lamps she and Michael made from glass battery cells lie on their sides on the floor. All the lights in the great room are on, and the refrigerator door stands fully open.

Then the silence hits Bibi. Except for the running tap, she hears nothing. Stillness has a leash on her home. She sees Victor's wake, but, from where she stands in her entry, she does not see Victor.

Since the door to the garage stands ajar, she opens it further to better see. The light is on, revealing the garage's far wall; what she notices makes her physically ill. The door leading from the garage to the outside stands wide open; crisp, brown leaves from outside have blown in and lie randomly on the entry mat. She could kick herself. With all her wisdom, she had stupidly left the side door to the garage unlocked. All Victor had to do was walk right into her house.

Her cheeks burn. How could she have been that stupid! Gad, this day.

She steps down into the garage. It looks like a tornado's skipped through it. Most of the camping gear Michael neatly arranged in the rafters lies on the garage floor, opened, as do his cigarette cases. The fishing rods are strewn all over the floor and the tackle boxes upturned. A pristine dune of spilled Tide laundry detergent rises where its box fell. The blue Coleman cooler rests atop Michael's car, and Bibi notices a small dent in the metal where it had landed. Bibi guesses Victor was looking for the box her mother had given her. Funny he should look there.

A wave of gratitude flows through Bibi, for fortune has it her treasure chest is still in Lars O'Leary's trunk. On a day like this, a small handful of luck seems more like a bushel. She looks for the lights, but doesn't see them.

Back in the house, Bibi heads to the kitchen to close the fridge and turn off the tap. On her way, she yells, "Victor, where are you? Answer me! I don't have time for this."

It doesn't take long for her to spot him in the great room, way down by the piano.

Bibi rushes toward him. Cigarette fumes linger in the air, agitating Bibi further. The closer she gets to Victor, the more she realizes he's at it again. Doing his familiar shtick. What's hers is his. He's pulling out music she guesses he's planning to take home with him, including her new *Ballades* book. He's already started several neat little piles of record albums, books, and pictures, which he's placed on her fireplace's hearth.

"What are you doing?" She starts picking up the stacks to reclaim what is hers, but throws them back down on the hearth, because that's not what's important here. Forcing herself into his space, she grabs the sheet music out of his hands. "You ran over my cat. You need to leave now!"

He rises up, and seems taller than she's used to. He wears two shirts and a sweater, as if unaffected by today's weather. His hair's a tangled mess, on the verge of becoming dread locks. He yells back at her, "I want the information Mom gave you."

Bibi wavers, but remains rooted in her spot. "You ran over my cat. You noticed, right?"

Victor's glare bores into and past her as if he's trying to figure out what she means. A question rises in his eyes and stays long enough for Bibi to realize he may not know what he's done.

"My cat! You didn't see? How could you not notice? Her fur's still on the driveway."

Victor looks incredulous. He shakes his head. Then his face reddens and he demands, "Where are the papers? You're a horrible liar, you know. Where are they?"

It's true what he says. Her face always reveals too much. Her skin reddens. Her eyebrows attest to her every thought. Besides, she doesn't want to lie. But she doesn't want to give him the information either, especially now that she's got it all arranged the way she wants it and knows the meaning of the contents. If she gives it to him, she'll never see any of it again. The worry that her car's trunk might not be locked crosses her mind. Then another issue pops up: her mother may not have told Bibi that she'd talked to Victor. Surely her mother would tell her if she told Victor; she wouldn't just leave Bibi hanging out like that. Or maybe she would. Bibi modulates her voice and wills her face to lie. "Mom's got them. Didn't she tell you that when you called?"

"I don't believe her."

At least her mother's not making this difficult for her. Bibi makes a show of looking around at the mess he's made. Sofa cushions everywhere. All their stereo albums strewn about the floor. Her black, silk embroidered Spanish shawl Bibi drapes over the piano lies in a puddle on the floor, along with the candlesticks that got knocked off. And that's just this end of the great room. What a friggin' son-of-a-bitch. A corner of her mind calculates what it will take to clean all this up before Michael gets home. "Tell me, did you find what you're looking for?"

He stops. His eyes jitter, as though he's trying to follow frantic thoughts. Finally, he says, "No." He steps over the pile of her piano music that he's made and looks at her piano in disdain. A simple reminder to her that he's still pissed as hell because their parents gave her the piano and not him, forgetting of course that when they gave it to her, he was living in a tree house.

And that's when she notices burn lines on her ebony piano's right shelf, on its music rack, and on the ivory keys! Burn lines caused by lit cigarettes left to smolder on its surface. Not superficial burns that can be rubbed out, but burns that have hollowed out shallow trenches, at least on the wood. And not just a few lines. She turns away in her refusal to count.

Her fists tighten. She looks for something to throw at him, but realizes she'd be wrecking her own things. She hates the snickering sneer pinching through his anger at her. How dare he do this to his piano, rather to her piano. Her mental slip does not escape her, and, in fact, distracts her from her anger like puzzles do. It should have been his piano; it was always going to him. But somehow a war over it broke out, and he lost that war. And she won it without even trying. Now she's paying the price for that. This war needs to end, that she knows.

Then she sees them. The dots. The sparks. The helpers. Just a couple of them. But enough. Yes, this war needs to end.

In her mind she assumes the high road, poised and pleasant. "Vic, you need to leave now, because I have to find my cat that you ran over, even if accidentally. I have to get back to the hospital because Michael almost died this morning. His chemo spilled out of his vein. He's reacted horribly. I mean chemo is meant to kill cells. You get the picture, I hope. I had to leave his side because of you. I don't know if he'll be alive when I get back to the hospital."

The whole impossibility of what Victor has caused stuns her. She realizes how desperately she wants to tell him about what she remembered this morning, and to ask him if he remembers anything too. But she can't or won't. She needs to get back to Michael. This is a travesty. Tears well in her eyes, and she bites her lips to keep from crying.

Victor's eyes slam shut. He covers his ears with his huge hands.

But Bibi keeps on. "Victor, I don't need this. I'm sorry for what you're going through. I don't know how to help you without hurting myself. You have to leave now."

Suddenly, his shoulders tighten, his back straightens and sprouts invisible hackles, and his cheeks and ears rage red. "No, not 'til I find it."

She backs away and maneuvers herself so a chair protects her from him. "Please," she says softly, reflecting how tortured but certain she feels in this moment, "you need to leave. There's nothing to find here."

He stares at her as though he were doubting what he was seeing. Then he looks toward the opened front door and walks toward it and her kitchen. "I know you have it," he mutters back to her. "I'm going to keep after you until you give it to me."

She points to the door and whispers, "Go."

When Victor reaches the top step, he suddenly turns back to her. He seems softer, his eyes glassy. He runs one hand through his hair, but his curls resiliently return to where they'd been. "Don't you ever think you're someone different from what you show the world? Don't you ever think you're something you're too afraid to admit to? And don't you remember things you won't allow yourself to remember?"

All this freezes the moment. Every question he asks begs her to nod, because it applies to her, even though he's making it sound as if it only applies to him. Of course, she is not who she shows the world. With her art, with her sense that she's really somebody else, with the voices she hears in her head but tries to ignore, with the lights she saw dancing in the garage and here in the great room, with her constant subterranean feeling that she is supposed to be something entirely different from who she is, and with thoughts of her father. "Yes, a lot."

He looks at her quizzically. "It's that gypsy witch in you, isn't it? Oh, you try to be really normal, really responsible, all that. But I know you. I remember you before you got married, when you were still in college. I know how quirky, off-the-wall crazy you can be. Why'd you stop painting? Why'd you stop thinking? You used to be the most unpredictable thinker in the house. All my friends loved you and thought I was lucky to have a sister like you, and I knew they were right. Where'd you go? I've lost you. I need you to be you."

Bibi's mind races. She knows what he's talking about, but can barely remember being like that. She was as he described when she didn't have parents around telling her how to be. The sorority bohemian. The painter. The occultist. The sexual abuse denier. Now look at her.

Suddenly Victor clutches his head in his hands, his fingers gripping so tightly, they practically claw into his skin. Then he looks up. The fierce redness has returned to his face. He directs his index finger in her direction. "You can see who I am. Admit it. You can see who I should be."

Bibi mentally sees him in a great hall, with a piano, a patent-leather black Steinway. She sees him with an orchestra to conduct, playing, writing, composing. Being great. Being lavish. She smiles. She does know who he should be.

"Damn it, don't laugh at me! If you can see who I am, why don't you explain me to others? Why don't you tell Mom and Dad? Why won't you do that for me? And why won't you remember when we saw her?"

Bibi doesn't know what he's talking about. Or she's not sure. Who is *her*? She needs time to think. "Go home. I'll call you. I have to take care of Ceres. I have to! I promise I'll call."

With his fist he bangs the kitchen table; everything on it jumps and jangles. Then he storms toward the front door and pauses long enough to say, "It's like you want me dead," before bolting out of her house.

Bibi scurries to follow him to make sure he really leaves. He disappears down her brick pathway toward the lawn, walking right past and ignoring Brandi Brownley who is walking up her driveway cradling the box holding Ceres.

Ella and Noah tag behind her; heartbroken tears streak their faces.

"Uncle Victor, you ran over Ceres," Ella bawls.

The sight is too much for Bibi. Hell, this day is too much. Gasping, she rushes out to Brandi and her kids, takes the box and motions for them to get into her car's back seat. She resists her impulse to pick up a rock rimming the flower bed at her feet and throw it at her brother. But she does not resist her impulse to peek at Ceres. "Dear God," she moans.

Victor pauses next to his truck's open door and watches the children. His color changes from yellow to almost white making his hair appear devilishly dark. Mist shrouds his eyes. Then he gets into the car and drives over the next-door neighbor's lawn and plants and skids off down the road.

She watches him drive off until the word Toyota is no longer legible.

She's got to be strong and get her kitty the help it needs and then go see Michael, and then make sure the kids are okay, because there they are in the back seat of her car weeping over the family kitty, freshly run over by their uncle.

§

At the vet's, Bibi sits in the middle of the turquoise Naugahyde bench with the box holding Ceres perched on her lap. Surrounding her are her two kids and their favorite sitter Brandi. The waiting room's yellow walls blare cheeriness. Bibi puts on her sunglasses. Her nose twitches from the vet's medical and grooming potions that saturate the air. Gad, how her heart hurts.

Ceres breathes loudly and laboriously. One of her eyes rests on her cheek, and many teeth appear missing. Most of her body is intact, because her great misfortune was not getting her head out of the way in time.

She's been such a precious, fluffy, little kitty, providing the family with tons of laughter because of her talent for falling out of trees and sliding off table tops. Her little white fur heart on her chest marks right where her heart is. Bibi loves her so much. She's even loved the smell of her cat food because it was hers.

Not really, of course. Ceres, who'd sit in a ball in the sink in the summer to keep herself cool. Who loves toilet water, sleeping on Bibi's kids' toes at night, and chasing her tail, which she predictably forgets is hers.

"Mommy, is she going to die?" Ella wails. She looks like she's been crying for hours. Little Ella, her baby who hates departures and has always taken them badly, cries her heart out, because it's the saddest moment in her life. Even sadder than the time she shampooed her beloved goldfish twins to death. Honestly, that about crushed tender Ella to bits.

Bibi nods, knowing this will just start her floodgates again.

"Like daddy?"

Bibi's heart gasps. She shakes her head hard and remembers praying to God. "No! Not like daddy. Daddy's getting well."

Noah's lower lip quivers, like it always does when she sings her little "Mommy Loves You, Daddy Loves You" song to him. He can be mournful sometimes when he thinks of his father, as though he already knows something sad's going to happen.

"No! Daddy's at the hospital getting well. He'll be home on Tuesday. He's just sick. He's not dying."

They both start crying.

Bibi looks up and sees, as if for the first time, that other people are sitting in the waiting room with their Pomeranians and Persians, and that the veterinarian's assistant, probably a young college girl, clad in a swimming-pool-blue smock, is walking toward her.

"Would you like me to take the box?"

"No. No, I'll carry it. I think we're going to have to put her, you know. . ." Bibi looks to the girl to intuit her next word, rather than say it around the children.

The girl studies Ceres a moment and then looks up at Bibi. Sorrow bleeds from every pour of the girl's face.

"You want to be with her when the doctor examines her?"

"Yes, please. It's the very least I can do." Bibi doesn't know how much longer she can hold back her tears. She bites her lips and opens her eyes wide. When she rises and walks toward the door, Brandi leads the kids out into the parking lot. Ella screams and weeps, and Noah, now stone faced, watches his mother carry the box of kitty to its death.

"It's okay," she whispers to them, before she has to set the box on the bench because she can't walk and weep at the same time.

At last, Bibi is led into a little gray room, where she places the box atop a stainless-steel table. The vet comes in, carrying his equipment in his hands and his concern on his face. Even though he's only been taking care of Ceres for maybe a year, he must somehow feel attached to her. "I'm so sorry," he tells Bibi.

He turns his back to her, and she knows he's filling the vial with a lethal dose. Before turning back around, Bibi watches him look up and sigh, as if asking God why or asking Him forgiveness. Then he turns back around and positions the needle in Ceres's front leg. She jerks slightly. He looks into Bibi's eyes. "Ready?"

Bibi can't speak. All the love, anguish, and sorrow of this moment lodge in her heart and throat. She nods and feels her composure completely fall apart. "I'm sorry, Ceres. I'm so, so sorry. I have loved you all your life. I'm so sad. I'm so sorry. I love you, little Ceres. I love you, little one." And then she watches her little dream kitty draw in her last breath.

Life, it's so fragile.

§

Yes, I know. Life is fragile.

Because of that, it must be given all the hope that's possible.

"Go out to your children," I tell Bibi. "They need you."

I know her human reaction is to sit here in the veterinarian's office and wallow in her misery. But she's actually making her misery worse. I can see it in her aura. She's feeling powerless. She remembers going into the chapel and asking God to keep Michael alive. The way her mind works, she'll eventually decide God chose to substitute Ceres for Michael.

This is not good. You know what I've said about decisions. In their own way, they materialize. Just like her decision that whatever is hers is Victor's. It seems innocuous.

I repeat, "Go out to your children. Now!"

She wipes her eyes and blows her nose with the Kleenex the staff left in the room. Then she stands and starts to open the door.

Her gray aura reminds me of Grace's on that November day when she walked her children into the ocean.

Bibi won't do that, I'm sure. But Bibi feels the same helplessness, the feeling nothing will change.

"What do you want?" I ask her. I repeat this several times, for answering this question is one of the most healing activities a person can perform.

She looks sideways at the right-hand wall. Pink hues dapple her energy. Her eyes seem brighter. But then they shut down again and the pink disappears.

"What do you want?"

Again, she looks sideways at the wall.

I can see that Bibi longs to think about what she wants, and yet she's afraid to do so. That's because she's protecting herself from the disappointment of not having what she wants.

Therefore, it should surprise no one when her energy materializes into disappointment.

"Go ahead," I tell her. "What do you want? See it."

For a moment she actually does. She sees Michael's health returning. And she sees Victor leaving her alone. And she sees herself finding her birth mother, but not ruining her family or herself. Then her children, sitting out in the car, appear in her mind. She gathers her things, pays the bill at the counter, and joins her children and drives them to Brandi's home, before driving herself to see Michael in the hospital.

§

September 3; Newport Beach

Bibi doesn't see Will anywhere. Maybe his shift has ended. She didn't get to see the doctor either because of Victor. The charts, the dripping tubes, the pinging monitors, the position of the late afternoon sun—they tell her nothing about Michael's state. Nor does Michael's own mien.

She kisses his nose, half hoping it'll wake him, something she rarely wants to do.

He opens his eyes slightly, and smiles weakly. "You look like a wreck."

That's because she is a wreck, thinks Bibi. If only she could tell him everything. Instead, she jokes, "So do you." She immediately regrets saying this. It presumes he's okay. "I'm sorry. How're you doing? Have you seen your nurse?"

His eyes lose focus, and then stabilize. "The cat?"

Bibi braces herself in an effort not to cry. She grips her lips together. She'll talk in a minute, when she's ready.

His ice-packed hand reaches for her, and she tucks her fingers in his and looks at the ceiling. When she's ready, she looks

Michael in the eyes and tells him, "She was too far gone. I had her put to sleep."

He shuts his eyes. Tears rim their edges. He purses his lips to hold in his sadness. She knows how much he'll miss Ceres. The kitty loved to ride on his shoulders and always tinkled on the lawn after he mowed it.

Then he opens his eyes; their redness speaks volumes. "How'd the kids take it?" He watches her.

"Badly. How else can it be taken?"

He focuses on the wall behind her. "And the car?"

"Car?"

"On the lawn."

He heard Will talk about that? Damn. "It was Victor."

"Your brother?" Michael glares at Bibi, suddenly full of life. "Was he sitting in his truck waiting for you? Asshole."

She inhales. Michael needs to recuperate; upsetting him will hinder that. There's so much he should know about her morning, but now's not the time. Tomorrow maybe. She weighs what to tell him. A big lie with a little truth, or truth with a little lie. "No, he was in the house."

Michael frowns. "How'd he get in?"

"He let himself in. He came in through the garage."

Michael frowns more deeply and his lips flinch, and then his eyes close.

Bibi's grateful he's going back to sleep, given that she'd have to think up some excuse for why the garage side door was unlocked. Sleep is the best that can happen for him now. He shouldn't be bothered with this family crap, not with all he's having to brave. She scans his charts at the end of the bed, trying to dissect what they mean. She inspects the bottles' contents, and tidies the spaghetti of tubes entering his arms, hands, and chest.

Facing his back, she draws his sheets higher to shield his shoulders from the hospital's chill.

Can he tell she hasn't told the whole truth? She hates lying to him. It's bad girl stuff. And she yearns to be a good girl. Good girls stay. Bad girls get punished and given away. But if she tells him the truth, that she's looking for her birth mother, or that her brother destroyed the inside of her home and killed their cat, she'll feel like a good girl who'll also be given away. All the lies she tells. All the lies she's told. My name is Bibi. Lie. This is my mother. Lie. I am a virgin. Lie. My father is the one who always took the best care of me. Lie. She's been taught to lie and rewarded for a job well done. Victor, on the other hand, refuses to lie. And look at him.

Michael's breathing deepens. She misses him at home. She hates these sessions because she gets used to living without him. Sadness moans inside her. She needs Michael well. She puts her hands flat on his back and wills healing energy into his system. Her hands throb and fizz. She sees dots of light in the air, and she smiles. She isn't alone. They're with her!

Michael opens his eyes suddenly, and turns his head toward her. "Give the shoe box to Victor. He'll never find her anyway. There are finders and there are lookers. Your brother's a looker. Think about it. He never finds anything he's looking for."

She walks around the bed to face him. He can't be right. There has to be something Victor has looked for and found. But she can't think of one. "You want me to just give him the papers?"

"Look by the fishing rods and stuff, in the garage. That's where I hid it."

Bibi steadies her face while thinking about the damage Victor did to their garage. "I'll look there. But what do we tell my mom?"

"Tell her the truth. Say what Victor did."

Well, there's a thought.

"And, Bibi, if you don't tell her, I will. I don't want him breaking into our home. I'm concerned about the kids and you. You don't do things like that to people who have children in the house. Cocksucker."

In a way, she's relieved. It's a pain keeping the papers from Victor. And yet, she doesn't want to give the letters away, either, for it is because of them that she's learning about and learning to love her birth mother.

Michael shuts his eyes. His breathing has settled. "Just promise me you won't try to find her."

An unfamiliar jolt strikes her. She wants to tell Michael the truth, but he needs to sleep. "Okay."

And the truth?

Bibi suddenly realizes that she wants to be the one who finds her birth mother. She wants to feel the thrill of victory. How many times in her life has she held herself back, to make it possible for Victor to appear the, well, the victor? Because he didn't complete college, what did she do? She didn't go to either of her college graduations. There's nothing to celebrate when it makes someone she loves feel miserable or makes her feel guilty. Still, she wants to win.

§

I follow Bibi as she moves down the hospital corridor, away from Michael and the promise she gave him, and toward the waiting room, with its lush view of Newport Harbor and the Pacific Ocean. Hot, bristling energy sparks and flares from her head and torso. At the same time a humiliated gray fog clings to her surface.

She dons her sunglasses and stands at the window to face the ocean. I hear counting inside her mind. And hopeless thoughts. I listen. "I never—. I can't—. " On and on her thoughts twirl around and around, never finding an off ramp.

I watch how these thoughts ignite hormones which in turn ignite physical responses in her. Her heart beat races. Her skin tightens. The taste inside her mouth becomes more acidic. Her stomach churns. She feels more alive and wants to sustain the feeling, as though it were a high. But she also hates the pain she feels.

"What do you want?" I ask her, hoping she'll hear me. "What will make you happy?"

I know she hears my second question, because for a mere second she imagines the joy of finding her birth mother. Pink and purple tinge her aura. But her mind slams down on this thought with guillotine speed.

Bibi's mind gallops in circles. "No one will let me. My family will hate me. It'll kill my brother. I'm a stupid girl." The pink vanishes, and the hot sparks return.

"Tell Michael the truth," I tell her. "Tell the truth. Lies always create more pain, ultimately. Always."

Bibi's breathing picks up. Her hands turn clammy. She knows I'm right, but doesn't believe me. Telling the truth, she knows, can create such trouble. She'll be yelled at, hated, mistrusted. Abandoned.

No, she decides, it's better to be allowed to stay and be in pain, than to experience abandonment. And death.

Eleven

Time is Not Itself

October 3; Huntington Beach

Bibi nervously flips on the kitchen light and answers the phone. She'd fallen asleep on the family room sofa, and the phone's ringing alarmed her.

The mahogany paneling behind the kitchen wall phone, with its haunting knots and threads, glares at Bibi, adding terror to the batter of misery and rage churning in her stomach. The voice on the other end of the telephone line could be her mother. The distinct pitch. The slow, controlled cadence, as if there is all the time in the world. And the purposeful silences that create the expectation of agreement and obeisance. Yes, the voice sounds just like Mrs. Andressen, except that it's Phoebe, Victor's wife.

Bibi turns her back to the wall and finds refuge in the visual disaster that her kitchen table is since her brother's visit. Torn sheet music. The Tri-Adoption pamphlet, which Victor must have noticed. An ashtray with a half-burnt butt smashed in the center. At least it had another purpose than ruining her piano. Cripes what a day. Bibi closes her eyes and resists lighting the butts. One. Two. Three. Four.

"Of course, Victor apologizes," Phoebe says. "How is Ceres? We hope she's getting patched up. Can we help with the vet bill?"

Bibi's chin slackens, as though the pin holding her head erect suddenly popped out. Images of little Ceres batting plush-stuffed mice across the kitchen floor slide through her mind. She holds the phone a foot from her ear to silence Phoebe's words and to hide her despair. Finally, she manages, "I had her put down."

"Oh, I am so sorry. So very sorry. Please tell me what it cost."

Phoebe's words jolt Bibi out of her sadness. The mess she came home to glares at her. "How about sending a cleaning crew to put my house back together again? My house is a wreck." Bibi hears the knife sharpness of her words, but feels no shame.

A studied silence precedes Phoebe's response. "Bibi, we are very sorry."

"Shouldn't he be apologizing, and not you?"

"Victor's having a very hard time. I hope you understand."

"This is hard for both of us."

"No, I mean he is having a very, difficult, difficult time. What you told him the other day, I think did more damage than you know."

Bibi pushes her mind to remember this morning, but all that comes is a mishmash of Ceres dying, Michael almost doing the same, memories of her father in her bedroom, Michael's mother coming by around dinner time and picking up the kids for an overnighter (thank God!) and wondering why their house was a total wreck, and Victor trying to steal her stuff and practically destroying her house. But then she remembers the moment when she was in her principal's office and decided to tell Victor about their near drowning. She meant it to punish him, which he deserved, at the moment.

But now she's not sure that was a great idea.

"You mean about the—." Bibi pauses, not sure if there are better words she can use. She turns from the distraction that is her kitchen to face the phone and the wall. "The drowning." She studies the paneling's faux knots contorting into screaming mouths and humiliated, wailing eyes. Cripes, she never meant that to be a cliff for Victor to jump off.

"Yesterday he didn't get out of bed all day. He missed practice. He wouldn't talk to me or anyone. I finally got the shrink to come over last night. He ended up going in the back room and hypnotizing Victor for what seemed a long time. When he relived the drowning, memories came back. Sure enough, Victor discovered how close to death he had been. He'd swallowed water. Someone got him to shore and pumped water out of his lungs. He remembered you touching him and calling his name. Re-experiencing that is one thing, I believe, that has sent him over the edge."

"One thing?"

"He also remembered when he was maybe eleven, when you and he were in the living room, and you both saw your birth mother sitting in her car staring up at both of you, while you stared back at her. He remembers running out the front door and racing down the steps to the driveway. He thought she'd come to pick you both up, and that you would be right behind him. He wanted to get in her car, but she'd driven away by the time he got to the driveway. He never saw her again. He thinks you refuse to remember this, but he knows you know."

Visions of these events frizz in Bibi's mind like *Twilight Zone* episodes. "I don't remember either of these things. You'd think I would, though." But Bibi wonders if that's even true, given her morning. The thought of dragging up old memories frightens her. She has no idea what to do with the memories she's already uncovered.

"Bibi, it all made him so angry. So very, very angry. But—."

Overwhelmed, Bibi doesn't know if it's Phoebe's exact words, or her tone, or that whole problem where Bibi experiences her brother's pain, but Bibi's insides are a jumbled mess, like tennis shoes and butcher knives tumbling in a dryer together. Carefully, she asks, "But what?"

"But late this afternoon, after he'd come home from your house, we were taking a nap. Something woke me. I discovered Victor was not in our bed. I searched the house for him, and even the outside. I finally found him again in the garage, sitting in the car with the engine running."

"Oh, Jesus!" Bibi's posture lets go. She slumps into the nearest chair. Her brother's face, in all the many forms she's known it throughout her life, appear in her mind, smiling from tricycles, standing atop the playground jungle gym, being whipped with a clothes hanger, and playing in the bathtub. Dear God, what has she done! This is impossible. This cannot have happened.

"I caught him early when I opened up the garage door. His keys are hidden now. He's out on the patio now. He's a wreck."

For a split second, Bibi feels relief that her brother is alive, but then her mind spins, and she imagines her brother, probably more terrified than distraught. Throughout her life, when things got really tough, she has watched him enter this trapped space where he became wild, like a fiend, and then dejected, and finally whimpering his acceptance of death. Bibi has saved him from these moments, in her own little ways. Fighting his tormentors, whether at home or on the playground. Taking blame for his actions. Belittling herself to enhance him. These moments swirl in her memory, uncatalogued and unsorted.

"Look, Bibi, Victor needs to find this woman. You must get the information and give it to him."

It would be easy for Bibi to just say, sure, come on down and get the box, and just hand her treasure chest over to her brother and his wife. But then it would be bye-bye letters. Shoot, she hasn't even finished reading them yet. No, she won't just hand them over. But she may figure out a way to make it up to Victor. "Have you talked with my mother? I mean, it's her choice whether to let Victor see the information."

"No. I haven't talked with her."

"Why don't you ask her for the stuff?" As soon as Bibi asks this, she regrets it. Better to lie low.

Phoebe chuckles. She knows what Bibi's talking about. "I've tried. Every time I've asked, Signe insists it will only break the family apart."

"Hmmm." Bibi searches for something better to say that would not also get her into further trouble, but nothing comes to her.

Then, like a hidden shotgun cocked and suddenly aimed at Bibi, Phoebe clears her throat, just like Bibi's mother does, to signal her final argument and to alert Bibi that she better acquiesce or something horrible from out of the blue is going to arrive in her life that will force her to regret her choice. Slowly Phoebe states, "Victor must find his birth mother. You are the only one who stands in his way because you know that if you ask your mother, she will give the information to you."

Bibi tries to protest, but Phoebe continues to talk over her.

"I really don't want to have to tell you this, but something peculiar is happening to our marriage. No. I take that back. This whole ordeal of finding his birth mother is destroying our marriage. Destroying it. This is the price of your stubbornness. Apparently, you want to keep your family together, but you don't care about mine. You understand that is how it appears, don't you? The very least you can do for your brother is to help him. The very least. We don't want him killing himself."

Bibi turns her back to the wall and its judgmental faces screaming accusations at her. She holds the phone at arm's length away from her face, protecting herself from Phoebe's untrue and manipulative accusations. But realizes her silence might convey consent. "Phoebe, this is not my fault."

"I understand how you can think that."

"Look, I don't know what I can do. That's all I can say. I can't promise you anything."

"I'm taking that as a yes."

"I didn't say yes."

"You didn't say no."

Realizing she has somehow successfully paved the way to give Victor what he wants, she blurts, "Would you do one thing for me, though? Tell my brother to call me and apologize for what he did."

"Please accept our apologies."

"No. I want his."

"And he wants the information."

Bibi smiles and hangs up the phone after saying good-bye. Despite how upsetting this conversation with Phoebe has been, she realizes that she is in a very good space. All she has to do is copy the letters and give them to him. The best of both worlds.

§

If you've ever driven a car a hundred miles an hour, and then suddenly slowed to sixty, it feels like you've completely stopped the car.

That is how Bibi feels in this moment, her hundred-mile-an-hour life suddenly slowed to sixty, sitting at her kitchen table, her home reasonably reassembled, her mug of freshly nuked coffee resting to her left, and her treasure chest set before her. She guesses it's around ten, but doesn't bother to check.

Thank God the kids are at Michael's mother's. What astounding luck! Bibi's swears she would have died an early death if it were not for Judith, her children's favorite grandmother, and the best substitute mother a daughter-in-law could ever have. Judith's the one who understands and loves kids. She's the one who mothered Bibi and taught her to cook, sew, and take care of the kids. Bibi's own mother never had a baby, and therefore could advise her on nothing. In fact, her mother had never seen an umbilical cord. She wanted Bibi to save Ella's in a bag so she could see it. Bibi had taken great delight in watching her mother open the bag and thoroughly inspect what eventually looked like a dried-up dog turd.

Bibi sips her coffee and savors its rich aftertaste.

She shouldn't be thinking these things about her mother. After all, she is lucky to have been adopted. She has students who should be as lucky as she. But they're not. They live their lives in one foster care home and then another.

The faces of those students stream through her awareness. She rarely thinks about their actual circumstances once they leave her classroom. It never occurs to her to wonder what happens to those kids, the girls especially, once the lights are out. She can't imagine what it would be like growing up without any siblings of your own, without anyone who really cares about your needs, basic or otherwise. Her own mother wasn't the most caring person, but her mother did care. There's a difference. And her father, he was incredibly caring compared to her mother, which she realizes makes a very weird equation.

She looks around for Ceres, for, with the kids gone, this would be the perfect time to hold her on her lap, massage her ears and the bridge of her nose, and listen to her purring's rhythmic cadences. But then she remembers there is no Ceres. Her eyes mist and then her intolerable weeping begins, while her vacant home throbs with silence. And possibility.

§

When Bibi's weepiness subsides, and she's blown her nose so many times it's parched, she tentatively focuses on the shoe-box treasure chest sitting before her on the kitchen table.

She snuffs and sniffs, and studies the box, and swears that it has suddenly sprung to life, emitting just enough of an aura for Bibi to imagine it wants her attention, if that is indeed what is happening here. She wipes the remaining moisture from the corners of her eyes, and pulls the box close to her.

The lid she opens, but drops back in place, as though not ready for any of this.

She gets out of her chair, walks to the fridge, back to the table, and back to the sink. The clock on the stove says it's ten-thirty. She shakes out her fingers. Resentment burbles beneath her surface. It's not fair that she has to give the information to her brother, just because Michael doesn't want Victor threatening her family anymore. He should get the copies instead. Besides, the only reason Michael wants her to give Victor the box is because Victor was a bad boy. Victor killed their cat, he vandalized their home, and he endangered their kids. Therefore, let's give Victor what he wants.

It's like when her mother wanted Bibi to buy her sofa bed from her for three hundred dollars, and when she didn't buy it, her mother gave it to Victor for free because he didn't have a job. That's fairness in this family: reward Victor for bad behavior.

God, she wants a cigarette. The refrigerator beckons her, but she counts to fifteen instead.

By the time she gets to thirteen in her abstinence count, she notices her treasure chest seems a glimmer brighter.

When she touches its lid, energy pulses from it and into her fingers, as though an idling engine were hidden inside. Its aura rouges slightly, and the six dots appear to dance in the air above it.

She draws back her hand. She must be imagining things.

While her eyes remain fixated on the box, her mind continues to scheme. If she waits until Monday, she can get to school early and Xerox everything. Except she wanted to go to Dalton's Bookstore to buy that *Adoption Triangle* book, or, what was it called? *Lost and Found*?

Or go to Dalton's after the hospital tomorrow, and she can make copies at the library after school, even though it will cost money. Then she can give him the copies, and she'll keep the originals, because originals are important.

She hears the phone ring once, but when she watches it and waits for it to ring again, she realizes it never rang in the first place. She shakes her head to clear it. The phone on the wall, she notices, appears to pulse, which she knows is impossible. Maybe she should get some sleep and start in on all of this first thing in the morning.

Instead, she imagines Victor getting the information. The mere vision of this relieves her, which in turn surprises her. Her shoulders loosen; the tightness in her torso fades. She'd never considered how having the information would actually help heal him. But now that she imagines it, the relief inside her feels monumental.

In fact, Victor should get the originals, for they would appease him. Maybe they'd inspire him to actually be a finder. Wouldn't that be something! Victor, finally, after all this time, finds what he is looking for. She should not get in the way of such an event.

But he might just take the box and burn it in a bonfire without even opening it. That would be just like him. He composed an opera for one of Shakespeare's plays, she can't remember which, and when it got noticed and he was offered a music scholarship, he burned the composition. Burned it!

Michael's right. Victor's a looker, not a finder. Perhaps he doesn't really want to find what he's looking for.

She shakes off the notion.

But then realizes she can't do the copying on Monday, because Michael could miraculously heal and come home early, which she must consider to be a real possibility. She doesn't want Victor coming to her house with Michael home feeling crummy, as he no doubt will. She needs Victor to come for the papers while Michael's still in the hospital.

Her mind searches for who could be open tomorrow that would have a copy machine, but comes up blank. It then occurs to her what's required of her.

She brings her old Corona typewriter and some paper into the kitchen and sets it on the table. If she works steadily, no screwing off, she should get what's in her treasure chest read and copied down in time to call Victor first thing in the morning to come pick the stuff up. Even if it means staying up all night typing. She sips her coffee and sets to begin.

Once she's removed her treasure chest's lid, she unceremoniously dumps its once-organized contents on the table. Letters, postcards, pictures, and business cards scatter about the table like autumn leaves. Dots to be connected. Memories to be pieced together. Bibi can't help but wonder, and worry, if the memories Victor wants her to recall will be cajoled by anything in this pile

The first things Bibi does is pull out the pictures and place them in a stack on her baker's rack. Victor'll never know they even exist.

She then begins typing letter after letter. First the ones from Mrs. Lacharite to some attorney named Lawson that explain Grace's whereabouts and her inconsiderate behavior considering all they've done for her.

Next, she types the letters her father Leif Andressen wrote to Mr. Lawson and Mrs. Lacharite, explaining why they should be selected to parent Beatrice and Evan. There's even a letter from the Los Angeles Sheriff attesting to the upstanding characters of Mr. and Mrs. Andressen, which causes Bibi to just about throw up when she reads it. Her father the congregation president. Her father the oil company executive. Her father the pedophile. Though nausea punctuates her thoughts, but she surges on, intent on reaching her goal. She'll deal with all that later.

Interestingly there are no letters from her mom Signe Andressen to Mrs. Lacharite.

There are three letters between the Andressens and the lawyer discussing the exchange of money with the birthmother. An emotional dagger stabs Bibi. To think there had been a fee charged for letting the Andressens steal Grace's kids, or at least that's how it sounds. A thousand dollars. That's what Grace had gotten for the sale of her children, and what the Andressens paid to acquire Bibi and Victor. No wonder her mother makes Bibi feel she owes them a debt. She does! Five-hundred dollars plus thirty years' worth of interest.

Despite the fact that this infuriates Bibi, she types on, making copies of all the correspondence as if it were about a normal transaction, like the purchase of a car or an investment in a land trust. The absurdity of it all makes her think this could not have really happened to her, so banishes all thought of it, and types away.

Finally, Grace's letter that Mrs. Lacharite forwarded to her mother surfaces, the one where Grace tells whoever has her babies how to care for them, as if she somehow lost them and has been trying like the dickens to find them again. Which, come to think of it, may be true. The letter is poignant to Bibi, and confusing, considering the letters hinting Grace accepted money in exchange for her children, which Bibi struggles to ignore.

The mere act of re-typing this letter fills Bibi with a divined knowledge about her birth mother, as though Grace's words settle first in Bibi's psyche before they stream through her fingertips, onto the keyboard, and eventually onto the paper wrapped around the roller. Bibi knows that her birth mother loved her and Victor with all her heart, in the same way Bibi loves her little Ella and Noah, and that her birth mother was crying when she wrote the letter, though the paper shows no evidence of tear drips. She knows her birth mother, like herself, loved books, and her birth mother embellished the stories to make them more alive and meaningful for her children. In her imagination, Bibi can see her birth mother holding their hands and walking them to the park, not thinking twice about buying each an ice cream cone, and laughing when the ice cream melts and dribbles down their chins. She can hear her mother singing her a lullaby after she'd been bathed and fluffed with baby powder, dressed in her toasty Dr. Denton's, and tucked in all cozy and tight in her little bed.

Through flooding eyes, Bibi types what she reads in this letter, weeping for herself, the lost child, kept from her own true mother; weeping for her birth mother, who for some reason lost her children, just like Bibi could have experienced that morning on the freeway; and weeping for a world where cruelty and unfairness is even allowed to happen.

But then she stops, her fingers springing away from the typewriter keys, for she realizes there is no way she's giving this letter to Victor. Having it won't help him find anything. Besides, it's the only proof she has that her birth mother loved her, and that something horrible, horrible happened in San Diego, and her parents, the Andressens, were probably not on the legal side of whatever it was.

She twists the typewriter's platen knob and watches the paper rise up out of the machine. She crumples the paper and lets it drop to the floor, where it bounces once and rolls off into a corner. After getting an old piece of clean pink stationery from the office, she retypes the letter without emotion, for all her efforts are channeled into making the letter look like a secretary transcribed it. She types "c.c." at the bottom. It looks dorky, but she doesn't care. It's all she'll give Victor of this letter.

It is ten after four when she completes typing the last letter.

She organizes them in a way she thinks will most benefit Victor. The easy stuff first, the letter about the fees about three-quarters down the pile, and she puts the retyped letter from her birth mother to her mother on the very bottom. She then slips them into a brown mailing envelope, licks it shut, and writes "Victor" in large letters across the top. She sets it on the baker's rack where it rests like a ticking bomb next to the stack of photographs.

She sets her alarm for nine, and crawls into bed to sleep.

When her alarm wakes her, she calls Victor, and tells him she has the information he wants and he can pick it up today.

She then places her retyped letters and the one original back in the Joyce shoe box, along with the stack of photographs. She closes the lid and sets it before her on the table. It's still her treasure chest, but missing many of its jewels. To her surprise, the dots and aura are there. She glances at the baker's rack, where she notes no light emanates from or sparkles around Victor's envelope.

She knows she is being helped and swells with the feeling of being part of a universe that is now taking care of her. She looks up. "Thank you," she tells the ether. Thank you for making her part of your plan. Thank you for showing her the way despite her blindness. Thank you for watching over her. And know, please know, that that she will pay attention, that she will stay on the path, and that whatever it is she is being shown, she will find it. For she is a finder. Of that, she is totally convinced.

§

October 4; Huntington Beach

With a mix of great joy and a little disappointment, Bibi sees from the office window that Judith is back with the kids on this sparkling Sunday morning. They spill out Judith's turquoise Cougar like puppies and romp up the lawn. They've been inoculated with the glee Judith adds to their lives, and they're happy to be home.

Bibi swings open the front door and waves to Judith, who is now getting things out of her car's trunk. A new yellow dress she stitched up for Ella, and what looks like green overalls for

Noah. Judith has obviously called for them to help her, for they rush to the sidewalk next to the car's trunk, their arms outstretched to take the bags and boxes she hands them. She looks like the sun walking up the brick pathway, with the kids orbiting around her.

"Fwank, Fwank." Noah insists. He uses his hands to help him get up the steps. Crispy white mucus edges his nostrils, which makes them look sore.

"We played at Frank and Lizbeth's last night," Ella explains. Judith has French-braided Ella's hair into two high puppy tails, making her look like the ballerina Bibi wishes she'd become, but at which Ella balks.

"Hot gods. Hot gods."

"And we had hot dogs." Ella helps Noah with his bag.

Judith's all jittery; as usual, she's probably worried she'll be a bother. "I'll just be a minute." She rushes into the kitchen and sets down a plate of coffee cake on the counter. Bibi and the kids follow her in. Ella hands her grandmother a tin-foil package of beef brisket slices or something like that, and Noah gives her his bag of three apples, all of which Judith sets on the counter.

For this simple moment, Bibi feels like she's in heaven watching her mother-in-law doing one of the things she does her joyfully best: feeding people.

Bibi takes the clothes from Judith's arm. "Wow, this is so great!" She gives her a kiss. "Thank you!" She eyes Ella and points.

"Thank you, Grandma."

"Oh, she's already thanked me." Judith then, just as quickly scoots toward the front door. "Give Grandma a kiss," she says, which the kids readily give her.

She turns to leave, but stops and turns around. Cheer has left her face. "How is he?"

Woe swims in the air. Bibi shuts the door behind her, keeping the sadness from leaking into the house for the kids to smell. "He's getting better. No emergency calls last night. Looks like the coast is clear."

Judith swallows thickly.

Bibi knows Julia's fighting back her tears. Such a brave woman. "Tell him I'll be by in a couple of hours."

Judith nods and leaves.

Bibi watches her walk down the path to her car. "Bye, Judith," she calls. She hadn't noticed it before, but Judith's walk is slower, as though she's resisting seeing her son. Bibi silently calls to her mother-in-law, "Don't think like that, Judith. It will do no good." But Judith's been such a trooper. Bibi doesn't think she'd be as strong if it were Noah in the hospital. After all, Michael is Judith's child. There is a difference. She waves as Judith drives off.

Back in the house, Noah shouts, "Dopted, dopted," at the top of his lungs, as though his words were gun fire.

Bibi covers her ears. "Noah. It's helicopter. Look at my lips. He-li-cop-ter,"

"No, Mommy. Grandma says you were adopted. She said your mommy gave you away. Did Bestamor give you away?"

The whole house falls silent. In less than a blink, Bibi is two years old again, alone with her guilt, wondering what she did that was so wrong that her mother refused to be her mother, that she became that child even her mother refused, and had, in fact, given away, had sold. Sold!

Worse, now her own children know the truth about her.

She dashes to the kitchen sink before she either throws up or starts her goddamned uncontrollable wailing. Just before her eyes squeeze shut and her tears erupts, she spots, there in the corner of her white porcelain sink, the stain that she has never been able to remove, seemingly darker or more obvious than she'd ever noticed before. Then her world disappears from view as she chokes, weeps, and sobs. Shame drips down her face and onto her arms and hands; her eyes have become a veritable sprinkler system of humiliation. She hides her face inside her sopping hands. She has been exposed as the bad girl that she is.

Ella pats the back of Bibi's knees. "Why are you crying? Don't cry."

Down in the great room, Noah marches to his new word. "Dopted. Dopted."

Bibi cannot stand to hear it. She runs down the hall to her bathroom and slams the door shut, wishing she could pour her badness into the toilet bowl and flush it down once and for all. There is no way she can redeem herself, no way to make her daughter see her in another light.

Ella bangs on the door. "Mommy, Mommy. I'm sorry, I'm sorry."

All the self-pity welled in Bibi's heart suddenly evaporates, for now she is doing what her mother had done. She ran down the hall to escape her children's voices, and in turn made Ella feel like a bad girl, when in fact she's a very good girl, a wonderfully good girl.

Bibi opens wide the door and holds her arms out for Ella to enter. She holds her Ella tight to her, smelling the Breck in her hair, and the Dove on her skin, as she weeps onto her little girl's shoulder. "You're a good girl, Ella," she purrs. "You're a really good girl."

Twelve

The Path is Blessed

October 4; Huntington Beach

"Go in my bedroom. Now." Bibi claps her hands quickly several times, trying to make the kids, who are down in the great room with their toys all over the place, understand that this is an emergency, but at the same time not scaring the bejeesus out of them, or making them think they've been naughty.

"But we're playing trains." Ella complains.

"I mean it!" Bibi claps her hands again. "Git! Now!! It's an emergency. And don't make a sound or I'll ... " She stops in time to not say "kill." "Git!" she yells in a furious whisper.

She guesses they see the horror in her eyes, for they actually run into her bedroom, their little bare feet padding along the ugly brown carpeting at break-neck speed.

She peers out the front door's peek hole, and sees Victor get out of his truck and cross the street toward her house. While she has no obvious proof he's in an angry, freakish mood, she senses it. He hasn't bothered to button his green-plaid flannel shirt, and its tails flip in the breeze he creates. She hurries down the hall and shuts her bedroom door behind the kids. "Shhhh!" she reminds them, feeling very much like the mother in Steinbeck's *Pearl*.

Back at the front door, she hears his quickening footsteps coming up the brick steps. She can't believe what little time it took him to drive from Santa Barbara down to Huntington Beach. Now that she thinks of it, he probably left his house even before she got off the phone with Phoebe.

He's now so near the front door she can practically smell him through the wood. Everything in her tightens, ready for battle, which she's trying like crazy to avoid.

He knocks.

She moves away from the peep hole and braces her back against the door leading into the garage, glad that she checked all her locks.

He pounds on the door, making it rattle and oomph. "Open up. It's me."

She holds her breath. There's really no need for her to talk with him. Or vice versa. Except she did ask for an apology. Bibi waits and listens.

Then she hears what she's been waiting for. His body leans against the door as he reaches down to pick up the brown mailing envelope she packed for him. He mutters something to himself and tears open the package.

She moves in front of her door to better see through the peep hole, but at first can only see his back.

His face again flashes in the peep hole, his nose made large by the convex lens. He pounds on the door again and tries the latch. "Fucking bitch."

She quickly stands out of the peep-hole's line of sight, just in case he can see in.

All is silent. No shuffling feet. No crumpling paper. Just the faint sound of the children wrestling up against her bedroom door.

His footsteps can be heard leaving her porch. Through the garage, she hears him open the gate latch on the other side of the garage and jiggle the door by the side yard.

Instinctively, she checks the lock from the entry to the garage. At the same time, she realizes he can probably look through the garage side door's window and see her car. She glances at the family room and down into the great room, looking for shadows or movements through the windows. The thought of him in her house scares the hell out of her.

Suddenly, his footsteps can be heard bounding back up to the welcome mat.

She levels herself against the door.

"I'm sorry. You hear me?" he yells, clearly not happy or sincere about the apology Phoebe's forced him to give. "I'm sorry." He jiggles the front door latch some more and gives the door one great pound, which shakes the wall around the door.

A part of Bibi gratefully registers Victor's apology, but another part prepares to make a run for it to her bedroom so she can hide in its bathroom, all locked up safe with her kids clutched next to her. As she waits, she realizes Victor's still standing at the door. Through the peep hole, she sees him looking at the stucco around the top of her door.

"And, Sis." He sounds suddenly repentant. "While I'm at it, would you please with a capital P explain to the family my secret? Explain to them who I am." He waits a moment, then adds, "I know you're home."

While she watches him sprint down the brick walk and across the street and get into his truck, she wonders what he meant asking her to explain his secret to the family. She expects him to squeal out in anger, but he just sits there for a moment, staring straight ahead with his lower lip jutting out. She scratches her mind for what secret he's talking about.

He then opens the envelope's flap, and takes out the entire stack of letters and papers at once. He reads one, crumples it up, and tosses it out the cab's sliding window into his pick-up's bed, as if it were the useless bag from an already consumed order of French fries.

Bibi's jaw slackens. "You jerk!" she yells to herself. To her, his actions are tantamount to stabbing a treasured Picasso. Of course, she'd known this might happen, but that he would actually do it astonishes her. She moves into the study for a better view, at the same time she asks herself why she'd even want to watch, for obviously he doesn't recognize the value of what she's just given him, or even the sacrifice she's made.

He reads another letter. It's probably something from the bottom of the stack. His hands cover his bobbing face; he's either crying or choking. He crumples another paper, this one pink, and throws it in the back.

Bibi stomps, bitches, and smacks the wall. And worries if she's done right by her brother.

Victor keeps this up for what seems forever. And so does she.

Until, from behind her, she hears her kids creeping down the hall, trying to be unnoticeable. Such puppies. They've done a good job being quiet. She wonders in what havoc they've left her room. She puts her index finger to her lips, and they get her point. But they want to see what she sees. She shakes her head no, but lets them stand clinging to her legs and wondering what's so special about Uncle Victor sitting in his truck.

Victor then starts the engine and revs it twice. He sits staring for a minute, both hands on the steering wheel, and then he tosses the brown envelope in his pick-up's bed, before squealing off down the street.

She'll wait until she's sure he's gone before looking for any letters that may have blown out onto the street.

"What's happening?" Ella whispers.

"Nothing. Not anymore. Go out and play. While you have the chance. In the back yard."

Ella stares at her.

Of course, her daughter doesn't understand what Bibi means, because it has nothing to do with her. "I'm sorry," Bibi says softly, for again she realizes she's just done what both her mothers have done to her. Bibi's problems are not Ella's problems. "Uncle Victor's having a really hard time today."

"Is it because he ran over Ceres?"

"Yes. He's sad about that. He's sad about a lot of things. He's going home now. Go play. Have fun. I love you."

§

September 4; Pacific Coast Highway

Bibi's fingers tightly grip her car's steering wheel; her blood pulses just beneath her skin's surface. It's past five, and she should be home by now. The light on Pacific Coast Highway blinks green. She shifts into first and steps on the gas. Home is twenty minutes away.

Since Victor left this morning, the kids are down at the Brownleys, bless their hearts, and she's been to see Michael in the hospital. Relief number one! At least Michael's coming home tomorrow. No assurances more than a pretty sure; they told her his bolting blood pressure had finally stabilized. Her visit at the hospital stole too much of her time, chasing down nurses, trying to figure out what was really going on. She thought back to yesterday morning when the nurse called and said Michael might die. It's shocking what hospitals tell you and don't.

And she's been to Dalton's where she bought both books she wanted. It amazed her they were even in stock. There must be a lot of adoptees in the area, or a lot of birth mothers. Not a pretty thought, she thinks. Lots of heartache going on.

Like a warm cinnamon roll, the books lie, still inside their white B. Dalton Booksellers bag, next to her on the passenger seat, on top of the five letters she found on the pavement after Victor shot down her street this morning. She can no longer resist the temptation. With one hand, she removes the top book from the bag. *Lost and Found.* "Lost" in big blue letters. "Found" in red. Patriotic colors. Or competitive, like they're separate countries or opposing teams.

Keeping one eye on the road, she turns the book over and catches this written on the back: "Do those who were lost consider themselves found?"

The word "lost" stares directly at her, waiting to be recognized and owned.

Bibi stares back at it and swallows. That word explains exactly how she's felt every single day of her life. Lost. Funny how she's never recognized this before.

She glances at the sentence again. This time she focuses on "found" and tries to relate to it. It seems alien to her. Found. The thought of being found and no longer a random fragment of the universe dropped from the sky, no longer belonging to no one and nothing, steals her breath and runs her mind onto new tracks. Around and around her mind spins, incapable of embracing the concept of belonging to something greater than herself, like a jigsaw puzzle piece finding its spot.

An opportune red light forces her to stop her car. She opens the book to a random page and reads about an adoptee, in her own words, describing how her parents would tell her if she misbehaves, they'll give her back to the Indians. The adoptee explained how she knew it was a common expression, but to an adopted kid it takes on a whole new meaning. She went on to describe how she learned to act in the approved manner so she wouldn't be given away.

The air about Bibi weakens, then caves in, and a great trembling bursts forth along her body's external walls, as though the air pressure around her can no longer maintain her shape. Tears drip from her eyes, and her throat burns with sadness. And yet hope finds its voice heard, for she realizes that she is not alone. Like the person quoted in the book, she too has tried to stay. She's tried hard to act like the Andressens, to do the right thing, to pretend she's Norwegian, just so she wouldn't be given away. And look, she's still here.

But so is Victor.

A car behind her honks, reminding her that she's in her car going nowhere. She snuffs her dripping nose and wipes her eyes with her sleeve. She puts Lars in first, and then second. She turns on the radio before shifting into third. It's the end of Kim Carnes singing "Bette Davis Eyes." She loves the song, and wishes she too had Bette Davis eyes. To have such power over people!

She opens to another random page and reads, though she is still driving.

A woman, Jackie, describes how when she became a mother, all she did was cry.

Bibi manages to set the book down on the passenger seat before she erupts into tears. She too had experienced that with Ella. If someone gave her a baby gift, she couldn't open the box because she would cry until she practically had a migraine. God, how she hates to cry. When her tears subside, she opens the book and reads from another page where another adopted girl says her role model is an infertile mother, and that she must remain the eternal child.

Bibi's entire vision blurs and collapses in on itself with those words. The lies of her life. The parents who are not her parents. The child they pass off as their own. The need to always remain that child. She cries out loud, like a toddler who's lost her mother.

Behind her, a horn blasts.

Cripes. She's stopped in the middle of the road. Doesn't even remember shifting down to neutral. She jams the gear into first and then second, and veers into the closest parking space. She finds herself parking in a quaint little strip mall that offers the Goodwill and Sam's Refrigeration Repair. God knows she doesn't want another incident with a policeman who thinks she's crazy.

She turns down the radio because she can't stand not knowing more. She flips randomly through the book. Never in her life did she think she would actually be someone's mother; she'd put it off as long as possible. She and Michael were married six years before Ella arrived. Arrived? No, Ella didn't arrive. She was born! Anyway, she just couldn't see herself with kids, which is funny since she spends all day with other people's children. Even now she doubts herself as a mother. Even now she thinks her own kids will give her away. She bets when she reads this book to the end, she'll find other women just like her who can't understand that their children are really theirs, and not someone else's. She can't even recognize herself in her own children, though other people do. But this book is showing her that she's not nuts. She's normal. And Victor's not nuts either. What's nuts is that her birth mother isn't raising her. What's nuts is that her mother has a letter from her birth mother who had no intention of giving her children away, telling her how to raise her birth mother's children. That's nuts. Bibi's normal. Really, really normal.

She turns up the radio. ELO belts out their zingy, romping new hit. "Hold on tight to your dreams," they sing.

When they repeat the line, Bibi pumps her fist and yells, "Yeah!" She looks in the mirror, not wanting to see Bette Davis's eyes anymore. She's looking right into her own eyes, as if she's found just what she's looking for. "Mom, Michael, I have to find my birth mother. I'm sorry. Disinherit me. Shoot me. Divorce me. I'm still looking for her. You're just afraid of what I'll find. I'm afraid too. I don't need you to leave me now. I need you to stay and help me. Just this once. I'll be a good girl from then on. Yeah!!"

She sets the book on top of the five letters. Michael's right. Victor's a looker, not a finder.

She's the finder, and she's going to have to deliver that little speech she gave herself in her rear-view mirror to her husband and her mother pretty darned soon. Heaven be with her.

§

Bibi's sure Noah and Ella love it when she's exhausted and out of time because then they're assured to be served one of her famous ninety-second dinners: nuked French fries and chicken nuggets. The only source of real vegetable nutrients comes from the globs of ketchup she allows them to pour over the feast.

She pulls two clean plates from the dishwasher, arranges some nuggets and fries on each plate, which she plops on the table in front of them, pulls the paper towel roll out of its holder under the cupboard, tearing a couple of sheets off and tucks them into the kids' necklines, sets the roll right in front of them, along with two containers of ketchup so they won't fight, and buckles Noah's bumper seat to keep him from escaping, even though he's capable of unlatching it all by himself.

With them busy, Bibi tears about her kitchen, pulling the rest of the clean dishes and sparkling glasses from her dishwasher, putting them all away in the kitchen armoire's shelves and drawers, and emptying her refrigerator of suspect food because she almost forgot that tomorrow's trash day, all the while listening for the dryer buzzer to go off so she can get the last of the laundry folded and put away.

She's exhausted.

It's six-thirty on a Sunday night. Michael's coming home some time tomorrow. She's got bus duty in twelve-and-a-half hours, so she has to get out of the house at 00:Dark:Early. And all she wants to do is get the house straightened enough so when she wakes in the morning, she doesn't feel like committing *hara-kiri* because the house is a wreck.

After unbuckling Noah, she goes into the family room and turns the television channel to *Disneyland*, so when the kids get down from their chairs, the TV can mesmerize them until it's bath time. After adjusting the volume, she steps back to see what's on. She immediately recognizes the music. Wagner. Disney's overuse of Richard Wagner's opera tracks cracks Bibi up. *Tannhäuser* for the sea life one. And now *Tristen and Isolde* as background music to a film showing the birth of a butterfly, or a moth, or something. She doesn't care. The kids'll be totally engrossed, which means she can accomplish twice as much. Besides, they're listening to classical music.

Just as the music hit its high point, the doorbell rings.

Guessing it's probably Brandi from down the street, Bibi doesn't even bother straightening up her hair or checking the mirror to see how she appears. She just flips on the light and swings open the door, allowing the night air and Brandi to invite themselves in.

Except it is not Brandi at the door.

The person Bibi sees is her obviously fuming mother, who stands on her porch charring the air around her.

Bibi is aware her jaw and heart have dropped, but aware of very little else except the look in her mother's eyes which screams anger and betrayal and sadness and all the worst that humanity can do to itself.

"Mom!" Bibi's first impulse is to slam the door in her mother's face. The memory of her mother slapping her across the face with a dishrag when she told her about Dad is too fresh and gigantic. Her mom didn't mother her. If she did, she would have protected Bibi.

But Bibi's too raw to trust knowing how to handle this. She'll wait; it's best for her to tell Michael first. She'll bide her time.

She stands back and holds her arm out to signal her mother may enter, which she realizes is odd, since her mother usually just walks right in. Her mother's forehead is livid red, and a crop of perspiration beads on her nose.

Her mother's steps tread heavily and slowly, without her usual entitled authority, and take her, not into the family room where she usually stops first when the children are there, but into the kitchen. The children's attention has left the butterfly, and they are now all over their grandmother, peeking into her purse, their fingers reaching into her baby-blue polyester double-knit jacket pockets. Feeling nothing, they just stare at her. Bibi is right behind them.

Ella gazes solemnly at her grandmother. "Bestamor, Grandma said you gave Mommy away."

Bibi puts pressure on Ella's shoulder and nudges her back to the family room. "Ella, no, go back in and watch TV."

Ella's words have ignited Noah. "Dopted, dopted."

Ella doesn't budge. She crosses her arms across her chest and stands resolutely, staring curiously into her grandmother's eyes for the real truth to shine through.

"Dopted, dopted."

Bibi avoids her mother's eyes and forcefully shoos the kids into the family room, and plants them in their usual spots on the floor. "No, Bestamor did not give Mommy away," she whispers loudly to Ella. "Grandma had it wrong. Forget you ever heard that."

"But—."

Bibi's answer obviously doesn't satisfy Ella, but Bibi will have none of this.

She presses her index finger to her lips and gives Ella the evil eye. Bibi's world is about to explode all on its own without Ella pouring gasoline onto the kindling.

Mrs. Andressen has followed Bibi and the kids into the family room. She pulls out the pack of gum the kids obviously missed, and unwraps it before she hands it to them. She then returns to the kitchen, sits down at the table, her knees held tightly together, which makes them a sturdy shelf for her purse. Her eyes settle on the Joyce Shoes box still sitting atop the kitchen table.

Bibi goes to the sink and rinses the kids' dinner dishes as though it's perfectly normal for her mother to stop by this late on a Sunday. "So, how've you been?"

Her mother clears her throat. "Victor called this afternoon."

Bibi's hands freeze, but she does not turn to face her mother. She's got to play her cards right in her family's high-stake poker game. "Un huh."

"Bibi, come over here so I can talk with you."

Bibi stands by the table, but does not sit down. She notices her mother's eyes resting on the treasure chest. She whisks it away and puts it in her pantry, as though it belonged there.

"Come back here. Why do you still have that box?"

"You gave it to me."

"Victor said he has it."

She walks back to the sink and turns to face her mother. "He said he has the box?"

"No, he said he has the information. Come back here, and stay!"

"Mom, I gave him the stuff, and I can explain." She tells her mother how Victor ran over her cat, broke into their house yesterday and vandalized it while she was at the hospital with Michael. She waits for this to sink into her mother's awareness. She avoids telling her mother about her memories of her father.

When the furrows, which had deepened with each new detail of Bibi's description of Victor's visit, between her mother's eyebrows relax microscopically, Bibi explains how Michael found out about this because the neighbors called the hospital and told him while she was still en route. "Michael told me to give Victor the box," she tells her mother.

When her mother's expression does not change, she adds, "And Michael has been your biggest supporter in not looking for our birth mother. But he said to give the box to Victor because he doesn't want Ella and Noah in danger, or me, nor does he want our home vandalized. Michael's got enough to handle without that added to the heap. That's the only reason he said to do it. Keeping the information was simply not worth the danger it put our family in. Mom, he's a family man."

All during this, her mother has been clasping and opening her purse. Open and shut. Open and shut. Bibi assumes her mother's just waiting for Bibi to get done with her stupid excuses for why she gave her thoughtless, ungrateful brother the information he needed to humiliate his mom by finding their birth mother.

Her mother's eyes study her, gauging what to do next. Her throat moves up and down as she swallows. "You don't have any of the information? The box is empty?"

"No." Bibi sits down. "I kept a couple of the letters and the pictures. I typed all the letters and information I gave him, and it's in the box."

Her mother's eyebrows leap. "Why did you do that? It wasn't necessary."

Bibi gets up and goes into the family room and returns with *Lost and Found*, which she places in front of her mother, and sits back down. "Because I am going to look for Grace."

Her mother's nostrils flare at the sound of her nemesis's name.

"Mom, all these things keep happening. A voice keeps telling me where to call, and when I do, the person who answers always knows something about Grace or me or Mrs. Lacharite."

Her mother just stares at her, incredulous. Her jaw faintly tick-tocks back and forth.

Bibi retrieves the box from the pantry and removes the yellow paper with the phone number. "I've thrown this paper away twice, and it keeps reappearing. Do you know whose number it is?"

Her mother takes the paper in her hand and studies it, shifting her trifocals higher on her nose, so that certain parts of her face seem remarkably larger than other parts. She shakes her head within a tight range. "This is not your writing."

"I didn't write it. Someone wrote it for me. The number's for Kettenburg Marine."

Her mother's eyes widen and her temples pulse.

"Yeah. And then when I read those letters, I realized I am like my birth mother in so many ways. I've never been like someone; in the way you are like your mother and sisters. I don't know what that's like. I want to know. I want to see my birth mother's face."

Her mother's complexion reddens, then deepens to a distraught purple. Tears well in her eyes, and her lower lip quivers ever so slightly. Her mother presses her upper lip against it, reining it in. Then she cries.

"Mom, Mom." Bibi holds her mother and pats her like she would do her children, for her mother's hurt and sorrow seep through her skin and permeate the air around them. The whole room tastes of sadness.

When her mother finally contains herself, she takes the hanky from her pocket and, without unfolding it, wipes her eyes, and then takes a fair amount of time to adjust her trifocals. "I'm sorry," she says apologetically.

It's clear to Bibi that she's said something that has stung her mother. "What's going on? You're so sad."

"Because of what you don't know." She flattens her hankie so it's perfect for the next time she unceremoniously bursts into tears, and lays it flat atop the table, near a little ketchup glop. "You know we couldn't have children. What you don't know is that back in the thirties, after I'd had all my surgeries, and I was pregnant, I had to have an abortion, or I would have died carrying the child. Abortions were illegal then, and we had to get a special court order."

She cries some more, but softly. "Dad had a vasectomy so we'd never risk my getting pregnant again."

Bibi takes all this in. Her father's vasectomy certainly explains a lot. But the fact that her mother could have died carrying a child scrapes at her heart. What an awful and frightening thing for her mother to have experienced. That would have made Bibi so intolerably sad if she'd been forced to abort a child whom she wanted with all her heart to have. The cruelty of it staggers her, the sheer and utter meanness of it.

And then it occurs to Bibi that if her mother had died, she, Bibi, might never have been adopted. She might have been put in an institution, made a ward of the state. She's taught kids like that and has always felts sadness for them. That could have been her. Then where would she be today? Those kids get no breaks, not like the kind she got.

"But what always makes me so sad, Bibi, is that I never saw my baby's face. Believe me, in my own way I know your sorrow. You want to see your birth mother's face. And, if you're lucky, you'll be able to."

Bibi's heart breaks for her mother. "And you'll never be able to see your child's."

"That's right. I'll never be able to."

"Jeez, Mom, that's so horrible and sad. It's like what I'm doing just reminds you of what you've lost. I don't know what to do."

Her mother straightens up. "Well, you have nothing else to do but to look. You at least have a chance of finding what you're looking for. I'm not going to stop you. You have my permission and my blessing." She breathes clearly. "In a way you have the permission I cannot give to Victor."

"Thank you, Mom," Bibi whispers, though she can only guess about what her mother means about Victor. The room glows with movement. The incredible feeling freedom provides soaks Bibi to her core, and the wall she's always felt erected around her starts its crumbling to the floor. She has permission. At the same time, making itself felt in the pit of her is a deep sense of guilt. Once again, her mother is giving her that which Victor feels entitled to.

Regardless, all Bibi has to do now is persuade Michael to let her look.

§

October 5; Huntington Beach

The instant the garage door opens for her to drive in, Bibi can see she's in trouble. She hadn't watched the time, and it is late. Michael stands in his robe, still sick from all his chemo, in front of their old gold refrigerator they've owned since they were newlyweds. He looks like the hunchback, the way he's bent. She'd have sympathy for him except for the growl on his face. He's probably wondering where she's been, and she really doesn't want to tell him. Gad, she should have watched the time.

He opens her car door even before she turns off the engine. "Where have you been? Do you know what time it is?"

She does know, and she should have been home an hour and a half ago. "I've been at the library. Why aren't you in bed?" She thinks of her treasure chest and the cooler and the fishing gear, and the way the place looked two days ago when she got home from the hospital on Saturday. She tried to put everything back in order.

"Because I'm worried about you. You didn't call and say you'd be late."

She gathers her school and search papers in her arms, and steps out the car. "I didn't want to wake you up." She opens the passenger door and unhitches first Noah and then Ella. They tumble out and hug their father.

"Daddy, play, play!" Noah tugs on his father's robe.

"You guys, go in the house." He's definitely sore about something, and it's not just about her lateness.

In the twilight, Bibi stands by the closed passenger door, holding her purse and papers and the Smurf sitter bag. Anything might set him off when he's like this. "How's your mom?" Thank goodness Judith brought Michael home so Bibi didn't have to miss a day of school.

"She's fine. The question is: How is *your* mom?" He reaches into his robe pocket.

Whatever happened between the time he got home from the hospital and now is a mystery to Bibi. But she smells something's up. "She's fine. She stopped by last night."

"Last night? Since when does she just stop by on a Sunday night?"

"I know. She'd heard from Victor. He told her I gave him the papers. She wasn't pleased."

He crosses his arms over his chest. "What'd you tell her?"

"What he'd done on Saturday. Killing Ceres. Breaking into our house. Vandalizing it." She stops. She hadn't told him about that. Or about her dad, for that matter. Or her decision to find Grace.

He looks around the garage, one eyebrow hitched higher than the other. He's too pissed to be bothered by his chemo, evidently. "He vandalized the house?"

"I'm exaggerating. But not entirely. I cleaned it up, kind of. Then I told her how you felt, and made her see your point of view."

"And?"

"She agreed with you." Bibi waits for this once-in-a-lifetime moment to register. A faint smile lights his eyes. "She understood. She actually seemed kind of happy you'd decided that."

"Really?"

"Yeah. And then I told her I wanted to find my birth mother."

His ears rise, pulling the skin on his temple back slightly.

Bibi keeps chattering so there are no vacant pauses for him to jump in and change the subject or her intentions. "I told her I wanted to see my birth mother's face. And then she told me she'd had to have an abortion way back in the thirties when they were illegal as all get out, or she would have died, and that she understands my need to see my birth mother's face, just like she wishes with all her heart she could see her real baby's face. Isn't that sad? It's like we had the opposite ends of the same experience. And then I told her I was a finder sort of person, not just a looker or a waiter. I can't explain it. I just feel that way."

His head angles as the meaning of her words strike him one by one. He inches closer to her. His hand is still in his pocket holding something.

"But," she holds her open palms up before her, so she can continue. "There's something I have to tell you, that I didn't tell her, because it seemed all wrong to tell her, and it seems wrong to tell you too, but you have to know because it's part of me. I don't know what you'll think of me after I tell you. Before I came to the hospital Saturday morning, before Ceres died, I was vacuuming, and I suddenly, out of the blue, totally remembered my father sexually abusing me for years, for my whole childhood practically."

Michael steps back in disbelief. His eyes search hers, seeking out the real truth.

"It was as though I forgot all about it, and yet, I know it had always been on the tip of my memory's tongue, and I kept swallowing it. But on Saturday, my memory wouldn't stay silent, wouldn't be swallowed up. It makes me wonder what else I've forgotten to remember about myself, or had decided not to remember. I need to find out."

He stares at her dazed, as though she's a stranger who's entered his life.

She wants him to hold her, to make her feel loved and safe. That's what the moment calls for, in her opinion.

But he recoils from her, as though she's spoiled property.

"What? Say something to me!"

He looks at the floor and shakes his head. "I don't know what to think of you."

"Think of me? I'm talking about what happened to me as a kid. How am I supposed to tell you the truth, if you hate me for it?"

His gaze focuses on her eyes, and she feels him reading her. She gazes right back at him, steady in her truth.

He removes a paperback book from his pocket and holds it up for her to see. Its red and blue lettering on the front immediately identifies the book to Bibi. Cripes, she must have left it on her night stand. His posture straightens. "Does this mean you're looking for your birth mother? I thought we agreed about that. In fact, you promised."

"I know. But I didn't know then what I know now."

"Like what? What could possibly change your mind?" He looks at the book's back cover. "Is it the book? Is it what your father supposedly did? What?"

She momentarily hates him for questioning what happened to her. But can't totally, because she's lied to him for years. She softens herself. "Maybe it's because I got that book at the store. When I started reading it, I realized how being adopted has affected me, how I'm always feeling as though I'm not really a part of anything, and feeling dropped from the sky, and never fitting in, and always feeling obligated to my parents, and always, always being an inch from being given away. I mean they control me because I feel obligated to them. They control me because I don't want to be abandoned. I know how you hate the control they have over me. Why do you think my father felt free to do what he did? He knew I owed him. He knew I'd do anything to stay."

She watches him nod in recognition. "From that book I realized that I am normal, and that what happened to me was not."

His eyes keep searching hers for what's really about to happen.

"And then I read some of the letters that were in the shoe box. I realized how I was kind of like my birth mother. And there were letters that made me realize she had been looking for me from the start. I just don't remember. And that maybe we were taken away from her, instead of her giving us away. But I don't know what really happened. I want to know."

His coloring reddens. The end of his nose dents in slightly. "You're not looking for her. I don't want her around my children."

"I never said anything about bringing her here."

"I know how this is going to end. She'll want to meet me and the kids. I don't want to meet her. If she didn't give you away, then she lost you. Mothers shouldn't lose their kids."

She feels the stony judgment in his tone and realizes his anger rises from his father dying when he was still in grade school, for death is a form of abandonment too. "Neither should fathers."

He backs up imperceptibly. He folds his arms across his chest like armor. "That was a low blow."

"I didn't mean it as one." She approaches him and places her palm on his bathrobe's lapel. It dawns on her how problematic being truthful with Michael might be. "Please, Michael, I didn't mean it like that."

He just stares at her. Hurt floods his eyes.

"How would you want me to respond if you discovered there was a way for you to find your father? I know it's not possible, and I truly wish it was. But would you want me to deny you that opportunity? I'm sure you'd want my blessing."

His right hand rises from his hip, and his index finger points right into her face. "You're evil." His lips moisten and quiver. She can't tell if he's about to cry or bite her head off. He spins around and shuffles toward the steps leading into the house, his head shaking the whole way.

How lonely, ill, and trodden he looks, with his shoulders stooped, his posture bent. And now his wife is asking him to bend on a decision in which he sorely believes. The world needs to be kinder to him, and she wishes she could give that to him, but she craves

finding her birth mother. She can lie about it, but she doesn't want to. She's sick of lying and sick of having an entire life based on lies. She remembers sitting in her car yesterday, imagining herself asking her mother and Michael for support rather than abandonment, and how good it felt to think these things.

"Please, Michael, say yes," she asks him. "Everything's going to be alright. Just tell me yes."

He acts like he doesn't hear her. He swings open the door leading into the house. Light from inside spills into the garage, along with the children's laughter from something they're watching on television.

At the top step he stops, and turns to her. "Okay, but will you keep the kids out of this?"

She can't believe her fortune. "I will."

"Promise?"

She hesitates, because she's already failed on one promise. "I do, and thank you." She feels the full weight of forcing him to let her do something he really doesn't want her to do, but which is rightfully hers to do. Especially since he doesn't feel well. "I promise."

And this is a promise she swears to herself she'll keep.

§

That dark night, in bed, Bibi and Michael lie awake next to each other, both of them still and alone, buried in their protective coffins. Outside their window, an owl hoots. Further away, a police helicopter circles, searching for its suspect. Its rotor blades thwop, thwop, louder and then softer, louder and then softer as it circles whatever it's patrolling.

Bibi dies for Michael's touch, just a finger nudging her so she knows that, angry as he is at her, he still loves her. Instead of reaching to him, she tightens her arms and hands around herself. She won't beg for what she wants. She needs him to touch her of his own accord, so she can believe in its authenticity. Her amethyst stone feels cold in her palm.

She knows he's not asleep; his breathing sounds awake. There is so much about which they need to talk, but she can't bring any of it up without upsetting him. All evening they've been silent. Silence, however, will get them nowhere. "How are you feeling?" she asks him.

Michael noticeably exhales out his mouth, perhaps in gratitude that she actually spoke to him. "Okay. The usual." His breathing stops for a moment or is too shallow for her to hear. "I've been thinking about you. About what you said in the garage, about your dad. It's hard for me to imagine it's true. Are you sure you're not making it up? Or you dreamed it?"

An understandable question. "I've been asking myself that since Saturday," she tells him. "How could I totally forget, and then suddenly remember? But I actually didn't totally forget. I always knew, but had trained myself not to think or talk about it. It's embarrassing. Humiliating. You're probably imagining in your own head my father—." Her lips silence her. She can't say the word.

"Did it happen more than once?"

The memories pour into her awareness, overwhelming her. Her father's hand sliding beneath her jammie bottoms as a three or four your old, and as a ten-year-old, and as a teenager. The waistband grating against her flesh as the elastic ribbing moved off her waist, past her hips, along her thighs and calves, and then over her feet. The way he'd insist she spread her legs apart and assure her that what he was doing was for her pleasure.

"It happened a lot. I have memories from when I was like three years old, and until I was seventeen. There were times in my life when it happened maybe several times a week. I know it happened a lot. I remember lying in my bed every night, hoping and praying the door knob wouldn't turn, and when it did, I lay as still as I could, so he'd think I was asleep, or . . ." She stops. She cannot tell Michael how she played dead.

"Did that stop him?"

"No, he'd wake me up."

"Didn't you tell your mother?"

"I remember drying the dishes, while my mother washed them. I was maybe fifteen or sixteen. I gathered my nerve. I said, 'Mom, Dad keeps coming in my room at night and touching me.' Before I could finish saying, 'Please make him stop,' she'd swung the wet dish rag across my face with such force I practically fell backward. I never mentioned it to her again. I think I might have told her another time, but the memory's so dim."

Michael breathes in deeply and slowly, his lungs sound like a gusting wind tunnel. "Didn't you tell anyone?"

His question forces her to think. "I prayed all the time, so God knew. He didn't care. My Sunday school teachers kept saying, 'God answers your prayers.' Well, guess what? No, he doesn't. For years I prayed, and for years nothing changed. He either wasn't listening, or he didn't give a shit, or he enjoyed watching. I have a bit of an attitude about God."

"I can understand. But where was your mother when your dad was in your room?"

Bibi shakes her head in wonder. "I don't know." She thinks about her brothers who had slept at the other end of the house. "Maybe she was in with my brothers." Suddenly that image doesn't seem the least bit out of the question. Her mother spent a lot of time in their room. "But I don't know. I just don't know."

"But how did you cope? Weren't you like nervous and all that?"

Cripes, Bibi had forgotten all this. "Starting in the sixth grade I was on Donnatal and Phenobarbital all the time. I had big jars of the stuff. Not those regular little prescription bottles, but jars. When I was in college, you know my sorority sister Janie, the six-foot-two Swede? She had a stomach ache, so I gave her one of my pills. That's what I thought they were for. Stomach aches. Which I had all the time. My stomach always felt like it was filled with broken glass. Anyway, I gave her a pill, and she didn't wake up for two days. Two days! I remember standing by the side of her bunk bed and worrying she might never wake up again, and wondering what the hell was in those pills my mother fed me on a routine basis.

"Now that I think of it, I don't know how I ever made it through high school, I was so drugged. I remember in my senior year my girlfriends asking me if I was worried about my test scores and getting into college. I had no idea what they were talking about. Nervous? Not me. At least I wasn't nervous about the same stuff that worried them. I'd taken my tests, but I didn't know they were important, and evidently my scores were somehow good enough. I knew I'd applied to the college of my parents' choice, but back then it hardly ever occurred to me that any tomorrow had real potential."

His hand reaches across the sheet for Bibi's. He takes it in his, and just holds it. Doesn't squeeze it. Doesn't pet it. Just holds it. Then, "What did he do to you?"

She relives her father's hand touching her between her legs, and his mouth by her neck and ears, and his whole body moving toward her, and then her hand holding his part, and, and—. Her psyche shuts down. "I don't want to say," she says rat-a-tat. "Don't make me describe it. I won't, I can't describe it." Her eyes squeeze tight. "It's awful. It's horrid."

He pats her hand. "Shhhh. It's okay. I don't need to know."

He keeps patting her hand and hushing the energy, until she says, "I'm okay. Sorry."

"No, no, don't be sorry." He waits. He's got timing. "When did it stop?"

Another thing she'd not remembered until now. "When I was a senior in high school. I'd just turned seventeen. My friend Suzanne was talking about her step-father touching her where he shouldn't. I told her my father did that all the time. She said, 'Tell him to stop.' I thought, wow, I can do that? And so that night when he came into my room and sat at my bedside, I grabbed his hand just as he was reaching into my pajamas. I said, 'Stop it.' That's all I said. And he did. He said, 'I'm sorry,' and got up and left. It was the strangest thing. And he never again touched me in a bad way."

Michael turns on his side to face Bibi. His right hand keeps holding hers, and his left hand smooths against her cheek. "But aren't you angry? You have never seemed mad at him."

She turns on her side to face him. "I know what you mean. But, no. I'm not angry at him. Or maybe I am. Maybe because he said, 'I'm sorry.' Maybe because, of my two parents, or rather of my four parents, he was the only one who made sure I got what I needed. He was the one who'd make my mother be nice to me. I always felt I was in danger whenever my dad was gone. It makes me feel so sad that, because I've remembered, I now need to hate him. But I can't hate him. I must seem crazy. "

"You're whole family's crazy."

"It is, isn't it? I never realized how nuts we are. I always thought we were kind of normal."

"Oh, no, you're family's not even close to normal." He waits. Timing again. "Why didn't you get pregnant? Weren't you worried?"

"I never put any of that together. Now that I think of it, it was family knowledge that my father'd had a vasectomy way back in the thirties when my mom had to have an abortion. Remember when I told you about my mother having appendicitis for like a week before she went to the doctor, and then she ended up flat on her back in the hospital for six months, her body cut open to drain out all the poisons? When they put her back together, she couldn't risk getting pregnant, or she'd die. In fact, she did get pregnant, and they had to go through all kinds of red tape to get an abortion. That's why my father had a vasectomy."

"Then tell me this, why did you tell me you were a virgin, when you obviously weren't?"

His question stuns her. It's true; she had told him she was a virgin. And she thought she was telling him the truth, but she also knew she wasn't. "My parents kept telling me to hold onto my virginity until I married. I thought I was a virgin." She laughs, but not because any of this is funny. "I can't explain myself. I have no idea how I was able to tell you that with all honesty, while also, on some level, I knew it was a complete and utter lie."

Michael rolls onto his back. He inhales and exhales through his mouth. "I wonder how much else of your life is a lie." He squeezes her hand. "I can't help it. I have to wonder."

She stays on her side, facing him. Her right hand bunches her covers and draws them close to her chest. "I don't know. I just don't know." She wonders what else there is to remember. And about the things Victor remembers that she seemingly can't. But maybe she can. Anna? Are you there?

Thirteen

The Ebbing Drift

October 6; Buena Park

From just behind her last row of students, Bibi stands teacher-firm, arm pointed straight forward to the three sentences she's written in yellow chalk on her classroom's blackboard. The sea of adolescent heads looks up from their desks waiting for her next direction. "Rewrite the three sentences on the board," she tells them, "so the predicate is at the beginning of the sentence. You may add words if you need to."

"Can we add a lot of extra words?" one bright kid in an old tie-dyed t-shirt asks from the front corner.

She smiles. God love these kids. "You bet. Just make sure the predicate's at the beginning of the sentence." She can't wait to hear what they come up with.

The sea of heads bobs up and down looking from the board to their papers. The sound of clicking pens gives rhythm to the air. Bibi remains standing in the back of the room, overseeing her estate of prime learners, the school's best and brightest, the oddball teenagers who love that they know so much and get a thrill from learning. She notes that the second-hand has swept once around the clock, when she hears Anna, the poet's voice, speak into her head. "Waldon Carmichael." Anna repeats it adamantly.

Bibi's shoulders sag. Cripes, she has a lesson to teach. But the name Waldon Carmichael keeps ricocheting inside her head. Just in case, she repeats the name to herself, hoping not to lose the sound memory of it in the time it takes for her to get to her desk at the front of the room, pull her composition book from her purse, and scribble the name on a new page.

She ignores her students and the fact that the room's sounds have changed to desks squeaking and creaking, low whispering, and the snapping and zipping of purses and backpacks. For by now she's gotten her book out of her purse and she's leafing through it looking for a clean page, while also noticing that, for some reason, she'd already written down the initials W.C., followed by a question mark. On the clean page, she writes Waldon Carmichael, her fingers giddy with excitement. To Anna, she whispers an internal thank you for pushing her where she had no idea she wanted to go.

The students' low whispering is now louder and overt, for they want her attention. She looks up and is tempted to tell them to keep chatting. She is lost in all the possible connections found in her composition book. But, the bell's soon to ring, and their learning is as important as hers.

She calls on the dark-haired girl in the front row, the youngest in the class because her mother had her skip a grade. "Cindy, read your new sentences."

The class groans.

Bibi should have allotted the readings more fairly to give at least three more kids a chance, but she wants this over with so she can find out who this Waldon Carmichael is.

"Standing in the store was a man with his wallet open." Cindy reads her other two sentences quickly and brilliantly. Another flawless performance. Except it's boring. The kid always follows the rules and plays it safe.

"Does anyone disagree with Cindy's answers?"

The class says nothing.

"Got something better or more interesting?"

A million hands shoot up.

"Jason, read your best one."

Jason clears his throat. "Standing in the recently burned down store was the man with his wallet out in hopes of getting a discount he could get on cooked candy bars." He looks up, as though waiting for applause.

Bibi laughs audibly and nods. "Okay, Angela, how about you?"

Angela blows her bangs away from her eyes. "Standing on a ladder in the Ever-Bright Lighting store is a man, the notorious prison escapee named Fritz Smith, with high hopes of finding a loose ceiling panel to give him access to the attic."

These kids! Bibi grins and shakes her head at the wonderful absurdity being read to her; yes, there is hope for the world. She looks at the clock. Less than a minute before the bell. "Tell you what, sports fans, on your way out, make a pile of your sentences on my desk. I can't wait to read them. I can tell by your faces you have not let me down. Anyway, go ahead and chat 'til the bell rings. But keep it down."

She has time to gather her purse, make sure she has a couple of working pens, and to think what she's going to say if Waldon Carmichael really exists and if he answers the phone.

After the bell has rung, and when the last kid has left, she hurries out the sliding glass doors in the back and girl-trots in her heels to the teacher workroom at the end of the next wing, where she knows there's a phone, and is soon thrilled to find that no one else is using it.

"Carmichael," she tells the San Diego information operator. "Waldon."

She waits, scanning the memos stapled to the wall: the bus schedule, the school-year calendar, the yard-duty list, and a note reminding teachers to "record your phone usage on the clipboard below."

"I have a W. Carmichael on Enchantress."

"That's good, I'll take that. Are there any more?"

The operator gives her the number and reports that there are no more W. Carmichaels.

Bibi calls the number, and while she waits for the phone to be answered, she obeys school policy and fills in the details of her call on the record-your-phone-usage memo.

An old woman answers, her voice pleasant, high-pitched, and quivering.

"Is Mr. Carmichael available?" Bibi asks her.

"Walden's not here. Would you like to leave a message?"

Bibi spontaneously smiles and turns around to see if other teachers in the room understand her good fortune, her two good fortunes, for she realizes for the first time in the whole search she can have people call her back at home. "I would." She gives her home phone number to the woman. "Are you Mrs. Carmichael?

"I am."

"I was hoping Mr. Carmichael could help me with a question I have. I'm looking for Grace Winslow."

"Grace Winslow?" There is a pause. "The brilliant pianist? Or she once was."

Bibi is floored. She never realized that about her mother. Of course, it makes perfect sense, what with Bibi's talent, and Victor's over-the-top genius. "Um, I think so." She doesn't want to totally commit, just in case there are two Grace Winslows, one who is not a brilliant pianist.

"I remember Grace. That was so long ago. After the war. She had such beautiful black hair. And all those children. Four, I think. But one died. One was a darling red head. She looked like Shirley Temple. I wonder what became of them."

Bibi's heart pumps its brains out. Four children. Red hair. That must be her. One died. It's too much to hear in a mere sentence. "Four!" she blurts unexpectedly, wishing she hadn't.

"How do you know Grace? Funny how you sound like her.

This catches Bibi off guard. "She's a, um, a friend of my mother's. And my mother's ill and she wants to reconnect. You know how it can be."

"Indeed, I do. Friends get lost, then found. As long as someone's around to do the finding."

Bibi's eyes widen. Yes, as long as someone's around to do the finding. She eyes the clock, and, out of her peripheral vision notices the Special Ed. teacher waiting to her right, arms across her incredibly ample chest, her matronly foot tapping temperately. "Mrs. Carmichael, can you have Waldon call me? I need to get off the phone."

"Can I ask you a personal question, though?"

"Sure. But let me give you my phone number first."

After Mrs. Carmichael jots down Bibi's home phone number, she asks, "How old are you?"

Bibi doesn't want to answer, but can't think of what else to say without being rude to the woman. "Thirty-four."

"Hmm. Thirty-four. You know, Waldon was a really good friend of Ernest's." She pauses slightly, then asks, "How did you get Waldon's name?"

"Can I tell you later, I really have to go. I'm a teacher. The bell's going to ring. Bye, bye."

She hands the receiver to the Special Ed. teacher, goes back to her classroom, and writes the following in her notebook:

Dark haired mother.
Red haired Shirley T.
Brilliant pianist.
All those children. Four. One died.
Whatever happened to them? Were they all adopted?
Waldon knows Ernest. Who's Ernest?

Bibi's mind clatters. The words she's written blur and wobble. She blinks and rereads the list. The force of her future racing toward her feels like a hurricane. It's all happening so fast and serendipitously. With mysterious voices helping her, it's as though she's a character in a cosmic drama authored by someone or something from another realm. Before her, several feet above her, the tiny dots blink. She wonders how close she actually is to finding this person she has demonized for most of her life and romanticizes about lately. Then what will she do? Nothing is turning out like she's imagined.

§

October 8; Huntington Beach

"Look, Noah, there's Uncle Victor's truck." Ella's voice resembles birds welcoming springtime.

A chill hurtles up Bibi's spine. She slams the refrigerator door, turns the heat off under the green beans, and races into the study to see what Ella's talking about. Michael's already there, arms folded across his chest. On the television behind them, the six o'clock news with Tritia Toyota airs footage documenting Anwar Sadat's death. They all watch Victor sitting in his recently-cleaned and politely-parked truck looking down at his lap.

"Stay here, Bibi. Kids go to your rooms. Now!" Michael goes around the corner, opens the front door, and posits himself on the threshold, legs spread, arms out, hands pressing against the frame, looking every bit like Da Vinci's *Vitruvian Man*.

Bibi stands behind Michael and, through the spaces Michael's body does not fill, she sees Victor's clean, red pick-up, politely parked alongside the curb, with Victor still in the driver's seat. He seems oddly calm, as he looks in his rear mirror, runs his hands through his curls, and gets out of his truck. It's been five days since Victor ran over Ceres and roughed up her house and tried to end it all; there's nothing she trusts about this visit of his. Sadness, anger, and dread writhe in her belly. She moves away from Michael so her brother can't see her from the walkway.

Michael's voice is thorough. "What are you doing here, Vic? Stop."

Bibi nears Michael again and puts an arm around his waist, confirming her support for him.

"I said stop." Michael politely attempts to bar Victor from barging through them, because that's all that should be necessary. But Victor barges past him and past Bibi, and walks into the family room, as though Bibi and Michael were invisible.

"Gad, Vic, what is with you? Stop already." Bibi takes Michael's hand, as they both face Victor and the great room behind him.

Victor claps his hands and points to the front door. "Bibi, I want you to come with me to San Diego."

"Now?" Bibi feels her skin cool. It never occurred to her that Victor would suddenly find Grace and expect her to accompany him to meet her without any kind of preparation. But, she reminds herself, it should have occurred to her considering how fate keeps dropping the unexpected in her lap. "You found her? In San Diego?"

"What?" Victor seems genuinely surprised by her question. "No, I haven't found her. I just want you to come with me. We need to talk."

The relief Bibi feels loosens her. "We can talk here," she cajoles him. "Stay for dinner. We have plenty. Want a beer? We're having Stroganoff."

For an elongated moment, Victor sizes up Bibi, then Michael, then Bibi again, then sort of smiles before turning and walking down the steps into the great room, where he keeps his back to them.

Bibi thinks Victor's hungry, so he might say yes. "And apple crisp for dessert." She and Michael move to the top of the steps.

Victor still doesn't face them. Staring at the fireplace, he tells her, "No. I said I want to talk with you." He turns to face her. "I want a lot of time. Remember how we used to do that? Get in the car and drive Pacific Coast Highway for hours. We'd stop at the beach at night and watch the phosphorescence light up the waves. We'd talk about who we were and what we wanted. Remember that? Connected. That's what I want; that's what I need." His face pleads.

Bibi longs for those days too. She remembers how safe she used to feel with him, how understood, and how alive with potential. But dinner's cooking. It's late. Michael will never agree to her going off this late, or getting home whenever. And she promised her students they'd get their essays back tomorrow. "Can we do it this weekend?"

He shakes his head. He turns to face them, with his back to the wide, brick over mantel that rises to the ceiling.

To Bibi, there are times like now when the great room seems a separate being from the rest of the house, like something added later to make the house feel complete. This sense grows stronger because the fireplace dominates the room in the way an altar dominates a church. All Victor needs to do to replicate a crucifix is to hold his arms straight out.

"Okay. We'll talk here."

Bibi's not sure this is such a good thing because Michael will be listening. She'll have to watch herself. She walks down into the room and sits in the rocking chair. Michael follows and sits in their black-leather Relling chair, his favorite. Bibi points to the sofa for Victor to seat himself.

But Victor remains standing, his hands in his pockets. "Have you done any looking? You had all those letters from Mom."

"You mean the ones I gave you? Not really."

"Not really, but kind of?"

On one hand Bibi feels like telling him about her conversation with Mrs. Carmichael, but she stops herself when she considers what Victor did with the packet of letters. "Oh, let me see. I talked to a lady at Kettenberg Marine who knows Grace. That was kind of weird."

"Kettenberg? Where's that?"

"In San Diego."

"Why did you call there?"

Bibi realizes she shouldn't have said a thing and changes the subject. "What have you found? You had all those letters."

"Nothing. They led nowhere."

Bibi realizes the position she's in. She's getting closer to finding Grace, while Victor's not even trying. At least it seems that way. Except, admittedly, he has not been faring well. The thought of him sitting in his idling truck in a closed garage seems impossible in this moment, but she gets the flaw in her thinking.

"Vic, remember when you were here on Saturday? The last time I talked with you?" She rushes her words so he can't answer and so she can avoid starting a fight. "You kept saying two things. You kept telling me to explain you to others. And you asked me why I refused to remember when we both saw her, whoever her is."

"Whoever her is?" He sits on the sofa. He stands back up. He faces Bibi head on. Anger and disbelief riddle his eyes. "Her is Grace, our mother. I know you remember that."

"But I don't." Glad as she is that she's managed to change to subject, she's alarmed by where the conversation is headed. She searches the ceiling hoping it will give her a clue. She looks back at Victor and shakes her head. She has no idea what he's talking about.

"Bibi, how can you not? I was on the driveway crying. I was eleven, or something close. I looked up, and there you were looking down at me through the view window. I'll never forget it."

Bibi freezes. She does remember this. "You were wearing that yellow and brown checkerboard shirt. Long sleeves. Corduroy. Right?"

Victor's eyebrows leap. "You do remember! Do you know why I was on the driveway crying?"

"I didn't know why you were crying. It made no sense to me. I was watching the fog climb up the canyon. I loved to watch the fog do that. It didn't happen often, so when it did, I was riveted. Fog is usually docile. But every once in a while, it's as though it's after something. It's chasing something up the canyon."

Victor waves his hands at her. "Stop with the fog shit."

"But—."

"Fog? That's what you were watching?" Victor looks incredulous. He walks to the great room's eastern windows, the ones that look at the side yard and the tall cedar fence separating her house from the neighbors. "Do you know why I ran down there? I mean we were both standing in the living room. We were both looking out the same window. You know what I was looking at?"

"No. Honestly I don't. What?"

He turns to face her. "I was looking at a white, maybe '51 Ford, and the woman sitting in the driver's seat. It was our mother. It was Grace. She was looking back at us, both of us, smiling. I thought she'd come back to rescue us and take us home. I assumed you thought the same thing. I raced out the front door, but by the time I got down to the driveway, she'd driven off. You don't remember any of that?"

"Jeez." The horridness of all this grips Bibi, especially the fact that she'd had an opportunity to see her birth mother and totally missed it. "I don't remember any of that. I couldn't figure out why you were crying. I thought Charlie said or did something creepy to you. Or Mom or Dad. Something. I had no idea. Why didn't you say anything?"

"I thought you didn't care. I thought it didn't mean anything to you. I thought you made a decision not to come along."

"Oh, Vic, I'm really sorry that happened." Bibi works to fathom all that her brother has told her. "My God, you've been carrying that around all these years. I don't know what to say. I don't know what to feel. I don't know what to do."

"But you remember it? Right?"

"Right. I remember you on your knees on the driveway crying your eyes out."

Victor shakes out his hands and shoulders, visibly unbridled or unburdened. "Then you've given me a lot. In some ways I thought I was crazy. I thought I was the only one who loved our mother. I thought I might have imagined it, even though I know it happened. Do you know what that feels like?" His expression and color seem dreamlike and casual, as though welcoming a new day.

Bibi glances at Michael, whom she's ignored throughout her conversation with Victor. She looks him straight in the eye, her kind of warning that she's about to do something brave and dangerous, and he better have her back. She stands and walks to the opposing windows and looks out at their backyard.

"Vic, were you sexually abused? Growing up, I mean." She turns to look for his reaction.

Victor appears taken aback by her question. "No. Why would you even ask me that?"

"Well, because I was. For years. Since I was little, until I was a senior in high school."

Victor winces and walks toward Bibi. "Who did it?"

"What?" Bibi thought the answer was too obvious to require a question.

"Who did it? Mom or Dad?"

Bibi frowns. Mothers sexually abuse their daughters? It had never occurred to her. "Dad. Not Mom."

Victor's eyes travel back and forth through his own history. He's so close to Bibi she can smell coffee on his breath. "Why didn't you tell someone?" he asks.

"I just told you."

"Yeah, but back then. Why didn't you say something?"

Bibi doesn't miss the irony of his question, nor the irony of what they kept secret from each other despite feeling they told each other everything. Still, his question embarrasses her. Why did she not say something? "Because I didn't want to be given away."

Michael reaches for Bibi's hand. "Bibi just remembered all this last weekend."

They both watch Victor mentally recall his Saturday and Sunday. "Last weekend?"

"Un huh," she says, as she too remembers that fateful Saturday, just five days old. She remembers vacuuming. She remembers counting. And she remembers remembering. And then trying to explain why she couldn't recollect what she'd known all along.

Victor's face reddens. Anger and sorrow flare in his eyes. He balks out the sliding door and sits on the kids' swing hanging from the willow's heaviest branch. Instead of swinging, he sways in a circle, with his feet never leaving the ground. Thinking. Mulling. Stewing.

Michael and Bibi watch him from the sliding doorway.

Ella and Noah, who had been spying from the family room, charge past their parents on their way outside to see what their uncle is up to.

Ella stands right in front of Victor. The breeze fluttering her hair softens the curious and resolute posture she has taken. "Why are you always mad, Uncle Victor?" she asks her uncle.

With no one around to stop him, Noah, apparently spurred on by his sister's tone, steps into Victor's perimeter and hits him on the knee.

Victor looks up at Noah, then Ella, stricken by their feelings toward him. "Hey," he says softly. "I'm not always mad. I'm only mad when things are terribly wrong, and they're terribly wrong right now."

Both children stare at him and wait for him to explain himself further.

But he has nothing further to tell them. He abruptly gets up, pats them on their heads, and walks back into the great room, followed by Michael and Bibi. He moves in haphazard circles as he talks rat-a-tat. "I finally understand why you're like you are, Bibi. I know why you always seem lost, even though you aren't. I know why you never trust, or never expect anyone to take care of you. Because no one has. None of your parents. Not one. Grace didn't. Our birth father didn't. Mom didn't. Dad didn't. No one." He looks accusingly at Michael before looking back at Bibi. "And, and this is the kicker, you never say a word. You keep it all inside, like you're the one protecting them. Like it's your duty to protect them."

Bibi hates Victor saying all this, especially in front of Michael and the kids. She covers her ears to stop Victor's gushing. "Stop," she yells.

But Victor's not done. "Don't you see why we have to find her? Don't you see we're destroying ourselves because of her? Can't you see that? Don't you wonder why you're the way you are? Doesn't it occur to you that maybe you're meant to be different?"

Bibi has removed her hands from her ears. She nods. Victor's right. She knows her silence protected her father. She flashes on times she has protected Michael by letting him get away with not helping her and by making excuses for him. And huge in her mind are ways she has protected Victor.

Matter-of-factly she says, "You're right. I know I've made you look good so many times in your life. You never graduated from college. I did. I even got my master's. Yet I never went to my graduations because of you. I'd make you look bad. Whatever you were doing, I couldn't do, or I couldn't do better, for fear that I'd make you look bad.

"You know why? Because if you screwed up and got given away, I'd be given away too. And I didn't want that. I hated being given away. All I know is that I've done a hell of a lot in my life to keep you and others looking good so I'd have a roof over my head and a family to come home to."

"You didn't have to do that. I didn't ask you to."

"I didn't do it for you. I did it for me. And I don't have to do it anymore."

Victor smiles. "You're right. You don't."

Bibi squeezes Michael's hand, aware of how she didn't have the nerve to mention the insidious ways she's also kept Michael from giving her away.

"You know what else, Bibi?" Victor continues. "I swear to God I'm going to find her. And I'm going to make her feel what it's like to be abandoned."

§

October 9; Huntington Beach

"Yes, this is Bibi." The woman's voice on the other end is unfamiliar, and the timing strange. Seven-thirty on a Friday night. No one except friends and family calls at this hour.

"I'm Laura Sorenson. My mother is Sadie Lacharite."

Bibi holds her breath. Lacharite. She cannot believe this is happening. The way she'd imagined this search to go, she'd be doing the phoning, especially after the Carmichaels never returned her call.

"A friend of my mother's gave me your name and phone number. She said you called her, and you sounded like Grace Jensen, I mean, Grace Winslow. Are you looking for Grace Winslow?"

"I am." Bibi thinks of Mrs. Carmichael. She looks at the ceiling and notices the six dots dancing in the air.

"I have a picture you might want to see."

"A picture?"

"Yes, it's a picture of you and your brother when you were small."

"You have a picture of me?"

"My mother recently died, and I was going through some of her things. I'll explain when you get here."

"Where are you?"

"In Seal Beach."

The next town north. Bibi's been searching for her birth mother in San Diego, and now she's looking in the very next town!

§

October 9; Seal Beach, California

Centered on the dining table of the house on Bayside Avenue in Seal Beach is a crisp, white business envelope. Bibi and Michael stare at it politely. Bibi's knees bounce impatiently, like a race horse at the starting gate.

"I'm sorry for the state of things. We recently moved. But I wanted to get this to you as soon as possible." Laura scoots the envelope toward Bibi. Nothing is written on the front or back;

just an envelope meant for no specific person, or no one to whom it belonged. "I actually have relatively recent letters from Grace and her husband down at my mother's"

Bibi picks up the envelope. In the worst way she wants to tear it open and see the photograph. She's never seen a picture of herself that was taken before she arrived at the Andressens.

But she holds back. Everything about Laura Sorenson spells fastidiousness and refinement. Perfect antiques. Thick-piled champagne carpeting. A professionally decorated home in tones of forest green and apricot. Laura in a fine dark green silk blouse tucked into tailored pink gabardine slacks that perfectly match her decor. And a bob that makes her look like Princess Diana.

Bibi's glad she left the kids home with Brandi. This is no place to flaunt the rules. "Where did your mother live?"

"La Jolla." She stared at the envelope in Bibi's hands. "I would have brought Grace's letters if I'd known for sure you were her daughter. The picture says Victor and Bibi on the back. I believe your mother who adopted you sent it to my mother, in case Grace wanted to see what you looked like as you grew older."

"That's our names. Victor and Bibi." Bibi's knees still and her shoulders drop. She hadn't realized that the picture would be one that the Andressens had taken.

"Well, go ahead and open it."

Bibi lifts the flap. She assumes she'll pull out a picture of herself and Victor fishing in the Sierras or in their Dr. Denton's on Christmas Eve. That would be so like her mother.

When the picture she pulls out is fully revealed, Bibi gasps. The small black and white photo pictures the extra-tall swing set from her back yard, the fruit trees that surround it, a lanky youngster Bibi recognizes as Charlie, and a pudgy tow-headed toddler who looks just like one of her cousins. She turns it over, and reads, "Victor and Bibi" written in her mother's distinct straight up-and-down, perfectly dotted and crossed writing. She turns the picture over, stares and shakes her head in astonishment.

Michael takes the picture from Bibi, looks at it, and reads the back. He sets the picture on the table and speaks to Laura. "This isn't them. Bibi was never a blond."

"Actually, it's a picture of my older brother Charlie and our cousin Tessa."

"But it has your names on the back."

Bibi laughs, though she's not amused. She can just see her mother fulfilling Grace's request to see how her children were faring. But instead of making it easy for Grace to spot her and Victor getting off the school bus or playing out in the street, her mother decided this was her perfect opportunity to throw Grace off track.

"May I keep the picture?"

"Certainly."

"When is the next time you're going to La Jolla? May I come down and look at the letters?"

"Tomorrow. We're actually going down tonight, after my husband comes home from work. He's a surgeon at Hoag. He's had a big day." She jots down the address. "You can have the letters. You know, some of them are from Grace's husband Nels Jensen."

When Bibi takes the paper from Laura, a warmth exudes from it that rises up her arm to her heart. It feels like a sunrise is happening right inside her chest.

Fourteen

Particles in Suspension

October 10; La Jolla, California

Bibi drives up the winding path leading to the late Mrs. Sadie Lacharite's most recent home, "a John Lloyd Wright" Laura had warned, in the La Jolla hills. Her fingernails click the steering wheel in anticipation. The scenery, the vegetation, and the serenity seem familiar, as though on the tip of her tongue. She enters the unassuming entryway to a modest, but exquisite jewel of a home. Oiled and smooth-sanded mahogany paneling bedecks the home's interior walls. At hip level and attached to the home's entire inner perimeter wall is a single bookshelf that travels through the living room, dining room, and bedrooms. The living room still holds a few of the Lacharites' impressive pieces. Eames chairs. A hand-carved grand piano, which seems oddly familiar to Bibi. Huge Persian carpets. Beyond on two sides of the home stretches an immense view of the Pacific Ocean and the northern view of the Southern California Coast. Bibi had grown up in Palos Verdes, but nothing in her experience prepared her for such a home.

Opera strains sound inside Bibi's head, as do piano concertos, and lively conversations bouncing with wit and smarts. She's been here before, she thinks. Maybe not exactly. But it's so familiar. And comfortable, like an old beguiling scent, or a long-worn moccasin. This should be her house, her life. This is what she longs for when she sits at her piano in her deep, empty great room that should instead be filled with people who are like her, but more interesting and more talented.

Laura's hand smooths across the Steinway's surface, her thumb bounces slightly as it traces the carved edges of the magnificent mahogany. "Victor was so excited when he saw this grand. He practically begged me to give it to him."

Laura's words snap Bibi out of her reverie. "What?"

"Victor. He was here this morning."

Bibi's fists tighten. She feels faint. "Victor?"

"Yes, he called soon after you left yesterday, and so I invited him down too. He's quite the early bird."

"He's been here already? Did you give him the letters?" Bibi struggles to hide how frantic she feels.

"No, actually he didn't want the letters. Only the envelopes. I guess he just wanted the addresses. Here, I've packed up the letters and put them in this envelope. And please, let us know how this all works out for you."

"He took the addresses? You don't have copies?"

Laura shakes her head. Her eyes at first seem confused and then aware.

Bibi knees go weak. The air around her ripples and throbs. She senses herself being suddenly small, a speck in reality. She searches Laura's eyes for motivations. All that's revealed is Laura's blatant yearning to do good.

And yet, by some peculiarity in how the world works, she has utterly failed.

§

Tonight, I worry for Bibi.

§

October 10; Huntington Beach

Back at home, the light of the midday sun cannot break through the cairn Bibi has erected around her soul. The morose drag of what happened in La Jolla stifles the air in her home and sucks the joy and love from anything that happens inside. Depression and humiliation grow up from the floors and down from the ceilings like stalactites and stalagmites, so her family is forced to tiptoe around these protrusions.

The family has been in Ella's room, playing Hungry Hungry Hippo, if for no other reason than to get Bibi to make a different face than the current lifeless one she sports.

"Come on, come to the kitchen" Michael offers her his hand, and she takes it, so it's easier to stand up.

"Mommy," Ella yells. She points at Bibi's knee. "A thumb tack."

Everyone takes a moment to look at Bibi's knee, which has a thumbtack stuck in all the way. Dried blood drips draw a meandering, maroon line sideways down her leg.

Bibi looks at and dismisses it. "Who cares."

"Stop." Michael bends down, and with his fingernail pries the thumbtack out enough to get a good grip on it to pull it out straight. He looks up at her and shows it to her. "You couldn't feel that?"

Her expression doesn't change. She shakes her head no.

They walk out into the kitchen. She just sits at the table, her finger tips over her mouth. She says nothing, looks at nothing, and feels nothing.

When the phone rings, she doesn't get up.

"It's your mom," Michael whispers after he answers it.

He disappears into the family room, the phone's long cord tagging behind. "Yeah, Signe, Victor got the addresses and things... I know, she's pretty upset...Victor called here last night when we were in Seal Beach, and the babysitter gave him the Sorensons' phone number...How were the Sorensons to know? No, we haven't heard from Victor. He better stay away from here if he knows what's good for him...No, haven't heard from Phoebe either. Okay, then, we'll keep in touch. Thanks for calling."

Hearing Michael recount Victor's surprise success leaves Bibi in an old, cold space. What is hers is his. What she's earned has become his prize. She has no worth, except that she might heighten his value. Her mind races in this loop, over and over, searching but not finding an off ramp, an exit, an emergency lane.

Michael sits down gingerly, careful to not further shatter any part of his brittle wife. He opens a beer and offers her a sip, which she refuses. "How does Ozzy Osbourne change a light bulb?"

She shrugs.

"First he bites off the old one."

She looks at him, and expresses one chuckle which can only be detected through her shoulders. Her face does not change.

"Stay with me. I'm trying my hardest. How many psychiatrists does it take to change a light bulb?"

She glowers at him.

"None, the light bulb has to want to change."

She puts an index finger up to her lips.

"Sorry," he whispers.

"You want some pizza? I'll order some."

She shakes her head.

"How about some TV?"

She nods.

But the phone rings.

Michael answers it and walks into the family room, hidden from her view. Michael's careful volume disappears. "What do you want, Vic?"

She freezes. He's already seen her birth mother. He's the golden child who got to meet her first. Her anger has heated to magma. It will not be contained. She leaps up and grabs the phone from Michael. "What do you want?"

"You can go see her now. I left the address on your front porch."

She throws the receiver down. She slaps the family room paneling. She picks up the receiver again and throws it down the steps leading to the living room. "That fucking son-of-a-bitch." She doesn't care if the kids hear her.

And then she dissolves on the steps, right next to her big plant, and she bawls her eyes out.

§

Every time Bibi perches herself up on her elbow, and peaks over Michael's sleeping body to read the clock on his nightstand, another ten minutes has passed. And now it is half past midnight on Sunday morning, and Bibi has been awake, but not necessarily alive, for every moment she's been in bed.

Her mind will not quell. The same images and Victor's words race around her mind like wind-up toys: "I've met her. You can see her now." The words will not let her escape. They drip through her like an opiate, depressing her, numbing her, murdering her, leaving her to face the abject grayness of her failure.

Worse, she cannot explain why Victor's words have literally sucked every ounce of joy from her. The answer must be obvious, but to her it is illusive, blinding her to the exit door from the miasma engulfing her. She cannot escape or shake this abhorrent mire that traps like mud burying her up to the neck. It seems like death, only worse, for she's here to witness it.

From a little place where her last ounces of sanity reside, a voice beseeches her to figure this out, urges her to search herself, dangles a carrot of hope in front of her. This is no way to live, it tells her, and she knows that. If Victor's words can do this to her, something is very, very wrong. All Victor said was, "I've met her. You can see her now." How bad can that be?

Except it is bad. In context it is very, very bad.

But what is the context?

Her blindness sinks deeper. Lead weights smother her soul. There must be a path out of this, something she can do to feel better. She begs her eyes to see and her mind to know.

She gets out of bed and walks down the hall. She's cold, though the house is comfortable. She turns on the TV, dims the sound, and plants herself on the sofa. A boxing match is on. Just what she wants: men hitting each other, while others watch. It disgusts her the way bull fights do, and dog fights.

She gets up and turns the channel knob. An old Paul Muni movie plays. He's underwater, breathing through a reed so he goes unnoticed, because he's escaped from something, maybe a prison.

She turns off the TV and faces the refrigerator in the kitchen. Bread. Mayonnaise. American cheese. She piles an unhealthy stack of comfort food sandwiches on a single plate.

She turns the TV back on and, chewing away, watches Paul Muni outsmart the dogs. She could give a shit. She gets up and turns off the TV. Back on the sofa, she sits, downing her sandwiches, thinking short useless thoughts, and hearing her brother's voice repeat, "You can see her now," like she's finally lucky enough to get his permission. Boy, that feels like an old story.

She goes back into the kitchen and finds the letters Victor had left on the porch without bothering to ring the doorbell.

"You can see her now." His words beat her over her head and infuriate her. That Victor saw Grace before Bibi did enrages her even more, but her madness dulls her anger to a deep muddy mire. It was, after all her fault that he got to the Lacharites' before she did. It's her shame to deal with. And yet, someone deserves blame. But who? Her mind circles and circles. She wants more sandwiches, but thinks she didn't taste or feel the first three.

She gets the Ouija board from the study closet and sets it up. "Why did this happen?" She asks it.

It spells out its usual expletive: F-U-C-K-Y-O-U.

"Should I see my birth mother today?"

It tells her to fuck off again.

Indignant, she crams the board and planchette back into the box and shoves it high in the closet, swearing she's tossing it the next chance she has. From the red Chinese candy box on the bookshelf, she removes her dowsing chain.

She writes “Am I doing the right thing?” on a piece of paper and dangles the chain over it, held tight between her thumb and index finger.

It does not move, not a stitch. How could a question be so dead?

Next, she writes on another paper scrap, “I see my birth mother today.”

As before, her chain does not move, not even a twitch.

How strange. She drops the chain back into the box and goes into the family room to get a deck of playing cards from the lamp table's drawer. Back in the study, she sits on the floor facing herself toward the desk, her legs spread before her in a vee. After tidying the deck, she places it face down before her.

She floats her fingers above the first card. "Red."

She flips the card over. Black.

"Damn."

She feels the next card. "Red."

When she flips it over, a black card appears.

After she got the thirteenth one in a row wrong, she throws the cards behind her in protest. She's connected to no one. Not herself. Not the universe. Not even those sparks of light that have been around her lately. Nothing. A distraught human body in an alien world. No, she corrects herself. The world is gray. And dull. And very, very distant.

But!

Perhaps she's mistaken about all this; perhaps, she is in fact dead. Many indications exist to support this theory. She can't feel anything, for one. More than that, she feels dead. That should count for something.

From her position on the carpet, she notices the mirror standing on the floor behind the desk. She'd forgotten how she and Michael had stuck it there until they could find a better place for it, which they evidently never did.

She moves the chair away, and crawls under the desk, where she experiences a distinct tomblike atmosphere. After moving closer to the mirror, she studies her eyes. They don't seem to trust her, not one bit. And she doesn't trust them either. She backs off a bit. Just because she can see herself in the mirror does not prove she's alive. She touches the mirror, which feels like glass, and not like her. Then she touches herself, which she can barely feel, but which she knows she's probably doing because her reflection in the mirror substantiates what's happening.

Or does it?

She's an inch away from the mirror now, peering into her eyes, searching for the truth, but comes up short. All she sees are dull, horrified, questioning eyes.

"Are you alive?" she asks her reflection, and waits.

Nothing is said, but her face stares back at her, her lips wrench and tighten, her brow furrows.

She wants an answer, but she's not going to get it from her reflection. Is she alive? Because if she's not, she'd like to get on with the rest of her death.

She scoots out from under the desk, realizing she really must know the answer. Whether she's alive or dead is not a rhetorical question. It's important. She must know. But maybe proving one is alive can be as impossible as proving one is sane.

From behind her she pulls the phone directory from the book shelf. In the yellow pages, she looks up Suicide Hotlines. There are several, including that church in Anaheim that used to be a theatre-in-the-round. "24 Hour Hotline," its ad reads.

She dials a number for an ad that promises Jesus loves her. She lets it ring ten times before calling the number again, just in case she mis-dialed the first time.

She counts thirteen rings before hanging up, all the while trying hard not to make assumptions about Jesus's love for her.

She has five more numbers from which to choose. She tries another religious one, though she realizes there's no reason why they should be better at this than one connected with county psychological services. Except, she's a teacher. If she is indeed alive, she sure as heck doesn't want the district finding out she's suicidal, which she isn't. All she wants to know is whether she's alive or not. There's a difference.

A guy answers the church's hotline. "This is Lynn. How can I help you?"

Suddenly she feels stupid. "I don't know if I'm alive or dead."

"I can hear you. That's a good indication that you're alive."

"But I feel dead."

"You may feel dead, but you're not."

"How do you know? How do you really know?"

"I'll tell you what. Get a pin. Stick it in your arm. If it bleeds, you're alive. If not, you're dead."

She hangs up on him. He's right of course, and she realizes perhaps she needs to start her inquiry a different way. Maybe she should give more information.

She calls the Lifeline Inc. number.

"Ray, here, how can I help? “He sounds nice enough.

"Hi, I'm having. . ." Suddenly it's a struggle to even talk. "I'm having a really hard time." She starts crying like a little kid, but doesn't make a sound. She feels helpless because she doesn't know how to fix herself, and she doesn't know what to say to help Ray fix her.

"Everything's going to be fine," he says softly. "Slow down. When you're ready, just tell me what comes to you. Okay?"

"Un huh," she blubbers. She gets herself together. He sounds so nice, like he's not afraid of what she might say. "I'm supposed to meet my birth mother for the first time today."

"Wow. Do you have a name? What can I call you?"

"Bibi." She knows she shouldn't have given the name. Now she can be accused of craziness.

"Bibi, is that what has you so upset?"

"No, it's that I found my birth mother. I did all the work, and my brother got hold of the information, and he went and saw her first."

"You're upset because he beat you to it?"

"Yeah, I guess, but I'm really upset because after he saw her, he called me up and said I could go see her now." These last words barely get out of her mouth because she starts bawling again.

Ray waits for her to calm down. "Let me get this straight. Your brother called you up and told you that you could go see your mother now?"

"Un huh."

" He gave you permission to see your birth mother? Is he always that big of a jerk?"

"What do you mean?"

"If my brother called me and told me that, 'You can go see our mother now," I'd be really upset."

"Really?"

"Of course. You don't need his permission."

"I don't? I mean I know that. But why does he say it to me? I don't know what to say. I don't know how to respond."

"Look, he's not in charge of what you do. I am, of course, assuming that you're an adult."

"I am. I'm married and have two kids."

"Did he admit he took your research?"

"No. He didn't really take it. He, um, just got lucky and it was handed to him."

"But you want him to thank you."

"Or something. At least admit it."

"Right, because you want the truth to be out."

"Yeah, you're right. I want the truth out."

"You know why?"

"Hum um."

"Because when one thing is happening, and everyone acts like something else is going on, it's crazy making. If he's got you believing that you always need his permission, and deep down you know that's not true, you're going to go crazy trying to make his premise fit into your world. You basically have to change your view of the world to accommodate the lie that he is advancing. Understand what I'm saying?"

"Kind of."

"Lies are crazy making. Even non-stated lies. Lies eventually send people into rages, enormous depressions, even suicide. If you know something is a lie, and your only option is to say it is true, you have to rearrange all the ways you think to make a lie be the truth. It's crazy making."

"Like if something's really sad, like the cat gets run over, and we all have to pretend it's really nothing, when it's obviously horrible, that's a lie, and it will drive us crazy." Her mind does a quick shuffle of the lies she's bought into on a regular basis. Being a virgin. Being Norwegian.

"Right. You do realize your brother's being a butt? He's making you believe the lie that you need his permission."

"Wow, you're right." The world looks suddenly Technicolor. Bibi can hear the clocks in the house. The browns in the carpet are now brilliant jewel tones of topaz, amber, and citrine.

"How do you feel?"

"Wonderful. Thank you so much."

"You have a great visit with your birth mother. And just remember, stay in touch with what you know to be the truth. Don't ascribe to other people's lies. You'll be all the happier for it."

"Thanks, Ray."

§

Bibi walks down the hall toward her bedroom, touching each child's smooth door on the way. Her fingers tingle; the children are doing fine. Crickets outside chirp. The kids' soap from their bathroom wafts in the air.

She slips into bed and faces Michael's back. What is the truth of right now? She's tired and grateful. She loves her husband and children very much. She is meeting her birth mother in a few hours, and she doesn't, in all truth, know what that's going to be like. Except she wants it to be good.

Fifteen

An End is a Beginning

October 11; Huntington Beach

Bibi walks down the hall all perfect in her white double-knit dress, the one that buttons up the back. She loves wearing white to important events. Her focus is in the moment. Her trusty mind dares not travel to what might be. In her hand she carries a padded box filled with pictures she'd taken from the shoe boxes filled with photos from her life: Little girl pictures, school pictures, photos of the house she grew up in, her wedding pictures, the children's photos. The whole gambit. Her life in retrospect to share with her birth mother.

"I'm ready," she tells Michael, who is plopped in front of the television watching four NBC sports commentators predicting the odds that the Dodgers will win game five of the National League Division Series. After all, they'll have the home field advantage. In a flash she knows it. "The Dodgers'll win today. You can bet on it."

He turns to her and smiles. "Thanks. I already have." He gets up. "Don't leave yet." He tightens his robe's belt. "Daniel is on his way."

"Daniel?" There was no reason for their good friend Daniel the Shrink to come this morning. "I'll talk with him when I get home. I gotta go."

"I don't want you driving until he's talked with you."

She balks. "Is this an appointment?" It dawns on her that he wants to be in a position of giving her permission, just like her brother.

"No. Stop it. I called him. He's on his way."

"I don't need to talk with him."

"You've had a rough twenty-four hours. How do we know visiting your birth mother today is the best thing to do?"

Again, he's forcing her to accept his permission. "Look, thank you for caring, and I mean it. But this is something I have to do. I've come too far to quit now."

Footsteps come up the pathway, saving the conversation from degenerating.

Bibi, being closest, opens the door. Daniel, who has dressed for the occasion, gives her a quick hug and hands her a bottle of Mumms. He's grown a short beard since she last saw him. It makes him look smarter. "Congratulations! That's quite an accomplishment, finding your birth mother!"

Bibi beams. It is an accomplishment!

She follows Daniel and Michael into the kitchen, where they arrange themselves around the table. Bibi describes what's happened, and the details of last night's conversations with the various suicide hot lines. "He told me I didn't need my brother's permission. I don't know why that never occurred to me before."

Michael turns to Daniel and asks, as if Bibi were in another room, "Well, what do you think?"

Embarrassed, Daniel hedges. "I think this is a joyous day."

"I mean, do you think she should go?"

Daniel stands up and puts a hand on Michael's shoulder. "I don't think you can stop her." To Bibi, whose facial expression he has been watching closely, he says, "You know, we marry our families."

Bibi blinks. What Daniel says sounds right, but she knows she'll need to think about it. Especially since her immediate family is gaining another mother. She does, however, know Ray's words from last night are right.

She covers Michael's hand with her own, intending her warmth and love to soak permeate his skin. "The truth is, Michael, I don't need your permission. The truth is also that I'm grateful that you love me enough to worry about me and asking Daniel over. And the final truth for this morning is that I'm going to kiss you good-bye and drive to Santa Ana right now. Wish me luck. I'll be home in a few hours. I love you."

Michael forces a smile. "Just think before you punt."

Bibi silently chokes. Last words before departing should never be so ominous.

§

Santa Ana, California

"Grace Winslow's room." Bibi stands in the lobby of an ancient hospital, that now serves as a ward for the county's elderly and infirm while they wait to die. From here, wax-slick, beige linoleum-floored halls lead outward in three directions, each clogged with cleaning trolleys, rolling lunch trays, and the attendants who work them. The air is ripe with the fermenting scents of antiseptic, urine, and baked goods. It must be lunch time.

The nurse comes back and announces, "There is no Grace Winslow here."

There's got to be some kind of a mistake. This is the address Bibi has. She pulls the envelope from her purse, and immediately recognizes her mistake. "Oh, I'm so sorry, Grace Jensen."

The nurse again returns. "Mrs. Jensen is in 619." She nods toward the elevator.

Once out the elevator, Bibi follows the arrows down a remarkably shiny and unlit hallway leading to Grace's room, at the end of the corridor.

She hesitates before entering. This is the first moment of the rest of her life.

She steps into the room and notices three women sitting around, something she had not expected. She scans the first woman, and then the next. It would be tragic to pick the wrong mother out of the line-up.

But then she sees the face.

"Dahling," the face says. "Itth tho good to thee you."

Bibi could burst into hysterics, so incongruous did she find Grace's first greeting after all these years, after the drowning and the abandonment, as though Bibi was an old friend who'd stopped in for tea. Dahling, so good to see you. It whirls in Bibi's ears and mind.

Ignoring the other ladies in the room, Bibi hurries to Grace and hugs her. The moment seems ephemeral, like a dream that can be lost forever once one awakens. Bibi hadn't touched her birth mother in thirty-two years, since that time when suddenly there was another mother for her to answer to.

She stands back and studies Grace's face.

How Bibi has longed and looked for this face. It dawns on her, and she regrets it immediately, that every time she looked in Signe's face, it was the wrong one. It was a lie. And it did send her into a rage, just like Ray said. But she didn't know why.

Signe wasn't her mother who bore her, and Beatrice knew the truth. Beatrice knew what her birth mother looked like. And everyone made her call this new woman Mommy, but she wasn't her mommy at all. And she also realizes she loves the mother who raised her, and that much of her anger at Mrs. Andressen primarily had to do with not seeing the right face.

She pulls up a chair and sits next to Grace, who, she notices has a sugary scent emanating from her. Bibi stills the box of photographs on her lap with her hands' weight. It occurs to her how the box, filled with pictures of her, contains no pictures of her as a baby. For the first time, Bibi allows herself to remember a yearning she's buried deep inside her. Throughout her life, when seeing her own friends' baby pictures, she would swallow her envy. She wanted to know if she had curious eyes like Ella's, or if they were full of mischief like Noah's, or full of sweetness like Michael's. Certainly, baby pictures reveal a lot about the individual soul before the world begins its assault.

Bibi removes the lid from the box and looks up at Grace. Carefully, with the same trepidation she felt when she originally took the Joyce Shoes box from her mother weeks ago, Bibi hands it to Grace. "I've brought pictures from my life for you to see." The meaning of this does not escape Bibi; she's trying to explain her life to a woman who has just returned from a thirty-year coma.

Bibi watches Grace intently. She can't get over the face. To think this is what she'd been searching for all these years—her mother's face. And now, here she is, convalescing and looking so much like Bibi. Frizzy white curls, combed into what appears an old lady's white afro. Her breasts sag down to her lap. She must be in her seventies. Her thick, wire-framed glasses create that aquarium effect, where it appears she has two sets of eyes, one set just a bit lower than the other. And there's something juicy and unsturdy about her eye balls, so that when she glances about, the stuff making up her eyes quivers, the way Jell-O does.

"Thank you, tho much." Grace lisps when she says this, for she has not a tooth in her mouth. She takes the box and settles it on her lap. Her eyes don't leave Bibi's face. "I love you tho much. I've thought about you every day of my life."

Bibi can't respond. She wants to believe Grace, but can't completely. She smiles in a way to let Grace know she appreciates her, and kind of loves her.

Grace picks up one picture and then the next. Bibi's high school graduation. Bibi's sorority picture. "You went to college."

"I did. I studied art."

Grace smiles. Her eyes quake. And her hands, the ones so resembling Bibi's, pick up more photographs. Her wedding to Michael. Ella. Noah. The black-and-white picture of the house in which she grew up. "I remember the house. It had turquoithe shutterth."

Shocked by this revelation, Bibi asks, "You knew where I lived?"

"Oh thertainly. You didn't look anything like thothe pictureth Mrs. Andrethen thent of you."

Bibi inwardly laughs at the irony of all this, and thus decides to ask, "So why did you walk us into the ocean?"

While the skin on Grace's face remains perfectly still, her eyes float back into her past before returning to Bibi. "I don't know what you're talking about."

"Didn't you try to drown us?"

"No, I'd never do thuch a thing."

Bibi knows she's lying, but chooses not to argue. Bibi's question should have made Grace at least a little angry if it was untrue. But Grace's composure remained the same. Bibi's focus escapes to Grace's two roommates, collapsed and sleeping in their wheelchairs; apparently, they haven't heard a word of this conversation. The window behind them reveals a graying sky, and a welcome cooling trend. A subtle tension disappears from Bibi's neck and shoulders. She returns her attention to Grace and patronizes her with a smile. "Tell me about my father."

Grace's eyes light up. "His name is Erneth. Can you imagine thomeone naming her child that?"

Bibi can't imagine someone naming her girls Beatrice and Delilah, either, but she keeps that to herself. "Ernest is his name? What's his last name?" Bibi thinks of Mrs. Carmichael, who'd been kind enough to explain what a great friend Ernest, her birth father, had been to Mr. Carmichael.

"Borg. Ernetht Borg. Look in the 1942 *Who'th Who*. Ernetht Borg. It'th in the library. He'th a phythician. A urologitht. Hith father wath too. Very well known."

While Bibi jots this down, she says, "I talked with Mrs. Carmichael. Do you remember Mrs. Carmichael, Waldon's wife?"

Her eyes float into her past again, and concern scrawls over her face. "You talked with Mrs. Carmichael?" She seems agitated.

"I did. They helped me find you. Mrs. Carmichael said you had four children."

Something in Grace's heart breaks apart. Sadness rearranges her brow. Her head lolls back a bit, and she shakes her head. "You have a thithter. Delilah. In Texath. My huthband will give you her phone number."

"Not four?"

"No."

Bibi knows more truth is being hidden. If the truth cannot be forced out, at least she doesn't have to be sucked into believing the lie. When she gets home, she'll contact her sister. She pauses a moment to let this fact sink in. She's always been the only girl in the family. She's never wanted a sister, or at least she's never thought about it. The uncertainty of all this jangles Bibi. She can't deal with this now, much less think how she'll deal with more family than she already has. She changes the subject, "So you were a brilliant pianist."

Grace closes her eyes and retreats back in time, and then opens them. "I wath. But I could not thtand the tenthion. It wath tho difficult. Frightening."

"Victor's a pianist." The instant Bibi mentions his name she regrets it.

"Evan? He wath here yethterday."

"I know."

"He thaid he found me."

"He didn't find you. He took the information from me, so I wouldn't have your address or last name. He did that so he could see you first."

"But he thaid he found me." Grace looks at Bibi as if to keep her from pressing her side of the story, that Evan cheated Beatrice out of what was rightfully hers. "I'm glad he found me firtht. He needed to do that."

Another lie she cannot change, but that she doesn't have to buy into either. But why Grace thinks it's best Victor found her first puzzles Bibi.

"He'th thuch a handthome man. Jutht like hith father."

Bibi nods. She doesn't want to think about her birth father Ernest. Dealing with today seems like crossing the Himalayas in bare feet.

"Do you know what he did yethterday?"

Bibi shakes her head. She really doesn't give a shit what Victor did yesterday.

"He walked in here and thaid, 'I'm Victor. I found you.' And then he turned right around and walked out the door. I didn't have a chanth to thay one word to him. It maketh me tho thad."

Bibi leans in. What an operatically cruel and contemptuous thing for her brother to do. "I'm sorry he did that. Perhaps he didn't feel well," she tells Grace.

And immediately regrets it. For herself, but not for Grace. Grace deserves an apology. What Bibi notices is that her old habit reappeared, the one where she must make him look good so she can stay. "I mean, I'm sorry that happened to you. I'm sad for you."

Sad that Grace missed the joy of watching her and Victor grow up. Sad that Grace didn't teach her all that she knew about music and the arts, rather than have it stifled out of her by well-meaning people who had little idea of her heredity. Sad that her brother and she let the gifts they've been given fall through their fingers like sand. Sad for all the lies she's told and endured for no other reason than to stay. Maybe staying isn't all it's cracked up to be.

§

Bibi lingers, just as she's entered her home's entry and realizes no one is home.

Like a cool, protective tunnel into a cave the foyer seems. She lets her purse drop onto the entryway floor and leans against the front door so it clicks shut behind her. Still holding the box filled with her lifetime's photos, she notices how her home rings with silence and how alive, but removed, the sounds coming from outside are. Robins twittering from the willow tree, the kids next door splashing in their pool, the dog on the other side of her back fence howling just like he does every afternoon, someone down the street mowing his lawn, a small plane taking off from Meadowlark Airport, a distant fog horn, and a fly or bee banging incessantly against her broad kitchen window.

Her home's hushed silence gives her the impression that it is actually a part of her, that she ends where its walls end, that her skin has dissolved and no longer acts to bound or limit her. A giddy hope wraps around her. In this moment, there's no one here to stop her, diminish her, advise her, deplore her, or distract her from whatever she wants or chooses to do next. Not only that, she's capable of anything because she's got help from the poem voice Anna, and from the starry dots in the air that help guide her. This moment, she realizes, is but a brand-new calendar waiting to be filled with what she wants. She has never felt this way in her life: deliciously alone to do what she wants, and yet surrounded by the most surprising and brilliant support.

She moves toward the family room and stops at the settee. Her fingers idly skim across its back and feel her family's presence. Now that she looks at it, of all the rooms in the house, this one explains their family best. The stuff constantly emerging from under the sofa, from between its cushions, from behind the television cabinet; the toy trucks and horses lying all over the floor; the television waiting for Michael and the kids to return; the Haight Ashbury posters hanging on the wall, mementos of the parents' giddy younger days; the ornate, brass andirons dressing up the fireplace, which Michael had given Bibi as a Christmas gift; and the draped end tables hiding Bibi's embarrassing horde of orderly boxes filled with miscellaneous crap she should, but doesn't know how to, get rid of.

A sudden dread grips her. Her body seems hollow, as though part of her has escaped. She clutches the box of photographs tighter to her. This is the same dread that enveloped her several times during her drive home. And with the dread, there came a question.

What has she done?

She knows that what happened today and the last few weeks will change her life, but how, she does not know. Michael is her main worry. He could get totally pissed, and turn against her. Worse, he could turn their children against her. No, he won't do that, she thinks. Then again, yes, he would.

Her mouth, she notices, has dropped open and that she's panting, as though experiencing a day-mare. She moves to the settee's front and sits down. The shoe box radiates warmth in her lap, and she looks down at its top. "Pappagallo" the white lid reads in the company's large, black, bubbly writing. When she turns the box on its side, she realizes this box held her white satin wedding shoes.

Bibi narrows her eyes and studies the room, looking sternly at the television, the sofa, the posters, the lamps, the trucks and horses. No, she decides. No, she doesn't want Michael to be angry. She wants him to understand. She wants him to put himself in her situation, and, she realizes, she must put herself in his situation as well. The idea disconcerts her.

But this is what she wants. She has to be able to tell Michael everything, regardless of how it changes his view of or respect for her. He must understand that she now has a sister, which certainly will change some of the dynamics, like putting another fish in an already full aquarium. She has another mother and father, who can't be her mother and father, legally or otherwise, but who must be acknowledged, like the true and forgotten inventors of a familiar product. Bibi carries their genes, their talents, and vices. Grace was a concert pianist, which Victor should have been. Ernest was a physician. Bibi wonders who she'd be if she'd always known this about herself.

Bibi stares at her opened palms and sees how obvious it is that she should want to play the piano, and would have been better at it and more committed to it if she'd known her origins. And her birth father was a physician, and therefore a scientist and explorer. A finder!

An amazed chill permeates her. Again, she feels uncontained. She knows she is so much more capable than anyone in her family had ever led her to believe. And she, like a fool, believed their assessments.

Then the dread reappears, along with the thought of Michael. He's not going to be impressed by any of this. She worries he won't be patient with her when her euphoria wears off and she's forced to come to grips with all the things she's experienced. Like the drowning, her father's horrible acts, and all the past lies she's told him. Brittle, Bibi shudders.

"What do you want?" the poem voice whispers.

Bibi forces herself to heed the voice. All during her dazed drive home from seeing Grace, Anna had encouraged her. "What do you want?" she had repeated in a cooing, patient tone that had given Bibi shivers and hope.

What does she want? This can't be that hard, Bibi had told herself. But it was surprisingly difficult. Not because she couldn't arrive at an answer, but because, with each thought and opposite thought, confusing waves of happiness and sadness stormed at each other like warring weather systems. Things she wanted would open an unexplainable, cavernous melancholy in her when she realized she also believed she couldn't have them.

Like this very moment. What does she want? Her first thoughts dash to her paints. Effervescence tickles her insides, and the top of her head fizzes; the gate for the muses to enter has opened. Paintings yearning for life appear in her mind. They dazzle and lure her with their depth, their shapes, and jeweled colors, and meaning. Her mind and heart, like lovers holding hands, race into the future.

Then the thud arrives, jarring open her pit of sadness. She realizes that Michael will probably return with the kids as soon as she makes her first brush stroke. That is what always happens.

Well, she can at least go down into the great room to play Beethoven's *Waldstein*. Or she can practice Chopin's *First Ballade*. In fact, it occurs to her that a great idea for Christmas would be to learn it for Grace. And for her mother too. She decides on that. It's what she wants, and it feels good to want it.

At the piano, she realizes that it is the *Waldstein* she really yearns to play in this moment, and sets about doing so. Her eyes follow the notes, her hands go where they should, her ears relish the tones, but her mind replays the morning over and over. Grace's puffy face and the eyes so liquid they undulate when they move, which Bibi hopes she missed inheriting. And Grace's denial of the drowning, and her confession that she'd always known where her children lived. All the probable lies and hopeful truths. In time, Bibi wants to know about her birth father. Right now, though, in this very instant, while she's all alone, she wants to hear her sister's voice.

Bibi stops her hands, shuts the cover over the keys and stands. How could she be so selfish and foolish to be using this precious time she has alone playing the piano, when what she should be doing is contacting her sister. Waves of thrill and fear lash about in her. She's never had a sister. But a sister will take time she doesn't have to spare. A sister can be a mirror helping to explain who she is, but she can't tolerate a sister who insists on being a part of her real family. She'd promised Michael she'd keep her birth family separate. But how unfair to her sister, who-ever she is.

She gets her purse from the entryway and fumbles through it for the paper having Grace's husband's phone number. Jacob Jensen, it reads. She sets the paper on her baker's rack and dials. The Edvard Munk faces in the paneling scream and moan at her, but she ignores them.

"Yacob here."

Cripes, another Norwegian, Bibi thinks. And he sounds even more ancient than Grace, who sounded a heck of lot creakier than her mother, who's about the same age. "Hello, I'm Bibi Am-ato."

Jacob breaks in. "I've been waiting and waiting for you to call. Grace was so happy to see you. You made her day. Don't get me wrong. I can't wait to meet you too. You'll love it here. We're right on a cliff in San Clemente. Dere's us, and den the ocean. It's a little old. And maybe small. Our apartment. Not de ocean. It's spectacular. De train runs along de beach right below us several times a day."

Bibi tries to imagine it all as Jacob tells it, and guesses they must have plenty of money. California coastal property fetches quite a bit. But then realizes she's only got so much time before her monster pack returns. "I'm calling because I want to get in touch with my sister."

"Ah, Delilah. Such a sweet bloom. She's in Texas, you know. In Lubbock. Hotter dan de devil's kitchen. Disgusting, it is. But don't share dat with Delilah. She'll want you to love everyting about her. You know, I need your address. I want to send you some tings so you'll understand our family. I'm Danish. Dat's important. What's your address? I got a pen and paper ready."

Bibi realizes she'll need to be rude. "Really, Mr. Jensen, I just want Delilah's phone number."

"Nonsense. And don't call me Mr. Yensen. I'm Papa."

Bibi freezes. Her free hand grips a rail of the baker's rack. He can't be serious. Surely he must realize he can't just become someone's father by decree. Except, that's what her parents, her adopters, did. All because her birth father wouldn't, for some reason, admit that he was her father.

"Relax," Anna's voice coos in Bibi's mind. "Give him your information. He'll give you his. All will be well."

"Anna?" Bibi whispers.

"Yes."

Bibi releases her grip. "Jacob, here's my address."

When she's done, she asks for Delilah's information, which she gets interspersed with lots of information about World War I and a promise that he'd send her a copy of his prized photograph showing all the kings of Europe meeting in Copenhagen or something before World War I broke out. Just what she wants.

With the phone back in its cradle, Bibi studies what she's written. Delilah Storm, Ransom Canyon, Lubbock, Texas. And a phone number. The individual words gathered together this way appear to warn her of something, though she knows she's reading too much into it.

"Call," the poem voice insists.

"Anna?"

"Yes. Call. Now."

Bibi picks up the receiver and dials. She realizes she knows hardly anything about Texas. Except she's been to Houston, where her soul almost boiled away in the June heat. And her cousins had weird accents and said, "Y'all." They also laughed at her when she said, "You guys."

"Hello."

The woman's voice carries no hint of Texas, and it sounds leery, but open, as if this call were expected. Maybe Jacob called Delilah to warn her.

Bibi jumps in. "I'm Bibi. I'm your sister, I mean your birth sister."

The woman chuckles like she's in on some private joke. "Well, well, well. It's about time you called. How many years has it been?"

Bibi looks quizzically at the receiver, as if waiting for it to agree with her that the woman's response was pretty darned inapt. "Is this Delilah? I do have the right number?" She glances at the number she'd written down and hopes she doesn't have to call Jacob back for a correction.

"Yes, this is Delilah, your long-lost sister. I didn't even know you existed until a couple of weeks ago."

"I didn't know about you until this morning. I knew there were four . . . "

Delilah interrupts. "But how did you find me? I mean us? I've spent a king's fortune and a half dozen years looking for you. No, that's not true. I've spent my life looking for my brother. You I did not know about."

Bibi turns her back to the wall and stares out the kitchen window at her fading morning glories. She hadn't expected to feel guilt, and isn't prepared to concede to it. "It was actually kind of weird. I heard this voice that kept telling me to call this number or to look up that person. It didn't take very long."

"But did you put your name in the adoption registries, like the Tri-Adoption agencies? I've had my name in there for years. Years! I can't believe you never looked there."

"I didn't know they existed. And really, I wasn't looking until like a month or so ago. Then this voice just started giving me information and telling me who to call."

"Yeah? Does the voice have a name?"

"Anna. She said her name was Anna."

"You mean Anne Marie."

"Nope, she said her name was Anna."

"Sorry. You didn't hear it right. It's Anne Marie."

Bibi wants to change the subject or win the argument, but she's as curious as she is irritated. "So, who's Anne Marie?"

"Our sister who died between us. She's the third child of us four. Anne Marie helped you find us."

Bibi plops in the nearest chair. Her hand covers her mouth in disbelief and amazement. This new knowledge forces Bibi to realize she cannot doubt that she's part of a larger plan, a larger story, one in which she is an actor with an important part to play. What that part is, she has no idea. But it is a part, grand or humble, and forces outside of her and outside of the earth plane are intent that she play her role, and make themselves available when she needs help. This knowledge lightens up her kitchen and brightens the sounds that the birds and trees outside make. Bibi's world and worldview can never go back to what she was yesterday, in the same way one never goes back to adding up seven eights once one knows and remembers that seven times eight is fifty-six.

"Are you there?" Delilah asks.

"I am. I'm just in shock."

Delilah purrs like a respected spiritual advisor. "Don't be. Anne Marie talks to me all the time."

Bibi feels suddenly possessive of Anna. Obviously, Bibi hears better than Delilah, or Delilah would have found her and Victor a long time ago. But bringing this up seems small, and Bibi has a feeling her sister, like her brother, doesn't take to being challenged. "Tell me about yourself. What's life like for you? What are you doing in Texas? Do you have a family? What are the highlights of your life?"

After Delilah describes the stellar moments of her rags-to-kind-of-riches life, she slowly articulates what she must have practiced saying since yesterday. "Mother never told me about you, though I always knew I had a brother. I will never do to you what my mother did. I will not pretend you do not exist. I will not abandon you. We must stop this family's cycle of abandonment. Mother abandoned you. But she was abandoned by her mother, who was abandoned by her mother, who was, well, you get the point. But the truth is our family is not right when any of its members is lost. It leaves a silent, gaping hole. That is why I will never abandon you."

Bibi feels a sudden sorrow for Grace, her abandoned birth mother, while also wanting in the worst way to give what Delilah wants in this moment: the vow that Bibi will never abandon Delilah. But she can't because she sincerely doubts that she'll ever allow herself to meld into Delilah's vision of her perfect family. It's hard enough dealing with the one she already has. Bibi struggles for what to say.

Anna interrupts Bibi's thoughts. "What do you want?"

For Bibi, the answer is simple. She wants to be free to choose what she wants, rather than fitting into Delilah's vision of how she should be. Except it feels awful to think like this, knowing her sister can't avoid feeling rejected by it.

Anna doesn't give up. "Then, what would make you happy?"

Like a blatant sunrise announcing a new day, Anna's words bare what Bibi really wants. She wants her sister to be happy too. And with this knowledge, Bibi blurts, "We're sisters. We're connected for the rest of our lives. There's no undoing that fact."

Delilah muses softly and with solemnity says, "I love your words. I love the sound of your voice. I love that you found us."

Bibi knows she has given Delilah the best she has to give. She pats her heart, and privately thanks Anna. "I love it too."

Delilah breaks the spell with a chortle. "Then tell our ass-hole brother to call me and to go visit his mother."

Bibi forces her lips together. Delilah may sound soft at times, but Bibi senses a lethal wickedness can emerge from her when things don't work out her way. This Bibi knows she must avoid. Just as she must dodge making excuses for Victor. He'll do what he'll do, and it's not her job to clean up after him anymore. No more poor Victor.

After Delilah and Bibi's conversation ends and they've promised to talk tomorrow, Bibi calls her mother. For some reason Bibi looks forward to hearing her mother's voice. She sees her mother's face in her mind and notices she doesn't experience the same terror she's felt most of her life.

"Mom," Bibi blurts, "I've met her, and I'm home. I love you and I thank you for helping me find her." Her own words surprise her. She doesn't ever remember telling her mother she loves her. Ever. Doesn't even remember thinking it.

Her mother is silent for a moment before she asks, "Did it go well?"

Bibi hears the strain in her mother's voice. And the worry, the neediness, and the hope. "Remember when we had that conversation about seeing the faces of your baby and my birth mother?"

"I do."

"I have to admit to you that in that first moment when I saw Grace today, I realized how upset I'd been all my life by seeing your face and not hers. Like, where'd Mommy go? And how did you get to take her place? It's alarmed me all my life, but I've never realized it nor known why. That's dissolved now. You and Grace are separate people. And you are my mother."

Bibi hears her mother's soft crying and wonders if what she said out of love has actually hurt her mother. "Mom, are you alright?"

"Yes. I just—. Thank you, Bibi. Or Beatrice. Yes, thank you, Beatrice."

Bibi notices her hands suddenly trembling and a smile breaking across her face. Subconsciously she'd always known her name had been Beatrice, but to hear her own mother call her that feels like heaven. It's as though a large, lost puzzle piece is finally found and placed where it belongs. She wonders how many other puzzle pieces still need replacing in her life, and, without dread, decides her future life is probably one huge project which she must complete.

After saying their goodbyes, Bibi walks down the steps to the great room and stands by the sliding door leading out to the patio and lawn. A swift-moving fog from the beach is replacing the day's grayness. She watches the fog, heaving and rolling like a vaporous, leviathan wave, crash into her yard and render it mystic and clandestine. She loves the fog, and how it eliminates backgrounds and accentuates that which is close. If only she could always live where grayness and fog are the prevalent weather. It would never get old for her.

The phone's ringing shakes Bibi from her trance; she hurries to answer it.

"Sis, congratulations."

It's Charlie, and Bibi hears the genuine cheer in his voice. "Yeah, it's kind of wild. I even have a sister. I mean, Victor and I have a sister. She's in Texas."

"So, you're going to become a Texan."

Bibi's radar picks up a blip, and with it her hackles stand on end. "Heck no. Why would you say that?"

"It makes sense. You have family in Texas. You're going to have to spend time there."

"Calm," Anna intones.

Oh, yeah, thinks Bibi. Focus on what makes her happy, like her family getting along and loving and helping each other, rather than competing. The thought dissolves her hackles and makes her smile, which makes her smile even more.

"Actually, no. Meeting Grace and talking with my sister makes me realize my family's here. You're my family. They're my birth family. I can't pretend they don't exist, but I also can't be equally in two families. Maybe some people can do that, but I can't."

"That's what you've decided?"

"Yes."

Charlie makes a sound like he's sipping beer. "Well, Sis, you've done a good job. I'm happy and proud for you."

Charlie's words dust across her heart like a clean cotton cloth wiping away the grime and smudges that dirtied up the family since Victor decided he had to find his birth mother. She knows the words she spoke to him assuaged his fears, if in fact he had any. But she also knows that her birth family will be part of her for the rest of her life. They hold the key to a trove of knowledge that she has, without realizing it, hungered for throughout her life. Whenever she thinks she's supposed to be living some other life, it's because of her birth family. They know, on some level, who she should be.

Which begs the question: If Victor's the one who all along realized he needed his birth mother to explain who he was, why didn't he engage with her yesterday?

After saying bye to Charlie, Bibi dials Victor's number.

When Victor answers, she asks, "How are you? From what Grace said you didn't have much of a visit. It didn't make sense to me."

"When I saw her there, pathetic and senile, I just wanted to hurt her. I wanted to give her what she gave me. I wanted her to know I could find her too, and then just drive off."

"Um, actually, I found her. You just intercepted the information from the babysitter."

"I still found her."

Gad, this pisses off Bibi. But she knows she's on the losing side of this argument. Victor sees it his way, she sees it hers. But he's wrong.

"Calm," says Anna.

Bibi ignores her. "You're a jerk, you know that? Don't you realize how rude you're being?"

"Who cares?"

"I care. Cripes, you go see your birth mother and barely say anything to her. You are going back to see her again, aren't you?"

"Probably not."

"Then why did you create all this turmoil in our lives? You're the one who insisted on finding her so you could discover yourself and make your shrink happy. Cripes, if it weren't for me, you'd still be looking. You realize that, don't you? And then when I find her for you, you not only ignore her, but you take credit for finding her."

"Calm!" Anna repeats.

"Stop!" Victor yells, as though he imagines her to be a freight train lumbering toward him. She can hear the moisture that must be forming in the back of his throat, she can see his nostrils flaring, and she can sense the anger, or terror, that must be radiating from his eyes.

Bibi struggles to heed Anna's warning. What does she want in this moment? Or, better yet, what would make her happy? For her brother, her sibling, her pal throughout her life, to find or get what he's really looking for, because, apparently, he hasn't found it yet. Yes, she thinks as she feels the warm, benevolent calm expand inside her, that would indeed make her very happy.

"I'm sorry," she tells him. "Actually, let's start over. What, and I know this sounds weird, but, what would make you happy?"

Her question seems to take him aback. His quiet gives Bibi hope. She feels herself drifting spellbound in space, waiting for the thing that will make both of them happy to be stated.

Finally, he says, "All your horoscopes and tarot cards, they never tell you anything about me that shocks you?"

She rifles through the possibilities, but none of them seem shocking. Sure, he's arrogant and ostentatious, but that's not shocking. He never combs his hair, but neither did Einstein. We all have our faults. "No, not really. You seem like you always seem."

"Can't you see it? Don't you notice?"

"No. What are you talking about?"

"I'm gay," he blurts.

"But—." She stops herself. Maybe he seems a little gay, but that's because he's artsy and bohemian. Except he's married. He's been married twice, in fact. Someone can't be both gay and married. Except, of course, someone can. With this realization, Bibi descends into a swirling, ill-boding pool of darkness. How horrid it must be to live with his secret. All the lies he must have to make up and manage, and all the lies he has to live with, he who has loved the truth his entire life. How horrible for him to know he is something so many people consider morally vile and despicable. Her brother, her creative, genius, usually-loving, law-abiding brother. She knows her mother will have a fit. She'll disown him and she won't let him in her house. And she'll despise him for something he was born with, like someone being hated for being blind, or pigeon-toed, or a freckle-faced redhead, which she is.

She holds the receiver close to her mouth and speaks low and softly. "How can I help? What do you need?"

The fear and anger have left Victor's voice. He speaks calmly and resolutely. "I need you to understand. And I need you to support me. And I need you to be the one who tells Mom. You'll need to do this soon because I can't go on like this much longer."

The gravity of his words weighs in her stomach. This is no frivolous request on his part. He needs her to help him in a way no one else can. She thinks of his attempted suicide and knows she must make sure he doesn't try it again. She knows she will find a way. She's a finder. "I will. I will do that." And she will.

"Help me," she whispers to Anna, as she places the phone back in its cradle. "Be with us for this."

"Yes," comes the reply.

It's another fifteen minutes before Michael walks in the front door, both kids trailing behind him with yellow and green stuffed bears he'd won for them at the Balboa Fun Zone, twenty minutes away.

Bibi rises from her chair at the kitchen table, where she'd been sitting dumbstruck by the day's events and the multiple directions in which her life has been thrust.

The children run to her with their new animals. She kneels down to greet them; their sticky cheeks reek of cotton candy and peanuts. She holds them to her and closes her eyes. Thank God she has them. And thank God she has never had the impulse or the need to abandon them or, worse, to literally exile them from their family of origin.

When she opens her eyes, she sees Michael standing in the doorway, leaning against the jamb, not moving toward her, but evidently studying her before making his next move. Perhaps she looks different to him. Or he suspects she has made some monumental and awful decision he asked her specifically not to make about her birth family. She can't blame him for thinking these things. He's right, after all, at least for now. She doesn't know this birth family. Things could get complicated in a heartbeat, even scary, if she doesn't pay attention.

She stands, releases the kids, and goes to him. "I've had a hell of a day." She slips her arms around his waist; his arms circle her shoulders. "I have a lot to tell you. Thanks for taking the kids to the Zone. I needed the time." She continues holding him, her mind thinking of Victor's request of her, and how Michael will adjust to having a gay brother-in-law. She thinks of her sister trying to fit in with her family, and vice versa. She thinks of her new relationship with her mother, and what that will be like for Michael. So much, so very much has changed.

When she releases him, he takes her face in his hands. "Tell me you love me."

"Ah, but I do."

"No, tell me."

His request flusters her, but she realizes her guilt. And understands it. "I love you. Very much." She kisses him so he believes her words, but also thinks how rarely she tells her own kids how much she loves them. And regrets it deeply. All because she couldn't allow herself to love her mother with the wrong face. Talk about punting.

§

I'm going to enjoy the coming times, working with Beatrice. She can hear me clearly, and what a difference that makes. You have no idea the problems that can arise when we souls are misheard. Tragic sometimes. But Beatrice has such a great antenna. A real radio-head. I can't wait to guide her to new ideas. To teach her to question, even me. For I know her soul like a sister. I know where she wants to go. We have no secrets.

§

October 12; Buena Park

The Monday-morning chaos of the teachers' lounge bombards Bibi with its energy and normalcy. She had one of the biggest days of her life yesterday, and none of her peers reads it on her face.

She spots Gloria and Pamela sitting at a corner table, coffee mugs set before them, both holding up the yellow morning announcements at eye level.

"You're going to love the new duty schedule," comes the low voice of the P.E. teacher behind Bibi.

"No, you're not," another guy adds.

"Why'd they change it anyway?" yet another asks.

Bibi's world of yesterday crashes into today. Being on the negotiations team means she'll have some assuaging to do regarding the new schedule, but that'll have to wait.

Besides, she's late. She grabs half a cup of coffee and heads for their table without pausing for creamer. There's so much to tell Gloria and Pamela.

In swift movements, Bibi sets her stuff on their table, sits down, and pats the table's surface.

"Good morning, Sunshine." Gloria's glasses lilt near the end of her nose. She nods to her paper. "Have you seen this?"

Pamela looks up at Bibi and blinks. "Did you go to the movies this weekend? Weren't you going to see *My Dinner with Andre?*"

Bibi blinks back. The thought of a movie hadn't occurred to her for days. She slaps the table again, a little louder. "I found my birth mother this weekend."

Gloria and Pamela both drop their papers and look directly at Bibi. "What?"

Bibi loudly annunciates so she doesn't have to say it again, "I found my birth mother. I met her yesterday." She looks around, but apparently no one else heard her.

Gloria pushes up her glasses and crosses her arms across her chest. Pamela sips her coffee and frowns. Unamused, they both stare at Bibi.

This is not the reaction Bibi had expected. She'd practiced in the car after dropping the kids off at the sitter's. After her initial announcement, they were supposed to look pleased and ask her a ton of questions. "Aren't you happy for me?"

Pamela motions to the sliding door leading to the atrium.

Perfect, thinks Bibi. No one else is out there. They'll have privacy. They can stand under the spreading magnolia and chat. She glances at the clock. Five minutes before the bell rings.

Outside, Bibi wastes no time. "I did it. I found my birth mother. She was in Santa Ana. It took me fifteen minutes to drive there."

To Bibi's alarm, Gloria and Pamela's expressions don't register happiness of any sort. But they're definitely listening. almost too hard. Bibi slows down, remembering what she'd forgotten. Despite their urging her to find her birth mother, she guesses this really wasn't a story they wanted to hear. "I have a sister in Lubbock, Texas."

They nod. Weird, stormy worry gathers in their eyes.

"I talked to her. Her name is Delilah."

Pamela's mood breaks for a moment. "Delilah? What kind of name is that?"

Bibi shrugs with her hands. "I used to be Beatrice. And don't start calling me that either." She wonders if she really feels that way. "My birth mother's name is Grace."

Pamela nods while she thinks about that. "Seems logical. Kind of fits the story."

Gloria is not nodding. Her nose has reddened, and she's biting her lips tight. Tears flood her eyes. She escapes to the back side of the tree.

Bibi and Pamela look to each other for answers, but have none. Bibi looks at the tree's sinewy trunk and hears the quiet sobs coming from behind it. How alive the trunk seems to Bibi, how brawny and protective.

They both move to the tree's back where Gloria still cries.

It feels cooler to Bibi, as though this side is more shadowed. She comforts Gloria, as does Pamela. In her mind, Bibi can't figure out what she said, if anything, to make Gloria cry. She knows there's not much time. "What did I say, Glo?" Bibi asks.

Gloria puts one hand on Bibi's arm, tacitly asking her to say no more, and she pats her own mouth, overtly trying to quell her emotional outburst so she can speak. At last, she says, "Grace is my middle name."

Despite the coincidence, it makes no sense to Bibi why having the same name as her birth mother would make Gloria weep so. Yet there must be something. "Is that making you cry?"

Gloria tears up again. She struggles to compose herself. She covers her mouth with both hands.

Pamela and Bibi continue calming her.

Gloria removes her hands from her mouth, and through tears, tells her friends, "When I was in college, I got pregnant. I gave the baby away."

Bibi's shoulders collapse from no longer having to wonder, and from realizing the brutal weight Gloria has carried around every day of her life. She flashes back to all the times she looked at Ella and Noah and wondered how anyone could have given her away. Now she knows that Gloria, lovely, funny, loyal Gloria was an anyone. In every way Bibi wants to protect Gloria from any judgment written on her face. She takes Gloria's hands in her own. "I'm so sad for you."

Gloria wipes her eyes. "And I know the baby's got another mother now, and he may look for me someday, but he's still my baby, he's still my child, my little boy, and I gave him away."

Fighting her own tears, Bibi closes her eyes. The tragedy that Gloria has borne all these years seems unbearable to Bibi. Next to Bibi, Pamela lets out a deep and primal moan, it scares Bibi into opening her eyes.

Pamela is looking at the sky through the magnolia's branches, like a wolf mother. She then looks at Gloria and then at Bibi and then back up again. When she's ready, she says, "I couldn't give birth. I couldn't carry. I needed someone like you, Glo, to give me yours. And my babies aren't my babies, but they are. God damn it, they *are* my babies!"

And then the bell rings. Classes start in six minutes. Nouns will be pluralized. Equations will be solved. Hypotheses will be tested.

The three women do not move from their stations.

Bibi sees the profound heartbreak haunting her friends' eyes. She sees the female condition, rather the human condition, for this must be felt by men too. She assumes her own eyes bleed yet another shade of the same despair. Yes, Pamela's babies are her babies, just as Gloria's baby is still her baby. And Bibi? She is the child of two women. Around her friends' heads she sees twinkles, and smiles.

"You know," she says to them, "think about what you want to have happen."

Bibi watches as their eyes, for just a moment, relay that her request registered in their minds. "Don't tell me now. Maybe at lunch. Or tomorrow. Just think about what you want."

§

In her future years, finding her birth mother will reinforce Bibi's desire to be the finder she is. She will meet her sister Delilah and be shocked by the many ways they are alike, while Victor will pretty much forsake his new-found sister.

Bibi will meet Grace's brother Gilbert and his wife, as well as their grandson, who not surprisingly resembles her own children. It is Gilbert who will tell Bibi, in the same New England accent as Grace's, "You look just like by mother."

Before meeting Bibi, Gilbert had sent her a letter written in pencil on lined, white paper, trying to explain his sister and his family:

> Oct. 27, 1981
>
> Dear Bibi and Family,
>
> I thought the stamps you sued on your letter to me a very touching addition to the total situation. I am still, after several days, absorbing the emotions—your emotions and Grace's.
>
> Your sister Delilah has been so patient in keeping me aware that I have a family out there. You see, Bibi I'm not family oriented. It seems that we do not shape our own destiny, but accommodate ourselves as best we can to the truly powerful forces, both within us and without. What I am going to say that is you, Delilah, and Victor are the second generation to be beset by the forces your grandmother, my mother, and her father, my grandfather. The families were split asunder (that is how this awkward paragraph started by my saying that I am not family oriented.) The emotional waves appear to have run their gamut and have, hopefully, receded to a quiet sea, making me and your other uncle Ted rather run-of-the-mill family people.
>
> I am an accountant working for the University of Rhode Island Foundation. You would love your Aunt Martha, who has one of those beautiful personalities that come from psychic strength.
>
> I called your mother Grace on Sunday, and I must say she was overwhelmed. But, of course, she would be. I must get the whole story because, as you no

doubt know, I just didn't believe that you kids really existed. You actually gurgled over the telephone to me when I was living in Minnesota. Your mother called me one midnight (she constantly forgot the time difference) and said she has you and Victor. But then I never heard more until Delilah came along, and then I was really confused as to the names, ages, etc. And I remember thinking: Grace is talking about Delilah; does she mean Beatrice, and what happened to Evan?

And then of course, there was silence for several years, and suddenly there was no more Beatrice or Evan, only Delilah. So I rationalized the whole thing by thinking Grace was on one of her great flights of fancy—some fancy—awful, horrible, living through a night, and I was too dumb or callous or busy with my own problems to read what was going on.

Anyway, can you imagine what it must have been like for her? Talk about Dante's *Inferno*. Where does reality end and fantasy begin? I can only conjure the storm of regret and guilt that must be thundering down on that quavering ship. I guess this is where compassion begins, or should begin.

Sincerely,

Your uncle Gilbert

In the years to come, Bibi will find her birth father's family, but not him, for he died in 1964, the same year she graduated from high school. He had two sons, both of whom Bibi will meet, though the oldest of the two, who looked disarmingly like her brother Charlie, will want little to do with her. The younger brother she will meet on several occasions, including a visit to

Austin, where he and Grace will regale in old times when she was his father's mistress, and he was still in his teens. His mother, apparently, had been institutionalized, and, as was the law at the time, could not be divorced.

Bibi will never feel part of either of these families, for in fact, she is legally not. Imagine that. The people with whom you should be legally tied are the exact people with whom you must be legally disconnected. Alas.

Instead, she will put her efforts to finding the one thing that she knew, but had completely forgotten. She will spend years exploring and healing the psychological ramifications of her adoption and her sexual abuse. Piece by piece, those wisps of herself which had left her to hover in the sky above, not daring to be inside her, those pieces too traumatized to handle what she went through, will begin reentering her. The more they reenter, the more her mind will remember what she knew, and yet forgot. For that is the human condition. Coming to earth with the knowledge of the universe and then forgetting.

And what, you might ask, will she remember? She will remember that her past experiences create her future experiences, for what you decide, you experience. Thus, to change her future, she must first change her past.

But that is not all.

She will also remember, with my help and the help of many others surrounding her, that we can each, with the powers of love, hope, and unlimited possibility, create new experiences for ourselves, about which we make more positive and loving decisions, and it is upon those decisions that our future experiences are created. She will remember the art of creating new beginnings. She will remember to live as a body and soul.

And that is what she came to do.

She will fulfill her destiny, as I will do mine.

Acknowledgements

Feedback from fellow writers is one of the best honing stones an author can have. I thank my Orange County writing group, led by the marvelous Louella Nelson: Deborah Gaal (especially), Fiona Ivey, Rosanne Lewis, Beverly Plass, Brad Oatman, Tim Twombley, and Herb William-Dalgart.

I thank my brave Anacortes first draft readers: Penny Barnard, Ellen Kaiser, and Barbee Cromack.

Advice on the production in many ways means understanding the story's deeper impact, and for that I thank: Kim Adams, Cheri Ault, Charlotte Backman, Frumi Barr, Sandra Barry, Chandra Fecktelkotter, Mona Hamlin, Annette Hawk, Michele Khoury, Phyllis O'Brien, Linda Seaton, and Linda Watkins.

In 1981 I was surrounded by close friends Ruth Cassilan, Marilyn Corbett, Pat Costa, Kathy McCann, Phyllis O'Brien, Carol Schmidt, and Linda Seaton. I am grateful to them for being with me through those tough times during and after finding Irene Nielen. They gave me perspective; I am humbled by their grace.

I have five siblings that I know of. Some are by blood and some are through adoption. I am grateful for all they added to my life.

I thank my husband David for his incredible patience and love. I thank my daughter Lisa Rodasta for her perception and advice. And I thank the poem voice.

About the Author

Joanne Rodasta Wilshin is a questor, teacher, and author. Before writing *The Findlings,* she found both her birth parents and their families. She has intimate knowledge of and sensitivity to the problems and ramifications of abandonment and adoption. Portions of *The Findlings* were short-listed by the Pacific Northwest Writers Assn.'s annual contest.

Joanne's two non-fiction books also followed intense quests: *The Happiness Path* (originally *Take a Moment and Create Your Life,* 1997) and *The First Mate's Guide to Cruising the Inside Passage.* Visit JoanneWilshin.com.

Besides boating, Joanne has been a lifelong writer, painter, and musician. For decades she taught English and critical thinking; she led the Gaian Sisterhood and Creating is Genius in Newport Beach for ten years. A native Californian, Joanne grew up in Palos Verdes, and then lived nearby before moving to Anacortes, Washington, and in 2010 with her husband David. She has degrees in art and education, and is a member of Mensa and ISPE. In 2006 she won the Worst First Sentence contest at the Santa Barbara Writing Conference. Her children Lisa and Nicolas live in Oakland and McMinnville respectively.

Read Joanne Wilshin's other books:

The Happiness Path (2015)

The First-Mate's Guide to Cruising the Inside Passage: Thriving and surviving the waters from Olympia to Glacier Bay (2017)

Made in the USA
Coppell, TX
04 June 2021

56885252R00239